ANGLE OF ATTACK

BOOKS BY ROBIN A. WHITE

The Flight from Winter's Shadow
Angle of Attack

ANGLE OF ATTACK

ROBIN A. WHITE

CROWN PUBLISHERS, INC.   NEW YORK

*Published by Crown Publishers, Inc., 201 East 50th Street,
New York, New York 10022. Member of the Crown Publishing
Group.*

CROWN is a trademark of Crown Publishers, Inc.

Manufactured in the United States of America

Book design by June Bennett-Tantillo

Library of Congress Cataloging-in-Publication Data

White, Robin A.
    Angle of attack / Robin A. White. — 1st ed.
        p.   cm.
    I. Title.
PS3573.H47476A83   1992   91-42238
813'.54—dc20   CIP

ISBN 0-517-57809-3

10   9   8   7   6   5   4   3   2   1

First Edition

DEDICATION

Some people maintain that the romance of flight is dead, that flying is nothing more than a crowded bus with bad meals, shrinking seats, and lost luggage. But they're wrong.

The dream is alive, because all flight is miraculous.

The kid at the airport fence knows it; the student pilot roaring down an empty runway, solo, understands; so does the tinkerer who sees the earth fall away for the very first time beneath a wing built with his own two hands.

The instrument pilot knows it as he plays a game of electronic pinball in the clouds, betting his life against his skill; the aerobatic competitor slicing the sky with the deftness of a surgeon knows it; and so does the Boeing captain who sweats to make it all look effortless; the attack driver barreling into his target at high subsonic and the fighter jock sliding into his prey's six, they both know it.

Most of all, the wise old pelicans who have seen wood and canvas become a tower of technology soaring from Kitty Hawk to the moon know it, even if they find it hard to say the words:

all flight is miraculous.

This book is dedicated to all of you who share these four simple words, and this dream, with me.

ANGLE OF
ATTACK

FOREWORD

A false dawn came early to the residents of Baghdad on the morning of 17 January 1991, courtesy of the armed forces of the United States. At just after four in the morning, black, invisible jets swarmed over the city like evil *djinns,* smashing generating plants, telecommunications buildings, and command sites. From the oceans came low-flying robot killers, missiles that knew the streets of the capital like mailmen.

The flashes and the crumps of the heavy bombs ceased as the sun hauled its way above the eastern marshes of the Tigris. A cutting wind had blown much of the smoke away, and the cold, gray light revealed a city that was remarkably undamaged. After half a year of imagining, of living under the lengthening shadow of war, people danced in the streets. *This is all they can do?* they cried.

Iraq still possessed an enormous, battle-hardened army. It had a well-equipped air force. A thousand tanks waited on the western border for the signal to advance into Jordan and beyond. It had secret weapons that even the Israelis feared. The war had begun. It would not end, it was said, until Iraq extended from the Persian Gulf to the Mediterranean Sea, until Palestine itself was but a western province of a new, Arab empire. The war had finally begun.

Only a very few knew it was already over.

Victory had come, not in the skies of Baghdad, not along the armored borders thick with tanks and mines, but at a remote site in the middle of the Libyan Sahara, sixteen hundred miles to the west. It was known to the bedouin, the mapmakers, and a select group of the world's best rocket designers as Dahr Nema.

There, hidden by half a continent of ocher sand and shattered manganese rock, billions of Iraqi petrodollars had been distilled into six slim cylinders, each forty-five feet long by four feet in diameter. Fully fueled, each missile weighed slightly more than twenty thousand pounds. Their warheads contained enriched uranium isotope jacketed in high explosive. They bore the name *Al Infitar:* the Cataclysm. From their launchers at Dahr Nema they could reach out four thousand miles.

Unlike the crude, slow SCUDs, there would be no defense against them. With *Al Infitar* ready to strike, no hand would dare rise against Iraq. It was the power of the Cataclysm that would hold back the combined might of an angry world. It was *Al Infitar* that would drive the hated Israelis into the sea. It was Saddam Hussein's hidden ace, his trump of all trumps, and it very nearly worked.

But when Iraqi tanks rolled triumphantly into Kuwait City in August of 1990, they were fighting a war that had already been lost in Washington, at a small grass airfield in the heart of Moscow, and at Dahr Nema. It is there that this story begins.

Wednesday Night, 18 July 1990

Col. Yuri Ermakov took a last swallow of hot tea, fastened the cap of his insulated flask, and set it carefully down onto the cockpit floor. His headset was wrapped around his neck, leaving his ears unprotected against the incredible buzz saw din coming from the old Tu-95's four turboprop engines. He listened and smiled. *Sweet.* The Bear was an old ship, but the pilot loved to feel the roar of its engines, not just in his ears, but right in his chest. He slapped the new copilot on the shoulder. "Hey, Roman! Where are we?" he shouted.

Capt. Roman Taskaev glanced up from his navigational log and pushed his earphones away from his head. "What?"

"Where are we?" Ermakov roared.

Taskaev shook his head and tapped his headphones.

He should have been a clerk, thought Ermakov. He had been trying to engage Taskaev for hours. But Taskaev, a new graduate of the experimental aviation school at Ramenskoye, was as quiet as a clod of peat. *We shall see how long that lasts,* thought Ermakov as he placed the heavily padded earphones over his head. He pressed the intercom button on the yoke. "Very well, Captain. Where have you put us?"

"Two hundred kilometers north of the Libyan coast." Taskaev watched the numbers spin down on the drum of his navigational display, then checked the scurry of his chronograph's sweep hand. It was nearly midnight. "Turn to one seven two in thirty seconds."

"Have I ever told you the story of my first flight at Ramenskoye?" asked Ermakov.

"No. Stand by for the turn. Get ready. Five, four, three, two, one, and mark."

"I remember my first operational mission," said Ermakov as he banked the big Tu-95 Bear south, then rolled level on the 172-degree heading. The bomber's eight propellers bit the thin air fifteen kilometers above the black Mediterranean Sea. The North African coast lay directly off the nose, still invisible over the horizon. "They gave me airway surveys to the Far East. You think you know cold? I will tell you of cold. The yaks huddled on the runway next to my engines to stay warm. Not like this milk run, eh? We might have been assigned to fly the Camel's Hump."

A massive military resupply effort was under way. War matériel of every description was headed over the Caucasus, the Camel's Hump, to Iraq. As many as fifteen flights per day were arriving at Baghdad International.

"To be sure," said Taskaev, but then he looked up and over. "I do have one question, Colonel."

"Yes? What is it?"

"Why do we fly halfway around the world to perform a mission we could just as easily accomplish at home? Don't we have rockets at Baikonur anymore?"

"Listen, Roman," said Ermakov, "every time we launch a rocket, the fucking Americans know everything, even before our own technicians. They watch us with their fucking satellites like buzzards. But they can't be everywhere."

"But Iraq is an ally. Why are we about to shoot down—"

"Allies. Enemies," Ermakov shrugged. "Who can tell these days? One day it is this, the next day that. One day we are friends, the next night, who knows?" He thumped the Bear's glareshield. It boomed like a bass kettledrum. "What I know is this, Roman. If the Americans knew what we were doing, they would shit in their pants. But they won't."

In this, Ermakov would soon be proven incorrect.

He stared out ahead as they drove south at eight-tenths the speed of sound. The night merged at the horizon with the black sea, and the brilliant constellations were themselves mirrored in the lights winking up from the busy shipping lanes below. He turned to Taskaev. "You know, I always wanted to be a cosmonaut."

"Colonel?" Taskaev looked up again.

"The stars," said Ermakov. "Go ahead. Look at them. Above us. All the lights on the sea below. No air outside our little cabin worth speaking of. Think of it, Captain. Here we are, surrounded by the dark. We might as well be in outer space, don't you think, Captain Taskaev?"

A poet, Taskaev thought as he glanced dutifully out the bomber's thick windscreen. "I suppose so, " he said, and then returned to his log. "Ten minutes to Point Anchor."

As they penetrated the Gulf of Sidra, the shipping lanes quickly emptied until the sea far below was utterly black. Libya had threatened any intruder with destruction: the famous Zone of Death. Ermakov glanced at the Sirena radar threat receiver. It was silent and dark. The Tupolev, all 180 tons of her, was still a fleeting ghost against the brilliant stars.

"Five minutes out." Taskaev glanced up. "It's time. We should alert our passengers."

"Scientists," Ermakov replied with a sneer. He reached behind and retrieved his rubber oxygen mask from the seat pouch.

The Tupolev's normal crew had been replaced by a team from the Serpukhov Institute of High Energy Physics. They were the cream of the Soviet technical crop. But as far as Ermakov was concerned, they could not be trusted to tie their shoes properly much less operate an oxygen mask. Who but whiskered academics would willingly surround themselves with a witch's brew of atomic radiations? Ermakov was glad for the thick lead shield behind the flight deck. He switched the intercom onto ship's circuit. "Professor Kessel? We are about to depressurize the cabin. I advise you to check your masks now for proper flow."

"Very well," came the high, nasal voice of Academician Valentin I. Kessel, the leading investigator for the highly classified and, from the standpoint of international arms agreements, highly illegal effort known to a very few as Project Stingray. "We are prepared."

A pressure-tight hatch nearly ten meters long had been cut in the top of the bomber's waist section. When it slid open, the Bear's cabin would be open to the thin atmosphere fifteen kilometers above sea level.

Hidden beneath that hatch was a miniaturized linear accelerator, an atomic cannon. At its heart was a resonant crystal the size of a soccer ball, made of purest, monocrystalline diamond. Ermakov smiled, remembering an American story he had once read, *A Diamond as Big as the Ritz*. Well, this one wasn't quite that large, but the effect it would have on history would be far greater. It wasn't a jewel, a bauble. It was the foundation stone for a system designed to shoot down ballistic missiles.

Aft of the cockpit, the Bear's cavernous body was an obstacle course of high-power cables, strange-looking plumbing, and thick lead shielding plates. The long fuselage had been broken into three internal compartments.

One space held a shielded vat of deuterium; a seething, radioactive soup of highly charged particles. The next section held the diamond-driven radio frequency quadropole.

The RFQ gathered the deuterium ions and fired them into the accelerator proper. Here, powerful superconducting coils set up an intense magnetic field that boosted the particles to velocities approaching the speed of light. Finally, stripped of its charge by a carefully crafted metallic screen, the invisible beam would emerge from the Tupolev, guided to its target by a powerful laser. The latter served as a tracer beam to help point the invisible energies of Stingray, but also cut an ionized path through the thin wisps of atmosphere that remained at their great height.

Stingray spewed forth a stream of atomic bullets flying at almost unimaginable speed. They could penetrate anything man-made. Unlike bullets, the beam could not destroy its target directly, nor was it meant to; Stingray killed with more subtlety. Like its namesake, it electrocuted its prey.

"Point Anchor in three minutes," said Taskaev.

The lights of the Libyan coast now fringed both eastern and western horizons. Benghazi sparkled off their left wing; Tripoli was to the right. Directly ahead the scattered coastal villages were backed up by the immense darkness of the Sahara.

The flat desert was a dry negative of the Mediterranean: an enormous expanse of wind-mounded sand and fields of shattered rocks that extended deep into Africa's heart. But dark as it might seem, Ermakov knew it was not entirely empty. They wouldn't be here if it were.

He glanced once more at the radar warning receiver (RWR). The instrument's glass face was dark. *Good.* It would not do to be discovered prowling around. There was enough to worry about without . . . He stopped in midthought as a spark of light flickered on the instrument. His eyes immediately locked onto the threat receiver. He tapped it, hoping against hope that a short had caused the light to glow. But it flickered once more, then began to flash in earnest. "Damn!" Ermakov looked out off their right wing, but the dark sea yielded nothing. *Who is out there?*

"Something the matter, Colonel?" said Taskaev, but then he saw the RWR's glow. "Libyan radar?"

"I'm afraid not." Ermakov pressed the depressurization warning tone. The beep sounded small and lost in the emptiness of the deep North African night.

Early Thursday Morning, 19 July 1990

"So you think it's really gonna blow?" asked Lt. William "Backster" Baxter as he sat in the rear cockpit of Cutlass 202, a Grumman F-14A Tomcat. A cool salt breeze funneled down from the cranked-open canopy as the USS *John F. Kennedy* sliced across the swells of the southern Mediterranean. He and his pilot, Lt. Richard "Ice" Eisley, were well into their second hour of alert duty. His legs were no longer registering any feeling, and his ass felt like rough cast concrete.

"Do I think what's gonna blow?" said Eisley.

"You know. Iraq and Kuwait," said Baxter as he squirmed against his loosened harness. He reached forward and stroked his good-luck charm, a Garfield cat he kept on his instrument panel. "The dope is we may have us a shooting war before too long."

"Dope's for dopes. They said the ice cream machine was going to be fixed last week, too."

"True." Baxter stretched his arms over his head again, trying to keep them from falling asleep. The radar intercept officer (RIO) watched a lone figure cross the empty flightdeck. "Anyhow, it sure is quiet tonight."

Eisley checked the fighter's panel clock. "Forty-two minutes and it's Miller time." Eisley leaned back and watched the big search-radar dish turn high atop *JFK*'s island, blotting out the stars as it swung round and round.

"Hey!"

A tremor ran through the ship, and the stars began to shift overhead.

"Oh, shit," said Baxter as he felt the carrier heel. *JFK* was turning into the wind. "I hate night cat shots," said Baxter as he strapped on his flight helmet. Like Eisley's, it was emblazoned with the crossed-swords insignia of VF-32. The deck-edge lights suddenly appeared, outlining the black flightdeck in red.

The pilot was already halfway through the prestart when the official word came over the booming loudspeaker mounted on the *JFK*'s bridge: "Launch the ready five! Launch the ready five!"

The flightdeck suddenly swarmed with activity under the red night-lights. A blue-shirted deckhand broke down the chains that kept the Tomcat tight to the flightdeck as a taxi guide stood off the fighter's nose, ready to direct him to the catapult shuttle.

Eisley's crew chief pulled the safing pins on the two AIM-9 Sidewinders mounted on their wing pylons and gave the pilot a thumbs-up. The pilot pulled the glass teardrop canopy closed and got both troublesome Pratt and Whitney TF-30s lit off and idling.

Following the taxi guide's glowing wands, he advanced the throttles and the Tomcat's nosewheel bumped over the shuttle and
locked into place with a slight shudder. "Everything copacetic,
BB?"

"I hate night shots," Baxter replied, stroking the stuffed cat on
his instrument panel.

"There goes the Angel." As the recovery helicopter lifted off
and began circling, Eisley heard the boom of his wingman starting
his engines. He looked over his shoulder and saw Lt. Charles
"Cotton" Mather signal that he was ready to taxi.

The voice of *JFK*'s Combat Information Center (CIC) came over
the secure circuit.

"Cutlass Flight, Screwtop Six has a Bear in the air for you
tonight. He's zero eight five at two twenty, course one seven eight,
speed four niner zero knots, angels four eight, repeat, four eight."
Screwtop was a high-flying Grumman E2C Hawkeye providing
round-the-clock radar cover for *JFK*.

"Christ. He's headed right down our throat," said Baxter.

"Cutlass two oh two copies," Eisley transmitted. He looked up
and saw the green-shirted catapult officer signal him to run up his
engines. He slapped the control stick through its full deflection,
watching the fighter's control surfaces move in his canopy mirror.
When he was satisfied, Eisley stomped on the brakes and ran both
engines up to military power, just short of the afterburner.
"Ready?" he asked Baxter. The howl of his engines screamed over
the intercom.

"I hate—"

"Let's go pay Mr. Bear a little visit, shall we?" Eisley ran his
throttles around their safety detent. Two cones of yellow afterburner
fire blasted back against the raised deflector. He thumbed the
throttle switch for his external navigation lights. The red beacon
began flashing. He looked over at the cat officer, gave him a
thumbs-up, and saluted.

The green shirt's glowing wand described a descending arc to the
deck, then slowly came level, pointing straight into the thirty-knot
wind streaming over *JFK*'s bow.

Eisley tightened his grip on the throttle guards. One heartbeat; two. He let out a breath. *Any second. Any second now . . .*

The catapult fired.

Ermakov pressed the intercom button on the heavy wheel. "Attention, attention! Stand by to depressurize. All masks must now be on and flow valves checked. I repeat: stand by to depressurize."

Almost immediately the red intercom light illuminated. "This is Kessel. We are all ready, except that it is very cold back here. Is there any more heat?"

Ermakov snorted. "Professor Kessel, it is"—he checked the thermometer set into one of the steel cross-braces that framed the heavy windshield—"minus forty-three degrees outside. Thank you for your concerns, Comrade Academician."

"Coming . . . coming up to Point Anchor," Taskaev said with a perceptible waver in his voice. His eyes kept returning to the radar warning receiver.

"Very well, Roman," said Ermakov as he gingerly advanced the propeller control on the right outboard engine. The 12,000-horsepower NK-12 fell back into synch. "Let's vent."

Taskaev spun the altitude-select wheel up from its setting of eight thousand feet to AMBIENT.

Ermakov felt his ears pop as the Tupolev vented her cabin pressure to the thin air. A cold breeze escaped through the heater duct and caught a drop of sweat on his brow. The fuselage creaked like an old freighter caught in a gale.

He checked the Bear's cabin pressure. "Well," he said into the scratchy intercom, "we are cosmonauts now." The air before him was now completely lethal. Ermakov pushed the circuit breaker in to the motors that would open the big hatch in the Tupolev's fuselage. "All right, Kessel. The hatch is powered and under your control."

They both heard the whine as the sliding hatch began to move. Ermakov felt the rumble of the slipstream as it blasted around the new opening in the Bear's backbone. As the Tu-95 shuddered and swayed, his mind was on the sea far below. And the Americans. They were somewhere out there, too.

The cabin lights dimmed as the electrical loads coursing through the old bomber's airframe changed. Kessel had summoned the sleeping energies of Stingray to life.

"Colonel!" Taskaev shouted.

"What is . . ." But Ermakov stopped when he saw what his copilot was looking at.

Taskaev was transfixed by the sight of an F-14 sitting motionless just beyond the safe confines of his cockpit. Its missiles were perfectly visible. He could see the dark shape of the pilot. He was waving.

Suddenly a brilliant flash exploded to their left. Ermakov swung around in time to see the spectral shape of the second American fighter appear out of nowhere, its twin tails a deeper black against the night sky. The F-14's nav lights came on and the red collision beacon turned in quick sweeping shafts. A second flash!

"A camera! He is taking our picture!" Taskaev exclaimed as he tried to scrunch down in his seat below the line of his window.

"Don't be an idiot," Ermakov snapped. He pulled off a glove and raised his middle finger, a gesture he had learned from the Americans themselves. He then pressed the cabin intercom, receiving a shock as he did so. "Professor, we have been intercepted by two American fighters. They are bracketing us."

"What?" said Kessel with alarm. "Are we still in international airspace?"

"Yes," the pilot replied. "And so are they." He watched as the fighter to his left angled off slightly, then turned sharply back in. Six meters, *five!* The roar of the F-14's twin turbines set the windshield glass trembling. The fighter ballooned in crisp detail out of the darkness, its nav lights brighter than any star.

"Look out!" Taskaev screamed as the fighter knifed in. He reached for the yoke, but Ermakov slapped his hands away.

"This one has balls," said Ermakov. He gritted his teeth and held on to his assigned course as the fighter tried to herd the Bear. But Ermakov would not be turned. He stared straight at his attitude gyro and ignored the rakish fighter whose pilot was nearly close enough to touch, separated by a narrow river of 500-knot air and two layers of bulletproof glass.

"Mother of God!" Taskaev watched as the right wingman pulled in equally close, the fighter's wing outstretched below the Tupolev's cabin. He could look straight down into the F-14's cockpit. He could *see* the glowing clusters of instruments! "Colonel!" he shouted, drawing in his breath as the fighter inched even closer.

Ermakov stabbed the intercom. "Kessel! I'm going to turn slightly to—"

"No! We are picking up the rocket! Hold your course!" Kessel ordered over the whine of the accelerator's power coils. His aiming device was extremely primitive; even a slight turn would throw it off.

Ermakov watched as the Bear's compass twirled into a dervish dance. *Useless.* An invisible cocoon of energy was beginning to wrap the old Bear in shimmering power. "Position check!" the pilot demanded.

"Point Anchor in fifteen seconds," Taskaev whispered, almost as though he were afraid the American fighter pilots would overhear. They were still there, perched as though connected to the old Tupolev on invisible steel beams.

Ermakov felt a tingle of shock through his gloved hands where he grasped the heavy metal wheel. "Ach!" The tingle grew annoying, then unpleasant. "Induced current," he muttered. A distinct smell of ozone cut into the stink of hot electronics and sweat. The cockpit flashed blue as tiny bolts of lightning no bigger than a needle danced across the windshield framework.

The red intercom light glowed. "We are ready," Kessel said calmly. "You might see some effect on your instruments, some false readings."

Ermakov watched as a miniature thunderstorm danced across his instrument panel. He put his arms under his legs, touching nothing. "We'll be watching, Comrade Academician."

"Colonel!" Taskaev shouted. "Look!"

Off to his right, nearly to the horizon, a soft glow erupted into a hard ball of brilliant flame. It climbed through the spectrum of heat, first red, then orange, finally blue-white hot. "Now just watch!" he told Taskaev, who shifted in his seat in time to see *Al Infitar,* the Cataclysm, blast into the night sky atop a ribbon of pure white fire.

"Did you see that?" Eisley said angrily as he held perfect formation with the huge silver Bear. "That little fuck gave me the finger!"

But Baxter was looking elsewhere. He had seen the strange opening on top of the Bear's fuselage. "This guy's got a moonroof, Ice," he said. "Climb up some so I can get it on video, okay?"

"Rog," said Eisley. "Cutlass trail," he called out to his wing-man, "hold what you've got while I film this bastard." He pulled up and leveled off right over the Bear's waist. "What does it look like, Bax?"

"Like weirdness," said Baxter as he swung the controls on the Tomcat's nose-mounted video camera. "Totally strange." He leaned over as Eisley banked the wing to give him a clearer view. "It's some kind of hatch. Hey, cool. I can see down inside it." But the image suddenly shifted.

The Bear began to bank with a slow, majestic tilt of its enormous wings. The turn put *JFK* dead off his nose.

The radio preset for the E2C Hawkeye radar plane came to life at once. "Cutlass two zero two, Screwtop Six. He's headed right for the bird farm. Get that bandit turned."

"Rog," said Eisley. "I think," he told Baxter, "this guy's in a real rut, you know?"

"Uh, Ice, I don't—"

"Hang on, BB." Eisley ran his throttles in and shot ahead of the Bear. Then, with a watchmaker's touch, he eased off, letting the fighter settle straight back at the bomber's nose. "Flip me the finger . . ."

"This is not funny, Ice," said Baxter as he watched the big bomber loom closer and closer. "Ice? I said—"

"I heard you. Hold on to your skivvies." Eisley drifted back toward the Bear's glassed-in nose. He could see its windscreen right behind his tail. All it would take would be a blip of Zone Five afterburner and he'd cook the bomber's stubborn flightcrew in their seats. Eisley broke out in an evil grin.

"He's got a refueling probe, Ice," said Baxter. "Don't you think we're a little close? He'll run that thing up our ass and—"

"Not to worry. I believe in safe sex." Eisley nudged his engines and stopped the drift. He held perfect position exactly fifteen feet in front of the Bear's crew. He wondered what they must be thinking with the twin orange suns of his PWs right in their faces. But the patrol bomber held its course. *Come on!* he thought. *Shear off!*

"Ice! We got a light!" Baxter yelled.

Eisley turned and saw the yellow master caution light burning. *Shit. What now?* He blipped his throttles to open his distance and pressed the ACK button. The caution message scrolled across the bottom of one of the three CRTs that formed the basic instrumentation in the F-14's glass cockpit. "Screwtop, Cutlass two oh two has a master caution light."

"Roger, Cutlass," said the "mole" peering at his radar aboard the E2C. "You have a ready deck and your signal at marshal is Charlie."

"Lead, this is two," his wingman called in. "I just picked up a master caution transient."

"Seems like we got us a contagious condition," Eisley replied. He banked farther away from the thundering Bear. The yellow light winked out. *Huh?* What had he changed? "Cotton, give Mr. Bear some breathing space." The second F-14 warped away. "Everything's okay now, right?"

"Yeah. How'd you—"

"This Bear's radiating some kind of bad news. Hold station about where you are and . . . Jesus!" A cocoon of St. Elmo's fire erupted from the Bear's eight counterrotating propellers. A snapping bolt sprayed blue light from the big bomber's tail as a pale green glow welled up through the opened hatch in the plane's back. One word came to Eisley as he watched the eerie pyrotechnics: *Fire.* "Screwtop Six! Cutlass lead! This bandit's about to blow!" Eisley flicked away. He was certain an explosion was imminent.

"Roger, Cutlass. Can you maintain station?"

"A-firm. But it looks like Mr. Bear's gonna go for a swim real soon." Eisley watched as ghostly fire licked along the leading edges of the Bear's wings, shooting out in weird patterns from every antenna. Eisley caressed the stick and the nimble fighter pivoted up on a wing in a graceful bank.

"Ice!" Cotton shouted. "Look out! Christ! There's a missile in the air!"

The words made Eisley's blood run cold. He snapped his head around and hunted for it, but all he saw was a thin streak of light against the southern horizon. His heart notched back down from its emergency setting. "Negative, negative. I've got a visual. That's way the hell off there," he transmitted.

"Wow," said Baxter as he watched *Al Infitar*'s fiery climb. He slewed the fighter's camera over and centered the flames in his field of view.

Eisley hit his transmit switch. "Okay, Screwtop, two oh two has an eyeball on some kind of a rocket launch to the south."

"Say again?" came back the puzzled man aboard the radar plane. "The Bear fired at you, Cutlass?"

"Negative!" said Eisley. "It looks like it's comin' up out of Libya somewhere." He kept one eye on the sizzling patrol bomber and the other on the rocket blasting up from the Libyan coast. A lot was happening all at once. "Jesus. It looks like Cape Canaveral out there. Like a shuttle goin' up. You taping all this back there, Bax?"

"Wow."

The glow from the Bear's open hatch grew brighter. A faint shimmering beam of green light suddenly appeared. Eisley looked back at the ascending arc of the rocket. It was streaking up from the south, becoming a supernaturally brilliant star in the constellation Scorpio.

"Cutlass lead, are you taping this?" asked the controller.

"Affirmative." Eisley watched the eerie pyrotechnics crackling around the Soviet bomber. "That light looks like a laser." The rocket was nearly overhead now.

He cautiously banked in toward the Bear. He stopped as a

brilliant flash of light high overhead smeared a smoking track across the night sky. *Holy shit!* As Eisley watched, it broke into fragments, each trailing a ribbon of burning gas. A shuddering thunder shook the F-14. "Cotton! You still with me?" Eisley transmitted, twisting his neck around to find his wingman against the burning chaos of the rocket's demise. "Where are you, two? I don't—"

"Two one five's in your eight o'clock," his wingman radioed. "That was one hell of a finale, shipmate."

"Wowser bowser," said Baxter, his head craned all the way back as he looked at the fireworks overhead. "I'm glad you asked me to come along, Ice."

Eisley looked over and saw the Bear go dark. As he watched, it banked away to the north, its roof hatch sliding shut. "Don't thank me, BB," he said to his RIO. "Thank the Bear."

2

Elena Pasvalys crossed the river Oka at the Serpukhov bridge, heading north along the Podolsk road. Her rugged little Lada, a Soviet version of an obsolete Fiat design, bounced and whined as it slowly accelerated.

The sun broke through the industrial murk rising from the city's smelters. She immediately felt its heat on her glossy black hair. A new day was dawning in almost every way imaginable.

Elena smiled. Once it would have taken an internal passport to travel the rutted highway. Now, if she felt like it, she could just *drive* to Moscow. Imagine! On a whim. Things were even changing back home in Lithuania. Slowly, of course, and not all at once. But changing for the better, changing forever.

She glanced at the fat letter her father had sent from Vilnius. Once it would have been crudely opened and resealed before arriving at her own apartment. Not anymore. The tape was untouched. The old machineries were falling apart. She chuckled. Who would have guessed her Lada would outlive the KGB?

As she traveled north, the industrial zone gave way to a more pleasant, open land dotted with stands of birch. The trees were like sharp white spikes against the black, peaty soil. Elena shifted into high gear and rolled down the window and began to sing an old song, one her mother had sung to her as a child.

Bayushki bayushki bayu. . .

"I *spell* you to sleep . . ." It was an old Russian lullaby, one her Lithuanian father naturally detested but that she still loved. *Thirty-four and I still sing children's songs.*

She conjured up an image of her mother, back before the scalpel of illness turned her unrecognizable. An ethnic Russian, she had given Elena her sapphire blue eyes. She also had her mother's pale, porcelain features. Her father had contributed his hair and his laugh, his Baltic irreverence.

Bayushki bayu . . . She heard the lullaby as though it were whispered directly into her ear. Even now, in the white days and white nights of a Russian summer in the miraculous year 1990, it summoned memories of crackling fires, vapors rising from piles of hot kasha, rose water and verbena.

She breathed in the morning air and let it out slowly. That was all the past. The future was what counted now. Her work at the Serpukhov Institute of High Energy Physics had flowered; the complex diamond-coating device she had designed was working without a hitch. At the throw of a switch, any material could be coated with a layer of purest, gem-quality diamond. Astonishing properties could be given to the commonest of materials: hardness, heat resistance, and under certain conditions, a limited kind of room-temperature superconductivity. The aftershocks of that technological breakthrough were still expanding out from Serpukhov like ripples from a skipped stone.

Fifteen kilometers north of town, a perfectly paved yet unmarked road veered into a small valley to the east. She turned onto the Institute access road. Huge power cables snaked overhead, branching off from the main line connecting Serpukhov and distant Moscow. Rounding a sweeping bend, she came to a high fence topped with barbed wire. Beyond lay an open, weed-choked belt sown with mines, and beyond that another fence rose to deter unwelcome visitors to the Serpukhov Institute of High Energy Physics. She drove up to the barred gate.

The guard emerged from his post. He wore the khaki and crimson uniform of the Internal Security Service. A whistle hung from his neck, flashing brilliant silver in the sun. A Makarov in a brightly polished holster was strapped to his side.

The man leaned into her open window and held out his hand for her identification. The red star on his cap was like a third inquiring eye.

She handed him her pass. "Another beautiful day," she said. "Is Director Velikhov in yet?"

"Since very early this morning." He handed her card back.

Early this morning? She checked her watch. It wasn't seven-thirty; how early had he come, and why? She shoved the reluctant gearshift into first and left the guard behind. In the rearview mirror, she noticed the guard was still watching.

The road ended at the small parking area beside the squat cube of the Accelerator Building. It was as brutally modern in design as it was cheap in execution. The concrete was spotted with leprous patches, and the previous night's thunderstorm had left it mottled with dark streaks of rain where the gutters had rusted through. Its mirrored windows leaked water like a sieve. What at first seemed to be curtains was in truth a lively green growth of mold.

Beside it, the big earth-covered ring of the accelerator itself looked like an ancient burial mound. Before Elena's diamond-coated circuits had allowed immensely powerful magnetic fields to be created using modest-scale equipment, the ten-kilometer ring had been one of the most important nuclear facilities in the country; indeed, the world. Now it was part of the past, too. A relic.

She pulled into her reserved space and switched off the Lada's engine. The small courtyard before the concrete building bustled with a detail of women brooming the walkway, sweeping and scratching like a flock of determined chickens.

Elena gathered up her father's letter and got out of the car. She wore a snappily tailored jumpsuit made of fine, olive linen. An outfit she had picked up on an overseas trip, it clung to her trim form in a manner that bespoke obvious foreign skill. Around her neck, hidden from all view, was a jewel quite unlike any other on the face of the earth: a pear-shaped pendant made of purest diamond.

Its size alone would make it noteworthy, but even stranger, trapped inside it like a mechanical insect in crystal amber was a silicon microchip. It had been accidentally created when the plasma gas reactor she had designed had run wild. Designed to apply thin films of pure diamond, it had instead built a diamond hailstone around the test part. Now it was a jewel, a medal of her technical triumph, warm with the heat of her body.

Inside, the Accelerator Building's stark lobby was so deeply tinted by the mirrored windows that the outside world seemed lit by the ominous light of an impending thunderstorm. She shook away the odd premonition and marched to the elevator bank.

Almost at once, the elevator door slid open to reveal the bulging pale-blue smock of an old woman, a member of the Institute's kitchen staff. She was holding on to a rolling cart with a tight-fisted grip. Her eyes were penetrating and wary. Elena saw why.

A tea service stood bright and steaming, surrounded by sweet poppy-seed pastries dusted with sugar. Elena breathed in a long, hungry lungful of air. The elevator was redolent with the heady aroma of fresh coffee. *Something is going on,* she concluded. It was so hard to find the real thing, especially these days. Elena breathed deeply as the elevator jerked upward. It came to a stop on her floor.

"Pajhouesta," the old woman said, and Elena stepped aside. The woman pushed by her, rubbing a trail of powdered sugar into Elena's linen-clad thigh as the cart maneuvered the tight corridor. Elena, as if in a dream, followed it down the narrow passage, her low-heeled boots padding noiselessly behind the squeaking wheels.

Where is she going? she wondered as the cart wheeled by Dr. Yevgeny Velikhov's suite of offices. Elena looked in and saw the double door to his personal rooms open, the office beyond unoccupied.

His secretary looked up and clucked her tongue. "Well. Good morning, Dr. Pasvalys. We were wondering when you would come in."

She checked her watch again. "Good morning, Gosplana. Where is Director Velikhov?"

"He's been here for hours. He's waiting for you in your office. He wishes to speak with you. Privately."

"Hours?" Her heart skipped like the engine on her Lada.

"I wouldn't keep him waiting if I were you." Gosplana turned once more to a pile of papers.

"Yes. Thank you," Elena answered. "I will. I mean, I won't." She felt her father's letter turn slightly damp with the sweat from her hand. It was all too clear. She felt her heart begin to sink. *Stingray has failed,* she thought as she followed the scent of the coffee down the hall.

Elena came to the door of her office. She turned and stepped inside. As Gosplana promised, Velikhov was there, standing by the window. But he was not alone. Academician V. I. Kessel was right beside him, a pastry already at his mouth. White sugar dusted his gray beard. A third man sat at Elena's desk. She knew him all too well.

Elena cleared her throat. Kessel's eyes went wide and he smiled when he saw her. "Elena!" he called out. Director Velikhov turned and peered at her, his thick glasses reflecting the light streaming in through the tinted window.

Col. Nikolai Sergeivich Slepkin, the Institute's chief watchdog and head of the KGB's Internal Security detachment, looked up. He was sitting at Elena's desk, her phone held close to his mouth. His pale gray eyes registered her presence. He nodded with a sweep of his hand for her to sit down, as though she were a supplicant and he the one giving the audience.

"Elena! Come in!" Velikhov urged. "We've been waiting for you all morning! Valentin is just back!"

"So I see," said Elena as she warily made her way into her room. Her office felt like captured territory, completely overrun.

"I came straight here. I haven't even slept," Kessel said with a look of self-satisfaction. His face looked like a balloon ready to burst.

"Well," said Slepkin with a sour purse of his lips. "You finally honor us with your presence." Slepkin hung up the receiver. His eyes were like sunglasses, so blank, so uninformative. His thin red hair was carefully combed to cover a growing bald spot. "We wondered if you were out practicing your flying this morning."

"Flying is my hobby," Elena said with forced evenness. "This is my work."

"Tell her!" Kessel urged.

She glanced at Director Velikhov. "They said you were here early. I came as fast as—"

"Don't look so worried, Elena," said Velikhov. The director's eyes seemed to hold an inexplicable sadness. "Eat a sweet roll. Drink a glass of this fine coffee. You might as well. It cost enough. I had Gosplana search all over—"

"To hell with the coffee!" Kessel blurted. "Don't torture the girl!" He turned to Elena. "The beam was perfect! It never once lost focus. Not *once*. We picked it up right after launch. First stage, second, then the third lit like a Roman candle! But my beam was right on it!" he gushed.

"Then why did it take so long for you to destroy that—" Velikhov began, but Kessel cut him off with a dismissive wave.

"Because I was tracking the damned rocket by eye!" he said with a scowl. "Elena, I tell you this, give me a real targeting system, a proper aiming device, *something,* and I will shoot down the moon!"

Elena let his words wash over her. She felt her face tingle with the flush of victory. "Does this mean that . . ."

Velikhov held up a finger to his lips, a sly, secretive smile spreading over him despite his best efforts.

Oh, my God! she thought. *Stingray works!*

Saturday Morning,
21 July 1990

Wyn Gallagher parked the Saab 900 directly in front of Building 1877 and shut the engine down. The harsh orange security lights bathed a nearly empty parking lot, blotting out all but the brightest stars. *Where is everyone?* he wondered. Three o'clock in the morning was early by the measure of the normal waking world, but to the computer wizards of Lawrence Livermore National Laboratory, it was absolutely prime time. But other than the swish and hum from the nearby freeway and the occasional yip of a coyote, the place was strangely deserted.

"Where the hell is everybody?" he said to himself as the Saab's engine ticked and cooled. Gallagher unfolded his long legs and got out, slamming the door shut with a solid Swedish *thunk*. At just over six feet, Gallagher made a fairly unremarkable Texan, an observation his mother in San Antonio still felt obliged to make; but his rangy, muscular physique and self-assured stance were more like an athlete's than that of one of the world's leading designers of miniaturized supercomputers.

What's going on? he wondered once again as he walked toward the low, modular structure that had been his home for nearly five years. Day and night, behind its double-locked entrance, Building 1877 was normally bustling with activity. Most of it was related to the Strategic Defense Initiative, and all of it was highly classified. A person could wind up spending hard time by mentioning what he did for the S-5 Group, the name of the supercomputer team at Livermore.

Gallagher was dressed in the informal uniform of the "propeller heads," cotton jacket, jeans, and running shoes. Unlike the other twenty computer jocks in S-5, he actually used the Nikes for running. Not because physical fitness was important to writing clean code. It wasn't. After all, Building 1877 was stuffed with junk-food stashes, cases of soda, even a small walk-in freezer filled with ice cream. But fitness was absolutely vital to Gallagher: when not buried in work at what the insiders called Teller Tech, he was a member of the U.S. Aerobatic Team. Every extra pound he forced his Pitts S-2 aerobatic biplane to carry took away from its ability to fly the extreme maneuvers that were necessary to win a modern aerobatics competition.

He came to the outer glass door and entered his access code. With a loud buzz, it swung open, admitting him into a brightly lit alcove. The door locked behind him as he entered a second number into the inner, wooden door. As he did so, the glittering eye of a security camera scanned him from the ceiling of the foyer. A second electronic lock buzzed its approval. He stepped inside.

The walls at Lawrence Livermore were painted in different colors that denoted the level of security demanded by the work done within. Red was the lowest; green the highest.

The corridor stretching before Gallagher was, like his Q-level identity badge, bright green. It was also strangely quiet. *Spooky.* His footsteps echoed in the corridor as he made his way to his own work space. *Must be an S-5 party tonight.* He was always forgetting them. He came to his office and snapped on the interior lights.

Gallagher's work space was neater than most, though he still had to make his way across a floor strewn with technical journals and piles of computer printouts. The walls were decorated with photographs of brightly hued aerobatic airplanes. A small wooden case held a clutch of colorful ribbons and medals, each one won in Gallagher's prized S-2 Pitts Special. Starting with the Texas Regionals, he went on to rise up in the rarefied realm of Unlimited aerobatics; bronze, silvers, and finally all the way to a gold at the Nationals at Fond du Lac, Wisconsin. His record had earned him a berth at the most prestigious event of them all: the World Aerobatics Championships, this year to be held in Yverdon, Switzerland.

His desktop was overwhelmed by three large computer screens arrayed around an elaborate keyboard. The one to his left was connected to the nonsecure system; the one to his right was the heavily shielded outpost of the Octopus, the ultraclassified Livermore supercomputer. But the one directly in front was even more special. Flat fiber-optic cables snaked away from it in all directions, covering the rest of his desk in black spaghetti. He reached behind and switched it on.

Little yellow *while you were out* notices were piled onto his keyboard by people who knew it was the only way to make certain they would be read. He grabbed the notes, tapped his start-up code for the evening's test run, and sat down to read while the system booted up.

The first note was from Lloyd Woodruff, the head of S-5. With the blithe disregard for niceties so common to genius, it simply read

SEE ME. "Sure thing, Woody," said Gallagher, tossing the note into the waste can. Woodruff had once been a creative thinker. He had been caught up in some of the zanier missile-defense schemes at the Lab and had yet to find his way back to earth.

The next, an invitation from the Lab's security chief, George Parrum, was executed in tiny, meticulous script. "I wonder what he wants?"

The last was a scrawled note from Gallagher's best friend at the Lab, Nari Brooks-Barrathur, an Oxford-educated Indian rocket designer from O Group.

Gallagher had met Nari the summer the Reagan administration had showered Livermore with unimaginable riches. Both of them were Stanford graduate students at the time, and both had been accepted as Kratos Foundation Fellows, a prize every bit as prestigious as those Gallagher had won in his Pitts.

Gallagher had applied on a whim; he had just broken up with the woman, a Chinese American graduate student in astronomy, he had always assumed he would eventually marry. When she told him her new boyfriend would be moving into their shared off-campus house, he saw no reason to linger in Palo Alto for the summer. Building computers at Lawrence Livermore sounded like a better deal. Gallagher had come through the gates an innocent. He hadn't considered the possibility that building a supercomputer the size of a soup can had anything to do with Strategic Defense. He was quickly proven wrong.

The screen before him suddenly came into focus, revealing a string of white lights flowing from right to left, and a similar procession of red ones going the opposite direction. It was a view of the traffic proceeding on Highway 580, courtesy of a very special wide-angle camera mounted atop a tower on the roof of Building 1877. Its computer-driven adaptive optics had taken more than a year to work out; even the tiny nitrogen chilling units used to cool down the infrared receptors were stamped Top Secret.

Tonight, despite the darkness, despite the miles of turbulent air between the Lab and the blacktop, the picture it beamed back was razor sharp. Gallagher slewed the scene with a joystick and ran in the magnification. Fixing the tracker onto the license plate of a speeding car nearly four miles distant, he could read the letters and numbers perfectly. *Good.* He tapped another command into his keyboard, and off in the far corner of his office, a small cooling fan began to whir.

There, sitting off by itself on a metal rolling cart, was the Prototype. What it was, in reality, was nothing less than a technological crown jewel.

The Prototype was almost exactly the dimension of a can of Campbell's soup. Its skin gleamed a bright gold under the incandescents. It was no illusion; the device, a high-density optical computer, was sheathed in the precious metal. It had cost five years of Gallagher's best efforts, and the magic that took place within the simple-seeming canister was worth far more than gold, more than its weight in pure diamond.

Lightning fast and packed with knowledge, the holographic computer was an optical, as opposed to electronic, brain. No longer tied to etched circuits and soldered wires, its digital arteries could be folded one atop the other in a three-dimensional matrix Gallagher called a data fog. It stored images as images, not as ones and zeros that required encoding and retrieval. The result was an immensely capable supercomputer that processed visual data faster than a score of Cray XMPs. It would someday be the eyes and the brains of what the open press called a Brilliant Pebble; the heart of the PALS, or Protection Against Limited Strikes, missile shield. Stripped of all its technical pretense, Gallagher knew it for what it was: the clearest-seeing, fastest-thinking gunsight the world had ever known.

A tone announced that the Prototype was ready for the first test run. This was the most frustrating time of all for Gallagher. All the truly glamorous work was over. The PALS Prototype was essentially complete. But there were millions of lines of computer coding to clean up and debug. Tiny flaws that had been unnoticeable seemed to pop out of the ether. *Let's see what you can do,* he thought as he punched up a command. A test menu came up in the corner of the screen. He typed in *HONDA*.

The screen dissolved, flickered, then the traffic scene suddenly

snapped back into view. Using the camera for its eyes, the Prototype assayed each and every car going by on Highway 580 until it
suddenly froze and zoomed in on a late-model Civic. A chime
announced its success, and a counter in the upper left of the terminal
recorded the length of the hunt: *00:02:23*. The Prototype, using its
storehouse of three-dimensional images of cars, had found its target
in slightly over two seconds. *Not bad.*

Gallagher entered the results in his test log, then typed in
TOYOTA. A rattletrap pickup truck blinked into view nearly at
once, the name of its manufacturer barely legible across its tailgate.
It was looking good. In space, the Prototype's offspring would be
programmed to seek out warheads, to ignore decoys, and to direct a
Brilliant Pebble interceptor to a collision with a warhead before it
could fall to earth.

Looking good, he said to himself as he began the third test run.
Gallagher typed in *FORD*. The cursor blinked as the rooftop camera
surveyed the highway. He tapped his finger impatiently, waiting for
the Prototype to find its target. The screen remained blank. *Damn!*
He reached up to bail out of the run when his STU-3 telephone rang
like an alarm bell. It rang again, echoing from the deserted corridor
outside his office.

"Gallagher here," he said without a trace of curiosity over who
might be calling him at three-thirty in the morning.

"George Parrum here," came the voice of the Lab's chief of
Security. "The Octopus autodialed me when you carded in. You're
working tonight?"

"I'm trying to," said Gallagher impatiently. The cursor on his
screen was still blinking. Was it a software problem, or was there
simply no Ford for it to find? *Maybe if I. . .*

"I take it you haven't been informed," said Parrum. "Your
access code has been decertified. You shouldn't have been admit-
ted."

"Uh-huh." Gallagher began retyping a new command, the telephone cradled on his shoulder. "What was that?" he said as he
erased *FORD* and entered *NISSAN*.

"Dr. Gallagher, are you alone?"

He punched the button to start the new test run. "Yes, why?"

"Your telephone is secure?"

A chime sounded as a Sentra appeared on the screen. "Secure?" said Gallagher. He checked to be certain the secure light on his STU-3 was illuminated. "Sure," he said. "What was that about my code? Do I need to change it again?"

"That won't be necessary. I'm sorry to be the one to tell you this," said Parrum. "But the word just came down from Washington today. From the Organization."

"Oh?" said Gallagher, knowing that the regular project milestone meetings were scheduled with the Strategic Defense Initiative Organization. He blanked the screen. "What word was that, Mr. Parrum?"

A long sigh was encrypted, decoded, and exhaled through the STU-3's earphone. "S-5 was cut," said Parrum. "They're shutting the supercomputer project down. You'll be given the option of—"

"They did *what?*"

The silence that followed was like the interval between distant lightning and thunder. The Prototype's cooling fans whirred softly.

"I'm sorry, Dr. Gallagher. I tried to reach you at home, and I did leave a note. I believe Dr. Woodruff also tried to contact you."

"You mean, they're cutting us out *now?* But we're ready to ship!"

"Dr. Gallagher," said Parrum, "I'm sorry. It's not up to me. It's not up to anybody here at the Lab. Now, you're going to have a problem getting out. Your access card won't work. It might even set off an alarm, so stay right there, gather up your personal materials, and I'll send a guard over to give you a—"

"Stuff it, Parrum," Gallagher seethed. "I'll get to the bottom of this my own way." He had the telephone directory open, and his finger was hunting the home number of the head of S-5.

"Dr. Woodruff left for Washington," Parrum said. "He won't be back for several days."

Gallagher stopped. Could this man read minds?

"I know you must be upset. But don't do anything foolish, Dr. Gallagher. Remember, the project owns all the results that S-5 has come up with to date. If anything is missing, or even damaged, some fairly serious—''

''I don't do sabotage,'' said Gallagher. ''Those damned fools in Washington are a hell of a lot better at it than I could ever be.'' He shook his head. ''We're almost *finished!*''

''I'll send an escort to your office.''

''Thanks.'' With that, Gallagher slammed the STU-3 phone back into its cradle. The secure light winked out.

He sat back in his chair. ''I can't believe it. I cannot fucking believe it.'' He listened, but the silent halls and empty offices were more convincing. ''Idiots.'' He slapped at the kill button. The whir of the Prototype died and the screen went dark. He looked over at five years of work crystallized into a gleaming gold cylinder. *I bet the Japanese wouldn't kill it.* He had a brief, treasonous thought that he stuffed back into its cage with surprising difficulty.

''Fucking idiots,'' he said aloud. Killing the S-5 project would mean that there would be no all-seeing eye, no lightning-fast brain to make a Brilliant Pebble anything more than a dumb boulder. And should America ever need an antimissile shield, limited or otherwise, it wouldn't be there.

Never mind a huge volley of ICBMs; the Russians were on the ropes. But even as the threat from their missile fields ebbed, new ones, more dangerous ones, were rising in other places. Which was worse, a superpower that had too much at risk to contemplate starting a nuclear war, or a myriad of little countries with nothing to lose? It was clear enough to Gallagher.

He looked at the blank screen. ''Well,'' he said, ''I guess that's about it. Five years. It's been fun.'' He suddenly pushed away from the desk, an acid taste rising in his throat. ''Shit,'' he said to himself. He stood up and grabbed his cotton flight jacket and walked out of his office, leaving the lights burning. When he came to the inner security door, he pulled out his green Q-1 card, inserted it, punched in his code, and the door buzzed. ''Figures.''

Well, thought Gallagher as he made his way back out into the quiet night, *now I can practice all day.* If PALS was dead, if the work of half a decade had just been erased at the stroke of a bureaucrat's pen, the upcoming aerobatics competition in Yverdon, Switzerland, was still very much on.

He walked out onto the deserted blacktop of the parking area. *Shit.* A few wisps of morning fog had drifted in, forming faint yellow halos around the security lights.

He cleared his mind and shook his long arms, flinging off the tension, feeling the wet air on his bare skin. *Begin.* The first Aresti symbol flashed in his mind, a faintly oriental shape of line and curve that was the written language of aerobatic flight. *Roll!* Gallagher leaned over, his hands together and outstretched, as he stepped through the complicated aerobatics routine he planned to fly in Switzerland.

Knife edge! Snap left and hesitate! One, two, three, four, and over! Both hands flew through the air in close formation. *Dive and pullout, then up up UP UP and vertical!* He swooped into a low crouch and stood his full six feet, his hands now high above his head, his fingers stretched out toward the stars, reaching for altitude, maintaining the purity of the vertical line. The next shape began to form. Suddenly, two bright headlights topped by a sparkling blue strobe appeared from the direction of the Lab's main gate. They swept over the deserted parking lot. A probing spotlight snapped on, catching Gallagher square in its beam. He held a hand up against the dazzle.

"Dr. Gallagher?" said the guard. "Are you all right, sir?"

Gallagher nodded. "Sure thing. I'm just getting a little—" He was interrupted by the hoot of the intruder alarm blasting from the loudspeaker above Building 1877.

Two guards got out, their sidearms out and ready. One made for the door and the other waited by Gallagher. A walkie-talkie crackled on his hip. "Nice night," said the one standing by Gallagher. He kept his automatic pistol out. "Must be a problem with the system."

"You know," said Gallagher, "that's exactly what I was thinking myself."

3

Saturday,
21 July 1990

The afternoon sun turned each flaw and scratch in the crimson Sukhoi's bubble canopy into a prism, flashing rainbows through the cockpit. Elena snuggled deep into the SU-26's sharply raked seat, the control stick light in her right hand, her elbow resting on her thigh. How lucky could one person be? Flying the very best aerobatic airplane in all the world on such a beautiful day? She checked left, then right, then banked back toward the one-kilometer-square cube of sky known to every aerobatics pilot in the world as the Box.

Elena had flown the intricate compulsory figures twice today, and they were beginning to get that solid, hammered feeling she knew they had to have. She glanced at the bright afternoon sun. It glittered in oily iridescence off the river below.

Once more? The championships in Switzerland were coming up fast, and it was impossible to practice too much. She smiled and reached down into the neck of her flightsuit, drawing out the brilliant crystal of her special talisman. The diamond sparkled as she brought it to her lips and kissed it for good luck. She checked the panel clock and drew in her breath. It was one of the most important instruments in the fuel-gulping Sukhoi; configured for aerobatics, the plane carried barely twenty-five minutes of fuel. She had been aloft for twenty. Practice or no, it was time to land.

Banking north, she pulled the throttle back, letting the engine rumble back to just under a thousand revolutions to the minute. The blades of the propeller flashed in the bright sun.

Elena slowed the Sukhoi to ninety knots as the single long runway west of the city of Serpukhov appeared over the nose. Home to the All-Union Aerobatic team, the white ribbon of concrete cut diagonally across a field the color of black bread. Beyond it, checkerboard patches of crops were interspersed with dark green stands of birch. The gentle terrain of rounded, glacial hills and fertile valleys marched to the horizon under a perfect cloudless sky.

It was all so beautiful. Here she was, soaring above the black-soiled croplands in the best, most capable aerobatic airplane in the world. And no apologies were required. The Sukhoi's design was not borrowed. The West had nothing like it. This was a *Russian* airplane, even if she would never say as much to her father. The old Lithuanian hated anything Russian, even the good things.

She snapped inverted with a flick of the control stick. The Sukhoi rolled around its axis as though on jeweled bearings, coming to a stop with deep green fields flowing by over her head. The combination of the best technologies with the most productive land on earth could provide the wealth that seventy years of mismanagement and stagnation could not. Why was it so hard for her father to understand something so clear?

The Vedneyev sputtered. Elena rolled back upright and dropped the nose of her Sukhoi to point right at the small building beside the single long runway at Serpukhov. She checked the panel clock again, then measured the distance she had to fly before landing. Elena laughed. *Why not?* She ran the throttle forward, and the airspeed indicator surged around its dial. The controls stiffened with speed. The air roared through a small crack where canopy met fuselage.

As she swept fifty meters over the runway, a stream of dots spilled from the wooden team building: her teammates. *Good!* she thought. *Let them watch!* She ran the throttle the rest of the way until it stopped dead in the panel. The big radial wound up into an uncharacteristic scream as it pulled the little Sukhoi into a high-speed low pass.

She fed in right stick and performed a quick victory roll. The runway blurred by, ending at a fence, and beyond that came a small lake dotted with white birds. She thought a command at the sensitive stick and leveled off. An almost imperceptible tug sent her up, up on a beautiful vertical line, the sky filling the Sukhoi's canopy, the red tail pointed straight back at the dark blue water of the lake.

She looked behind her, taking measure of the purity of her climb. When she looked ahead, a tiny white dot marred the perfection of the sky. Before Elena could react, it ballooned into the frantic beating of a gull dead ahead.

"No!" She slammed the stick over to avoid it as its wings tucked into a dive, but to no avail. She slewed right as the bird dived to the left. The gull flew directly into Elena's windscreen.

The thump was so light she thought for a moment that it had missed, but the blood and feathers smeared across the Plexiglas bubble said otherwise. For a moment she did nothing. The howl of the engine was normal, the arc of her propeller undamaged. All her instruments were unchanged. But a hollow feeling, half sadness and half wary superstition, made her throttle back, turn to her home runway, and land.

The engine began to surge as it drew the bottom of the fuel tank through its nine cylinders. The Sukhoi tapped its tailwheel down first, followed by the double bounce of its titanium-strutted mains. She cut the mixture, killing the engine, letting the speed of her landing roll bring her all the way to the team building. As Elena cracked open the canopy, the smell of the nearby fields flooded in with the wild cheering of her team. A feather flew over her head and drifted to the runway.

Khalida Makagonova, the youngest member of the women's team, ran up to the ticking Sukhoi, her face alight. "You looked like a hawk! What a beautiful pass it was! I thought . . ." She stopped when she saw the blood. "Elena! Are you . . ."

"I am fine, Khalida. I hit a damned bird." Elena scowled as she unbuckled from her harness and stood up. Try as she might, like aviators everywhere, Elena felt that killing anything with wings was a bad sign.

Kashum Nazhmudinov, the team trainer, threw open the door to the operations building, his face a thunderhead of wrinkles. He tossed a cigarette aside as he came. The four other women fell instantly silent. He stalked over to Elena as she stepped from the Sukhoi's wing. "You came in very quietly," he said. "And you were so low you hit a sea gull. Should I bother to check the fuel tank?"

"No," she said softly. Elena swallowed hard. "It's empty. And the bird came at me so fast I couldn't avoid it, Kashum. There was no—"

"Someday," the trainer interrupted, "you will learn that it is easier to be careful than lucky." He clucked his tongue as he brushed away the last feathers glued to her canopy by blood. "As I thought. Cracked. Another few centimeters and it would have come straight through and hit you in the face. You were going, what, perhaps two hundred kilometers per hour?" He turned. "We all are in such awe of your intelligence, *Professor* Pasvalys, but tell me. Do you know what would have happened then?" His voice built to a shout. "Showing off! For what? What skill is there in it? Do you think you are here to prove how daring you can be?"

"I'm sorry," Elena said, hoping to forestall an even worse eruption. "I'll be careful."

"No more showing off! Fly your routine and fly it safely. Is that understood?" He swung to face the other women. They were all watching, waiting. "Well? What are you all gawking at?" he thundered. "Back to work! We will be in Yverdon before you know it!"

Saturday Morning, 21 July 1990

Gallagher pulled the Saab off the taxiway and onto the stubby brown grass. At seven forty-five in the morning, the sun was still burning its way through the lingering fog. Gallagher got out and walked over to his hangar. It was the very last in the row, close by to a storage yard stacked twenty feet high with old radial engines, each in a barrel labeled with faded dates and signatures. He glanced over at the blinking beacon atop the Livermore control tower. It was still IFR, or instrument conditions. But the sun was hot and patient. The fog wouldn't last. To the east, just over the wind generator farms atop Altamont Pass, Gallagher could already see a slot of blue sky. By the time he was ready to take off, the last wisps would be gone. The conditions would be perfect.

He took off his cotton jacket and tossed it down to the tarmac. It was going to be a hot one over the pass, and his flameproof Nomex flightsuit, its green fabric covered with patches from old aerobatics competitions, was all the clothes he needed.

Just beyond the strange, weeping forms of the deodar cedars that lined the airport fence, the nearby freeway hummed with morning traffic. Even weekends were workdays for the many high-tech start-up firms drawn to Livermore by the presence of the Lab. But not for Gallagher; not anymore. George Parrum's call at three-thirty in the morning had put an end to that.

Gallagher put his shoulder to the first door and shoved it open a foot. *Parrum. After five years, I get the boot from a dumb-ass cop,* he thought as he slipped the hangar key into his breast pocket. He eased between the opened doors and into the cool dark of his hangar.

More by feel and memory than by sight, he maneuvered around the invisible wings of his Pitts Special. He touched the cool, taut fabric of the tiny biplane's upper wing. It resounded with a small, satisfying drumroll to Gallagher's inquisitive fingers. *Good morning,* he thought at the machine. *Ready?*

He knew the answer to that one. Some experts claimed the Pitts, a design pioneered some thirty years back, was too old for Unlimited competition; that the future belonged to the brutal, exotic planes coming out of specialized aeronautical laboratories.

Airplanes such as the Extra 300 and the Laser series were starting to dominate world aerobatics. The Russian Sukhoi, with more than a hundred extra horses in its bulbous nose, was scaring everyone. But just the same, Gallagher knew *this* Pitts was ready to go anywhere he had the nerve and skill to fling it. He had won medals in her before; he would win some more before he was through. *She may be old,* he thought with a smile, *but she ain't broke.*

The muscular biplane was barely chest high, a functional sculpture of steel bones and fabric skin. It was the big two-place S-2 model with a second cramped cockpit for a passenger. It was, he reflected, mostly wasted space. His work had come to dominate his life, especially after that terrible summer at Stanford. The Prototype only got better as he worked on it; the same had not been true of his broken-off relationship.

His eyes grew accustomed to the dark. The brilliant yellow and black stripes of its bold design seemed to glow within the dim hangar. On the snub nose of the biplane was the name given by its original owner: a cocky macho name that fit Gallagher's mentor, an old naval aviator, better than it did Gallagher: *Anytime Baby.* A black, round bomb with the number 8 at its center was painted on the S-2's tail. A snaking, sparking fuse coiled away from it.

Gallagher remembered his old aerobatics instructor's craggy, permanently sunburned face; there were folds cut in his leathery skin so deep they never saw the light of day. The old man had ended his flying career and his life at a country airshow while flying a stranger's airplane, an old Waco. The bones of the old biplane showed through its skin like an old horse's rib cage. The plane had come apart after a six-g pull-up. The lower wing had collapsed up and over the cockpit, trapping him. The wreck had burned furiously for hours.

Even now after the passing of five years, five airshow seasons, it still surprised him that *Anytime Baby* had been handed over in the will. "Stud," he had once told Gallagher, "with a name like Wyn you'd better get good in a hurry."

Gallagher had laughed but took the admonition to heart. It had been a long, tough climb up the ziggurat of aerobatic competition. But Gallagher had arrived. Regional champion; the nationals at Fond du Lac. In a few weeks, he would join four other men and five women. Together, they would represent the United States at the

World Championships at Yverdon, Switzerland. He stood a real chance to come home with the title *best in the world.*

He stood quietly for a moment, then pulled the canvas cover from the canopy. The Plexiglas shimmered like a jewel in the light cast by the half-opened hangar. He turned at the sound of a soft scrape of tennis shoe on tarmac.

"Hey! Is anybody home?"

Gallagher turned. "Hey yourself."

It was Sara Avilar, a young woman Gallagher had taught to fly aerobatics three years ago. The Prototype had eaten up so much of his time, he had only occasionally found the chance to fly with her since. He was dimly aware that she had gotten quite good.

Tipping the scale at just under a hundred pounds, Avilar and her tiny, single-place Pitts S-1T were made for each other. She had been an avid student, and today she was an up-and-coming advanced-level competitor in her own right, even if she needed pillows under her seat so that her legs could reach the rudder pedals. "What's up, Wyn?" she asked as she walked up to Gallagher. Her curly, dark hair barely reached his shoulder. "What's going on? I thought you Lab ghouls hated sunlight. You're not supposed to be here in the A.M."

"I was getting in a rut," said Gallagher as he shoved the hangar doors completely open. "Give me a hand pulling this thing out, will you?"

"Anytime," she said, scampering over to the far wing. She would do a great deal for her teacher, even if Gallagher was entirely oblivious of the fact. Small as she was, her enormous dark eyes gave her a far larger presence. More than a few times, Gallagher had caught her flashing them squarely at him. He had frozen as solid as a deer caught in high beams. This morning she wore a sky blue flightsuit and running shoes. A pair of laughable granny-style glasses sat perched on her freckled nose. Her hair was curled even tighter by the fog. "So how come you're not at work at the Bomb Factory?" she persisted as they rolled his Pitts outside.

"Hey. Enough, okay?" Gallagher gave her a fierce look. "What got you out of the People's Republic of Berkeley so early? I thought you liked to go hang out and drink coffee with your weirdo friends on Saturdays."

"Weirdo friends? Just because they don't choose to build hydrogen bombs is no cause—"

"I don't build bombs, Sara."

"You might as well. Weapons of peace. What a lot of BS. If SDI's ever used, we're all history. And if it won't be used, it's just a bunch of bucks in a big, black hole."

"Sara . . ."

"Okay. Anyway, I thought I'd catch some breakfast over at the golf club and then go fly. I have some secrets of my own. Only my secrets don't go boom. Unlike some other guys I know."

"I just bet you do." Gallagher sighed. "Look, Sara, I'm going flying, okay? I don't want to talk shop. I'm kind of on vacation."

"Oh, yeah? How come?" She stopped as Gallagher continued to pivot the biplane around to face the runway.

"Never mind," he said as he walked over and grabbed his thin-pak parachute from the Saab. The hatchback hissed shut. Gallagher locked it and carefully placed the key atop the rear tire. He didn't want anything in his pockets while he was flying; you never knew where a loose pencil or a handful of change might wind up when you were inverted. People had been killed that way. "Work still fun at Siliconix?" he asked.

"Just." Sara, like many other people in the San Francisco Bay area, did something with computers. He wasn't sure just what it was. "The Japanese always killed us in quantity," she explained, "now they're doing it with quality, too. If orders get any slower, I'll have to learn to knit. Maybe I'll be an aerobatics instructor."

"You and me both." He buckled the parachute's chest strap and cinched it tight.

She watched his face. Something was definitely wrong, and he didn't seem to want to go into it. She decided to hit his flank. "So tell me, Wyn. What are you going to practice?"

"If I told you," he said seriously, "I'd have to kill you afterward."

Aerobatic routines came in two varieties: known and unknown. The first were assigned, the last you made up in the hopes of astounding the competition. The unknowns were considered as classified as the PALS Prototype was at Lawrence Livermore.

"Hey, come on, secret-agent man," said Sara. "What am I? The KGB?"

"If you were," said Gallagher with a chuckle, "you wouldn't be so dangerous."

"Dangerous? Me?" She smiled. "I like the sound of that."

"You would."

"So?"

"So I'm going through my freestyle first," he said. "If that feels good, I'll fold right into my four-minute. You know what's on the freestyle card. You don't get to know what my four-minute looks like."

"Fair."

Gallagher had been working secretly on this last series of figures for well over a year. Revealed only a few days before the competition, the sequence included maneuvers that took the Pitts right to the ragged edge and then, when there seemed to be no more to give, pushed the flight envelope one notch beyond.

He saw she was still watching him. "Something else I can do for you, Sara? You want to schedule a lesson later today or what?"

"Hey, Wyn. Word," she said as she watched him snap the last parachute strap into place. "Take it easy this morning, okay? Seriously. You're looking a little wasted."

"Wasted? Me?" he said as he double-checked the gleaming metal D ring connected to his rip cord. Then he stopped and shook his head sadly. "Well, hell, maybe I am." He unlocked the canopy stepped up on the wing, and swung one long leg up and over th cockpit sill.

"Fly well, Wyn," Sara said, stepping away from the plane. "E careful up there."

He gave her a thumbs-up and began his prestart check.

Small as it was for his six-foot frame, the cockpit felt like hor Gallagher could close his eyes and reach out and identify every l

control. The stick grip fit the inside of his palm to perfection, the rudder-pedal straps, adjusted as far forward as they went to accommodate his long legs, slipped over his Nikes as though by their own choice. *Welcome back,* the Pitts seemed to whisper.

He snapped the five-point restraint buckle onto each of the heavy webbed belts and snugged each one tight. Letting out breath to take up even more slack, he retightened each one again. Upside down and pulling negative g, the Pitts doing its best to fling him from its back, too tight was not nearly tight enough. He left enough room at the shoulders to keep his back from compressing in the sudden maneuvers, then, when all was to his satisfaction, he wrapped a final, ultimate belt across his waist and clipped it into place. If all else failed, this would at least keep him and the Pitts together.

"Clear!" he shouted. Gallagher energized the starter.

The big Lycoming in the nose of the Pitts turned the flashing blades once, twice, then caught into an irregular stumble of fire that smoothed out as Gallagher adjusted the mixture. A fierce, challenging wind blew back across his face, setting the fabric of the airplane drumming. The stick controls trembled in the slipstream, tapping his hands and feet impatiently.

He left the canopy open and fed in throttle. Sara Avilar waved, and he nodded back. The Pitts danced eagerly away from the confining hangar and out onto the taxiway. The prop blast whipped her curly hair as he went by.

He pressed the stick trigger and the radio popped and hissed in his headset. "Livermore Ground, Pitts One One Whiskey Golf at the east tee hangars, taxi."

"Mornin', Whiskey Golf," came back the familiar voice from the tower. "We just went VF and R. Taxi to Runway Two Five Right and call when you're ready."

"One Whiskey Golf." S-turning so that he could see ahead and over the high snout of the Pitts, Gallagher came to the run-up pad. With both feet stomped on the toe brakes, he brought the engine up to takeoff power. The 310-horse Lycoming roared its approval.

Left mag, right mag, both, and check, he thought as he tested each of the two independent electrical systems. *Altitude zeroed.* He

swung the altimeter needle from the actual field elevation to zero. At two hundred knots upside down, there was no way to interpolate your altitude unless you began with a stone-simple zero. *Set*. He pressed the stick trigger and spoke again.

"Pitts One One Whiskey Golf is ready. We'll be headed to the practice area over the pass. We'd like a special departure."

"You're all clear, Wyn," came the same voice. "Special's approved."

Gallagher reached back over his head and pulled the Plexiglas canopy forward. The intense rush of air now flowed smoothly over the nicely faired cockpit. He swung the nose of the Pitts out onto the runway, pointing directly at the dark wall of the East Bay Hills.

"Here we go," he said aloud as he lined up on the long white centerline and eased the throttle in. The biplane was small for all the horses up front. Long before Gallagher's hand had pushed the throttle to the stop, the machine bolted forward, its small wheels skipping across the dark runway pavement. The tail rose before a hundred feet had flashed by, and then, with that sweetest of feelings, the biplane's stubby wings bit air and took hold. The earth fell away as Gallagher inched back on the stick and shot into the air. The Pitts felt perfect.

Feeling his weight and his worries fall away as the ground streaked below him, he hauled back on the stick, pointed his nose straight up, and blasted into the cool heavens, his windshield filled with nothing but sky. At fifteen hundred feet, he rolled and pushed over level, his course now nearly due east.

"Appreciate the show," said the tower man. He was used to Gallagher's very special arrivals and departures.

"Whiskey Golf is leaving the pattern to the east," he triggered, and then reached over and toggled the radio to silence. Now only the throaty rumble of the big engine and the sandblast sound of the air flowing back at one hundred knots filled his ears. Directly ahead, the low sun struck the thousands of windmills spinning atop Altamont Pass, turning them into a flashing sea of steel flowers sprouting from the dry summer earth.

As he followed the course of Highway 580, the big cluster of buildings at Lawrence Livermore passed under his wing. Building 1877 was hard to distinguish from up here; there were a great many low, sprawling buildings just like it.

But Building 111, once home to Dr. Edward Teller, the father of the hydrogen bomb, was perfectly plain from an altitude of four thousand feet. Gallagher checked left, right, then rolled the Pitts inverted. Teller Tech went by overhead like an architectural planning model. He considered buzzing Building 111. It would be dead easy. *Well, Parrum,* he thought, *you wanted to see me? Here I am.* His hand tensed on the stick, but at the last moment, he simply rolled upright. What would those bored security troops do if a small plane was spotted heading straight for Livermore's nerve center?

Gallagher pulled back on the stick and entered a big barnstormer's loop. *Feels good,* he thought, his blood rushing to his scalp and his shoulder straps biting into his arms as he went slightly negative g over the top. He touched the feather-light stick and the Pitts corkscrewed upright with a small, almost unnoticeable shudder, its nose pointing steeply downhill. The shudder went away as mysteriously as it had arrived.

"What's that all about?" Gallagher wondered with a small frown. He checked the engine instruments. Every needle was deep in the green. *Perfect,* he thought. *Loosen up, partner.*

Altamont Pass fell behind him, and the vast flats of the Central Valley were all his. Way in the distance, a ragged line of snow stood guard atop the high peaks of the Sierra Nevada. He ran the throttle forward and stormed into the practice area, all thoughts of Prototypes and phone calls and wasted years far, far behind.

With a sudden, savage pull he threw the Pitts into knife-edge, then inverted once again in a hesitation roll, back to upright. *No surprises,* he thought at the Pitts. *Okay?*

The straight, glittering path of an irrigation canal below would be the fixed reference against which he would measure the perfection of the lines he would slice through the cool morning air. He took a deep, relaxing breath and formed up in his mind the first Aresti ideogram. *Begin. Accelerate to one forty, level, perfect level! Line up and pull!* The Pitts stood on its tail, the brilliant sweep of the prop a crystal circle against the pure blue sky, straight up. *Roll!* The S-2 swung in sure, precise arcs around the pure vertical line of the zoom. *Airspeed!* The needle plummeted to zero, but still the Pitts held on by the immense effort of its big engine and swinging prop, hovering like a mad bumblebee.

NOW! A hard kick of rudder swapped the Pitts end for end in a perfect hammerhead stall. The windshield was filled with the brown earth. *Roll ninety.* Gallagher flicked the Pitts inverted. *Pullout on the outside.* He recovered from the inverted dive upside down, his cheeks pulling from the minus four g's that registered on the accelerometer. *Snap roll up!*

"God, I love this!" he exulted above the bellowing engine.

An hour passed in the rapid countings of rolls, loops, and snap maneuvers. "And now it's time for something completely different!" Gallagher scanned the skies for intruders, and finding none, he leveled once more and rammed the throttle to the stops.

He began the four-minute sequence in a roar of power and a rush of acceleration. The airspeed indicator needle surged around its dial. As the speed built, the stick felt solid yet almost unimaginably sensitive, as though the smallest twitch could send the Pitts careening through the sky in great, elegant slices of air and cloud.

One sixty, one sixty-five, okay, hold it, hold it, NOW! Gallagher pulled into a zoom climb that turned into a vertical roll. The Pitts spiraled up on an invisible winding tower of thrust. *RIGHT stick LEFT rudder!* Three ascending spins flung him against the cockpit walls as the airspeed bled off to nothing. The engine yowled as he spun upward. *Throttle back!* The Pitts once again hung in the air, did a horizontal pirouette, then fell from the sky with a vengeance in a flat spin. His eyes flicked to the madly unwinding altimeter. Five thousand feet; four thousand feet; he was dropping like an iron leaf. It was time.

OPPOSITE rudder, INSIDE stick! Still hanging from his straps inverted, Gallagher rammed the sensitive stick against his knee. He heard a faint metallic *clink!* from someplace at his feet. The Pitts started to recover from the spin, rolling nearly upright, but then it stopped. The airspeed needle sagged. The nose shuddered and fell, the wings corkscrewing around tighter and tighter into another, unplanned spin. *What?*

He stomped opposite rudder and the gyrating spin snapped into a pure clean dive. He throttled back the racing Lycoming and pulled the stick aft for a normal recovery.

The stick moved back an inch and stopped.

What? He pulled back harder, then pushed. The stick froze in earnest with a sickening grinding sound of binding metal.

Shit! The nose was now tucking under as the forward-jammed control stick commanded it. Gallagher yanked back hard and felt the metal tubing bend, nearly break, but not budge. Something was jamming his elevators into a dive!

He felt the hot rush of fear course through his blood as the Pitts tumbled inverted, obeying the last and immovable control input. *What's going on?* He eyed the unwinding altimeter. Altitude was money in the bank, and Gallagher was fast going broke.

He shot a quick glance down to his feet as the Pitts dropped drunkenly through vertical again and onto its back. *Nothing!* He saw nothing in the complicated joint the control stick was mounted on. *Do something!*

The ground rushed up as the S-2 plummeted.

No! The altimeter was now fleeing through two thousand. Another few seconds and there wouldn't be enough space between Gallagher and the ground for the parachute to take hold. The memory of his own instructor, tumbling down from the sky in his crippled biplane, cut through his memory like acid. Suddenly there was no more when, no more if. There was only *now*.

He grabbed the canopy jettison handle and yanked it back with one hand. The other punched his restraint buckle. The five-point harness sprang loose. All of a sudden it was very windy. Gallagher tried to stand up and vault out of the cockpit, but something grabbed him around the stomach and held on. He was caught! He saw the altimeter hurtle through five hundred feet as the Pitts nosed inverted. It threw him hard against the reserve strap he had forgotten to unhook. The force of over nine negative g's snapped the nylon webbing like a dry stick and fired him straight down at the swelling earth.

Gallagher tumbled. Up and down, the purity of his vertical line, all lost now in a roar of air and the rush of adrenaline. He swatted at the D ring on his chute, but the slipstream made it joggle away from his hand. The wind whistled up from between his legs as the unforgivingly hard earth hurtled up at him.

He concentrated on the flashing D ring and slowly, oblivious of the nearness of the rising rocks, he grabbed it with a violent pull. *Too low,* he realized. There was a stand of trees, some kind of orchard, right below him. It was no longer a geometric square; it was individual trunks, branches. A metal fence rising up to smite him.

A bomb burst of white nylon exploded overhead as the parachute opened. He had the impossible sensation of being fired from a cannon up into the sky. It was a short-lived illusion.

It shattered an instant later as he crashed through the high branches of an almond tree. The shroud lines tangled and caught. He jerked to a stop, limp and only half aware, his body falling only now into shock.

Then he heard it. He let out a long, pained groan and shut his eyes. Half a mile away, his beloved Pitts struck the earth in an explosion of spars and wings. *It's over,* he thought as the blackness swallowed him whole.

4

George Parrum put down the pencil he had meticulously razored to a fine point. A small cone of shavings marred his otherwise perfectly clear desk. He carefully swept them into his shredder and tapped the foot switch. The metal jaws snapped shut and ground them to powder.

It was one minute before eight in the morning, and Parrum was ready to begin his day with a row of gleaming yellow pencils, perfectly sharpened by hand.

George Parrum believed in order. It was the only thing the fifty-two-year-old former intelligence officer trusted. He had lived and worked in the shadows long enough to see everything else melt away. Even his hair was disciplined: a steel gray brush only now beginning to thin. He checked his watch. *Now.*

Parrum gathered a few briefing papers on the bizarre accident that had befallen Dr. Gallagher and made his way out of his spacious office and down a carpeted hall. He paused by the closed door leading to Dr. Edward Teller's office. The eighty-two-year-old director emeritus was off, as usual, stumping for SDI. The joke at the Lab was that he had swallowed a bit too much uranium over the years, for his energy seemed inexhaustible. When would the old Hungarian ever slow down?

Parrum continued walking down the hushed hallway. Lawrence

Livermore wasn't like Langley, but there were compensations. Here there were *real* secrets worth protecting. Even better, unlike the hobbled drones operating amid the ruins of the CIA's Clandestine Directorate, Parrum had the freedom to do real work here, and that suited him just fine.

Parrum was short, but built like a wrestler. His midsection was as hard at fifty-two as it had been at twenty, and he wore his hair the way he had worn it back when the Agency was more than an address.

At the end of the seventh-floor corridor, he walked through the last doorway. A young woman sat at a small, lustrously polished desk. A large pot of African violets stood on one corner. A security camera winked red from a corner. Another door was right behind her, partially open, leading to the director's conference room.

"Is Dr. Nichols going to join us?" Parrum asked her.

"No. He won't be in for another hour. But you can go in. Mr. Enstrom is expecting you."

Parrum felt his pulse quicken as he walked up to the dark oak door. He had never had an audience with the pope, but he imagined it wouldn't feel much different. He hesitated. Then, as the sweep hand on his watch passed twelve, the director of security at Lawrence Livermore National Laboratory stepped into the small conference room.

"George," said William Hewlett Enstrom with a nod. "Please. Sit down." He held his hand out for Gallagher's file as Parrum pulled out a heavy wooden chair. A crystal decanter filled with ice water sweated onto the table. There was only one glass.

Parrum slid Gallagher's file across the gleaming mahogany. He noticed the thick folder Enstrom had been reading before he arrived. His eyes caught the Top Secret stamp from across the table. Parrum sat down and silently watched as Enstrom read.

Dr. Edward Teller had been the Lab's founding father; its current head, a man whose specialty was exotic, third-generation weapons, was his protégé. But William Enstrom, and the Kratos Foundation that he chaired, had always been the true power behind the throne. Silver hair, bespoke navy suit, and keen, appraising eyes, Enstrom looked as though he owned the place. In a way, he and the Kratos Foundation he chaired *did* own it.

Formed in the late 1950s, the Kratos Foundation funded the Lab's summer-intern project, sweeping up the best and the brightest young researchers from all over the world, bringing them to Lawrence Livermore and turning them loose to daydream.

It wasn't a matter of simple altruism; whenever a Kratos Fellow's daydream struck pay dirt, the Foundation took care to channel it into the appropriate slot in the private sector. Indeed, Enstrom's old aerospace firm, Norton Aerodyne, had been the ultimate recipient of a gusher of lucrative breakthroughs pioneered at the Lab and thoughtlessly abandoned by an uncaring government.

William Hewlett Enstrom, classics scholar, Princeton class of 1944, had spent much of his adult life issuing commands. Now, as he sat reading through Gallagher's personnel file, he exuded a natural and irresistible aura of power so strong it seemed like ozone in Parrum's nostrils.

"Interesting," said Enstrom as he closed the file and looked up at Parrum. "George," he began, "it may seem tangential, but do you remember the 1964 presidential campaign? Goldwater against Johnson?"

Parrum cocked his head. "Vaguely. Why?"

"Goldwater was a simple truthteller. It destroyed him, of course. But he said something I've always found compelling: *extremism in the defense of liberty is no vice.* Do you remember?"

"No, sir," said Parrum. "I was out of the country back then."

"Of course." Enstrom smiled knowingly. It evaporated in a blink. "George, I believe in those words. I think you do, too. We may be nearly alone in this. I don't need to tell you what's happening in Washington. Congress is cutting the heart out of our nation's ability to defend itself. The peace dividend is what they're calling it, but you and I both know it's just a lot of politics. Where will it end?"

"Things are getting real tight here." Parrum nodded. "The Lab would be in tough shape if it weren't for the Foundation. Even with it, we're shutting down a lot of programs. Losing docs. Gallagher's

own project was just canceled,'' he said, looking at the Top Secret
file folder before Enstrom.

"That couldn't be helped,'' said Enstrom. "Even Kratos can't
hold back the tides. Not single-handed. We need some help.'' He
leaned forward, pinning Parrum in his gaze. "We need your help,
George. That's why I've come this morning.''

"We?'' asked Parrum. He knew Kratos, for all the billions at its
command, was Enstrom and Enstrom was Kratos; its corporate
headquarters was a postbox at the Livermore station, and its sole
employee was a part-time secretary. Everything else was taken care
of capably, and quietly, by Enstrom himself. "What kind of help
are you talking about?''

"George,'' Enstrom continued, "what we're about to discuss is
sensitive. But I know you, and I know your history. I know what
happened to you at the Agency. In a way, it has just happened to me
at Norton Aerodyne.''

Parrum narrowed his eyes. "I heard rumors.''

"We're no longer deemed necessary, you and I. Defense is
obsolete. Forget the thirty thousand nuclear weapons that are tar-
geted on us. Forget the Middle East. Forget that the Japanese can
throttle eighty-seven percent of our defense industry if they decide
to hold back producing microchips. Forget them all. The politicians
have decreed that it shall never rain again. Who needs purveyors of
umbrellas?'' Enstrom let a shadow of anger flit across his expression. He pushed the report on Gallagher's accident aside and pulled
a packet of photos from the other folder on his desk. His bright blue
eyes seemed to deepen to violet.

"A lot of time and sweat has gone into making strategic defense a
real possibility,'' Enstrom continued. "But Washington sees chaos
in the camp of our old enemies and finds that somehow reassuring. I
do not.'' He slid the glossies over to Parrum. "What do you make
of these?''

Parrum opened the cover sheet, noted the standard Agency warning and disclaimer form, and examined the first picture. It showed a
nighttime explosion. Tendrils of smoke and flame blew out in an
expanding fan of debris like the biggest fireworks shot of the show.

"Looks like a bomb going off," he said. "Conventional explosive. No structure. No background terrain. I presume it's midair."

"Good," Enstrom agreed. "A range safety device detonating a missile. An Iraqi missile. It even has a name. *Al Infitar.* It means the Cataclysm. I assure you, it's no exaggeration."

Parrum looked up. "I haven't been briefed on that one before." Parrum knew that Iraq possessed short-range, Soviet-designed missiles: the SCUD. He even knew of the Condor, a Brazilian missile the Iraqis were tinkering with. But the Cataclysm?

"It was a little secret they were keeping with the connivance of their Libyan friends. Or trying to keep. The Cataclysm is a true intercontinental booster developed by a rather disagreeable, and reckless, despot. Do you understand what that means?"

Parrum nodded. "Saddam Hussein could hold the region at risk."

"No!" Enstrom slammed his hand down on the desk. *"Not* the region! The *world.* From Iraq, from *anywhere on earth,* our own cities can be held hostage. We've spent forty years fixated on the Soviet threat. But now look what has happened. Do you think Saddam Hussein will be as reasonable, as fearful, as a Nikita Khrushchev?"

"Not from what I've heard," said Parrum as he shuffled the enlargement under. The next photograph showed a large multi-engined aircraft, conventional enough except that its swept wings sprouted propellers, not jets. It seemed to glow an eerie green against a black background. "A Russian Bear?"

"A Soviet Tupolev in night infrared," Enstrom explained. "It is a highly modified reconnaissance aircraft that *happened* by during a test of the Cataclysm. The photograph was taken by one of our fighter aircraft that *happened* to be there. Look at the next one."

Parrum put aside the strange figure of the spectral Bear and saw a perfectly conventional, daytime photograph of an Air Force transport retrofitted with an odd, bulbous turret just aft of the cockpit. It looked like a tumor clinging to the top of the converted 767.

"Cobra Star," said Enstrom. "Norton Aero took it on as a Skunk Works project back in 1974. We cut metal in 1979 and had operational hardware up and running four years later. It was our first attempt to mount a chemical laser, a beam weapon if you will, in an aircraft. It almost became operational, just like Gallagher's S-5 targeting computer. Almost.''

Parrum took out the picture of the Bear. ''I take it the Bear is the Russian version of Cobra Star?''

''Not Russian. *Soviet*. But yes. Excellent,'' Enstrom replied. ''Apparently, chaos or no, the opposition has a thriving strategic defense effort under way. One that has been permitted to bear fruit.'' He poured a glass of ice water. The cubes tinkled in the silence. ''An Iraqi ICBM. A Soviet SDI breakthrough. Meanwhile,'' he said as he sipped the ice water, ''we're left with nothing. Now. What about the computer designer from S-5?''

Parrum reached into his breast pocket and brought out a small, silver key. ''I have friends over at the Federal Aviation Administration. They found this item in the wreck of his biplane. It's the only piece of evidence that explains why his airplane's controls were frozen. He was lucky.''

Enstrom held out his hand. ''Not as lucky as he's going to be.''

Parrum handed over the key.

''Astonishing.'' Enstrom held the key, letting it flash in the light streaming in through his window. ''Absolutely astonishing,'' he said, his eyes distant. ''You know, George? Sometimes I can almost believe there is a God.''

''I don't follow, sir.''

''Then listen closely. That Soviet beam weapon? It came from the Serpukhov Institute of High Energy Physics. Now, I've read the biographies of the principal investigators at Serpukhov. Most of them are hacks. But one,'' he said, ''is interesting indeed. And she shares something with Gallagher.''

''She?'' *What is he getting at?*

''Dr. Elena Pasvalys is her name. A physical chemist. She's a half-Lithuanian, a member of the All-Union Aerobatic team.''

''I still don't see the connection with Gallagher. Other than sharing an interest in flying.''

Enstrom smiled like a crocodile approaching a lunch. ''Tell me,

George, wouldn't you like to know how Serpukhov made that beam weapon? How this Pasvalys woman made it possible? Wouldn't the development of it be a real shot in the arm for the Lab?''

"Of course. We could drop our wheel-spinning and concentrate on a practical technology. Not to mention busting open the whole ABM Treaty for their violation. It would work to the Lab's advantage."

Enstrom rewarded him with a nod. "And don't you think we rather need such a reinvigoration just now?"

"Yes, sir," Parrum agreed. "Just knowing the outlines of how the Russ . . . the Soviets did it would be a big help around here. After all, knowing what's possible makes the development of a workable shield much simpler. You can concentrate. Is the Agency going to take a look at this for us?"

Enstrom laughed. "Don't count on it. They'll find a hundred things to do before they take this on. No. I don't think we can count on too much help from the Agency." Enstrom waited, then, with a slight shrug, dropped a bomb. "We shall have to do it for them. And the Pasvalys woman is the key."

"We?" said Parrum. There was that troubling word again.

"You."

Parrum let Enstrom's message sink in. "But how do we gain access to her?" he asked. "We don't have the assets to work a job like that."

"Oh?" said Enstrom with the same cool smile. "Come now. Think more strongly, George. The S-5 man? This Gallagher? He's supposed to fly in Switzerland in a month, yes? The World Championships?"

"Yes . . ."

"But George, what will he fly? He crashed his airplane, if I understand you correctly." Enstrom reached under his desk and pulled out a simple leather briefcase. He unlocked it with two cracks from its hasps and pulled out a folded sheet of paper. He handed it to Parrum.

It was a sales brochure for the Sukhoi Design Bureau. The cash-starved company, seeking to earn hard currency, was selling the world's premier aerobatic airplane, the SU-26MX, for $200,000 FOB Moscow.

Enstrom then slipped a check, already signed, across the desk to Parrum. It was drawn from a Kratos Foundation account, made out to Wyn Gallagher.

Parrum scanned it and looked up. "We're buying Gallagher an airplane? How does that gain us access to this new beam weapon they've built?"

Enstrom merely raised a bushy eyebrow, as though disappointed by the slow progress of an otherwise promising student. "George," he said at last, "the Pasvalys woman flies a Sukhoi. The entire All-Union team flies them. According to the pattern they have established for the last several years, they will operate from the Sukhoi Design Bureau facility in Moscow for the week prior to the world competition. Gallagher would pick up his own Sukhoi airplane at the very same place. Now," he said with a chuckle, "do you see?"

"But that means Moscow," said Parrum as he stared at the check, then up at Enstrom. "And she's bound to be guarded. How will . . . ?"

"Fortune. Providence," said Enstrom with a smile. "The joker of the universe. Concentrate for a moment. Turn it around. How would you react to the information that someone here at the Lab, say, perhaps, Gallagher, was meeting secretly with a Soviet national?"

"He'd be out so fast he wouldn't know what hit him. Why?"

"Because," Enstrom explained, "at the very least, we can make that happen to her."

"We're going to *burn* the Pasvalys woman?" said Parrum, his face blank but his brain spooling up fast in an effort to stay abreast with Enstrom. "But Gallagher's an amateur."

"Of course. I wouldn't dream of assigning such a mission to someone like Dr. Gallagher alone. He will only cast the shadow over her, plant the seed, if you will," said Enstrom as he sipped his glass of ice water. He nodded at Parrum. "*You* will bring her out."

5

Elena stared numbly at the letter her father had sent, the one she had slipped into the top desk drawer and in the excitement of the moment had forgotten. It contained a copy of *Atgimmimas,* the official newspaper of Sajudis, the Lithuanian independence movement.

The news it contained was not good. Not at all. It was filled with stories of Soviet security troops breaking in and occupying Lithuanian state offices and radio stations. What had happened to the atmosphere of change? This sudden chill was as ominous and as inexplicable as the sun's dimming on a cloudless day. An unpredicted eclipse, dangerous in its foreshadowing.

But there was more; the careful taping pattern she and her father had established as a kind of code had been intact when she had slipped it into her drawer. No longer. Someone had entered her office, unlocked her desk, slit it open, and . . . her thoughts came to an abrupt halt when three knocks sounded from her door.

"Come!" she said angrily.

Valentin Kessel stroked his beard, hesitating, rocking from one foot to the other. She was so brash, so difficult. It would have been far better, far simpler, if Stingray had failed. But it had not, and that was going to make the message he carried all the harder for her to accept. He knocked again.

"I said come in," Elena called out again. Her door eased open.

"Ah, here you are, Elena," he said, peeking in. "I see you're very busy. Perhaps I'll come back when—"

"Not at all, Dr. Kessel. I can use the company just now." She slipped the violated envelope under a pile of papers on her desktop. "I wondered when you would stop by. Please. Come in."

"You're sure?" he said as he entered her office. He took note of Elena's outfit, a clinging sort of dress made from bright swatches of silk. Didn't she know the importance of invisibility? She would shortly learn that lesson, he suspected. He pulled out a chair and sat down. "You say you expected me?"

"Of course," she explained. "We need to put our heads together for the next test flight. But first, how much time do we have to make changes in Stingray before you fly it again?"

"Well, ah, you see . . ." He stopped, nodding to a hidden voice playing within his head. "You see, I, ah . . ."

"Yes? What is it?" She cocked her head. Why was Kessel so nervous? What did *he* have to worry about? Nobody was reading *his* mail, or were they?

"I met with Director Velikhov this morning. The department heads were there. And representatives from the Academy of Science. I . . ."

"What kind of meeting?" she asked, her heart beginning to thump a bit faster. *Academy?* What did those dinosaurs want this time? Its ranks were filled with Party hacks and well-connected incompetents. Working scientists in the Soviet Union called it the Boneyard. "Why was I not informed?"

"It was a private sort of meeting. Well, actually," Kessel said, looking into her eyes at last, "it was about you."

"Me? What about me?"

"The view was that you should take on a new assignment. In honor, you see, of all that you have done here at Serpukhov. Stingray being the latest of—"

"New assignment? Just what sort of assignment would that be?" she asked, her eyes narrowing to gunslits.

"A very important one. And in Moscow."

"Moscow?"

"The Academy is lending a hand with bringing our best science to the world market. You know how badly we need foreign investment. It is a prize assignment, Elena."

"We will sell Stingray for hard currency?" she said, her eyes wide. "Don't be ridiculous, Valentin. What is it really?"

"Not Stingray. Other things. It's official. You'll be leaving us, I'm afraid. Imagine: you will now be *Academician* Pasvalys. On to a bigger and better life. They've even found an apartment for you to—"

"I can't just leave for Moscow!" she shouted. "Stingray is barely off the drawing boards! And what could I possibly do at the Academy? It's nothing but a bunch of doddering old fools, toadies sucking up to . . ." She stopped and grabbed her telephone. "We'll see about this," she said as she dialed the director's exchange. The phone buzzed over and over in her ear.

"He isn't there," said Kessel. "Believe me. Even if he is, he isn't." His dark brown eyes looked incredibly sad. It was a cruel piece of business for Velikhov to have given him above all others this onerous job. He looked around nervously. "Elena," he said, "please. Listen to me. There are times to stand tall, yes? And there are times to blend in. To go to ground. Look at me. How have I survived so long without knowing a few things?"

"By doing nothing!" She slammed the phone back onto its cradle and breathed in slowly, letting it out, then in again. When she had calmed herself, she looked up at Kessel again. "Valentin," she said with forced evenness, "I do not work at the Institute to blend in. *Why are they burying me?*"

Kessel winced at her shout. "Please. Keep your voice down and stop with this *burying* nonsense. It makes me nervous."

"Is it because of this?" she asked, pulling out the letter from Lithuania and waving it at him. "Because I was born in—"

"It didn't help." Kessel shrugged. "It may be someone is worried about your, your heritage. But it could also be something else, too."

"Like what?" she said, crossing her arms over her chest.

"Have you ever considered that destroying an Iraqi missile was not—how shall I say it?—an example of internationalist solidarity? Do you know how much hard currency comes in from arms sales to the damned Arabs? Maybe it's that. Who knows? I say, take what is offered. It's better than anything they gave to me. Better than a lot of . . ." He paused, searching for the word.

"Other Lithuanians? Is that it? So I am no longer worthy of trust. Is that it?"

"It's all a matter of politics, and the world of politics is very mixed up right now. You of all people should know."

"I am not a politician," she said. "I am a scientist."

"*Academician* Pasvalys," said Kessel, gathering himself up, "my advice is simple." He stood up. "Put in your time at the Academy. Enjoy Moscow. You will be back at work before you know it. One thing thirty years has taught me, Elena, is that the world is round. You'll be back. It's just politics, and even politics can change."

Elena reached into the neck of her dress and pulled out the diamond pendant, the jewel with the printed circuit at its center. "This isn't politics," she said, "this is real. I *made* this." The artificial diamond flashed, but not as hotly as Elena's eyes.

"Forgive me," said Colonel Slepkin. He poked his head through the door. His red hair was plastered onto his scalp. Of course, he had not bothered to knock. "I heard voices in here and I thought it best to look in."

Slepkin wore a loose gray suit that draped from his thin frame like sails hauled up on a windless day. "After our triumphs on the battlefield of science, I wish nothing unfortunate to happen to our own secret weapon." Slepkin eyed Kessel as a man might regard an insect.

"Triumphs!" Elena fumed.

"I was just offering Dr. Pasvalys some professional advice," said Kessel as he quickly stood up. "I was leaving."

"So I see." Slepkin smiled patronizingly. Smiles came easily to him, but his eyes never joined in. "You will excuse us?"

"Of course," Kessel replied. "I was finished anyway." Kessel turned and made a slight bow to Elena. He scurried to the door and pushed by the KGB man.

Slepkin walked up to Elena's desk. His after-shave cascaded down. She wrinkled her nose as he perched his gaunt frame on the corner of her desk. "I have been informed by the center that security operations will be a little different for your trip to Moscow. Your technical success makes them value you even more than . . ." He stopped. "What is it, Elena?"

"I didn't know you dabbled in comedy," she said bitterly.

He cocked his head. "Oh? Why would you say that?"

"As if you don't know. Your friends in Moscow are burying me. Why have you come by? To throw the first shovel of dirt? As if you haven't heard."

Slepkin raised an eyebrow. "I see Valentin has spoken with you. Yes. I have heard. There is little that happens here that I miss. You don't seem pleased with your new assignment."

"I don't need your understanding, Colonel."

He nodded. "Very well. Then we shall discuss business only."

"Yes." She felt a tear trying to escape from her eye, but fought it back. She would not give him the pleasure. She blinked it away. "We will speak of business. Why have you come?"

"This will be our last time working together," he said. "After the Championships, your case will be transferred to another officer. In Moscow. But until then, you are my responsibility. We need to discuss the security arrangements for the trip to the Sukhoi facility in Moscow. Like last year and the year before that. Nothing more."

Elena shook her head, her eyes unfocused, her mind elsewhere. "Please. Continue."

"You will be staying with the rest of the aerobatics team at the Aeroflot dormitory at Moscow Central, just like before." The large hotel was built in front of the old, grass airport still in occasional use right in the heart of the capital city. The Sukhoi Design Bureau maintained a final assembly hangar there as well as a repair shop. "The Antonov will fly us directly to Switzerland from there."

She shot him a quick look. *"Us?"*

"Didn't I mention that?" He gave her a look of earnest puzzlement. "Perhaps I forgot. My team and I will be attending the competition along with you and your team." He leaned over, and then, to her complete surprise, he took her hand.

Elena shuddered at the touch of his cool flesh.

He smiled, revealing one steel tooth set beside its tea-stained brethren. "I know this seems like a difficult time for you. That's why I will be there to help. Think of me as your sword and shield against a dangerous world. Strikes. Protests. Thieves and hooligans. Moscow is a very dangerous place for you," he replied, then checked his watch, a gold and silver Soviet imitation of a Rolex. It had stopped. Slepkin shrugged. "You will be in the best of hands. You have my promise." He eased off her desk and without another word left her office.

The smell of his after-shave lingered behind like a musky cloud. Elena went to the window and flung it wide.

**Wednesday,
25 July 1990**

The condominium complex was a deserted maze of white stucco buildings and shaded outdoor corridors fringed in belts of dark green ice plant. Brilliant, midsummer sunlight beat down on the buildings nestled against the low hills of the Livermore Valley. It was high noon, and the fog had burned off completely, leaving the air still and dusty. Most of the residents worked at Lawrence Livermore, and the Lab could be seen in the distance, beyond the freeway.

Parrum set the parking brake on the dark government sedan and watched as a mailman stuffed letters into Gallagher's mailbox. A yellow and black biplane was painted on it, flying upside down; Gallagher's Pitts S-2.

Parrum had seen for himself the remains of that very same airplane. It had looked like something caught up in a harvesting machine run wild: Gallagher's prized Pitts had been reduced to a ball of yellow fabric, bent tubing, and frayed wire.

The mail truck trundled off, and before it had turned the corner, Gallagher's front door popped open. Using a cane to ease his pulled leg muscles, and wearing a white brace around his neck, Gallagher hobbled out.

Parrum grabbed his briefcase and slammed the door of his car loud enough to gain Gallagher's attention. "Dr. Gallagher?"

Gallagher stopped, peering in Parrum's direction.

Parrum approached. "I'm glad to see you're up and about," said Parrum heartily. He marched up beside Gallagher. The computer designer stood a head taller, even leaning on a cane. Parrum automatically extended his hand, but then, with a chuckle, retracted it. "Forgot," he apologized, nodding at the cane. "How's the neck?"

"What can I do for you, Mr. Parrum?" said Gallagher. He wore a loose-fitting flightsuit, the collar open to accommodate the neck brace.

"We were all worried at the Lab," said Parrum. "When we heard, I mean."

"I'm happy to hear it, but in case you forgot, I'm defunded. Why have you come? To outprocess me? I didn't know spooks made house calls these days."

"Spook? You give me far too much credit. I'm just an employee of the Lab. No. I've come to discuss your future with us."

"What's there to talk about? You want my Q-1 back?" It was Gallagher's prized Top Secret clearance. "It's inside. You're welcome to it if—"

"No. What I'd like is the chance to chat with you. But I'd rather do it inside. By the way," he said, opening his dark suit jacket and pulling out a small, shiny key. "I believe this is yours."

Gallagher stopped cold. Parrum could see at once he had struck pay dirt. "Where did you find this?"

"Inside the wreck of a Pitts aerobatic biplane," said Parrum. "It was lodged in the control cluster. You know? At the base of the control stick."

"Jesus." Gallagher kept staring at the bright silver key.

"I thought you'd be interested. The key must have fallen out of your pocket. It wasn't your lucky day, was it?"

The sun telegraphed a brilliant beam of light onto Gallagher's forehead.

"On the other hand, here you are. Alive and on the mend," Parrum continued. "I suppose you just forgot to clear your pockets. Damned good thing the parachute worked, or we wouldn't be able to have this talk, would we?"

"Jesus," Gallagher said again, and rocked back on his cane. "What a damned stupid way to . . ."

"You were lucky," said Parrum.

Gallagher pocketed the key and looked at Parrum, shaking his head. "Okay, Mr. Parrum. You bought yourself a chat." He turned and hobbled stiffly back into his town house.

Gallagher's living room was a sun-filled space with a tall cathedral ceiling. A marble fireplace was tucked into the stairs that led up to the dining room and kitchen. The stairs folded again up to the third-floor bedroom level.

"Nice place," said Parrum.

"It's rented," said Gallagher.

"I know."

"I guess you would." Gallagher flopped down on a cream-colored leather sofa. He put a foot up on the coffee table. On the glass top was a model of a yellow and black Pitts S-2. "Go ahead," said Gallagher to Parrum. "I'm listening."

Parrum nodded. "I won't waste your time. So let me come directly to the point. Your work at S-5 is done. But there are other sources of support at the Lab we might be able to tie you into. Your work at the Lab doesn't have to be finished." He snapped open his briefcase and handed Gallagher a folder. "What do you make of this?"

Gallagher scooped it up. Inside, the same series of photographs of the Iraqi missile, the Bear, the explosion, were reproduced. Gallagher flipped through them. "Wow," he said, lingering over the shot of the Bear wreathed in electrical fire. He tossed them down onto the glass tabletop. "Lots of pyrotechnics there, Mr. Parrum. But it's not my field of expertise."

"What's your opinion?"

"Look, I'm just a propeller-headed computer jock. But my dumb eye says the antimissile treaty just got smoked." He looked up at Parrum. "The Russians got there first, didn't they? We screwed around trying to make the world's best gunsight, and they went ahead and made a gun. Figures."

Parrum smiled. "Not the Russians, Dr. Gallagher. The *Soviets*. And of all the Soviets, one in particular."

Gallagher picked up the photo of the lightning-sheathed Bear. "You're saying you know who designed this thing?"

"Yes," said Parrum. "And so do you. Her name is Elena Pasvalys."

Gallagher squinted as the name sifted through his memory. The image of a Sukhoi aerobatic monoplane flitted behind his eyes. "Okay. Now I remember her. Short gal. Dark hair and blue eyes?"

Parrum nodded. "She's a physical chemist. We think it was her breakthrough that allowed that beam weapon to be made small and light enough to fly, and still pack enough wallop to take out a missile. I believe it's called *brightness*."

"If we know so much, how come Washington killed my project?" said Gallagher with a huff. "And tell me something else while you're at it: How come if I'm out of the loop, you're telling me so much?"

"You first came to Livermore as a Kratos Fellow, didn't you?"

"You know I did," said Gallagher. "What's that got to do with it?"

"Is it so tough to imagine that Kratos doesn't like the idea of losing talent at the Lab? They spent a bundle bringing you here, after all."

"Young flesh hard to come by these days?"

"Good brains are always in great demand, Dr. Gallagher. And no, the Foundation is still able to support the search for them."

"So?"

"I met with a Kratos representative. I talked this out with them at some length. We both feel that you can still play a very important role at the Lab." He nodded at the photographs of the Bear. "Not to dramatize, but maybe you can save it."

"Is that all?" Gallagher laughed. "Come off it, George. If PALS is dead, and S-5 Group's a goner, what are you suggesting I do? Write code for Accounts Payable?"

"Dr. Gallagher," said Parrum suddenly, his eyes suddenly zeroed in and unblinking, "are you in condition to fly the competition in Switzerland?"

"Huh? Sure," said Gallagher, unconsciously reaching up for the neck brace. "Why?" What was Parrum getting at?

"What airplane will you be flying?" Parrum reached into his briefcase again.

"I don't know yet. There's bound to be something I can find. I've got a couple of weeks yet."

It was time to set the hook. "No, you have exactly twelve days." Parrum pulled out a single sheet. A smaller piece of paper was clipped to one corner. He handed Gallagher the sales brochure to the Sukhoi SU-26MX. "What about this one?"

"What about it?" Gallagher stopped when he flipped open the folded Kratos Foundation check for $200,000. "Jesus," he whispered, licking his lips. "Do you know what this . . ."

"The price of a Sukhoi 26, picked up at the Moscow factory. I'm told you can buy them more cheaply if you haggle, but as I said, none of us has much time left."

"But why would . . . I mean, you want to give me . . ." Gallagher's words trailed off. A square of yellow sun flashed across the glossy paper of the sales brochure.

"Of course," Parrum went on, "you'll have to pay taxes on it, but the insurance on your Pitts should just about cover it." He chuckled amiably. "I'll give them this: these Kratos people have thought this through quite thoroughly."

Gallagher looked up, stunned. "You want me to go to Moscow? To pick up an airplane? But what does this . . ." Gallagher stopped. "She'll be there, won't she?"

Parrum nodded. "Each of the last three years, the Russ . . . I mean, the Soviet team has spent the week prior to the international competition fine-tuning their planes at the Sukhoi plant. That is precisely where you will go to pick up the new machine. There will be opportunities, Dr. Gallagher. Opportunities for us all.''

"Now I get it.'' Gallagher laughed. "You want me to go, you know, strike up a conversation? Ask her how her work's going? Come off it, Parrum. I design optical computers. I'm not a spook. She won't let herself be seen in the same room with me. She'll have people like you to make certain of that.'' He tossed the brochure down. The check slowly refolded itself along its crease. "I'd like to help out. Believe me, I really would. That little hummer is the hottest thing flying, and I could . . .'' Gallagher stopped and forced himself back to reality. "I wish I could help you.'' Gallagher's eyes were drawn to the image of the SU-26 on the sales brochure. "I really wish I could.''

"You can. What I have in mind is really quite simple. A delivery of a small package of papers. You will not be compromised in any way. I will be there, right beside you.''

"You'll be in Moscow? Then why don't *you* take care of it?''

"Simple. *You* would have no trouble arranging to be near her. You're a flier. You're there to pick up an airplane and you've got a wad of hard cash to back you up. On the other hand, if *I* tried it, well, you can see what I'm getting at.''

"But you said you *would* be there. Beside me.''

"Figuratively speaking.'' Parrum nodded. "But the fact remains that nobody can get nearer in the time we have left.''

Gallagher sighed, looked at the check, the sales brochure, and then at Parrum. "I still say she won't come within a hundred feet of me.''

Parrum smiled. "Not so. I think she'll be quite interested in talking to you. I can guarantee it, in fact.''

"How?''

"Simple,'' said Parrum. "You see, Dr. Elena Pasvalys wants to defect.''

6

The USS *John F. Kennedy*'s engines drove the carrier through the Mediterranean night at twenty knots, plowing a foaming wake across a furrowed seascape of building swells. Her two smaller escorts, the frigate *Samuel B. Roberts* and the destroyer *Moosebruger,* endured a rougher ride as they struggled to keep pace. The fleet resupply vessel *Seattle,* loaded to the gunwales with the instruments of modern war, plodded along behind. Suddenly, on command of an unseen signal, all four vessels turned north.

Lt. Richard Eisley's inner ear informed him of the course change. The metal walls of the squadron ready room seemed to tilt as the ship rolled broadside to the swells. He could feel the low, omnipresent throb of the carrier's screws, even though the Swordsmen's ready room was in the ship's forecastle. He sat back in the comfortable, theater-style chair, his knees hard against the back of the seat in front of him, waiting for the brief to begin.

"Heads up," said Baxter, his backseater.

"Attention on deck!"

Eisley snapped his boots to the floor and stood with the other pilots as Capt. Henry Reynard, commander of *JFK*'s air group (CAG), strode into the room and up to a wooden lectern.

Reynard was a lanky six-footer with big ears and a worry-creased face that had earned him the nickname Hound Dog. The CAG was not an optimistic man. Indeed, he believed it was his deep mistrust of both high-performance aircraft and the wisdom of higher authority that had kept him alive long enough to make captain.

"Hound Dog looks pissed," whispered Baxter.

"Join the club," Eisley replied. All the pilots were edgy, itching for something real to do, Eisley more so than most. Why were they steaming around in circles off Libya when rumor put the real action in the Persian Gulf?

Reynard put on his gold-rimmed glasses, cleared his throat, and everyone in the room fell silent. "Be seated," said the CAG. He took in a deep breath and let it out slowly as the assembled fighter pilots and their backseaters shuffled into their chairs. The deck tilted as the carrier rose up a steep swell and sliced down into the trough.

"Gentlemen," he began, "as you all know, we've been in something of a holding pattern out here. I know it's been wearing a little thin, so I scheduled this brief to fill you in on what we know."

Reynard shuffled through his briefing papers, gazing down over the tops of his half-glasses. He'd been forced to start wearing them only a few months back. "We'll start with the strategic and work our way back to the tactical. In the Persian Gulf," he said, "Iraq has massed upward of two hundred and fifty thousand men along the Kuwaiti border. Four thousand tanks plus, and a similar number of armored personnel carriers, all supported by several front-line air divisions of fighters, ground-attack jets, and early-warning AWACS-type ships." He looked up with a sour expression. "The word from the State Department is that it's all designed to move Kuwait into a better negotiating position vis-à-vis oil production and pricing. I think all of us in this room recognize what the real position is."

"Spread-eagle?" someone responded amid a chorus of laughs.

"Affirmative," said the CAG. "Gents, there's an old Arab expression: don't spit on a man's mustache unless it's on fire. Well, this shitbird Saddam Hussein's called the emir of Kuwait an oil thief. I doubt very much whether this will settle out of court." He tossed the official word down and picked up a sheaf of flight schedule forms. "As a direct result, our air operations are going to change real soon."

The news brought clapping and a few war whoops from the pilots.

"Quiet," said Reynard. "The bad news is, we'll be off the Libyan coast for a while longer."

The clapping dribbled away to silence, then more grumbles.

The CAG held up his hand for silence. "I know some of you may not be pleased with the state of affairs. Accept my apologies, gentlemen. As you all know, we try to keep everybody happy. But let me assure you," he said, "if what we think is happening right here is even half-true, *JFK* is going to get her licks in firstest and mostest. Lights?" An aide darkened the room, and the projection screen lit up with a photograph taken from orbit.

"I see the beach," said Baxter. "But where's the ocean?"

"Mars," said Eisley.

Reynard ran in the zoom control. "Gentlemen," he said, "meet Dahr Nema."

The oblique satellite shot showed an enclave of geometry against a backdrop of broad fields of ruddy sand. An arc of chocolate brown mountains stood as a shield to the north. Fans of alluvial rubble spread out from their flanks across the flat desert. A white tank farm dotted one corner of the site; a cluster of metal buildings huddled in the center, and extensive earthworks sprawled across the far side. A single runway underlined the facility in a long black ribbon.

"Dahr Nema. Four hundred miles over the beach, right in the middle of the Libyan Sahara," said Reynard, using a light pen. "Someone went to a hell of a lot of trouble to make this place hard to find. They almost succeeded."

"What's it supposed to be?" someone asked.

"Dahr Nema is a missile testing site the Iraqis have assembled in the middle of nowhere with the help of our good friend Colonel Qaddafi."

"I think I'm beginning to smell a mission," Eisley whispered.

"Wonderful," Baxter replied.

"Cut the chatter, gents," said Reynard. "Dahr Nema is designed with one thing in mind: the flight-testing of long-range rockets. Not SCUDs, and not the souped-up version that can go five hundred miles or so. We're talking a potential intercontinental capability here. Next slide, please."

The image dissolved into a hemispheric map that extended from the east coast of the United States all the way across the Mediterranean and on to India. Broad red circles were inscribed on the map, and all of them were centered on Dahr Nema.

"From this site," Reynard continued, pointing at the circle's focus, "they can test-fire their missiles into the heart of the West African desert. They're buddies with the Mauritanians and the Algerians, so no problem. They can also fire them north, into the Libyan Gulf of Sidra, or out into the southern Atlantic. Now, you may well ask, why should we care?"

"Definitely a mission," said Eisley excitedly.

The light pen's dot jumped across the blue waters of the Atlantic to Washington, D.C. "From Dahr Nema, an ICBM of the sort we believe is under testing can reach all the way to Foggy Bottom with a flight time of twenty-three minutes. Though nobody back in Washington is willing to state as much, that, gentlemen, is why we are here."

Eisley sat up straight. He was beginning to like what he was hearing. A lot. "But they don't have nukes to arm the missile with, do they?" he asked.

"Lights?" said Reynard. "That's a good question," he replied as the slide dimmed and the lights came up. "The answer is, not as far as we know. The problem is, we don't know everything. Gentlemen," he said, his brow crinkled up into a hundred creases, "Iraq has the third-largest oil reserves in the world. Libya is a proven terrorist nation. There's a line a mile long to sell both of them anything they might want in the way of modern weaponry. Money, greed, and terrorism are not the kind of mix that leaves me with warm, fuzzy feelings."

"So when do we take it out?" someone said. The room filled with shouts of assent.

"When the president orders it," Reynard said with a worried look on his face. "Okay then. That's the strategic picture. Now let's talk turkey." The CAG dropped his papers and somehow managed to pin each and every pilot to his seat with a single glance. "The situation in the Persian Gulf is heating up fast. Intel says that Iraq is threatening to hit Kuwait by the middle of August, right after the talks Saddam Hussein has scheduled with the emir. My official reaction is that Intel doesn't know shit from shineola. It could happen tonight, and by Jesus, I won't have a Beirut fuck-up on my watch. As such, we're going to be ready to launch on a plus-fifteen basis."

In 1983, *JFK* was ordered to strike guerrilla training camps in retaliation for the bombing of the Marine barracks in Beirut; it had been micromanaged to the point of absurdity, and in the end half the strikers launched with only partial bomb loads and less idea about what the hell they were supposed to be doing.

Reynard nodded to his aide and the young lieutenant commander began passing out threat sheets to the assembled aircrews. They were products of the brand-new tactical aircraft mission planning system (TAMPS) recently installed on *JFK*. If an air strike against Dahr Nema was a symphony, these TAMPS sheets, specific to each aircrew, were the score.

"Okay," said the CAG, "the Libyans have learned a lot since the last time we bloodied their noses. You'll notice that between Dahr Nema and the beach, they've set up a string of radar sites, triple-A, and SAMS in a dense, interlocking net. Libyan fighters are based at Benina, Al Burayqah, and over to the west at Ghurdabiyah. They can scramble 'em on short notice to a slew of rough strips in between. You guys had no trouble munching the colonel's cookies last time, but this could be a different show. The presence of Iraqi air support, including third-generation MiG-29s and Sukhoi 27s, cannot be dismissed. These aircraft demand your utmost respect, especially the Fulcrums. They're damned small and hard to pick up visually. If you paint 'em, they know you're coming. If you don't power up your radars, you're down to your mark-one eyeball. I don't need to remind you rollers that the '29 has a decent infrared search system that will let them spot you before you spot them. In short, going in and cleaning out Dahr Nema's a real porcupine pie.''

"Great," whispered Baxter.

"Now, for the next several days," Reynard continued, "we will continue our inshore patrol. But flight ops will change. While the suits back home try to work out some kind of diplomatic solution, we'll be taking the measure of Libyan coastal defenses. We can expect them to notice, and to vector out snoopers to make our lives miserable. As we learn their setup better, your TAMPS sheets will change accordingly.''

"Are we flying fangs-out, sir?" asked Eisley.

"That brings me to the rules of engagement," said Reynard, summing up. "There will be no hotdogging out there unless *I* say so. If they come up to play, you play. If they go nose-on, you do the same. But nobody, repeat nobody, goes weapons-free unless they fire first, or you hear it from me. Is that clear?''

"That could get a little late," Eisley whispered to his RIO.

"When do we start?" asked Cotton Mather, another F-14 driver.

"Right now," said Reynard. "We'll be flying heavy Combat Air Patrols round the clock. Ditto with the E-2s. We'll have one Screw-top up and one ready to shoot at all times, and the same for the Texaco drivers.'' Reynard stepped away from the lectern. "I hope you sleep well tonight, gentlemen." The ship shuddered as it rose and fell. "As I said, we're due for a little weather, but that keeps life interesting. We'll start the formal aircrew briefs at oh four-thirty. Eisley," he said, turning to face the young lieutenant, "I see TAMPS has you on the boards to lead the first section up tonight.''

"Yes, sir," Eisley replied, scanning his mission sheet.

The CAG's eyes focused like two fifty-calibers boresighted deep inside Eisley's skull. "Remember the rules of engagement. If you wind up starting a war before the official invitations get mailed, I'll personally nail your pecker to the flightdeck. Understood?''

"Yes, sir," Eisley said glumly.

"Good. Okay then, gents," said Reynard, "if you want any more details. I'll be in the wardroom working out the wrinkles. Any more?''

"One last thing, sir," asked Eisley. "What about the Russians? The Bears? What if the guy with the moonroof shows up again? Do we treat him as a friendly or as a hostile?"

"You leave him be," said the CAG.

"But sir, that guy with the zapper—"

"Eisley," Reynard broke in, "you don't know what that Bear was packing, and so far as I know, nobody else does either. Maybe the weenies back home have a notion. Until you hear different, belay the 'zapper' terminology. We've got enough on our plates without you dreaming up a Russian death ray. Am I getting through loud and clear?"

"Yes, sir," said Eisley.

"Good." Reynard stood stiffly as he gathered his papers. "Good night, gentlemen. And sweet dreams. Tomorrow we go to work."

Friday Morning,
27 July 1990

"Cutlass two zero two, Sentry Six," came the voice from *JFK*'s airborne warning aircraft, a Grumman E2C Hawkeye. "Target, twelve o'clock and sixty miles. Course one eight five, four hundred seventy knots, and level. Vector zero nine five and your signal is buster."

"Rog," Eisley replied as he hunted the moonlit clouds off his nose for a sign of the intruder. "Let him go buster himself," he said to Baxter over the intercom.

The word *buster* meant he and his wingman, Cotton Mather, were to apply all possible speed in the intercept. But one eye on his F-14's dwindling fuel state and the other on the thick clouds masking the carrier far below told him that would be dead stupid. It was going to take some work to get aboard the boat tonight, and he needed all the gas he could save.

"Fifty miles," said the radar mole on board the Hawkeye.

"Fuel is four point eight," Baxter reminded him. "And we're headed right for Libyan airspace."

"I know, Bax." He hit the transmit button on his stick. "Okay, two," he called out to his wingman, "go military." He nudged his throttles forward until they came to rest on the afterburner detent. Under full military power, the F-14 accelerated through five hundred knots. "Talk to me. What do you see?" he asked his back-seater.

"Diddly on video. You want to light him up?"

"Negative. Leave your radar dark and just keep looking. I don't want to warn the fucker." A bright moon beamed down on a mountainous terrain of mounded silver clouds. Brilliant stars hammered down from on high. It was a beautiful sight at twenty thousand feet, but he knew that down on the water, underneath the front, it would be black as a coal mine, all the way to the carrier's rain-swept flightdeck.

"Still no contact," came the call from Eisley's wingman. The two F-14s cast twin black moonshadows onto the ragged tops of the clouds as they sledded along them at over five hundred knots.

"Twenty miles," said the radar controller. "Warning, Cutlass: you'll be in Libyan airspace in twenty-two miles."

"Roger, Sentry." He glanced up in the canopy rearview mirrors and caught sight of Baxter's face bathed in green instrument glow. "Screw it, Bax. We're getting too damned close. Let's zap 'em," said Eisley as he banked around a towering thunderhead and arrowed through a narrow black canyon.

"In their face." Baxter switched the powerful Hughes APG-71 radar from standby to search. "Contact!" he sang out. "Bandit is inbound, on the nose and level, range fifteen!"

"Tallyho! Two has a visual," called Cotton. He had seen a glint of moonlight off metal.

"Take it, Cotton!" Eisley slipped back into loose combat trail, allowing the pilot who had his eyes on the target to lead the way to the intercept.

"Something weird about him," Baxter said as he tried to optimize the radar picture. "He's all big and fuzzy. Paints like an airliner, but . . ."

"We'll shave him down some," said Eisley as he kept an eye on the twin orange balls of fire of his wingman's engines. He reached up to his armament panel and flipped up a protective cover. "Cotton, go tactical." Both fighters switched to a different frequency. "This guy may be an airliner, and then again, he may be something else. Remember that Bear? I got surprised out here the last time, and I don't like surprises. I'm going master arm on," he radioed his wingman. A white cross blinked onto his heads-up display (HUD).

"Say again?" said Cotton.

"I don't like surprises," said Eisley again.

"Roger. Master arm is on."

"Uh, Ice?" said Baxter. "That isn't what we're supposed to do. The CAG said not to—"

"Can it, shipmate," Eisley interrupted. "I'm not waiting to see the whites of his eyes."

"Just stay cool, Iceman. He's not too far off the airway," Baxter persisted. "He really could be an airliner. And the CAG'll go tits up if he finds out."

"Don't worry. I don't smoke airliners. Besides, the CAG said it himself: no more Beirut fuck-ups."

Baxter reached up and stroked the Garfield cat on his glareshield. "What about a Tripoli fuck-up?"

"Cutlass flight, Sentry six. The bandit is ten miles out and descending," called the airborne controller.

"Like an airliner," Baxter reminded him again.

They lanced through a wisp of cloud, and there, directly ahead, were the broad wings of an IL-78. The Soviet four-engined jet gleamed like pewter in the moonlight.

What's he got under his wings? The tricolor insignia of the Iraqi Air Force was painted on its tail. "Tallyho!" Eisley called. "Sentry, Cutlass two zero two has an ID. We have one India Lima seven eight running with his lights out, and a big ol' Iraqi flag painted on his ass." He reached up to shut down his armament panel when a sudden flicker of motion froze him in his seat. "What . . . Jesus!"

"Watch out, Ice!" shouted Cotton as two dark, finned objects exploded from underneath the Ilyushin and roared off on four yellow streamers of afterburner flame. "Fighters! Two of 'em!"

"Where the fuck did they—" Baxter began.

"They were hiding in his baffles! Bax! Lock him up, Cotton! Break left!" Eisley screamed as he shoved his throttles full forward and around the detent into reheat. The Tomcat surged ahead. *Energy energy energy!* Eisley silently chanted as he hauled the fighter into a steep right bank, trying to stay nose-on with the enemy. It was a losing battle. "Jesus!" The unmistakable shape of a MiG-29 slashed by and began curving back in behind him.

"Bandit at four o'clock! He going inside us!" Baxter yelled. The MiG had plenty of energy and was more maneuverable than a mongoose in heat. If the MiG wasn't playing games, they had seconds.

"Hang on!" Eisley slapped the stick full right, rolled inverted, and dove for the deck in a high-speed split. The undulating mass of moonlit clouds rushed him like an avalanche. The F-14 smashed through and into their roiling heart. Flying on pure instinct, Eisley hauled back and rolled level, letting his speed build up again. "Where is he, Bax?"

"Looking!"

"Cutlass Flight!" shouted the controller. "What's going on out there? I show multiple . . ." Eisley ran the volume down as he looked straight up through the teardrop canopy, but there was nothing to see inside the cloud.

"Radar contact!" yelled Baxter. "Ice! He's right overhead!"

"Good!" said Eisley.

"Good?"

"Stand by," said Eisley as he silently counted. It would take a watchmaker's touch to make this come out exactly right, and anything less than right was very wrong indeed. "Stand by, stand by . . . *Pull!*" Eisley stood the Tomcat on its tail and climbed on a tail of afterburner fire. One moment they were wrapped in thick cloud; the next they were blasting free and into clear air like a Shuttle heading for orbit.

"Tallyho!" Baxter called the bogey, but it was unnecessary. The MiG's exhausts were dead ahead, two bright orange globes against the black sky.

"Sneaky little fuck," Eisley said under his breath as his right thumb selected the F-14's Vulcan cannon on the stick switch. There were too many aircraft around to fire a missile. *Where's Cotton?* he wondered as the word *GUNS* popped up on his HUD. The range-to-target display flashed ever lower. The death dot flashed and Eisley jammed his finger down on the stick trigger.

Nothing happened.

"Fuck!" he screamed as the MiG sat like meat on the table square in his sights.

"Cutlass Flight! Cutlass Flight!" called the controller on board the E-2 Sentry. "Knock it off! Repeat! Knock it off! You're over the goddamned line! They're headed for the beach! You're in the Libyan ADIZ!"

"Break it off, Ice!" Baxter shouted. "Break it off!"

"Cutlass! I say again! You are in Libyan airspace!"

"Ice!" Baxter shouted. He knew a target trance when he saw one. "Ice! You heard the man! Knock it off! We're in Indian country!"

Eisley hesitated, and in that fraction of a second, the MiG banked up hard on a wing and dove for the nearby Libyan coast. The second MiG had already joined with the escorting tanker. Ice felt his heart pound for the first time. The engagement had lasted exactly twenty-eight seconds. "Fuck," he said quietly, and deselected the cannon. The *GUNS* annunciator went dark.

"Ice, two has you in sight," called Cotton. "I'm joining up." There was a distinct waver in Mather's voice. "The bogey was all over me! He could have—"

"Okay, Cotton," Eisley said with a slight, chill shiver. "Settle down and join up. We'll debrief when we get aboard. Say fuel."

"One point one. I mean it, Ice! I was meat on that MiG's table! I didn't even—"

"Let's take it back to the barn, Cotton. You've got the lead."

"Me?"

"Take it!" Eisley checked his master fuel counter. He had under a thousand pounds himself, and down under the clouds, a night landing on a heaving carrier awaited them. What had Reynard promised them? That things would get interesting? His wingman began to calm down as he slipped into the lead of the two-ship formation, just as Eisley hoped he would.

"Hey, Ice," said Baxter, "I don't know about you, but the only time I have too much gas is when I'm on fire. Let's tank before we trap, okay?"

"Okay, BB," he said. Cotton's Tomcat was in his one o'clock, its gray skin bathed in bright moonlight. He hit the transmit button on his stick. It was right next to the Vulcan's trigger. "Sentry, Cutlass Flight's gonna head upstairs for a drink before we recover."

"Roger," said the controller. "Vectors to the Texaco are three three eight for sixty, angels thirty. Your signal after the tankup is Charlie. And the CAG wants to see you both after you come aboard."

"Thanks, I needed that." Both fighters banked away from the Libyan coast and began to climb to the waiting KA-6 tanker.

"Who do you think was on board that thing?" asked Baxter. "I mean, fighter escort and all, it's probably a VIP, don't you think? And the markings were Iraqi. Maybe it was Saddam himself. Maybe we should have shot the mother down and saved the world the bother."

"I tried," Eisley replied.

The Iraqi IL-78 lined up on the single long runway at Dahr Nema, its landing beams brilliant against the powdered stars of the desert night. The two fighters that had escorted it all the way from the nuclear facility at Tuwaitha were right behind. The big jet touched down with a scream of reverse thrust and quickly made its way to a huge, half-buried shelter. Deep tunnels made of interlocking steel and concrete rings connected the hardened hangar with the launch tower a half mile distant.

The Ilyushin nosed inside. Before its engines died, the blast-proof door was already closing behind it. The cargo ramp at its tail whined as it descended. The cabin lights snapped on, revealing half a dozen cylindrical objects lashed to the cargo deck, each the size of a casket. A crew of Libyan laborers stood by on the ground, awaiting orders.

A short man appeared on the jet's cargo deck, dressed in a lead bib. He walked down the extended ramp, stripped off the protective garment and hood, revealing a dense shock of black hair, glossy under the hangar lights. He had the odd, rolling gait common to sailors and saddle-sore cowboys as he made his way over to a blond-haired man standing with a clipboard. "Reiner?" he said.

"*Ja*. And you are . . .?"

"Wei." The small man bowed stiffly from the waist. He was the liaison from Koko Nor, the Chinese nuclear weapons design and test facility. The Chinese had a long history of copying the instruments of death, refashioning them into simpler, more reliable designs, then selling them to an insatiable world. They had done it with the early MiG series; they had done it with the AK-47. And now they had done it again.

"You are late, Herr Wei," said Reiner, the German designer who had overseen the final assembly of *Al Infitar*.

Wei smiled and nodded, without apology or explanation. "Baghdad is now on a war footing." He turned and watched as the first lead-wrapped cask was wheeled down the Ilyushin's tail ramp. "We brought all six."

"So," said Reiner with a nod. It was no coincidence that there were six isotope warheads in the Ilyushin's cargo hold. There were six rockets in final stages of assembly at Dahr Nema.

Each tapered warhead contained four hundred kilograms of intensely radioactive material surrounded by a shell of high explosive. A small amount of the uranium, the purest U-235, had come from the French. Some had come from the Soviet Union. But the majority had come from South Africa. Their rich deposits and pariah status had found a perfect match in Iraq's willingness to supply them with cheap oil, and in a more complex arrangement, with China's interest in supplying certain African rebel groups with simpler arms. Taps were opened and closed. It was a deal on many levels, with many forms of currency exchanged.

The six warheads were nuclear weapons, and they weren't. No

mushroom cloud would rise from their aim points. No gamma flash would radiate from a million-degree fireball. Instead, the six warheads, properly spaced and exploded at medium altitudes, were meant to blanket a wide area with persistent, deadly nuclear dust. Whole regions could be rendered uninhabitable for generations.

Iraq had more than six enemies in the world. What Arab nation didn't? But of all the possible enemies, one stood above all the rest: a keystone whose removal would cause the vast architecture stirring itself to resist Saddam Hussein to collapse, and in doing so would weld together the whole of the Arab world.

The six isotope warheads, mated with the long-range reach of *Al Infitar,* had but one true target, and its name was a curse. That name was Israel.

7

Thursday Afternoon, 26 July 1990

"Wyn!" said Sara Avilar as Gallagher walked into the small airport lounge at Livermore Municipal Airport. He kept his sunglasses on against the hot light streaming through the plate glass window. "What are you doing out? You should be in bed or something, shouldn't you?" She rushed up to Gallagher and hugged him.

"Easy," he said as his muscles complained. He wrinkled his nose at Avilar's patchouli-oil perfume. Where did she find that old stuff? "It's nice to see you, too, Sara," he said, fending her off with his cane and making for the dilapidated couch.

"I was worried when, I mean, after the grief I gave you that morning, you know," she stammered, "the Dr. Doom stuff. It was a joke, you know? But then when you . . . when you . . ."

"Crashed?"

"I'm really sorry. Really." Her eyes glistened. "I know your Pitts was really special to you."

"Was." Gallagher eased himself down onto the couch. "Don't be sorry. It wasn't your fault. I did it to myself. I'll tell you all about it when I'm through being pissed off."

She sat back down on an old chair held together by duct-tape patches. A worn leather jacket was draped over her bright white cotton T-shirt. "I'm sorry. It's dumb. But I was really worried when I heard . . . I mean when it came over the news that a plane had gone in over by Tracy. I thought, I mean, I never thought it could be you until they . . .'' Avilar stopped and brushed away a tear. She shook her head. ''Sorry. You had me worried. I should have known you could take care of yourself. That's your specialty, right?''

''You bet. Just the same, take it from me, Sara. Jumping out of airplanes is just no fun.''

She wiped at her eye distractedly. ''But what are you doing here? You look beat-up.''

''I thought I'd clean out the hangar. You know. Think.'' He glanced out at the bright afternoon sky. ''Looks like a nice day to aviate all right. Going up again?''

''Later.''

Gallagher rested his cane on the edge of the couch, but it clattered to the linoleum. He leaned over to get it, and when he did, the Sukhoi brochure and the Kratos Foundation check fell out of his jacket pocket.

Sara jumped up from the ratty chair and retrieved them. She had almost handed the brochure back before her eye caught the brilliant crimson airplane on its cover. ''Hey! Is that a Sukhoi?'' She unfolded the check clipped to the corner and saw more zeros than she had ever seen before on something negotiable. ''Jesus . . .'' she whispered. ''This says . . .''

Gallagher snatched it back.

She looked up at him, her dark eyes big and round with wonder. ''Wyn, is that for real? I mean, *two hundred thousand dollars?* I mean, why would . . .'' She paused, shaking her head. The words would simply not come. ''Is it really real?''

''Real enough. Two hundred thousand's the going rate for the new export model. Bigger gas tanks, instruments done in feet instead of meters, little bitty baggage compartment. You know.''

''I almost think you're serious.'' She looked at him closely. Her eyes betrayed a lingering question. ''Wyn, I don't mean to pry or anything—''

''Then don't.''

She glanced at the Sukhoi brochure. "Tell me one thing: Who do you have to kill? How come Kratos is, like, all of a sudden in the airplane business?"

"They've been in that business a long time, Sara," he said, thinking of Norton Aerodyne. "Just not little ones, that's all. It's kind of like a thank-you for all my years at the Lab. Some guys get lunches, some guys get gold watches, I—"

"You get a two-hundred-thousand-dollar airplane? *Right*." She crossed her arms across her chest. "I repeat: Who gets rubbed out? Or is it your firstborn child? Did the dude with the long black cape just hand it over, or did you have to sign something?"

He laughed. "What makes you think I made a deal with the devil?"

"Number one, you work at Teller Tech. Number two, you think you're this mystery man from Texas. The Lone Ranger. Like, who was that masked man? *Wrong*. I know you. If this was something legitimate, you wouldn't be moping around looking so grim. You'd cash that check and buy yourself an airplane. Especially *that* airplane. Wow. A Sukhoi." She said the name as though it were a holy incantation. "Besides, nobody tosses out two hundred K without wanting something in return. Not even the boomheads at Kratos. Case closed. Am I right or what?"

"Maybe. That's all I can really tell you, Sara. Maybe after I help her out and—"

"Her? What kind of help will you give this *her?*"

Gallagher shook his head.

"I see." Sara eyed the Sukhoi brochure. "Okay. You've got your private life. You want to be known as the techno-gigolo of Livermore Valley, it's none of my business—"

"Correct," he said with a cool frown.

"But tell me this: What if you get caught?" It was a stab in the dark, but she saw by the way his face lit up that she had struck a bull's-eye.

"Remind me not to play poker with you, Ms. Avilar," he said as he eased his sore neck down onto the back of the couch.

"So when are you supposed to go help this damsel in distress?"

"August first. I'll be back after Yverdon." Gallagher smiled. "I'll come back overgross with gold medals."

"Sure you will. I know you can do it." She bit her lip. "Hey, Wyn. Honest Injun: I don't know what you're doing, but I just have this feeling, okay? Don't do it. Rest up this year. Yverdon won't be the last WAC competition."

"You and your feelings." It came out crueler than Gallagher had intended. "Sorry, Sara. I didn't mean it that way."

"Fine. You know what you're doing." Her eyes hardened as she stood up to leave. "Just think about it, okay?" She turned to leave.

"Sara!"

Avilar stopped. "Just think about it," she repeated, and left.

Tuesday Afternoon,
31 July 1990

A light rain fell as a Grumman Greyhound carrier on-board delivery (COD) aircraft appeared out of the low gray mist and turned up *Kennedy*'s wake on final.

Eisley heard its engines and popped his head out of his fighter's forward gun bay. His Tomcat was spotted aft of the carrier's big island, next to the deck vehicle parking lot known as the mule pool.

Eisley's plane captain was hunting for the reason the fighter's Vulcan cannon had hung fire in his aborted dogfight with the Iraqi MiGs. Hedge, so named for the cut of his dense Afro, had half his body wedged inside the rear cannon bay. He was sweating and cursing as he tinkered with the big ammunition drum.

Eisley watched the courier plane's approach. *High,* he judged. The COD's twin turboprops were pulled back to idle, followed by a little dip of its nose. *Better.* "Mailman," he said.

"About time, Mr. Eisley," said Hedge, his voice echoing from inside the Vulcan's guts. "Maybe they'll have some new tapes. *Wabash* didn't send any over with the gas."

Eisley watched the Greyhound glide toward *JFK*'s ramp. He could just see the carrier's two escorts in the light rain; a third ship, the fleet tanker USS *Wabash,* had already melted into the gray mists. Wherever the old cow had been headed, Eisley figured it was better than staying here.

Dahr Nema or not, there certainly wasn't much action in the southern Med. The Libyans were lying doggo, and a week of probing had failed to provoke a reaction from their defenses.

He watched the C-2's wings lurch as it flew through the wake turbulence spilling off the carrier's island, then, trailing its double-forked hook, it slammed down to the flightdeck. The Greyhound hooked the number two wire and came to a shuddering stop, wiggling like a fish on the arrestor cable. Its twin engines throttled back, and both wings began to fold up and aft as the pilot taxied forward.

"Got you, you little sucker," said Hedge as he picked a crushed 20-mm casing out of the cannon's drum. The Vulcan returned spent cases to the ammunition drum to keep them from flying into the Tomcat's jet intakes. He held up the wrinkled case with a look of disgust and tossed the shell into the back of a yellow tow tractor. The mist that spattered his face was mixed with beads of sweat. He swiped it clean with a rag and looked over at Eisley. "Sir? How come we got to be the ones to fool with the A-rabs? Why don't we just leave 'em alone?"

"Good question," said Eisley. The delivery aircraft taxied close by, moving forward of *JFK*'s island. Its propellers sheeted the rain back across Eisley like hail. "The heavies think they've got a rocket in their pocket."

"Oh, yeah?" He'd heard that much already. "I thought that shit was under control."

"Money still does the talking."

"Yeah," said the plane captain. "And we still do the walking. So now we got to glass 'em 'fore they glass us, is that it?"

"Sounds familiar, doesn't it?" said Eisley. The COD's engines died and its two paddle-blade props began to freewheel. He watched a man in Air Force blues drop to the deck. A black briefcase was locked to his wrist with a bright silver chain. Head bent low, he scurried to a hatch in *JFK*'s island. *What in hell is an Air Force puke doing here?* he wondered.

"I don't know, Mr. Eisley," said the plane captain, "I guess it all comes down to the green. But I wish we'd just get it done, you know? Stop *bull*shittin' off Libya and get it done. This ain't nothing but cutting holes in the ocean. I mean, for what? For all the good it's doin', we might as well go home."

"Hedge," said Eisley as he watched the Air Force officer disappear into the island, "I have a feeling something's about to change."

**Wednesday,
1 August 1990**

The distinctive roar of the Tumanskii R-27 jet engine was all the alarm Capt. Kamel Sayid needed. He was out the door and running across the sun-blasted ramp of Dahr Nema even before the Klaxons began their howl. Despite the fact that he and the other MiG-29 pilot were being kept on the ground and hidden, these endless alerts were wearing him paper-thin.

Sayid reached the metal sun shelter that protected his fighter in time to see two MiG-23s begin their takeoff roll. *Pigs,* he thought derisively at the old Libyan jets. They were no match for the Americans he knew to be lurking off the coast. Sayid knew his own fighter was more than a match for them, even if one of the Americans had given him a scare the night of their arrival. Things would be different next time.

The two Libyan fighters clawed up into the white hot sky.

Captain Sayid could feel the thunder of the Libyan jets long after they had disappeared to the north.

He kicked a piece of concrete loose from the cracked apron, picked it up, sent it sailing, and stomped into the sun shelter and leaned against his MiG. It felt warm, alive. The '29 was every bit as good as the Tomcat. And Kamel Sayid knew he was a better pilot. All he wanted was the chance to prove it.

In this, Sayid would shortly get his wish.

8

**Wednesday Morning,
1 August 1990**

"Finally," said Gallagher as the blue and white Aeroflot jet pushed back from the San Francisco gate. The four big turbofans on the IL-96's wings began to whine as their fires took hold. The cabin lights flickered once, then went out, leaving the portholes pearly gray with the dim light of a foggy morning.

The first-class cabin, designed for eighty passengers, was nearly empty; Gallagher counted only fourteen.

He pulled his seat belt tight across his lap. Tugged to its limit, it was still two fingers' loose around his slim frame. The cabin lights in the Soviet jet blinked back on. The IL-96 shuddered and the loudspeaker began to hum.

"Good morning to all our passengers from California. Welcome aboard Aeroflot's experimental service, Flight Two, from San Francisco to Moscow." The woman's voice was clipped and professional, with more than a hint of a British accent. "Aeroflot is the world's largest airline, with scheduled service to every continent. Please take this time to—" The announcement suddenly stopped when a commotion erupted behind them.

Gallagher turned in time to see a blue-suited stewardess attempt to block the doorway leading from the nine-abreast tourist-class cabin. A group of young men and women, all dressed in bright red track suits, stood pushing, arguing for passage. The stewardess held

a tray of crystal tea glasses, and each time the intruders pushed, they teetered closer to destruction.

As Gallagher watched, one of the group, a tall, slender man with close-shaved hair and a chiseled, wolflike face, suddenly reached out and snatched the stewardess's tray. She shouted angrily, but in an eyeblink, one, then two, then four glasses, were sent sailing into the air.

Jugglers?

The beleaguered stewardess gave up as the rear cabin erupted in applause. The tea glasses sailed round and round, faster and faster. The juggler's neck muscles were ropy and knotted in concentration, and he held a long wooden match between his clenched teeth.

Not one tea glass dropped to the jetliner's carpeted deck. One of the troupe's women, a tall blonde with short, lustrous hair, took off her red warm-up jacket, revealing a sequined bikini top. She bowed deeply to the appreciative passengers in the aft cabin, and the applause promptly doubled.

The group pushed by the angry stewardess and streamed forward into first class in victory. Still juggling the crystal tea glasses, the juggler walked up to Gallagher's row and stopped. Suddenly, as the glasses whirled in glittering arcs, the performer somehow manipulated the match in his teeth and struck it. A long white flame flared, reflecting from his eyes.

The sequined woman shook her head and urged the juggler forward. He paid not the slightest attention. She smiled at Gallagher and shrugged, as though an errant child had misbehaved. She pushed the juggler, speaking in angry Russian for him to move. The juggler, match still burning bright between his teeth, scowled and then went forward to join the others in the front of the cabin, directly behind the galley.

"Please take a moment to check your seat belts," the voice of the stewardess continued, although there was no sign of her or the rest of the crew. "We will attempt to depart shortly. Thank you all for choosing Aeroflot. Beverages will be available to all passengers after our takeoff."

"Attempt?" Gallagher peered through the porthole. The fog was

barely above the control tower. "I hope they put this thing together right." He eyed the rivet heads on the airliner's long wings. They seemed uneven, didn't they?

The group of Russian gate-crashers made no movement to be seated as the jet taxied out to the runway. Packages were unwrapped; prizes of their stay in America were displayed. Gallagher looked back into the rear cabin; seat belts were dangling into the aisle, unused. It was a hell of a way to run an airline. The FAA would go into terminal apoplexy.

The jet pivoted out onto the runway and lined up, pointing north. Gallagher looked up at a sudden burst of laughter and clapping. The juggler had taken off his jacket, revealing long, bulging arm muscles. He was doing a handstand in the aisle. "Oh, Jesus," Wyn said.

The pilot brought all four D-90 turbofans up to full throttle, keeping them pinned in place by brake power alone. The brakes moaned as they slipped a few feet. The jet shook as if it had the flu. The overhead bins rattled. One came free and dropped with a loud thud, nearly putting Gallagher through his seat belt. Nobody else seemed to take the slightest notice. Suddenly, the pilot let go of the brakes and the half-loaded Ilyushin began to roll ahead of sixty tons of smoking thrust.

The ride was hard with none of the oceanic rise and fall of a 747 on the run. The IL-96 seemed to chatter as it accelerated, transmitting the runway seams straight into Gallagher's teeth. The acrobat doing the handstand swayed, but he did not fall.

The nose popped free of the ground, but the main wheels rumbled like thunder under Gallagher's feet. *Come on!* The rumbling fell away as the Aeroflot jet broke from the ground. Rhythmic clapping came from the circus group. The acrobat was now balanced on one hand! "I don't believe this."

An instant later they pierced the bottom of the deep gray fog. The cabin tilted as the pilot banked steeply. *Easy . . . easy!* Gallagher looked out the window. Streaks of water blasted by the porthole. The bank steepened even more. "I don't like . . ." he began, but just then they broke free into brilliant sun. Mount Diablo stood

above the white sea to the east, and the distant Sierra Nevada could be seen beyond. The small Livermore Valley was totally socked in. Gallagher let out the breath he had been holding and looked up. The circus troupe was now gathered around a man shuffling a deck of oversize cards.

Gallagher peered out behind the tall winglet perched on the tip of the Ilyushin's wing. Down there was Lawrence Livermore National Laboratory. *I hope I'm doing the right thing.* He closed his eyes. *I hope I'm doing the right thing,* he thought again, *and I hope Elena Pasvalys is for real.*

The IL-96 climbed as it turned northeast. They crossed the Sierra Nevada with the sapphire blue of Lake Tahoe glinting in the morning sun.

When he awoke and looked down, icebergs bobbed on a dark blue sea. Two tones sounded from the speakers overhead.

"Ladies and gentlemen, please take your seats. Aeroflot Flight Two will be going down now. Our stay in Anchorage will be very brief, so excursions from the cabin will not be permitted. An informative film will be shown during refueling. Thank you."

Somewhere in the far nose of the Ilyushin 96, four throttles were pulled back to flight idle. The big airliner, still hundreds of miles out over the North Pacific, began its descent to Anchorage.

Thursday, 2 August 1990

"I wonder what that Air Force puke had in that briefcase?" asked Eisley as he banked southwest. They were flying great ovals above the Libyan Gulf of Sidra, Qaddafi's Zone of Death. "Must have been hot. The sucker was manacled."

"Whatever it was," said Baxter, "he can keep it." He slewed his joystick, sweeping the sky ahead of the fighter with the nose-mounted video camera. He and Eisley were leading a two-plane section on the afternoon's combat air patrol. There was little enough to see. Even Libyan coastal radar was shut down, showing up only occasionally as a peep and a flash on their threat receivers.

"Anything out there?" asked Eisley.

Baxter ran in the magnification, then switched back to the wide-field. "Negative. Even the buzzards are walking. I wonder where—"

Suddenly, the radio squawked in his headset.

"Discrete! Discrete! Discrete! All aircraft on this frequency, maintain radio silence and return to base. Repeat! Maintain EM-CON and return to home plate."

"Huh?" Eisley was slow to comprehend. "Was that for . . . hey, Bax, did you just . . . ?"

"Shit," Baxter cursed. "Was there supposed to be a drill to-day?" The Discrete code was an emergency message of the highest order. Neither of them had ever heard it uttered in earnest.

"I didn't hear about one. I wonder what's up?" Eisley said, banking the Tomcat to the north. The band of clouds hugging the North African coast fell behind their twin tails. His wingman fol-lowed suit. "You think it's for real?"

"I think I'd like to go home now," Baxter said with not a trace of humor.

"All aircraft on this frequency, stand by to copy new marshal instructions," the urgent voice aboard the carrier repeated.

Baxter copied down the new vectors to where they could expect to find the *John F. Kennedy*. When he was done, he checked them again.

"Where are we headed, BB?" asked Eisley.

"Remember the CAG's stirring speech about taking out Dahr Nema?" said the backseater. "And the Air Force type with his briefcase?"

"Yeah? What about them?"

"I think the manure is about to hit the turbine."

Eisley let out a war whoop as he shoved his throttles to the stops and banked east. The innocent peace of the August day was ancient history, and *JFK* and her air group were now at war.

Thursday Afternoon,
2 August 1990

"How interesting," said Colonel Slepkin as he took a deep drag of his cigarette, letting the smoke swirl around his face and on up to the stained tiles of his office ceiling. It was an American Marlboro, a favorite not only for its taste but for its status: in Moscow it was known as the cigarette with *blat,* or pull. There were few doors a carton could not spring open. "Yes. Yes. Of course," he said into the old black telephone. "I realize the danger. Her state of mind is not the best."

The KGB's head of security at the Serpukhov Institute shoved aside a pile of papers, cleared a small space, and opened a brown personnel file marked with a crimson slash across its cover. A color photograph of Elena Pasvalys was stapled to the first page, along with a full set of fingerprints. "Very well, Viktor. I appreciate the warning," he said. "No. I doubt it, too. Send what you can. Have Zarkich come straight away, just as soon as he lands. I'll want to speak with him about the plan. And a recent photograph would be best." Slepkin nodded and drummed his fingers nervously on the scarred desktop. "Of course. That was wise. My thanks. Good-bye."

Slepkin hung up the phone and tapped a long finger of ash onto the floor. He drew in another lungful, and the Marlboro glowed red. He stared into Elena's face on the page of her personnel jacket. Was that the tiniest hint of a defiant smile? A wrinkle around the eyes? How could a person stand for an identification photo and still look smug, superior?

He stabbed out the cigarette, gathered up Elena's file, and locked his battered desk. He checked his watch. She would still be at the practice field, readying her Sukhoi for the trip to Moscow. It was time to have a talk with Elena Pasvalys. Slepkin snatched his jacket from the hook on the back of his office door. He was half out of the room when the old phone jangled again.

"Now what?" He hesitated, tempted to not answer it. The phone rang again. "Yes, yes. Very well," he said as he walked back to his cluttered desk and snatched up the handset. "Slepkin."

A quick stream of words gushed out. Slepkin's cheek began to tic and a flush of red suffused the pale skin of his thin neck. "When?" he said. Another gusher of excited Russian flowed. "But I thought—"

"This morning!" the man, an old contact at the KGB headquarters in Teplyystan, shouted. "Iraq invaded Kuwait this morning!"

9

Parrum opened the heavy velvet curtains of his hotel room and watched as a surge of demonstrators passed by below on Zhdanov Street, southbound for Marx Prospekt.

He smiled as he watched effigies of the Soviet president sway in time to the beat of drums. Posters of Boris Yeltsin's impish face sprouted from the sea of protesters like sunflowers. Over the steeply pitched roof of Detsky Mir, the giant toy store across the street, Parrum could see the riotously striped domes of St. Basil's; the ball atop the Ivan the Terrible bell tower burned a brilliant gold against the clear blue sky.

The mob sloshed over the curb like a river in flood and began to press against the buildings; across Zhdanov Street, blank, horrified faces peered out from the huge arched windows of Detsky Mir at a world turned upside down.

Parrum opened the window, and from his perch on the fourth floor of the Hotel Savoy, the voice of the crowd out on Marx Prospekt rose like pounding storm surf. Suddenly, some critical pressure was achieved, and the marchers began to flow south; an angry, surging river pointed straight at Red Square. Parrum chuckled and shut the window. *Welcome to democracy, folks,* he thought. *Enjoy it while you can.*

Parrum let the curtain drop closed and checked his watch. It was nearly eight in the morning. Two minutes later, he stepped out onto Zhdanov Street.

Parrum wrinkled his nose. The air was already rank and oily. Green mold sprouted from the mortar joints scoring pastel yellow and tomato-soup red walls. Drunks, washed up into alleys by the demonstration, passed bottles from one to the next, oblivious. He turned left, straight toward the imposing edifice of the Lubyanka Prison, the former headquarters of the KGB.

The air was humid and diesel-laced. Parrum crossed over the tram tracks and approached the statue of Feliks Dzerzhinsky, the founder of the KGB. "Piss on you, pal," he said with a smile. The gaunt figure with its devilish little goatee had just been swamped with protesters, and the image made Parrum chuckle. He stepped up his gait as he turned the corner, heading north.

Parrum caught the sudden stir at the news kiosk on the corner. Two suited men were standing reading the same bleak headlines over and over again. One caught his eye and quickly looked away. *Amateurs,* he thought. He stopped and checked his watch again. It was just after 8:06.

Parrum began to heat up as he half-walked, half-marched. The great stone facades facing the inhumanly wide street were already beginning to sweat. At the Boulevard Petrovsky, Moscow's inner-most ring road, he stopped, stepped out onto the street, and held up four fingers. The effect was immediate.

Three cars dove for Parrum, only one a cab, squealed their brakes, and weaved over to pick up a prize fare willing to pay four times the normal rate. A long black Chaika, obviously an official's limousine in between assignments, pulled rank and glided to a stop. Parrum got in.

The Chaika was huge. Parrum could stretch his legs straight out and not come near to touching the back of the driver's seat. The interior reeked of tobacco. "The Planetarium," he said.

"American?" said the driver with a big smile.

Parrum reached into his jacket pocket and pulling out a five-dollar bill and a pack of Marlboros. He handed them forward, and the limousine's tires chirped as it pulled smartly into traffic. Parrum looked behind. A gray Fiat had pulled from the curb, keeping a measured distance behind.

The beehive-shaped Planetarium was a favorite of Parrum's from the days when Moscow had been his home turf. It had been designed with the efficient movement of vast numbers of people in mind, and so while it had one main entry, it had a dozen exits around its circumference. The dark, starry dome within made it the perfect place to lose all but the most determined tail. It was a switchyard. Indeed, back in Parrum's Moscow days, they had called it the Roundhouse.

He bought a fifty-kopeck ticket from the disinterested clerk at the main door, stood in a mercifully short line of blue-and-white-uniformed schoolchildren, and entered the dark, hushed interior.

Overhead the winter constellations burned down brightly on a fanciful cityscape of onion domes and ultramodern spires. Comic little aerial cabs drifted from skyscraper to skyscraper like jet-finned fireflies. The flare of rocketship traffic headed for orbit lit the horizon. It reminded Parrum of nothing so much as the old, laughable World's Fair visions of the future; a cartoon paradise the real Moscow was in no danger of ever attaining.

Parrum let the flow of schoolchildren push him along, but when he came to the outermost aisle, he turned right and quickly made his way to one of the many exits. He pushed through and back out into the light. The broad square leading to the zoo was nearly deserted. There was no sign of the opposition.

Five broad blocks and ten minutes later, as the second hand on his watch swept through nine o'clock, he walked by the two Moscow Militia guards stationed at the stone steps of the United States Embassy.

Van Zandt Wilkerson, the new Moscow station chief, was expecting him. "Perhaps you'll tell me what you're up to, Mr. Parrum." Wilkerson waved a cable that had arrived overnight from Langley. His long, patrician face transmitted pure contempt. "I don't believe I know you, and to put it bluntly, you're on my territory." He gazed down at Parrum as though someone had left an inexcusable mess in his chair.

Parrum's first reaction was to remain silent. After all, there was probably not a single building on earth less secure against bugging than the United States Embassy in Moscow. Then he remembered that some of his words could, indeed, *should* be overheard. "I guess there just wasn't enough time to dot all the *i*'s," Parrum said at last. "We're working on some fairly fast-breaking information. Time wasn't on our side, cooperation-wise." He eyed the CIA station chief. Since when did officers start looking like TV weathermen? From his carefully shaped salt-and-pepper hair, to the slavishly preppy yellow-dot tie, Wilkerson was a virtual model of the new breed at Langley. An insider who had never known the world of the outside.

"There was enough time to get this ticket punched back home," said Wilkerson, the decoded cable in his hand. "Things just don't work this way anymore. Frankly, I rather doubt they ever worked this way at all."

"Just lucky, I guess," said Parrum with a smile.

"Yes," said Wilkerson slowly. *Knuckle-dragger,* said his eyes. He knew rather more about this smug man than he was letting on, and everything he knew spelled trouble. "And another thing," said Wilkerson. "Since when does Defense Intelligence run NOCs in Moscow?" It stood for non-official cover, a dirty little clandestine corner that Wilkerson clearly did not approve of. "I get the whiff of a rogue operation, Mr. Parrum. Please tell me I'm mistaken."

"We may have put this together quickly, but that cable in your hands says we're legit," Parrum replied. "But what do I know? After all, I'm just the water carrier." He shrugged.

"Yes," said Wilkerson slowly. "Parrum. George C. The C stood for Clandestine once upon a time if I'm not mistaken."

"That was a long time ago." Parrum's eyes narrowed slightly. "Nobody does that anymore. You know. It's technical means from here to Sunday. Spies are only in novels."

"Yes. That's what it should be. But here you are again. A Defense Intel NOC running loose in my town. It's bloody unheard of."

"I'm sure you're right."

"Most of your compatriots—or should I say cohorts?—are on the street. At least, those that stayed out of prison. I was under the impression that Clandestine got mucked out fairly thoroughly."

"Once a barn always a barn," said Parrum with an easy smile.

Wilkerson screwed up his mouth as though he had taken a bite from a hard persimmon. He tossed the cable onto his desk. "This thing. It doesn't say what the object of this exercise is, but we'll leave that for the moment." He looked back down at the decoded document. "This is to be an independent op, no Agency authorization. That means you're on your own. No backup." Wilkerson looked up, his bland expression incompletely masking malice. "You *do* work for us, don't you?"

"Of course," Parrum replied.

"Do you know how difficult it is to maintain a safe house here in Moscow? Much less two of them?"

"I have some idea."

Wilkerson said with a pen to his lips, "I suspect you do. What are they for?"

Parrum shook his head.

"Just asking. After all," said Wilkerson bitterly, "it's rare when a mere station chief gets to meet a real old-fashioned spook. I thought they stopped making them back when the Cold War ended."

This, finally, elicited a nod. "They did. About those houses?"

Wilkerson pursed his lips again as he brought out the keys. "One is out by Moskfilm. Setunskaya Street. Right on the river. Isolated approaches. Disaffected bohemian characters all over the place. Watch out for the starlets. They'll ID you faster than our friends from the Committee. They're trouble. Some of them *are* the opposition."

"Don't worry. And the other?"

"Number six Archipova."

"The old Jewish quarter?" Parrum said, objecting for form only. It was the very safe house he had requested from his old, and deeply entrenched, friends back in what was left of Clandestine.

"Very good, Mr. Parrum. You seem to have studied the map.

And yes, the main Moscow synagogue is there, too. Is that a problem?''

"No."

He handed Parrum the two sets of keys. "Take very, very good care of these, Mr. Parrum."

"Don't worry."

"Worried?" Wilkerson's smile suddenly evaporated. "I don't worry about you, Mr. Parrum. You see, compartmentalization goes both ways."

"How's that?"

Wilkerson leaned across his desk. "If by some chance you start to smoke, don't come here yelling fire." He scrutinized the keys in Parrum's hand. "Because I'll have no choice but to let you burn."

10

Elena buffed the cowl of her Sukhoi until its bright red paint gleamed ruby. Like the diamond pendant that hung from her neck, the powerful SU-26 was a tangible piece of absolute perfection. Indeed, it was one of the last ones left to her. She was getting thrown off Stingray, after all; why not the All-Union Aerobatic team?

The last week had been merciful. She had worked hard, harder than she ever had before, immersing herself in flying, in honing her skills, in forgetting. In the sky she was her own master, and it was a powerful restorative against the abrasion of the last week.

Six hours of flying full-throttle aerobatics had coated all but the wingtips in an oily sheen, but now, standing back, admiring her work, the SU-26 looked as new as the day it had been built. It was ready, and so was Elena, yet every time she stopped to remember Kessel's message, she felt a chasm open at her feet; a flaw cutting through the perfection she and her airplane created together. *Forget it,* she thought. *And forget them.*

She wiped her face with the last clean rag and began tying the wings of her plane to the iron rings set into the parking area. Eight other red SU-26s stood in a neat row, already tied down for the night; the tenth, belonging to a member of the men's team, had already been flown ahead to Moscow. The technicians from the

Sukhoi factory there could cure its nagging oil-temperature problems more capably than anyone.

The team building behind her was quiet, everyone else having gone out for the traditional pre-flyaway dinner with the team's cranky but able trainer, Kashum Nazhmudinov. Elena had stayed to practice one last time; to practice and to savor being alone in the presence of perfection.

She glanced up at the still-bright sky. Leningrad and Vilnius both had their white nights, and so did Serpukhov. In the heart of the Russian summer, it stayed light long into the evening.

She tied the tail wheel tight to the ramp, feeling the heat of the day radiate up from the still-tarry blacktop. The sound of a car approaching made her look up. What she saw made her heart sink. A black Chaika was rolling up the access road. *Slepkin*'s. She yanked a rag from the back pocket of her sweaty flightsuit and began rubbing the Sukhoi's flanks again. Her heart throbbed in her chest as the chasm she sought to forget opened up once more.

The car glided up to her and stopped. The driver's door opened. "Well, now. Here you are," said Colonel Slepkin. "I thought you might be out flying. We all were wondering if you were under the weather."

"There's work to be done," she said tightly. "And they still let me do it here."

"Always working. It is the sign of a true professional." The KGB man leaned against his car, watching Elena. "I take it everything is ready?"

"Quite," Elena replied.

The evening sun was still bright in the west, but its heat was gone. Slepkin forced himself to remain calm, in spite of the news of the Iraqi invasion, in spite of the news that a key American defense researcher was on his way to Moscow to buy an airplane just like the one before him. "I was told you struck a bird the other day. Nothing damaged?"

"The Sukhoi is ready," Elena answered as she slowly rubbed circles into the already immaculate metal.

"Excellent." He paused, counting the instants. Information was his job, and he, too, was a professional. "Have you heard the news?"

She stopped the polishing and looked at him. "News?" *Could they have changed their mind about her reassignment?*

"You *have* been busy today," he said with a smile.

"What's happened?" She tried to read his face, but the afternoon light came from behind him, nearly silhouetting Slepkin, turning his features black.

"Well," he said, drawing it out, "for one thing, you and I and everyone else will be leaving for Moscow a day early. Tomorrow instead of Saturday. I just was told this."

"What? Why?"

"The weather," said Slepkin with a shrug. "Not even Moscow can schedule the rain, it would seem. Not any more than they can keep their trusted allies in line."

There was something about his smile that told Elena there was more. "Which allies?"

"There's been a bit of nastiness in Southwest Asia. Baghdad," said Slepkin simply, as though he had been let in on the invasion by President Saddam Hussein himself. "Iraq invaded Kuwait this morning."

Elena felt a slight cool breeze chill her sweat. "It finally happened." She shivered. "What will come of it? What will it mean?" She hoped he would tell her that the Bear with Stingray in its belly would fly again, that the war would bring her back to Serpukhov. But in this she was disappointed.

"That's for others to determine," said Slepkin. "Why do you look so troubled? It's not as though he invaded *us*."

Elena tossed the oily rag to the ground. "Is there something else you wanted to speak with me about, Colonel? I was up flying since early this morning. I am very tired." Her arm muscles ached and her knees were vibrating with fatigue even as her brain buzzed with the news of the invasion.

"As a matter of fact, there is something," said Slepkin. "Let's take a walk, shall we?"

"Walk?" Elena was exhausted, her legs sore and her belly

bruised from the Sukhoi's tight harness. All she wanted now was a hot shower and to be rid of this pesky policeman.

"Just for a few moments. I have another piece of news to share with you."

Her ears perked at this. What was Slepkin trying to tell her? "Is it about me?"

"Very much so." Slepkin slammed the door of his Chaika shut. He peered up into the pale blue sky. A breeze sent dust spiraling up from the sun-baked blacktop.

Elena shivered again. She was certain he was about to tell her the Championships were canceled. First Stingray was taken from her, then the one event that illuminated her year was switched off. She was sure that's what it was. Her flightsuit was soaked with sweat. The diamond pendant hanging from her neck was slick with her exertion. It felt like a cube of ice. She nodded. "Very well, Colonel. We shall walk."

"Elena," he began as they paced along the small runway, "there have been some developments I feel obliged to discuss with you."

Elena stopped. "Switzerland? It's canceled, isn't it. Tell me the truth."

"Canceled? No. Don't worry. But please tell me, have you ever heard of an American, a pilot like yourself, by the name of Wyn Gallagher?"

The faces of the top aerobatic competitors flashed in Elena's mind. It took an eyeblink for her memory to frame one face from the few. "Of course," she said. "He's ranked third on the American team. What of him?"

"You know what he is? What he does?"

"He flies an old biplane rather well. That will be his mistake this year. Our Sukhois will eat him alive."

"Don't count on it," said Slepkin with a secretive smile. "But that's beside the point. You must listen well, Elena. It is imperative that you go nowhere near this man Gallagher. Not once."

She laughed. "Don't worry. The Swiss will be careful to keep our accommodations quite apart, even if you had not made sure of that already."

"Not the Swiss," he interrupted. "Not at all. Gallagher arrives in Moscow this evening."

"*Moscow?*"

"Yes." Slepkin loved knowing what others did not. He was ready to let the last bomb drop. "Gallagher," he began, and then corrected himself, "or shall I say, *Professor* Gallagher, is coming to buy a Sukhoi." He watched the shock spread across her face. It was worth it for this one moment. How many years had she ignored him, paid him less attention than she gave even to that Jew Kessel? "Just like yours."

"Are you serious?" she said at last, her voice a whisper. "But how can he? Who has let this happen?"

"What a question. The Americans have looted the world for fifty years. Why shouldn't he have enough hard currency to buy whatever he might want? Why not *ten* Sukhois?" Slepkin smirked as Elena silently played out the meaning of his words. "Now you know, Elena. You and he will both be in Moscow. A big city, to be sure, but sometimes not big enough. This time we must take extra precautions. Ignore him. And never, *never* find yourself alone together."

Suddenly, it all fell into place for her. "Tell me, Comrade Slepkin," she said quietly, a note of amusement in her voice. "Does Moscow think the danger is with Gallagher, or me?"

He waved away her words. "I thought we put that all to rest. No, I have no worries other than my wish to protect you. This Gallagher might well want to know what you know. After all"—he reached over and tapped the bulge of Elena's diamond, right above her breast—"you have given us this."

At first she was too shocked by his sudden intimacy to move, but then she twisted away, her neck flushed with anger.

"A priceless gift," Slepkin went on, "but that will not keep the world from wondering whether it might also be for sale."

"So? If the alternative is to bury it under a mountain of secrets, perhaps it should be."

Slepkin scowled and ran his hand through his slick hair. "I will forget you said that." He took her arm lightly and guided her back toward the Chaika. Her own wheezy Lada was parked just outside the little airport's perimeter fence. "Come on. I'll give you a lift to your car."

"No thank you, Colonel," she said, untangling her arm from his. "I'll walk."

11

The sun edged closer to the Bering Sea as the airliner climbed out from Anchorage. North America grew smaller as the Aeroflot jet ascended; smaller and more distant, a rumpled, frosted carpet of mountain and valley, an island; finally a dark line on the far horizon. *Now it's all up to me,* thought Gallagher as the first iceberg dotted the sea below. The thought both excited and scared him as the world lost all its shading, its gradation; all the complexities vanished in a world of black, frigid sea, and polar white.

By the time the IL-96 leveled off at flight level 320, the Bering Sea had solidified into one giant floe from horizon to horizon. The last light of a very long day turned the Ilyushin's wing the color of old pewter.

Gallagher pressed against the Plexiglas porthole, watching the flash of the airliner's wingtip strobes. A brilliant star twinkled low on the horizon. It was like a diamond, a chaos of chromatic sparks to which the wing strobes flashed their dull, metronomic reply.

"Excuse me?"

Gallagher turned, and as he did so, the smell of sage fell over him from the tall, blond woman standing in the aisle. She was the juggler's apprentice; the woman in the sequined bikini top. But now she was wearing both parts of her red and gold track suit. It didn't detract from her spectacular figure in the least. She didn't wait for an invitation before settling into the seat next to Gallagher's.

"Hello?" said Gallagher uncertainly.

"Hi," she said, swinging the short bangs of her golden hair from her eyes. "May I join you?"

Gallagher had never seen eyes quite that color before. Were they blue, or green?

He must have stared a bit too long, for the woman laughed, reached up to one eye, and popped out a tinted contact lens. Now she had one eye the color of the sea, another the color of ice. "Is this better? My name is Lyuba."

That scent! Gallagher breathed in the sage perfume. "My name's Gallagher." He extended his hand.

She took it and shook it firmly. "A pleasure. I'm from Moscow. Do you know Moscow?"

"Not yet."

"Oh. You will. Are you from California?"

"Texas."

"We loved performing in your country. Everyone was so wonderful. San Francisco is so beautiful. So bright. I have never seen so much sun over a city before. Everything is clean and new. You feel wealthy, just breathing. Who needs money?"

"So I saw." Gallagher nodded at the juggler sprawled across two seats up at the head of first class. "Tell me something, Lyuba. Does he always get you upgraded to first class that way?"

She laughed and looked forward to where the rest of the troupe sat. "Kolya is such a clown. But sometimes he is a very useful clown." She turned and made sure the juggler was not eavesdropping. "He is also full of himself. But Gallagher," she said, turning to face him, "you should come and see us perform in our own theater. It's right in Moscow. Gallagher is your first name?"

"No. It's Wyn."

"Wyn," she repeated. "So you will come?"

"I don't think so. Maybe next time. I won't be in Moscow for very long. Just a few days. I'll be leaving Sunday morning."

"So short?" she said, disappointed. "Why do you travel so far for only a few days?"

"I'm not on a tour. I came to buy something."

"Really?" She sat up straight. "You have come to *buy* something from *us?* What could you possibly find worth buying in *Moscow?*"

Gallagher wondered what he should say. But why not the truth? "An airplane. A Sukhoi airplane."

"A *Sukhoi?*" She leaned close and whispered, "Is it very expensive?" The smell of her perfume enclosed them in a velvet cocoon.

"Yes." Gallagher nodded, a bit dizzy. "Very."

"Good!" she said loudly, clapping her hands. "We need it!" Kolya the juggler heard her and looked back over his seat. His face was dour and disapproving. A new wooden match dangled from the corner of his mouth. She caught his glance and stiffened almost imperceptibly before turning her smile on Gallagher again. "Well, Mr. Gallagher," she said, making ready to stand, "I suppose I should—"

"Wyn."

"Wyn." Lyuba extended her hand. "I must go. I hope very much that you enjoy Moscow." He shook it, wishing she wouldn't leave just yet, but Lyuba stood up with a fresh wash of her perfume. "If you can, come see us. The Central Puppet Theater. Number three Sadovaya Street. That's where you can find us."

"Puppets? I thought you were in the circus."

"Whatever made you think so?" With a final laugh, she rejoined the others up forward.

The airliner arced over the pole. At some mathematically perfect instant, its northbound heading turned into a southerly course. Just before eleven o'clock Moscow time, the four D-90 turbofans were throttled back. The Ilyushin descended toward the black, invisible ground, banking over isolated islands of yellow lights. In the distance, Gallagher could see the bright galaxy of Moscow itself, its spiral arms extending out into the countryside like roots.

The jet's landing gear extended with a whine and a thunder of air. They flew low over a highway, then a tall building studded with red marking lights, and then with a loud squeal of tires and a roar of reverse thrust, they were down, rolling out along the main runway at Sheremetyevo 2.

Gallagher had arrived, and the next few days seemed to stretch before him like a runway. Landing in Moscow was just like taking off in his old Pitts. His future, his survival, was completely in his own hands.

"Welcome to Moscow, and thank you for choosing Aeroflot, the world's largest airline. Please remain in your seats until the crew has left the aeroplane," came the final cabin announcement. The forward crew hatch cracked open, the flightdeck emptied out first, and only then was the main cabin exit unsealed.

Gallagher stood up and stretched out his weary, stiff legs as he retrieved his one and only piece of luggage from the overhead bin. The brown and green L.L. Bean duffel was tiny; it had to be. Gallagher had researched the matter with some care. The small duffel, less than two feet long, was the largest object the Sukhoi 26's tiny baggage compartment could contain.

A stewardess urged him to the hatch. He nodded woodenly, followed her, and stepped out onto the stairs.

The air was warm and humid, laced with the cutting stink of kerosene. The stars were blotted out by the bright yellow security lights beaming down from the big terminal building. A distant flash illuminated the southwest horizon. Gallagher waited, but there was no thunder.

Gallagher descended the airstairs and climbed into the waiting blue and white bus. He checked his watch. They were twenty minutes shy of a new day. Suddenly, the doors whooshed shut and the bus moved away from the airliner. He sat his brown duffel on his lap, clutching it tight to his chest. He felt his heart beat in his throat as the bus moved along a path of blue lights toward the terminal.

It stopped in front of the Customs gate, where two sleepy-looking border guards were posted. Gallagher, certain that he exuded an odor of absolute guilt, folded into line behind the disheveled businessmen he had shared the first-class cabin with all the way from San Francisco.

They were dressed in suits; Gallagher wore blue jeans, a light sweater, and his decorated cotton flight jacket. A spare change of clothes plus a flameproof flightsuit were in the duffel. At least he didn't have to bring a parachute. A very good one was built right into the Sukhoi's seat. Still, he was sure he stood out like a gate-crasher. But he was wrong. They paid him no more attention than the businessmen.

Inside the Sheremetyevo terminal building, the entry lobby resolved into ten long lines of Passport Control. Only three were manned at this late hour. The unmistakable sounds of American Muzak could be heard spilling from the ceiling speakers. The lighting was much brighter than in an American facility. A knot of men in uniform, some others dressed in leather, plus a few women with push brooms stood near a wall-hung television monitor.

As Gallagher passed close, he could see that it was, of all things, a CNN broadcast. He chose the longest line of the three on the theory that the inspector would be more harried by the time he came to him.

"Gallagher? Wyn Gallagher?"

He turned at the sound of his name. A young man with a sky blue Sukhoi cap perched jauntily on his brown hair stood behind the chest-high barrier, his face up against the wire security mesh. He wore a red, white, and blue jacket with the emblem of the Experimental Aircraft Association sewn onto one breast pocket, and the words *Oshkosh 1989* over the other.

"Over here!" he said, indicating the shortest line of the three. "You are Wyn Gallagher?"

"That's me all right," said Gallagher, although his brain was so fogged from his travels he nearly opened his passport to confirm the fact. "You're from Sukhoi?"

"Yes. Evgeni Frolov. At your service."

Frolov was every bit as tall as Gallagher and was dressed in clothes an American might wear for hanging about the local airport. Then Gallagher remembered: Frolov was none other than the chief test pilot at Sukhoi.

"You picked some time to travel!" Frolov called out, nodding at the CNN broadcast playing on the screen. "Meet you at Customs!"

"Huh?" said Gallagher, but Frolov was already gone. He shuffled up to the brown-uniformed official. The brilliant crimson band on his hat was finished with a bright gold hammer and sickle.

The official scrutinized Gallagher, his eyes falling to his casual dress. His eyes held the slightest hint of disapproval. "Passport, visa, flight ticket, and landing card," he said wearily in heavily accented English. Gallagher handed across the papers and his passport. The packet received a cursory examination.

The official frowned when he came to the entry visa. The three purple sheets contained his date of entry, his place of residence while in the country, and the border station he would cross on leaving.

The official's finger went back over the date entered at the top. He licked his thumb and separated the purple pages, looking again at the exit stamp. He looked up at Gallagher, now keenly interested. "You are staying in Moscow only until Sunday?"

"Yes, sir,"

He held up the purple visa papers. "You are leaving from Lvov?"

"In the Ukraine," Gallagher said with a quick nod.

"Where is the authorization for your trip to Lvov? How are you going to get there?"

"I'm flying."

The official scowled and flicked an annoyed glance at the nearby Aeroflot desk. "Aeroflot must have made another mistake. They are always—"

"No, not Aeroflot," Gallagher interrupted. "I mean, *I'm* flying. I'm in Moscow to pick up a Sukhoi and fly it to Switzerland. I'll be crossing into Czechoslovakia at Lvov."

"Wait." The official picked up the black telephone under the counter. Another phone rang somewhere within earshot, and Gallagher saw a figure detach itself from the group clustered around the CNN program. The border guard shot a stream of excited Russian into the handset; the other man, no more than thirty feet away, replied loud enough for Gallagher to hear without the phone. The passport official nodded, shrugged, and hung up. "Thank you, Mr. Gallagher. Enjoy your very brief stay. Please proceed to Customs."

"I'm only bringing in this," said Gallagher, holding up the L.L. Bean duffel.

"Next," said the man with the crimson hatband.

Gallagher felt his heart begin to pound again as he walked by the luggage carousel. It was quiet; Aeroflot had not managed to empty the jetliner's holds yet. He was the very first person into the empty Customs Control area. All three customs officials watched as he walked, their glances zeroed in on the small brown duffel bag as though it contained a ticking bomb. His heart throbbed in his neck.

Each aisle terminated in a small, enclosed hut not much larger than a telephone booth. *X rays?* he wondered as he came to the booth. *Confessional?* Beyond the barrier, he could see Evgeni Frolov waiting for him. He stepped inside. A switch snapped and brilliant lights flooded the interior. Gallagher squinted against the dazzle. What the hell was this all about? He looked up at the ceiling, trying to spot a camera, anything, but it was like looking into a welder's arc.

A door clacked open, then shut. The new official, dressed in a dark olive uniform with the same, bright red flash of color on his officer's cap, stepped in from the far side and impatiently motioned him to drop the duffel onto the small table. *"Deklaratsiya,"* the guard demanded.

Gallagher handed him the card he had filled out on board the Ilyushin. The list was exhaustive, containing the large draft made to Sukhoi for just over $200,000, right down to his St. Christopher's medal and Rolex Air King wristwatch. The guard scrutinized the list, then handed back Gallagher's passport and visa. He made a motion Gallagher assumed indicated he was free to go.

That was easy, he thought with a wash of relief. He picked up the duffel and reached for the exit door handle.

"Nyet!" the guard shouted, and Gallagher froze. "Open it," the official demanded. "The bag."

Gallagher swallowed and calmed himself just the way he might on the run-in to an aerobatic routine. "Sure," he said, his voice catching. He unzipped the brown duffel.

"Uniform?" the official said when he came to Gallagher's Nomex flightsuit. "You are soldier?"

"No. I'm a pilot. A *private* pilot." The guard seemed annoyed and puzzled. How do you explain a private pilot in a country where they didn't exist?

The flightsuit was covered with patches from his many aerial competitions. The border guard held the wrinkled Nomex disapprovingly and turned it all the way around, unzipping the many pockets, hunting for who knew what? The lights spilled down, the hidden cameras recorded everything.

Suddenly, the far door snapped open and the Sukhoi test pilot stuck his head in. "What's going on?" Frolov demanded. "What's the hang-up?" He pulled his blue Sukhoi cap down and unleashed a torrent of Russian so forceful the guard's face blanched. His uniform seemed to deflate. He tried to edge a word in, but Frolov was having none of it.

"Come on," he said to Gallagher when it was over. "Let's get out of here, okay? Who does he think he is? Gorbachev? It is so incredible."

"Sounds good to me," Gallagher agreed. His heart was still racing. He zipped the duffel closed and nodded to the guard. What had Frolov said to him? Whatever it was, it had worked. "See you around," he said, and stepped out into the soft lights of the terminal.

Frolov took Gallagher by the arm and pulled him into the waiting area on the safe side of Customs. Gallagher was too tired to protest the physical closeness. "Welcome to Russia!" Frolov said, guiding Gallagher. "The world is falling all to hell." Frolov pronounced it *hall*. "But here everything is still on the track. Okay? There's a car outside." He nodded at the small duffel. "That is everything?"

"Everything that will fit. But why do you say the world is—"

"Then it will be easssssy," he said, relishing the word on his tongue. "I almost forgot you will be leaving Moscow for Yverdon. Quite a flight. You will know the SU-26 before you get there. You'd better."

"That's the general idea," said Gallagher. "But what did you mean about things falling apart?"

Frolov stopped. "You have not heard?"

"Heard what?"

"The war? They said nothing?"

"Who said nothing? What war?" Gallagher's travel weariness and his run-in with the guard were making him edgy.

Frolov whistled. "This morning. Boom! Iraq invaded Kuwait. It's all over. Poof. Like the Nazis. Tanks. Planes. Who knows? We sold them everything they wanted. It worked." He snapped his fingers. "Done, Finished. *Eassssy*. The Kuwaitis? They had no chance."

Gallagher felt his brain try to rev up to meet the news, but he was just too damned tired from the trip. "I thought there was going to be some kind of meeting. That's what I read in the morning paper."

"The free press is free to be wrong, yes? Anyway, it won't matter now. Not anymore. Come," he said, clapping Gallagher on the shoulder, "there is much to get done if you will live to arrive in Switzerland."

Gallagher dumbly trailed Frolov through the huge, almost deserted lobby and outside. There, a Mercedes, black as the night, was waiting, its engine nearly silent, purring. The driver took his little duffel as though it were made by Hermès and placed it carefully in the huge trunk. The lid closed with a pneumatic hiss.

Gallagher got in, then Frolov. They moved off from the curb and headed into the night. As the car joined the main highway to Moscow, they passed a series of enormous metal sculptures by the side of the road. They looked like a pair of child's jacks, if jacks were built twenty feet on a side.

"Tank traps," said Frolov, catching Gallagher's stare. "We build them big in Russia. Too bad they had none in Kuwait."

Gallagher frowned. "And nothing is happening? I mean, we aren't retaliating or something?"

"Words. What else is government good for?"

"You'd get along real fine in Texas, Mr. Frolov."

"Please. Evgeni. As for Texas, I have been. The girls are the very best anywhere. It's true, yes?" He picked up a black canvas bag in the limousine's footwell and pulled out a heavy bundle of hardbound books. "Here are your manuals. You must study very well. We want you to go back and make everyone in America want to buy a Sukhoi. But first, you must live, yes?"

Gallagher took the stack of documents. They had the size and heft of a good-sized dictionary.

"Flight manual, mechanical drawings, engine specifications, and overhaul guide. It is all there," said Frolov. "We will start in the morning with preflight, and perhaps, if there is time, we will fly, too."

"Uh, thanks, Evgeni. But where do I put it?" said Gallagher. He knew the SU-26's baggage compartment wouldn't hold this pile and his duffel, too.

"You memorize it first, and then we'll ship it ahead for you. First class, yes? For two hundred thousand, it should be."

"Memorize?"

"Just the important parts. Don't worry. Mr. Gallagher—"

"Wyn."

"Wyn," said Frolov. "Don't be too concerned. I have read your file. You can fly. Our team thinks you can fly even a little too well. Wait when they realize you now have a Sukhoi. Gold medals like snow! But business is business I always say."

Gallagher nodded. "I was wondering, Mr.—"

"Evgeni, please. We are now friends."

"Evgeni," Gallagher finished. "How much does it really cost Sukhoi to build an SU-26?"

"Who knows?" Frolov shrugged. "How much did you pay? That is what it cost."

Gallagher chuckled at this. "They've got a little company back in Texas that works just the same way."

"Oh? Which one?"

"General Dynamics." Gallagher suddenly felt his eyes grow heavy. He leaned on the limousine's window, staring at the stands of birch forest sweeping by. As suddenly as if someone had thrown a switch, the trees were gone, and in their stead, rows and rows of tall apartment buildings appeared. Each was angled the same forty-five degrees to the highway. The brilliantly lit spire of the Northern Ferry building passed by silently on their right as they plunged deeper into the heart of the city.

"Right there," said Frolov, nodding at a large blue sign that read *Aeroflot*. "That is where we will fly tomorrow."

They sped by what was obviously a hotel. "Where?"

"The airport is behind the hotel," Frolov explained. "It was once the only airport for all of Moscow. Two thousand meters of grass. A little short for big airplanes, but not for the SU-26. You are doing something wrong if you need two hundred meters, never mind two thousand. But it will make you more precise. Perfect to learn from, yes? Easssy."

"Sounds all right. What about the practice area? I assume I can't fly anywhere over Moscow I want to."

"Correct. The last one who tried learned to ice fish for a year. The German."

"Mathias Rust," said Gallagher, referring to the young pilot who had evaded the vaunted Soviet air defenses all the way from Finland to Red Square.

"That was the name. The practice area is very small. Very regulated. But what is so new? Can you fly over the White House?"

"Just once," said Gallagher with a smile.

"There. You see? It is the same. There are apartment blocks on two sides, and the river off the departure end. But you will be careful, yes?"

"I never cared too much for ice fishing."

The buildings got larger as they sped across the outer Garden Ring road and turned left onto the inner Boulevard Ring. The Hotel Savoy, sitting just outside the inner sanctum of Red Square, was brightly lit as the limousine pulled up and stopped. The driver got out, retrieved the small brown duffel from the Mercedes's trunk, and opened Gallagher's door.

"Tomorrow morning at seven we will start work," said Frolov as Gallagher got out. "Oh, you did bring the money, yes?"

Gallagher patted the duffel.

"Excellent. See you at seven." Frolov pulled the door shut and the limousine pulled away.

Gallagher stumbled down the marble stairs into the lobby of the Hotel Savoy, passed the casino, passed the restaurant, passed the desk as well. He made it to the ancient, ornately decorated elevator before he realized he hadn't a clue where to go to find his room. White marble statues of female nudes in classical poses stood guard from nearly every corner.

"Good evening and welcome to the Savoy, Mr. Gallagher," said an immaculately uniformed bellhop. "Do you wish your dinner, sir?"

"Bed," Gallagher grunted.

"I'll show you to your suite."

Ten minutes and a hard-currency tip later, Gallagher, still in his blue jeans, fell into a deep feather bed. Thoughts of war, of invasions, of risk and benefit, evaporated like high-octane aviation fuel spilled onto a hot runway, and in their place came a sleep of flashing propellers, crimson airplanes, the smell of sage on morning dew, and a clear, clear blue sky.

12

"Did you sleep well?" asked Evgeni Frolov as the limousine turned off Leningradskaya Prospekt and up the access road to Moscow Central airfield. He peered intently into Gallagher's face. "I assume you have memorized the operating limitations? Starting procedures? Stall and maneuver speeds?"

"I read them over breakfast," Gallagher replied groggily. He looked at his watch, trying to figure out what time it was back in California. He gave up.

"They had better be right here," said Frolov, tapping his forehead. "But remember two things above all else." He held up one finger. "Never get slower than one hundred and sixty kilometers per hour."

"That comes to ninety knots," Gallagher agreed. "What's the other thing?"

A second finger joined the first. "Only this: the SU-26 is stressed to survive twenty g's. You are not. Understood?" Gallagher nodded. "Good. Then we can fly right after the preflight. Listen," he said, "I want you to concentrate, yes? Forget about everything. Forget about the war. It's over anyway. You will need to be very sharp this morning. All my students must be sharp." He glanced at Gallagher's brown duffel bag. "You brought the check?"

"Right here." Gallagher patted the L.L. Bean bag. They sped by

117

the big Aeroflot Hotel and straight through a security gate. A sentry stood at rigid salute. "Who does that guy think we are?"

"A black limousine," said Frolov with a shrug. "Oh. I forgot to mention. There will be a few people at the hangar this morning."

"People? Who?"

"You will see." Frolov smiled secretively. The long black limousine nosed between two old, decrepit-looking hangars. "Moscow Central," Frolov announced. "It might as well be a park. No one ever flies from here anymore. Except," he said with an arched eyebrow, "for you. You will have no competition. It will be easssssy."

The view opened onto a broad field of green, hemmed in on the far side by a solid wall of white apartment blocks. At the foot of the grass runway, he could see the sluggish Moskva, its waters reflecting the hazy summer sky. And in the middle of the field, in the very heart of Moscow, Gallagher saw a bright orange wind sock waving in the morning breezes. It was the same the world over. Wherever a wind sock filled with air, a pilot found a home.

"Over there," said Frolov, nodding toward one of the arch-roofed hangars. "There is a small surprise. You will see."

Four Sukhoi airplanes were tied down to the grass, their fat, round cowls pointed skyward; four muscular, wind-carved shapes seemed ready to leap up and take a great bite out of the sky. Their forms shouted performance, but they also whispered danger. A knot of figures stood to one side, apparently waiting for Gallagher's arrival.

Three of the SU-26s were painted in crimson and white. One was different. Instead of the factory-standard paint scheme, it was done in a dazzling combination of dark blue with an electric-pink lightning bolt emblazoned along its side. Bright red stars glowed from the rudders of three of the planes; the fourth ship was again distinct.

"Hey!" said Gallagher as they drew close to the line of airplanes. Frolov chuckled.

The last blue Sukhoi had a black, round bomb painted on its tail, the number 8 at its center; a sparking fuse snaked down the Sukhoi's slim tail. It was the same eight-ball insignia that Gallagher's Pitts once wore.

"How did you . . . I mean . . ."

Frolov smiled mysteriously and clapped Gallagher on the shoulder. "Research."

As the black Mercedes glided up to the tie-down area, the group of people standing next to Gallagher's new ship began to applaud.

Christ, thought Gallagher. *What now?* Some of the group wore the white coats of technicians, others the blue smocks of metal workers. A few were dressed in business suits. A photographer stood to one side, watching. All of them were bedecked with medals fastened to their chests. The gold and silver and crimson medallions glittered in the sun as they clapped. "Who's the reception committee?"

"A few people from the factory. They wish to show their appreciation. Come on," Frolov said, opening the door. "Let's get it over with."

"But . . ."

"Don't forget the check," Frolov said, and then got out.

Gallagher grabbed his duffel bag and followed, and the applause promptly doubled in intensity. It gradually coalesced until all eight people clapped as one, louder, louder, like a football rally cheering on the home team. Gallagher wasn't the home team, but it didn't seem to matter. They pounded their hands together as though he were. He smiled weakly, embarrassed, remembering that he was here not to help Sukhoi build airplanes for the world; he was here to help Elena Pasvalys make her escape to the West. Gallagher held up his hand for them to stop, but it took Frolov waving his arms to get them finally quieted.

A blue-smocked assembler from the Sukhoi plant stepped forward, pulled out a piece of paper, and began to read.

"Just a few more minutes," whispered Frolov as Gallagher stood there, listening to the man speak. Who knew what he was saying? Finally, the speech ended and the photographer stepped forward, followed by one of the two men dressed in business suits.

Frolov nudged Gallagher and nodded at the duffel bag. "Now," he whispered.

Gallagher unzipped the bag and withdrew his check for $200,000. It fluttered in the strengthening breeze. He put on a smile and handed the check over. The shutter snapped, a motor winder whined, and the shutter snapped again. When it was over, the man in the suit reached out his hand. "Thank you very much, Wyn Gallagher!" he said in stumbling English. "Peace to all the world!"

If you only knew, thought Gallagher as he extended his hand, thinking the ordeal would end with a civilized handshake. The next thing he knew, he was caught in a powerful bear hug getting kissed, his breath whooshing out. He dropped the duffel to the grass. The grip relaxed, but a line had formed. Eight more hugs, sixteen more kisses followed before the ceremony reached its preordained conclusion. The check was passed from one to the next as though in proof.

"You see?" said Frolov as the factory group retreated back into the big hangar behind the tie-down area. "That wasn't so bad. Now we go to work. Here." He handed Gallagher a heavy iron key that looked as if it would open the cab of a locomotive. On it, the round bomb with the number 8 was reproduced.

Gallagher hefted it. It must have weighed a pound. "What's this for?"

"The canopy lock," said Frolov with a scowl. "I thought you read the manuals."

"I did, but . . ."

"Well, then? Are we going to begin or not?" Frolov stood back and crossed his arms over his chest. His Sukhoi ball cap was pulled down at a rakish angle over his forehead.

Gallagher flipped the key in his hand again. *I won't leave this one in my pocket,* he thought as he stepped up to the blue Sukhoi with the eight-ball bomb on its tail. He inserted the heavy key into the canopy lock and turned it. With the smooth, well-oiled click of a bank vault opening, the teardrop canopy moved up and back. Gallagher reached over and swung it full open.

A gust of warm air, scented by new leather, washed over his face.

Gallagher closed his eyes and breathed in. It reminded him of a
brand-new baseball mitt. "Nice," he said. He leaned over and ran
his hand across the top of the wing. It was like touching the wind
itself; there was not so much as a dust mote to mar its ultrasmooth
surface. From the nine-cylinder radial in its nose to the number 8 on
its slim tail, the Sukhoi looked as though it had been grown from a
single, perfect crystal, not assembled by mere men. He looked back
at Frolov.

"Yes?" Frolov said with a proud smile.

"Evgeni," said Gallagher, "this thing's too pretty to fly."

"Go ahead and sit in it. It won't bite you. At least not here on the
ground."

Gallagher stepped up onto the narrow wingwalk. The small
airplane rocked beneath him like a kayak, its titanium landing-gear
legs flexing under his weight. He glanced back at the Sukhoi hangar
building. He could see faces peering from one of the windows.

He settled himself in the steeply reclining seat. Gallagher's feet
were almost level with his chest, an asset when eight g's were
draining a pilot's head of all his blood. Set back at nearly forty-five
degrees, the seat's odd angle, though limiting the view over the
engine, quickly felt natural. The joystick was a massive, goose-
necked sculpture rising from the floor and ending at eye level. He
found that by resting his right arm on his leg, the stick fell perfectly
into his hand. He wagged the controls. There was not the slightest
trace of slop in them. *Perfect.* He turned to face Frolov, his face
glowing with pure delight.

Frolov nodded, recognizing the simple fact that Gallagher was
falling in love. "May I ask you a question?"

Gallagher roused himself from his reverie, his guard belatedly
deployed. "Shoot."

"The Sukhoi, it is a very good airplane. Much better than the
Pitts. But why did you wait until just before Yverdon to buy one? It
will not be to your advantage. It takes time to know an airplane."

The sound his stricken Pitts had made as it crashed flooded
Gallagher's memory. "I lost my regular airplane. Just last week."

"Lost?"

"Crashed."

Frolov's mouth formed a silent Oh. He squinted at Gallagher from beneath the Sukhoi ball cap. "Well," he said as he digested the news, "you will not lose this one. Not if I have anything to say about it."

"I'm with you, Evgeni," said Gallagher. "Let's begin."

"Yes," Frolov agreed as he opened the flight manual. "Let us begin."

**Friday Noon,
3 August 1990**

"There they go!" Slepkin shouted over the roar of Elena's engine. Her plane, Number Seven, roared aloft from the Serpukhov strip. The heavy rumble of the powerful Vedneyev resonated in his chest. He leaned back on the hot steel of his black Chaika and watched.

Kolya Zarkich tracked the crimson airplane as it rose, his gray eyes reflecting blue like two small, perfect mirrors. With a wooden match dangling from the corner of his mouth, he had the look of a hungry wolf watching a herd of deer. "I thought all Lithuanians were tall," he said. "Is she a Jew?" Dressed in a bright red track suit and standing a full head taller than Slepkin, Zarkich's neck was ropy with muscles. His hands had the chiseled look of roots gripping stone. One of his eyes was surrounded by a bruise the color of eggplant.

"Please," said Slepkin. "I have enough problems to worry about."

"Did you get to screw her?"

Slepkin scowled at his taller subordinate. "Tell me, Kolya, what happened to the eye? One night in Moscow and already you are losing fights?"

"Moscow is full of hooligans," Kolya Zarkich replied with a twitch of his mouth. His tongue rolled around the match he had dangling from his lips. The match suddenly disappeared inside his mouth. When it emerged, it was on fire. He spat it out, a flaming comet arcing to the grass.

"You love your little tricks, don't you?" Slepkin said as he ground the match out with his shoe. "So what happened?"

"A disagreement." He didn't mention that the fight had taken place only moments after his arrival at Sheremetyevo Airport, or that his victim, a tall blonde named Lyuba, had been sent to the hospital. "There's no respect for order anymore."

"So true." Elena's Sukhoi receded to a tiny red dot at the head of a vee of identical red dots. "Nobody knows his place. Nobody knows what to do. Tell me, how can this be?"

Zarkich knew he was not really being asked. "We should do as we are trained," he said.

"Bravo, Kolya," Slepkin agreed. "I remember something Lenin once said. It was 1923. Famine, intrigues. The whole world was turning to shit everywhere he looked."

"Like now."

"Yes. Like now. Do you know what he said?" Slepkin's eyes seemed to glaze as he looked up. "He said, '*We aren't shooting enough professors.*' I wonder if we might not do well to remember this."

Zarkich snorted and broke out into a grin. From some hidden reserve—where did he keep them?—another wooden match dangled from his lips. He rubbed his bruised eye. "When do we start?"

Slepkin waved at the Chaika's passenger door. "Now."

It was a tight formation; dangerously so for any other than a group of the world's best pilots. Elena flew close enough to the other four SU-26s of the women's team to feel the rumble of their engines against the glass of her canopy. The work it took to fly so close kept her from thinking too much.

To her left, the four other ships of the women's team were tucked in tight, the nose of each plane a precise two meters behind and below the wingtip of the one ahead. To her right, the men's team stepped away in equally precise formation. Just beyond them,

Kashum's two-place Sukhoi trainer nipped at all their heels, keeping them together like a sheepdog minding a flock.

Still more than fifty kilometers distant, Moscow's tall buildings already broke the northern horizon.

She checked her fuel gauge again. With only seventeen gallons in the tank ahead of the cockpit, her Sukhoi could remain aloft for only twenty-five minutes. It would take nearly that long to reach Moscow. There would be little left in the tanks on their arrival.

"Formation break in eighteen minutes," called Kashum, the team trainer.

The two teams would fly in formation, sweeping over the heart of Moscow. Then, at the five-hundred-meter Ostankino TV tower, they would turn in trail for the landing pattern at Moscow Central.

She moved the sensitive stick almost imperceptibly. Her eye told her that her SU-26 was all over the sky, but she knew that from the ground it would seem welded in formation. A trickle of sweat fell down her neck and between her breasts. The morning sun was hot, and it took hard work to create the illusion of perfection.

"Fifteen minutes out," called Kashum. "I want everyone to look good. Anyone who screws up will find themselves flying gas masks to Baghdad. Red Nine!" he shouted. "Back into line! Have you forgotten how to fly?"

Elena turned and saw Khalida's plane slip back into its proper position. Kashum's threat was a joke, but the war going on was very real indeed.

The smokestacks and apartment buildings of Moscow grew larger directly ahead, through the spinning arc of her propeller.

"That's better, Red—" Kashum began, but his transmission was suddenly drowned out when a new voice came over her headset, a loud, booming voice that rode a whining but powerful carrier wave.

"Big Bird One is orbiting Ostankino," it said. "Are you there, Elena?"

Elena jumped at her name, her head cocked to one side. Who, or what, was Big Bird? Who would call her name across the sky? Who knew she was—

"Well?" came the voice again. "Must I ask twice?" She could

hear, against his voice, the sound of jet engines. The voice in her headset suddenly doubled in volume. *"How is this, Red Seven? Is this any better, Squirt?"*

"Who is on this frequency?" demanded Kashum.

"Yuri!" Elena exclaimed involuntarily. He was an old friend and onetime suitor whose girth had gotten him kicked out of fighter training and into transports. They had met at the university; she a math tutor, he an unwilling student putting in a mandatory sentence required by the Air Force. It was Yuri who had started Elena's love of flying; a love that despite all his attempts had not blossomed beyond aviation. Was he flying the huge Antonov? It certainly was a fitting assignment. "Is that you?" she asked.

"So you *do* hear me. Very good," said Yuri. "I'm flying the Big Beast! We'll land right after you. The crew will be staying at the Aeroflot Hotel. I am in room seven one four. Repeat! Seven one four. Do you copy, Red Seven?"

Big Beast? "Seven fourteen," Elena repeated, a red flush rising up Red Seven's neck.

"It sounds like Red Seven will be flying tonight," said someone from the men's team.

"That's enough!" bellowed Kashum. "Nine minutes out!"

Elena remembered Yuri and their first flight together; it had been her first flight ever. The university flying club had a few old Yak trainers available, and Yuri, big, ungainly Yuri, had been as smooth and as graceful as a Baryshnikov at its controls. Earthbound, he was one thing. But the man had brought the gift of flight to Elena. *Maybe he will be lucky tonight,* she thought.

The sun blazed down through the Sukhoi's cranked-open canopy like the hot beam from a magnifying lens. Gallagher, his eyes closed, reached out and touched each of the plane's controls, reciting their names and their functions from memory. Sweat trickled down his face. The far-off whine of a big jet was the only sound he could hear.

"Fuel pump," said Frolov.

Gallagher reached out to the lower right side of the narrow cockpit. "System pressure," he said, turning the handle one way, "and engine prime," he said, flipping it the other.

"Good. Emergency fuel shutoff?"

His eyes still closed, Gallagher reached with his left hand and tapped a big red handle that would kill all fuel to the engine in the event of a fire.

"Correct," Frolov said again. "Trim?"

Gallagher nodded and extended his arm to where the trim used to live in his old Pitts. His knuckles struck bare metal.

"Hah!" said Frolov. "I thought so!"

"Sorry, Evgeni," said Gallagher sheepishly. "I forgot." The SU-26 had no trim system at all. His brain was still laced with the memory of his old Pitts.

"You forgot? Let me tell you of something that I remember," said Frolov with a wag of his finger. "It was with a girlfriend. A very pretty one. At—how shall I say?—a very delicate moment, I shouted a name." Frolov shook his head sadly. "The wrong name. She threw me out, of course. Now," he continued, "what will happen if you must react like this." Frolov snapped his fingers. "Your body is in a Sukhoi, but your brain is flying another airplane. Very bad. Understood?"

"Understood," said Gallagher. A rivulet of sweat worked its way down his neck. He glanced up into the hot sky. It was like southeast Texas around here; hot and muggy. If only he could start the Sukhoi up and let its big propeller blast him with wind!

"Then that is that," said the Russian test pilot. "We have drilled you enough I think. Well, Wyn Gallagher? Do you think you might survive one little flight? Would you like to try?"

His hand gripped the stick hard, too hard. He willed it loose. "A lot," said Gallagher. Alien though it was to him, just sitting in this hummer made him feel powerful, as though some of the Sukhoi's strength flowed right into his body through the control stick. His old Pitts had felt much the same way, although it had taken years to achieve. The Sukhoi managed the same trick in one morning. Was it a trick, a fatally reassuring illusion?

"You are certain?" Frolov asked. "You will not leave it some-place inconvenient? I warn you. The Moskva is very wet."

"Evgeni?" he said, holding up the heavy key. "Hold this for me, will you?" He tossed it to Frolov.

The Sukhoi test pilot smiled as he snatched it. "I have never lost a student. We can go over some more—"

"You won't lose me," Gallagher finished. "Untie this thing, Evgeni, and let's see what she can do."

"If you kill yourself," said Frolov as he loosened the tie-down ropes, "don't expect a refund."

Time to concentrate. He pulled the double lap belt tight and hooked it, followed by the shoulder straps. He let out a breath and cinched them all tighter still. He was now part of the machine, a single, forged unit from its three-bladed prop to the black eight ball on its tail. He snuggled into the combination seat and parachute pack. Once he was off the ground, only his own skill would bring him back alive.

Gallagher looked over to the ramshackle control tower. "And you're sure I don't need to talk to anybody?"

"Them?" Frolov waved dismissively. "The controllers have been on strike for a month now. They visited America and now they all want to be paid real money. No," he said. "Don't worry. Fly no higher than two thousand meters. The river, the Moskva, is the boundary." He swept his arm around. "The apartment blocks are the other three sides of the box. Do not let yourself get blown, Wyn. They do not like little airplanes over Red Square anymore."

"Got it." The entire flying area was barely twice the size of a thousand-meter aerobatics box; it would take some care to keep inside it. "I'm ready." Gallagher handed him the operator's manual.

"I hope so." Frolov reached into the cockpit and tugged at Gallagher's belts, one at a time, and gave him the thumbs-up. "Full throttle for takeoff, and let it fly itself from three point, yes? Don't push." Frolov indicated the joystick. "There is little clearance to the propeller. After takeoff, climb at eighty percent, do a circuit, power back, and land. Again, do not strike the ground nose low! You will hit the propeller. Very expensive noises will result, yes?"

"Stick back and three point all the way in," Gallagher repeated. He tapped the fuel gauge. The SU-26MX, the export model, carried far more fuel than the ships flown by the Soviet team. He could fly her all morning if he wanted to.

Frolov held up three fingers. "Three takeoffs, three landings. After the third, if I wave you to go back up, then go. If not, you come back and I will tell you where you are making the mistakes, okay?"

"Okay."

"Remember to relax," said Frolov as he stood back. "She is eassssy to fly. But very hard to fly well. Good luck."

"See you in three, Evgeni." Gallagher extended his Nikes into the rudder-pedal straps. "Brakes set!" he called.

Frolov stepped up to the big three-bladed prop and gave it a tentative pull. With Gallagher's feet on the brakes, the Sukhoi rocked back and forth but did not roll an inch. "Switches?" called Frolov.

"Off," Gallagher replied as Frolov pulled the prop through to cleanse the bottom cylinders of residual oil. After three blades, the Sukhoi pilot stood to one side, his own face beaded in sweat. Gallagher energized four rocker switches at the bottom of the instrument panel, bringing on a row of annunciator lights. "Switches are hot," he called out as he worked the sliding throttle a couple of times and left it cracked open a half inch. With his other hand, he stroked the priming pump, sending raw fuel to the Vedneyev's nine gaping cylinders. Gallagher's hand paused above the starter lever. "Clear!"

"Be careful!" Frolov shouted as he danced back from the prop.

Gallagher hit the starter, and with a loud, snakelike hiss of compressed air, the propeller began to whirl. As it spun up to speed, he snapped on the magnetos. In a loud belch of blue smoke, the Vedneyev caught and stumbled, firing on one, then two, then five, and then on all nine cylinders. It smoothed out into a low, confident rumble.

Gallagher left the canopy open, letting the blast of air dry his face. It felt damned good, but he wasn't here to feel good. He was here to fly. He reached back and pulled the heavy canopy down. It locked with a smooth, satisfying click. It was time to fly. The prop wash made the slim wings tremble.

Frolov stood to one side. He gave Gallagher the thumbs-up.

Gallagher nodded. "Now," he said to himself. "If I can just keep this hummer from killing me . . ." He advanced the throttle a fraction of an inch, and the massive engine pulled the Sukhoi with the eight ball on its tail out of its parking slot and onto the grass runway.

He had no visibility at all over the cowl as he snaked his way down the grass toward the end of the runway. By the time he got to the run-up area at the far end, the Vedneyev's vital signs were touching the tops of their green operating ranges.

He tapped the left brake and swung around. Six thousand feet of smooth grass faced him, ending at the blue line of the Moskva River. The engine temperatures were still climbing. Gallagher stomped on both brakes and pulled in full power.

The Vedneyev roared, but the note was strange to him. He scanned the instruments as the radial tried to pull against the brakes. The tach needle was right where it should be. Instead of the 2,800 RPM snarl of the Pitts, the Sukhoi had, appropriately, the deep, rumbling roar of an angry bear. He checked both magnetos and then the propeller pitch control. They were set. He pulled the throttle back to idle and checked the sky. It was empty. The smell of hot oil cut through the cockpit as he swiped a salty bead of sweat from his eyes. The back of his flightsuit was soaked through.

The stunning fact that this would be his first flight since he crashed the Pitts flooded through him. He had been thrown, and now he was getting back on the horse, but this horse was wilder, more dangerous than any he had ever ridden before.

Okay, he said to himself, *are you here to fly or what?*

With three calming breaths, Gallagher pushed in the throttle. The engine note rose to a thunderous shout. The Sukhoi accelerated like a gunshot.

Almost . . . what? The little plane was swerving to the right! Of course! The Sukhoi swung its prop the opposite way from his old

Pitts! Gallagher stomped on the left rudder pedal just as the tail came up as if by its own decision, then, with a bounce, the main tires lifted free of the grassy runway. He had yet to advance the throttle halfway, and they were already flying! Gallagher was way behind this airplane and they were scarcely airborne.

He shot a glance at the airspeed indicator as its needle surged to life in the rush of wind. Gallagher pushed the stick forward and leveled off twenty feet above the rapidly passing runway. The rows of white apartment houses passed in a blur to both sides. Ahead, the river rushed toward him. There was no longer a question of simply landing the Sukhoi straight ahead. He was flying, or more accurately, he was hanging on as the Sukhoi flew, and there was only one safe way back to earth. "Fly the airplane," he said quietly. "Fly the airplane."

He nudged the stick back and the Sukhoi barreled into the Moscow sky like a black-powder skyrocket. He pulled back on his power and tried to level, but the Sukhoi kept right on going, higher, higher. He risked a quick look to the side. There was Red Square. There was the Kremlin. The boulevard rings of Moscow receded below him like a map. He pulled off even more power, and only then did he wrestle the powerful plane level. He eased the stick over to one side and the Sukhoi lurched into a steep bank. "Jesus," he said, weaving back level. It took a watchmaker's touch to fly this damned thing! Gallagher was no neophyte. He'd been classed with the very best pilots in the world. But he was ham-fisting the SU-26 like a rookie.

He brought the nose around onto a downwind heading and began slowing up for the first landing. The wind was blowing him in toward the grass runway. Using two fingers on the stick, he corrected for its effect, swept the instrument dials for anything amiss. *Don't get below ninety knots,* Frolov had warned him. He had nearly 120 on the dial as he pushed the nose over and banked onto final approach, close in, high, and blisteringly fast. The black, hawklike shadow he cast flitted over the Aeroflot Hotel and across the verdant green runway.

"God damn!" he roared as the airstrip streaked below him. He was going to miss the whole runway! He yanked off all his throttle, shoved the prop control forward, and threw the Sukhoi into a steep slip.

The effect was instantaneous. He was thrown forward against his straps. With the idling propeller generating pure drag, Gallagher plummeted toward the grass like a dropped piano.

An instant before he hit, Gallagher blipped the throttle forward a touch as the ground rose to smite him, cushioning the impact only slightly. With a squeal of protesting titanium and one long, looping bounce, he brought the Sukhoi back to earth, stabbing the rudders to keep them straight. Then, with a sweep of the throttle, he accelerated again and took off, his motions more sure, more subtle this time than before.

The first landing had been a crash in everything but the result; the second landing was passable. The third, whether by luck or by skill, was a whisper-smooth touchdown, the plane's wheels kissing the blades of grass ever so gently until their rumble announced the reality of the landing to Gallagher's ears. He shot a glance to where Frolov stood. The Sukhoi pilot was waving for him to go back up.

"Okay," he said, lining back up, "here we go!" He buried the throttle into the panel and the SU blasted forward. Gallagher tugged on the stick and they shot into the sky. He was beginning to feel like a pilot again, and not just a passenger. As the Moskva swept toward him, he pivoted up onto his right wing, turned toward the center of the practice area, and leveled. The airspeed surged as the big engine thundered over the grass runway.

"Now!" He swept the stick back and stood the Sukhoi on its tail. The wings were at a perfect right angle to the horizon; his tail was pointed straight back down. He waited for his airspeed to decay, but long after his old Pitts would have given up the ghost, the Sukhoi was still flying, rock solid, up, up, a vertical line cut into the Moscow sky. *Jesus!* When was it going to slow up? The hands of the altimeter raced around the dial. With full throttle, the Sukhoi seemed headed for orbit.

It was a reverie, a rapture akin to that experienced by deep-sea divers. It was a reverie of freedom; no matter that Red Square was right off his wing. He pulled back the throttle, kicked left rudder, and danced the SU-26 into a perfect hammerhead stall. The green grass of Moscow Central filled the windshield as he dived. The Sukhoi would do anything he wished, point anywhere he chose. It was perfection. He had only tasted it so far. Now it was time to take a deeper swallow.

He swept level a scant hundred feet above the grass and rolled, first one way, then the other, before pulling back into another vertical climb. Gallagher let out a yell as the blue plane rocketed straight up. He didn't level off until the altimeter read nearly six thousand feet. Now he had enough breathing room for some serious maneuvering.

He quickly swept the air around him for other airplanes. Then he remembered: the city spread below him was Moscow! The huge open expanse just off his wing was Red Square. There were no other airplanes here. He had the place to himself. He smoothly fed in right stick and the Sukhoi rolled inverted.

Gallagher grinned as his shoulder straps bit into him. He looked up and watched Moscow pass under him. The looping, indolent line of the Moskva River, the giant open squares; the off-white mushrooms of a dozen sports stadiums. He looked off his wing. The tall spire of the Ostankino TV tower was a golden needle stuck into the hazy sky.

The engine sputtered, bringing him back to the business at hand. He rolled back upright, feeling the blood flood down from his head, and shoved the throttle wide open. As the airspeed indicator wound up through two hundred miles an hour, he fed in left stick and kicked hard right rudder.

The Sukhoi snapped around with a yowl from its singing prop, the nose ending precisely on heading. Gallagher's grin doubled. He snapped again, this time to the left. The recovery was just as perfect. When had snaps been so easy before? Was it his flying, or was it the Sukhoi?

It was easy to fly fast and ballistic; flying more slowly was far more demanding, far more revealing. "Let's see," he said to himself as he brought the power back again and raised the nose, slowing the Sukhoi. He kept the nose rising, higher, higher, the plane hanging on its propeller as it slowed. The airspeed needle was dead against its peg before the wings shuddered and let loose in a full stall. *Nice manners.*

He recovered with a blast of throttle and swung around, checking for traffic. With the exception of a single large jet circling to the north, he had the Moscow sky to himself. His first few maneuvers had been grade-school tricks; it was time to take the Sukhoi to college.

He let his speed build once more as the ground flashed below. When it felt right, when the controls had that satisfying stiffness, as the Vedneyev roared its approval, Gallagher swept the stick into his gut and went vertical, rolling as he rose first one way, then the other. As the airspeed decayed again, he slammed the stick into the far right corner of the cockpit and stomped down hard with opposite rudder: a classic spin entry.

If Gallagher had barely started grade school, the Sukhoi was about to give him a final exam.

The spin entry looked normal, but before Gallagher knew it, before he could stop it, the plane came around again in a vertical cartwheel, once, then again, tumbling crazily, the propeller slashing the air as they dropped toward the grass runway far below. Blue sky flashed to green grass to blue sky as the plane wound up tighter and tighter. Gallagher was thrown first one way and then the other inside the small cockpit. His head slammed against something hard.

Gallagher fought against the controls, but he couldn't find the rhythm. He was not only free-falling, he was tightening the spin. A glance at the unwinding altimeter proved the impossibility of doing nothing for very much longer. *No,* he vowed through his tightly clamped jaw, *not again.*

He watched, his eye measuring the Sukhoi's incredible sensitivity as it fell, spinning, spinning. "Now!" He stomped the rudder pedal to stop the accelerated spin and neutralized the stick. The Sukhoi recovered demurely as though nothing out of the ordinary had taken place. Gallagher's eyeballs were still spinning, the earth and sky still tilted crazily, as he leveled off. A wave of dizziness struck. He willed the horizon still and held on grimly for it to pass. *Now that was different.*

The Moskva River passed below him as he rocketed back to a safe height. "Let's try that again," he said to the Sukhoi. With a finger-light touch, Gallagher put the Sukhoi into a crisp spin. An equally light recovery and the SU-26 came out on heading as though it were riding rails in the air. Gallagher was impressed.

He swung around in a tight bank, feeling for a moment the spirit of the aircraft flow through him, the wings like extensions of his shoulders, the powerful Vedneyev an expression of his will, his drive to be the best. He'd have to get a lot better fast. He checked the fuel level. He had fuel for perhaps another fifteen minutes. *No traffic in sight.* All was clear. *Now or never.*

The first Aresti shape formed in his mind. *Begin.* He ran through the first figures mandated for the known compulsory section of the upcoming World Championships. The radial engine snarled as he looped and rolled, right side up and inverted, all the way to the last figure of the routine, an inverted spin.

Now! Gallagher swept the stick over until he hung from his straps. Engine throttled back, he fed in forward stick and kicked the rudder. The Sukhoi shuddered and fell straight down. The world was a pinwheel as he spun inverted, white blue green, white blue green, faster, faster, the altimeter unwinding. He was about to kick out from the spin when a sudden flash of red cut across his vision. Then a second crimson streak hurtled by. A third! The roar of radial engines rumbled against his canopy.

"What . . . ?" He kicked out of the spin. Gallagher was square in the middle of a rapidly disintegrating formation of airplanes. They were SU-26s, beautiful against the blue sky. He would have admired them except that one, its propeller glinting in the sun, was flying right at his eyes.

Any moment now . . . Elena waited for the lead plane to begin angling down toward the green grass of Moscow Central airfield. To her right was the huge expanse of Red Square. The striped

domes of St. Basil's sprouted from the acres and acres of brick like exotic weeds.

"One Flight! Two Flight!" called Kashum. "Ready. Stand by to begin your descent—" He swallowed his next word. "No! Stop!" he yelled over the radio. "Stop! Get out! Break! Formation break! Watch out, Seven!"

What? A sudden odd, jerky motion caught Elena's eye. She turned and looked over her left shoulder. Khalida's plane was just fine. What was Kashum yelling about? She turned forward, and the whole sky was filled with the edge-on shape of an airplane: a blue Sukhoi. *God in . . .*

"Elena!" screamed Kashum from his perch above. "Break left! *Break left!*"

As the intruder ballooned larger and larger, Elena threw her stick into the far left corner of her cockpit. The Sukhoi obliged, but her eye told her it was too little, too late. The collision was inevitable. *I hope they crucify him,* she thought as the blue intruder flashed beneath her tilted wing.

Gallagher had suddenly materialized in a world chock-full of re airplanes. He was paralyzed with the swelling vision, the bright a of Elena's propeller bearing down on him like a flying buzz sa When he saw the red Sukhoi suddenly pivot up on a wing, p instinct took over. With the sound of the other airplane a roar in ears, he swung the stick hard, slicing left as the other plane mo right. It was almost, but not quite, enough. The red plane shot not more than a foot from the top of his canopy.

As he looked straight up at the oil-stained belly of the crim Sukhoi, a loud *crump* came from behind his head, doubling vision, shoving his plane downward, snapping his head agains canopy. The blue Sukhoi staggered on the thin edge of cont

Gallagher shoved on full throttle and dived away, hoping no important had busted behind him. He shot a glance up and b him and saw the red Sukhoi weave away in a yaw like a broken Something was very wrong with it. It moved crabwise, cri

and something dangled from the bottom of its fuselage. He realized it was one of the titanium gear struts. "Oh, shit." He had broken its landing gear! It didn't occur to him to wonder what he might have broken on his own plane. A chill coursed though his nerves. *Goddamn! That was a midair!*

The cloud of red airplanes dissolved into chaos, some climbing, some fleeing from the confusion at full throttle; two hadn't seen the collision and proceeded to land. A larger plane, though red like the others, dived from above and joined up on the crippled ship's right wing. It was then that Gallagher, stunned by the collision, noticed that his fuel gauge showed almost empty. There was nothing he could do for the plane he'd hit; all he could do now was save himself.

With one final glance toward the Sukhoi he had struck, he swung back toward the grass strip. There, with two other red airplanes ahead of him in the pattern, he gingerly flew downwind, base, then final. *A goddamned midair collision!* As the grass rose to meet him, he cut his throttle and pulled back on the stick.

The tail struck first and immediately began vibrating, shaking the instrument panel so badly that Gallagher couldn't read the faces of the dials. "Shit!" He *had* taken some damage back there! He fought the shudders with stabs on his rudder pedals, slowing, slowing, one eye ahead to where the other red planes were. The last thing he needed was to hit one of them! The shaking grew less as he slowed. With a final jab of brake, he swung off the grass and toward the place he had left Evgeni Frolov.

The Sukhoi test pilot was standing very still, one hand over his eyes, peering up into the sky, as Gallagher taxied up and killed the engine by pulling the mixture control to idle cutoff. Gallagher cracked open the canopy. Loud, excited voices came from the Sukhoi hangar. He turned to face Frolov.

"I didn't see . . ." he began. "I think there's something wrong with the tail. It—"

"You think they told me? Idiots!" Frolov shouted. "They weren't supposed to arrive until tomorrow! I will—" He suddenly stopped. Frolov was staring into the hot, hazy sky.

Gallagher twisted in his seat. "Christ," he muttered to himself as his hot engine ticked.

The crippled Sukhoi was turning from downwind to base with a second plane, the larger one, impossibly close by. Their wings seemed almost overlapped. Then Gallagher saw that they *were* overlapped! "What . . . ?"

"Come on! Get down," said Frolov as he jogged by and joined the line of others standing at the edge of the runway.

Gallagher hit the quick-release lever at his midsection and all five straps sprang free. He was up in an instant, over the side of his cockpit, and onto the narrow wingwalk. He jumped down to the grass and made after Frolov at a dead run.

What happened? wondered Elena as she swung her plane ninety degrees to runway heading. Something was very wrong. Number Seven weaved left, then right, but she hadn't moved the stick. She had felt the tremendous jolt when she had struck that fool. What was he doing up there, flying around? Didn't he know . . . She stopped worrying as her ship suddenly began to swing like a drunken metronome. She stared at her hand. It was shaking.

"Ach!" spat Kashum, his voice full of disgust as he leveled off ten feet from her right wingtip. "It's broken!"

"What's broken?" she radioed back to him, but he didn't answer. Instead, Kashum's bigger SU-29 moved closer to her, six feet, then two, its wing edging under her own. She could see him in the rear cockpit of the tandem trainer, scrutinizing something.

"Listen, Elena," he said. "Forget I said anything. We will land together, all right?"

"Yes, but Kashum, you are getting very close—"

"No buts!" he roared, then his voice calmed. "Land a little faster than normal, but when we touch down, kill your engine. Get ready for final approach, and please, Elena. For once just *do as you are told!"*

"What is the problem?" came the impossibly loud shout from Yuri's powerful transmitter. "Hey, Squirt! Are you all right?"

"Get off this frequency!" Kashum's tone of command was such that he hardly needed a radio at all; the whine of Yuri's radio promptly went off the air. "All right, then, Red Seven," said Kashum more calmly. "You fly nice and even. I will do the work."

Elena nodded to him. It was so strange. There he was, not ten feet from where she sat, yet he was as utterly distant from her as a cosmonaut. She loosened her tight grip on the control stick. *When I find out who that idiot was . . .*

"Power back to twenty percent!" Kashum ordered.

Elena pulled back the black-knobbed throttle. The heavy nose sagged at once. Kashum, in his two-place ship, kept close station off her right wing. The larger SU-29 seemed welded to her wingtip.

"Get ready for the turn," he commanded. "Now."

Both crimson Sukhois banked gracefully together. The grass runway swung into view directly off the nose.

"Good. Three hundred meters. Power to ten percent."

The throttle came back again. The four-hundred-horse radial drove her prop so slowly now, Elena could count each blade passing in front of her.

"Elena," said Kashum, "you will feel something when we level out. Just fly and don't worry, all right?"

"Of course," she replied. What was broken? Was there a panel hanging down, creating a disturbance to the airflow?

"One hundred meters. Lock your tail wheel now."

Elena pulled the control lock on her tail wheel. Directly ahead she could see two other airplanes of her team, lined up, and then she saw the other one. The blue Sukhoi. *Bastard!* she seethed. The ground rose up as they descended. *I will find out who that idiot was who . . ."*

"Fifty meters. Fly very steadily, Elena. Very steady, very smooth."

Suddenly, with a slight crunch, like footsteps on dry snow, Kashum edged his wing under Elena's. "Kashum!" she shouted, fearing she had struck her trainer's airplane.

"Fly your airplane!" he commanded.

The grating of wing against wing set her teeth on edge, as though her own body was being injured, but she fought the urge to bank away. Kashum was doing this for some reason. He was holding up her right wing! Was it going to fold up, to fall off without him?

"Ten meters! Ready on the power, ready on the power," said Kashum. "Remember! Kill your engine when we touch down!"

It was the smoothest landing Elena had made in a long time. Both Sukhoi airplanes kissed the grass together. As her wheels rumbled onto the grass, she pulled back her mixture control and the engine promptly died with a clanking of hot cylinders.

"Straight," said Kashum. "Easy, easy. Straight. No brakes! Just let it roll out."

They slowed, sixty knots, forty; then twenty. The world slowed as they rolled straight ahead. Soon they were going no faster than a man could walk. Then, almost without realizing it, Elena was stopped dead center on the grass. She looked to her right. Kashum was grinning. She unlocked her canopy and threw it open, hitting her quick release at the same time.

A flood of hot city air laced with industrial fumes swept in. She killed the electrical system and stood up, one leg over the cockpit rail, then the other. Her Sukhoi wobbled beneath her. She hopped down to the grass and looked below her wing as the other planes of the All-Union Aerobatic team landed without incident behind her, pulling off to one side to avoid the two Sukhois with locked wings. She nearly staggered backward when she saw what had happened to her plane. *Mother of God!*

One landing gear bowed out normally under the weight of her ship. The other dragged backward, leaving a trail of disturbed black earth all the way to where she and Kashum had touched down together. Now she knew why he had flown his wing under her own: by lending her his undamaged landing gear, he had kept her from swerving uncontrollably, cartwheeling her beloved Number Seven into a ball of wreckage. She felt her anger swell as she turned to face the ragged line of people running from the direction of the hangars. She quickly identified the two from the men's team. And was that Frolov, the factory test flier? But who was the tall one? A sound made her look back up into the hot, bright sun.

From somewhere in the yellow sky came the powerful whine of a brace of jet engines. It was Yuri, of course, in that aluminum overcast of an airplane he flew. Even at a distance, its wings seemed wider than the whole of Moscow Central's runway, its fuselage longer. It seemed to fly impossibly slow, but that was just a trick of its size.

"When I get my hands on that hooligan, I will squeeze his throat!" bellowed Kashum as he leaped down from his two-place Sukhoi. He bent down and inspected the damage to Elena's plane. "Look at it!" he shouted. "Just look at it! It will never be repaired in time for Switzerland! Who in hell was playing games where he had no right to be? What is the world coming to?" The roar of the Antonov's four engines became thunder, but Elena could scarcely hear it.

She turned again. Frolov was fast, but the stranger with his foreign running shoes and long, long legs ran faster. She knew without thinking that this one was the man who had nearly killed her. *Who . . . ?* Then her thoughts stopped dead, a cold, icy chill running down her neck, down her sweat-slicked arms. She remembered Slepkin's admonition. It gave the running man a name, a name that escaped her lips like a half-spoken curse. *Gallagher?*

"Oh, Christ!" said the tall American as he ran up to her. "I'm sorry! I just didn't see you!" His breath came fast as he glanced up at the Antonov. *Jesus!* It was huge! Each of the four engines hanging from its wide wings looked as big as a regular airliner's cabin! He turned to face the woman in the sweaty red flightsuit. "I didn't . . ." He stopped, peering directly at Elena. A wash of recognition swept over his face. "You're . . . I mean, aren't you . . . ?" he said, his voice strangely squeaky. "Dr. Pasvalys?"

A low growl seeped from her throat. It was her only reply.

"I thought . . . I mean you're . . ." He almost said, *You're much prettier than your official picture.* Her dark hair and blue eyes gave her an exotic beauty that was lost in the little black-and-white Parrum had given him. *Is this the person who's going to revolutionize SDI?*

Frolov came to a stop in a cloud of dry grass and fine dust. He saw Elena's eyes turn dark, two blue lasers firing needle rays of utter contempt at the American. He saw her fist ball. *"Nyet!"* he shouted. "It was my fault! Nobody bothered to tell me you were coming a day early!"

Kashum looked up from the broken gear leg and saw what was coming. He knew Elena; knew her temper to be almost, but not quite, as hot as his own. And twice as dangerous, for he could control his. *"Nyet!"* he shouted as she took two steps up to Gallagher, her head coming up only to the neck of his green flightsuit. *"NYET!"*

Yuri's Antonov appeared low and fast over the end of the runway, its wide wings spanning nearly the entire width from apartment block to apartment block. A cocoon of cold silence dropped over Gallagher and Elena as the shadow of the great AN-124 blotted out the sun. Yuri hauled the big ship into an impossibly steep bank, using the turn to slow. All sixteen bogeys of its landing gear popped out as it turned around to land.

"Elena!" Kashum shouted, but it was too late.

Elena Pasvalys stepped back and reached behind her back the way an archer might reach for a fresh arrow.

"I really didn't even see—" Gallagher began, but he never finished the sentence. With an overhead swing, Elena drove her fist down onto the bridge of his nose.

13

The ready room was absolutely hushed as Captain Reynard waited for the airmen to finish copying the strike data; not a word of banter came from the assembled aircrews of VF-32.

The Swordsmen knew this was no training exercise. It was for real. A misplaced frequency, an omitted heading, could spell the difference between landing back aboard *John F. Kennedy* and going for a long and lonely swim in the Libyan Gulf of Sidra. Each piece of strike information they committed to memory jogged the odds in their favor, and so nothing, not even the number of wrinkles on Hound Dog Reynard's forehead, was beneath consideration.

Reynard watched as first one, then another, then nearly all the pilots and their backseaters looked up at him, waiting on his next words.

"Okay then," he went on, "our watchwords for Operation Deep Canyon will be fast in and fast out. I don't want the bastards to know what hit them. What's more, I don't want to give the other side a chance to launch on warning. Given the range we think this missile has, it could be headed anywhere, Saudi Arabia, Tel Aviv. It could be headed for Washington. I think you get the idea."

"How long does it take them to fire?" asked one of the pilots. "If they pick us up over the beach, can they flip one before we take them out?"

"So far, we've caught a lucky break there," said Reynard. "Their birds are liquid fueled, so Intel says a minimum of six hours from the time they drag a rocket out of the bunker to when they push the button." Reynard hit the slide changer, and another satellite image came up on the screen. "This overhead shot was taken this morning. As you can see, the launch tower is empty. So we know, at least as of this morning, the six-hour clock wasn't ticking. That could change at any time. It might have changed already."

Reynard waited, then spoke again. "You will be tasked with flying fighter cover for the strikers. I don't want so much as a goddamned buzzard aloft without you putting your eyeballs on it. When this is all over, I want the three most feared words in the Libyan Air Force to be *cleared for takeoff.*"

Even this didn't bring forth the usual warlike howl from the high-strung Tomcat drivers. Just the scribble of their pencils. He wanted them to go out of this room feeling like winners, and yet he knew that war had no room for winners, only survivors. He had learned that over North Vietnam. They would learn that all for themselves over the Libyan Sahara.

Reynard cleared his throat. "From offshore, the Hawkeyes will coordinate the flight from launch to recovery. The Prowlers will lead the first wave in." The Grumman Prowler was an electronic-warfare version of the venerable A-6 attack jet. It carried jammers plus HARM missiles designed to home in on and annihilate enemy radar sites.

"Once the Prowlers blind the bastards and the first layer of defense is peeled back," Reynard continued, "we'll send in the A-6s to do the dirty work. The range is such that they'll have their own tankers with them. Some of you will ride herd on them all the way in, some of you will fly top cover for the main strike force, and some of you will man up a BARCAP to keep any leakers away from the boat. I don't need to remind you all that one Exocet punching through the defensive screen could ruin our day on *JFK.* Any more questions?"

Eisley stood up from his chair. "Sir! When do we go?"

"Eisley," said the CAG, "if it were up to me, we'd have hit

them last week. We go when we get the word from the heavies. Given what's happened overnight in the Persian Gulf, I expect that word to come at almost any time. Next?''

"Suppose Dahr Nema launches a missile first? Before we get the go?'' asked another pilot. "You said it could be carrying a nuke, right?''

"Correct. Then we all better hope it loses its way.'' Reynard shuffled through his briefing folder. "Now,'' he said as he stepped away from the projector screen, "if you'll excuse me, I'll go give the A-6 drivers the good news. Dismissed.''

"Attention on deck!'' someone shouted, and the young pilots of VF-32 stood rigid as Hound Dog Reynard, his face even more deeply wrinkled in worry, passed by and out of the ready room.

"What I want to know is,'' said Eisley to his RIO, Baxter, "who the fuck is selling the Arabs all the hardware? ICBMs. Maybe nukes. They sure as shit couldn't come up with it themselves.''

"Probably us,'' said Baxter.

Capt. Kamel Sayid watched as a crew of Libyan armorers hoisted the last air-to-air missile onto his MiG-29's wing pylon. He was well dressed for this morning's activities: a G suit bound his slim body into a tight package beneath bib-style flight overalls. He held his white helmet under his arm as he watched them finish. *At last,* he thought with a smile as he regarded his beautiful fighter.

The buried hanger was bathed in yellow sodium light; the armored door leading to the runway was shut tight against unauthorized eyes. Three medium-range AA-10 Alamos and three slim AA-11 Archers hung from his rakish fighter's wings. On its tail was painted the tricolor Iraqi insignia, three stars at its heart, and underneath, in newly added script, were the words *Allahu Akbar:* God is great.

God is great, thought Sayid as he watched the arming crew work, *but six missiles are better.*

"All set,'' said the chief armorer as the hoods were pulled from the Archers' infrared-sensitive eyes. They, like his 30-mm cannon, were designed to kill at knife-fight range. The big Alamo rockets rode their own radar beams. They were his long punch. A ground power cable snaked across the hangar floor, connecting the MiG to the Dahr Nema grid.

"It took you long enough," said Sayid as he climbed the metal ladder to his cockpit. He stepped over the canopy rails and sank deep down into the ejection seat.

The instruments arrayed before him would not have seemed out of place on a 1960s-era Western fighter; analog displays and round dials dominated the flat-gray panel. But if there was no cathode-ray tubes and exotic digitals on board, what was installed was simple, reliable, and given Sayid's extensive training, perfectly adequate.

He plugged his oxygen, G suit, and communications connectors into the left sidewall of the cockpit, right under the twin throttle bars. The canopy swung down and locked with a barely perceptible hiss. Over the MiG's long snout, the steel blast doors began to cycle open. A scalding line of white heat appeared as the desert sun blazed into the half-buried hangar. Sayid pulled his dark visor down.

The ground crew now stood at a respectful distance as Sayid brought on first the right engine, then the left. The RD-33s surged to life with no hesitation. Sayid knew they were the best engines ever installed in a fighter, simple to start on the ground, exquisitely responsive in the air. He could forget them in a fight, knowing they would not let him down.

The exhaust-gas temperatures stabilized at 750 degrees C, right on target. He gave the signal to the ground crew chief. The ground power cable was pulled. Sayid nudged his throttles and taxied out into the hot desert sun.

The heat was immediate and intense, even with the air-conditioning dialed up full. Sayid made his way quickly through the maze of mounded, half-buried structures, and out to the end of Dahr Nema's single long runway.

The voice of the field controller came into his helmet. "Falcon One is cleared for takeoff, depart immediately for Patrol Sector Red."

"Falcon One," said Sayid as he stomped on his brakes and brought the powerful RD-33s up to military power. Heat waves shimmered off the runway. The ship's nose dipped as the brakes held it firm. Then, as Sayid raised the protective latches on the throttles and slipped into afterburner, he released the brakes.

The acceleration was instantaneous. Even with a full load of weapons and fuel for a long patrol, the MiG shot down the runway, breaking ground as the airspeed surged through 230 kilometers per hour. Sayid leveled off and built up his speed, pulling in the flaps and raising the landing gear with smooth, practiced movements.

As the runway flashed below, he pulled up into a steep climb, his G meter registering four. He felt himself shoved hard into his seat, the G suit swelling around him to cut off the flow of blood down from his head. The needle-nosed fighter blasted through twenty thousand feet as the last of the runway passed far below him. He leveled off and banked to the north; that was where the Americans would be coming from.

He glanced down ahead of his wing. The gravel road that connected Dahr Nema's launch tower with the buried rocket assembly rooms cut the desert with a fine geometer's line. But then he saw it.

Crawling like a caterpillar across the blinding white sand of Dahr Nema, a rocket transporter was making its way toward the skeletal steel launch tower. Sayid grinned behind his oxygen mask and visor. *Finally*, he thought.

He brought his engines out of afterburner and checked the armament panel. Sayid's MiG was now a flying SAM site; six rockets and a good 30-mm cannon would leave their toll on any force foolish enough to come at Dahr Nema over the Libyan deserts. *Let the Americans come* he thought. He could already imagine their black funeral-pyre smoke rising from the sand. *Let them come*.

He swung to look back at the rocket making its way to the launch tower. From twenty thousand feet, it seemed not to have moved at all. The trip from the assembly room to the tower, a distance of about a mile, would take *Al Infitar* about forty minutes, twice as long as its flight time from the heart of the Libyan Sahara to downtown Tel Aviv.

Friday Afternoon,
3 August 1990

"So how is the nose?" asked Frolov.

"I'll survive," Gallagher replied as he watched the activity around Elena's crippled Sukhoi. Technicians from the Sukhoi hangar had streamed out at the roar of Yuri's Antonov, pulling the two planes off the runway.

The huge transport had touched down light as a feather at the very edge of the grass; lightly loaded and with thirty-six wheels to bear its weight, it had left no more of a scar on the firm grass than Elena's broken gear leg.

Two technicians maneuvered a jack under Elena's right wing. Then slowly, carefully, they lifted the plane off Kashum's two-place trainer. Elena Pasvalys stood by, watching, directing them as they tried to go about their jobs. Every now and again she would turn and glare at Gallagher.

"Idiots," said Frolov as the broken Sukhoi was dragged into the factory hangar. "The All-Union Aerobatic team. Pah!" he spat. "Prima donnas. Too important to let the world know they are coming a day too soon. All they had to do was to call ahead. But no. The world must accommodate *them,* even if it gets one of them nearly killed." He turned to face Gallagher. "Let's go look at what you have done. Come on," he said, nodding at Gallagher's blue Sukhoi. Gallagher touched his swollen nose as they walked to where he had left the plane.

The smell of hot, dry grass mingled with burned kerosene as they walked. "Two things I must warn you about," said Frolov. He held up a finger. "Russian women"—a second finger went up—"and Russian airplanes. Looking at the nose, I will say you did very poorly with one. Let's see how you managed with the other."

The blue Sukhoi's canopy was still open, the engine still warm. Gallagher checked his watch. He wondered how long it had really taken to nearly kill himself and Elena Pasvalys. It felt like hours. It was certainly no more than a matter of a few minutes. What would George Parrum say if he *had* killed her? *Good work*, probably.

"You say it vibrated after you struck?" asked Frolov as he ran his hand along the top of the Sukhoi's fuselage. He came to a dark smudge about five feet behind the cockpit, the place where Elena's tire had struck Gallagher's plane.

"No," said Gallagher. "Not in the air. Just on landing."

"Hmm," said Frolov as he pressed in against the discolored panel. Faint crinkling sounds came from within. "Something is broken. Maybe just the skin panel. The steel is all right." He continued to press hard against the plane's composite skin, feeling for signs of internal damage. No doctor could have been more gentle, or more thorough. "Well, you were lucky. You hit right where four tubes come together in a weld. The strongest part of the airplane." He pulled his ball cap down over his eyes against the hot sun. "I don't suppose you locked the tail wheel before you landed?"

"I . . ." Gallagher stammered. "I don't remember."

"You don't remember?" Frolov walked back forward to the open cockpit. He peered down at the tail wheel locking lever. "As I thought. There is your vibration." He pulled the locking bar, reached up, and swung the clear canopy down, brushing off his hands after it clicked shut. "You were very lucky," he said, reverting to a more formal tone. "You still have an airplane, and that is more than I can say for that woman. On the other hand, her nose is much smaller than yours. But this"—he thumped the blue Sukhoi—"this is nothing. A little epoxy, a little blue paint"—he snapped his fingers—"and it will be ready for Switzerland like that."

"What do you think I should do? About her airplane? I feel responsible."

"Responsible?" Frolov laughed, wagging his head. "You forget. This is the Soviet Union. We don't feel responsible here. Not for anything. Not yet, anyway. Now," said Frolov as he pulled at the long bill of his ball cap, "leave it to me. I gave you permission to fly. And in any event, it is really all their fault. *They* were the ones who didn't bother to inform *us* they would be a day early."

"What about this plane?" asked Gallagher, nodding at the blue Sukhoi. He still couldn't bring himself to call it his. Would he ever? "Shall I push it back and tie her down? Or do you want me to wait?"

"Stay right here." Frolov pointed. "Don't move it. Don't start the engine. Just wait right here. I will go speak with Kashum—you know who he is?"

Gallagher shook his head.

"Just as well. You would not like him today." Frolov turned to face the big Sukhoi hangar. The rolling doors were closing, Elena's Sukhoi safe inside. They stopped, leaving just a dark crack. "I will go face two lions in their dens." He took two steps and stopped. "Actually, one lion and one . . . how is it said?"

"Lioness," Gallagher said ruefully.

"Be careful!" Elena shouted as a workman shoved a sawhorse under her broken plane's wing. "You'll scratch the skin!" He ignored her and walked away.

A fine grit suffused the air, gold dust tumbling through the hot beams slicing through the hangar's high windows. Pigeons called from their nests up in the latticework; the rattling of a rivet gun hammered in a separate workshop. It sounded like any busy factory might, but there were more people standing around the perimeter than working.

"Kashum," she said, her dark hair plastered to her head with sweat, "I want to know what will be done about this."

"I don't know yet," said Kashum softly. "Don't worry about the paint. This airplane will not fly for a while. Come on, let's go have lunch. We will figure out what to—"

"No. I will wait right here until the engineer makes his survey," she said, stamping her foot on the hangar floor. "And I want to know what will be done about that fool who nearly killed me."

"You tell me," Kashum said with a sigh. "Shall we send him to internal exile, or just be done with it and have him shot?"

"Shooting is too quick."

"Let's be serious. But first let's eat something, all right? All that perfect flying I was forced to do has made my stomach growl."

"Go ahead. I'll wait here. If that idiot comes near, I want to be able to protect my airplane."

Kashum's dark tan turned red. Elena had no idea how difficult it was for him to remain calm. "Look. This idiot you keep jabbering about is an American. He—"

"I know who he is. I know all about him," she stormed. *Why isn't that policeman Slepkin around when he might be useful?* she wondered angrily. "Why should he leave Moscow with a Sukhoi in the first place? It isn't enough he rams mine, but he gets to fly one in Switzerland, too? What kind of justice is that?"

"The best justice his money can buy?"

A white-coated engineer arrived from a workshop, carrying a thick roll of technical drawings under his arm. He spread them out on the wing of Elena's plane and slowly, maddeningly slowly, flipped through them until he came to the detail of the landing gear structure. He crouched down beneath the jacked-up plane and began his investigations, making small grunts of displeasure.

"Well?" asked Elena as she watched him tug on this, wiggle that, and shake his head. "What is it? Can it be repaired?"

He looked up owlishly. "Yes," he said. "Of course. This is the Sukhoi Design Bureau."

"Ah," said Kashum. "You see? Now, can we go eat?"

"Wait," said Elena. She turned again to the engineer. "How long will it take?"

He shrugged. "It's only a preliminary estimate. I wouldn't want you—"

"How long?"

The engineer gazed up into the hangar rafters. "Five weeks. The landing gear torque box will have to be cut out and replaced. You will need a new landing gear leg, too. Surplus titanium is hard to come by just now. Our quota has already been delivered for the year. Composite panels, paint. I will have a full repair estimate ready in a day or so." Without further explanation, he rolled up his drawings and began to walk away.

"Five weeks? What repair estimate? Wait! Stop!"

The engineer stopped and turned, his face a studied mask of boredom. "Yes?"

"Is there another plane available?" asked Elena. "While mine is getting fixed?"

"Of course." He sounded offended. "We have four ready for purchase. They are all MXs. You know. Export models. But other than that—"

"Purchase? What do you mean, *purchase?*"

"I will have our business manager come and discuss this with you." The engineer turned on his heel and left, his heavy shoes making loud *clop clop clop* sounds on the bare concrete floor. The rivet gun beat out a ragged tattoo, then stopped.

"Hey!" She made to follow him, but Kashum grabbed her by the shoulder.

"Come on," he said. "We will eat and discuss—"

"That idiot has destroyed my airplane!" she shouted, her voice echoing through the high arch of the hangar roof. "And *that* fool wants me to buy a new one! What does he want me to use for money! Diamonds? *I am on the All-Union team!"*

"Elena, calm yourself. We will get this worked out our own way. But for now—"

"Kashum?" called Evgeni Frolov as he eased through the main doors of the hangar.

Elena spun. *"You!* Where is he? Where is that damned—"

"He is sitting out under his wing, maybe with a broken nose. You want to try again and be sure? What were you thinking about, flying in here a day early?" Frolov turned to the team manager. "Kashum," he began, "why was no word sent about your arrival time? I would never have let him fly. Didn't you think it was important to let us know?"

Kashum scowled sheepishly. "Someone always takes care of that."

"Someone? Please, who is this someone? *Someone* doesn't work here anymore. It is time we learned to take personal responsibility," said Frolov, wagging his finger.

Kashum's eyes went wide as though someone had delivered a kick to his stomach. "Don't lecture me, you little twig!" he thundered, unable to control his temper any longer. He had had enough. "You and your blue jeans and your fancy flying clothes. Who do you think you are? An American? Just because they let you dress like one? Wear a clown suit! That is more like it! It is your fault," Kashum shouted. "You'd sell your mother for a dollar! What would you sell for two hundred thousand—"

"Your fault, my fault," Frolov interrupted. "What difference does it make? For years we hand over airplanes to you and your team for free. Do you think *they* get airplanes for nothing? They have to *pay* for them. Every time we throw one at you, we lose more hard currency than you've seen in your whole miserable—"

"You *sell to an American, but you won't help a Russian?* What kind of world is this?" Kashum exploded.

"Hey! Squirt!"

Elena, Frolov, and Kashum turned to see a new figure appear at the cracked-open hangar door. Without waiting for the electric motors to open them, with a grunt and a powerful heave, Yuri Komarov, Elena's old suitor and commander of the huge Antonov 124, shoved the doors open enough to admit his massive frame. "I came as fast as I could!" he said as he pushed into the hangar. The pilot walked toward them with the rolling gait of a sailor.

"This gorilla was the one on the radio?" asked Kashum, narrowing his eyes and readying a new barrage. He knew he would have to reach some arrangement with Frolov, after all.

"In the Antonov." Elena nodded. "Excuse us for a moment, will you? I can take care of him."

"Who gave him permission to call out over the air? What does he think it is, a telephone?"

"Please," said Elena. "He was an old friend."

Kashum's eyes narrowed. "Then he can calm you down. I certainly can't."

"Look, Kashum," said Frolov, "maybe we can make an arrangement to borrow an airplane. I think I can find one on those terms. The manager owes me a favor. But you'll have to offer him *something* in return."

The team trainer snorted. "Maybe he'll accept a carload of cabbages as a deposit."

"Anything but rubles," said Frolov as they walked off, leaving Elena to meet Yuri head-on.

"Elena Pasvalys!" he bellowed. His voice boomed from the cavernous hangar. He came right up to her and hugged Elena more avidly than she wished. She felt her breath driven from her. "So skinny!" he said as she felt the buttons on his tunic drill into her breasts. "What a big surprise to meet here in Moscow! And think! We are even staying in the same hotel! How long has it been?"

She doubted it was much of a surprise. Yuri had probably planned the meeting with all the subtlety of a general plotting an invasion. "Enough!" She squirmed in his bear hug. "It is always a surprise to see you." He relaxed his grip enough for her to breathe. "I see they made you a colonel." She pretended to examine the row of emblems on his uniform. "Tanks, is it? Was that in preparation for flying the Antonov?"

"Colonel?" Yuri's beefy pink face seemed puzzled for a moment. He let her go, checked his insignia. "Tanks? What tanks?" Then he looked back at her with a laugh like the rumble of an old radial engine. "Remember the old times? That little Yak? Boy, were you impressed."

"You always leave an impression, Yuri."

"That Antonov is some airplane, eh? Not so easy like a Sukhoi." He made delicate little motions with his hands as though Elena's Sukhoi were a child's toy. "It takes great skill to tame the Antonov, to make it fly like a fighter. It takes *finesse*." He pronounced the word with a distinct and deplorable Italian accent, making it erupt like an overshaken bottle of seltzer.

"Finesse? Now *that* would be truly a worthwhile addition to your skills."

"Yes. Absolutely," he agreed. His bushy eyebrows knitted together like an approaching storm front. "We had a bet, the copilot and me. How much of the runway would we use?"

"You're lucky you didn't sink down to your wings on this grass."

"What? The An? Nah," he said. "We were light as a feather."

"A two-hundred-thousand-kilo feather, perhaps."

"I bet him we'd touch down the first hundred meters and stop before a thousand. I really slowed him up," said Yuri, referring to the Antonov by its proper masculine. He pinched his fingers together and his eyes glinted. "We were this much away from stalling. You know what he did? My copilot? This is true! He began to cry. I couldn't concentrate. So I thought, what is a few more meters? So we put down a little longer, a little faster. But what a ship!"

"That surely is the right word for that thing." Elena nodded.

He glanced at Elena's damaged Sukhoi. "So what happened? You broke something? You look all right."

"I didn't break anything. Someone was playing at being a pilot in the pattern. Doing spins when we arrived."

"You hit?" asked Yuri, his voice hushed.

Elena nodded. "And now they say it will be five weeks to fix my airplane. Unless," she said acidly, "I wish to buy a new one. Can you believe it? They expect me to buy my own airplane now."

"Everything is changing," Yuri agreed. "And things are not so good right now, you know? This business in Iraq. I think there will be a big war before long. I'm glad it's so far away."

"Yuri, you don't have to travel very far to find a war. Look around you. There's a war going on right here."

He pretended to look around the hangar. "Where is this war? Here? Who is fighting? Tell me and I will put a stop to it myself!"

Despite herself she started to laugh.

"Much better." His face brightened. "So, Elena. Here you are. Here I am. What could be better than that? Remember the university? You taught me calculus. I taught you to fly. What can we teach each other now?"

"I can think of some things," said Elena, glancing outside, her hand balled into a fist.

"You know, Elena," he said with a mischievous wink, "when I am flying over the farmlands, all the cows look up. I can see them from my cockpit. They stop chewing grass and look at the Antonov! Do you know what they say?"

"I could not possibly guess."

"What a bull!" Yuri roared as he hitched his trousers. "Elena, I was thinking. Perhaps you and I can meet for dinner tonight. A plate of meat. A glass of Armenian brandy? Eh? You see! I remember what you like after all this time. What do you say?"

"Why is everyone so hungry? All I want is an airplane."

Yuri looked around, then back out through the cracked-open hangar door. "There were plenty of airplanes out there. My crew is loading four brand-new ones to take with the team to Switzerland. I tell you what. I will make you a present of them!" He opened his mouth wide and brought his teeth together with a snap. "A present! Take your pick"

"Yuri," she said. "I would like to sit here and think this through. Alone. Later we can conspire against the State."

"You are sure? It would be no problem. A little paint, a lost paper here, a little bottle of something on the side, we could make the switch, and by the time somebody found out, we'd all be dead. Just like that." He snapped his jaws again, though who the intended prey might be was not at all clear to Elena.

"I'm certain. Maybe I'll see you at the hotel after I get this mess cleaned up."

"Very well," he said as though deciding for the both of them, "I'll be back at the Hotel Aeroflot by five. Room—"

"Seven fourteen," she finished.

"You always had a head for numbers." He nodded at her sweaty flightsuit. "You brought better clothes, I hope."

"I'll see you at the hotel."

"Don't forget me, Elena," he said, turning to leave.

"How could I possibly?"

"That's right!" he agreed.

She watched him leave, and then she sat down beneath the broken wing of her Sukhoi, watching Yuri strut back out through the open hangar door. She reached into the neck of her flightsuit and pulled out the diamond crystal that held a silicon chip at its center. Elena rubbed it like a worry bead. First she was too Lithuanian to be trusted with Stingray, her own creation. Now she was too Russian to afford to buy a new airplane. *What shall I do?* she wondered as she heard the pigeons call from up above. *What shall I do?*

14

Gallagher took the heavy iron key Frolov had left behind and unlocked the blue Sukhoi's canopy. Now the smell that rose was partly new leather, and partly his own sweat. It was as it should be; an aerobatic airplane had to grow to be an extension of its pilot's body. *I hope I get to know you, Sue,* he said, and then came up short, startled. Why had he called the Sukhoi by name? He reached in and stroked the quilted seat cover, noting the dry, white salt stains his sweat had left behind. *Silky Sue,* he thought.

"Hey!"

Gallagher spun. It was Frolov. He was walking briskly from the Sukhoi hangar.

"Everything is okay!" he called to Gallagher. "We worked it all out."

Gallagher breathed out a long sigh of relief. "What did it take, Evgeni?"

"Simple. They take an MX to Switzerland, keep it available as a factory demonstrator, and sell it to the highest bidder after they win their gold medals. The team keeps whatever is left after we fix hers. You see?" he said with an impish grin. "We are learning, yes?"

"I'd still like to apologize."

"Don't," Frolov warned him. "She is very emotional. Give her a day. In fact, give her a year. Maybe then it will be safe." He

157

checked his watch. It was getting on to two o'clock. "Well, what are you waiting for? There's still plenty of daylight to fly."

"Fly?" Gallagher's ears all but leaned forward. "You're serious? I can take it up again?"

"If you promise not to hit anything else," Frolov said seriously. The sound of a fuel truck starting came from across the field. "That gorilla pulled the Antonov off the runway far enough. Well? Do we fly?"

Gallagher thought once more of Parrum's envelope, then he tossed the heavy canopy key to Frolov. "We fly."

"They will even paint a seven on the tail for you," said Kashum. "All you have to do is to fly with potential buyers in Switzerland. In the two-place, of course." He grinned. "Did I not do well for you?"

Elena nodded. "I wasn't thinking very clearly before."

"And now?"

"Now I am." She smiled and brushed away the dark bangs from her forehead. "Thank you."

"You're welcome. Now," said Kashum, "unless there is another little problem to solve, perhaps we might go and find something . . ." He stopped.

They both heard the chuffing sound of a radial engine starting, ragged at first, then building to a low, powerful rumble.

"Who is going up?" she asked.

"Come on," said Kashum, taking her by the shoulder. "Don't torture yourself. You beat him this morning. We will beat him in Switzerland. What more do you want?"

"I want to watch."

"Elena, are you—"

"Come on," she said.

"She doesn't do as she is told," said Zarkich, a wooden match dangling from his white teeth.

"No," said Slepkin as he watched Elena and the Soviet team manager leave the big Sukhoi hangar. "She doesn't. But in a few weeks it will be someone else's headache. After Switzerland."

"She needs to learn."

Slepkin grunted but said nothing. It had taken nearly an hour and a half to drive up from Serpukhov; it had taken only a few moments after his arrival at Moscow Central Airfield to learn that his charge had disobeyed him in a most serious fashion. *I warned her,* he thought. *I told her to stay away from him.* That old fool Kashum was lecturing her as they stood together, watching the American taxi his blue airplane to the end of the grass runway. *Hot,* Slepkin thought, and mopped his face with a soaked handkerchief.

With a roar of his engine, Gallagher began his takeoff roll, faster, faster, his plane bouncing along the grass, until it lofted free and clear, up into the muggy afternoon sky. The sound of distant thunder rolled across the field, and a tiny cool breeze troubled the grass.

"Perhaps we will have to teach her to obey," Slepkin said to Zarkich. "I want you to go back and check with the hotel liaison. Find out if anyone was videotaping when she hit him. Maybe we'll be lucky."

"You want to know if anything was passed, is that it?"

"Just go and find out," Slepkin repeated. "And on your way, inform Professor Pasvalys we will meet before dinner. Six o'clock. She needs talking to."

"As you say." Zarkich loped off in the direction of the KGB's liaison office at the Hotel Aeroflot.

The roar of Gallagher's engine washed down over Slepkin. He shielded his eyes against the hot afternoon glare, watching the American climb higher and higher. "Such impudence," he swore under his breath. To fly, to fly within spitting distance of Red Square itself! What would they do next? Sell guided tours to missile bases? Gallagher began to fly a fancy routine, up, down, his engine louder than the thunder coming from the dark southern horizon.

A shadow of premonitory dread passed over Slepkin like a cool wind on a hot day. *Could she be up to something?* Elena was rebellious, just like all the other damned Balts. It was in their blood.

The Balts, the Georgians, the Armenians, the Tatars. They were destroyers, all the seditious factions chipping away at the Soviet Union. It was like a giant dam beginning to show a spiderweb tracery across its blank, imposing face. But for all that, Slepkin reserved his greatest scorn for the man who had first opened the floodgates.

Something was going very wrong, a rot, a decay that spread from its source in Moscow out until its foul tendrils touched everything that had once been proud and sacred. Even the Army. Had he not just read how Red Army sergeants were selling off their uniforms to German tourists? And Iraq! An old and trusted ally for how many years? *Abandoned.* It was incredible that so much could fall apart so fast. Only the KGB remained as a bulwark against collapse, and Slepkin knew without knowing that there would come a day, sooner, perhaps later, when the decay would be cauterized and order would be restored.

The sound of heavy footfalls came from behind him. "Yes? What is it now, Kolya?" he said without even looking. But it wasn't Zarkich.

Suddenly, a burly man dressed in a navy blue jogging suit marched right by, his eyes forward toward the Sukhoi hangar, his fists pumping up and down as he went. *A jogger?* What kind of idiot would be out exercising in this heat? Then Slepkin caught the man's profile.

The big man seemed to sense Slepkin and he turned. There was no recognition in his eyes.

But Slepkin knew him. If the shark has no need to consider the remora, the reverse is certainly not true. When Slepkin had first learned of Gallagher's arrival, this one's face had been at the very top of the briefing folder forwarded from Central Files. *What,* he wondered as the man jogged away, *is George Parrum doing in Moscow?*

Friday Afternoon,
3 August 1990

Five thumps and a kick came from Eisley's door. He swung out
of his bunk and snapped on a light. The tiny stateroom was hot
and musty. Despite the air-conditioning, the tropical heat found
its way into the carrier's interior. Eisley shook his head clear.
"Come."

It was Baxter, his radar intercept officer. The young lieutenant
kicked the door shut behind him. "Morning, Ice."

"Morning? What time is it?" Eisley checked his watch. It was
nearly 1700. They weren't due to brief for the evening's combat air
patrol (BARCAP) for another hour. "What's cooking, Baxman?"

"The world, Mr. Eisley. I just intercepted some very interesting
poop. The heavies finally got it together. Deep Canyon's a go."

Eisley came to instant attention. "When?"

"Tomorrow morning at oh dark thirty. But there's good news and
bad news."

"Yeah? Like what?"

"The good news is that flying BARCAP's off for tonight, at least
for us."

"All right." Eisley nodded. He knew how much Baxter hated
night catapult shots. "So what's the bad news?"

"We're flying top cover on the first wave into Dahr Nema."

Eisley grinned. "Bax? Don't forget. Bring the cat. Old Garfield
wouldn't miss this one for the world." *And neither,* he thought,
would I.

The distinctive rumble of Gallagher's engine rose and then fell as
the blue Sukhoi circled over her head, climbing up for a safe reserve
of altitude.

"Come," said Kashum. "You know what a Sukhoi looks like.
Enough of this. Let's check into the hotel."

"Quiet!" Elena watched the blue intruder, so familiar yet so foreign. "You go on without me," she said, her eyes on Gallagher's airplane. "I'll meet you there in a while."

Kashum let out a long breath through his teeth. "Very well. I will see you back at the hotel. We are all having dinner together. The entire team. Six o'clock." With that, he turned and walked briskly away.

A faint shudder tickled her ear as a low roll of thunder passed over. Thundershowers in the afternoon in muggy summertime Moscow were as predictable as the tides. Even now, a herd of fat cumulonimbus clouds was bearing down on the capital from the southwest. The mounded white clouds split, letting a thin beam of golden sun play across the grass runway. In the momentary brilliance, a telegraphic flash beamed from Gallagher's wings into Elena's eyes. She looked straight up. Its dark blue was very nearly the same color as the building storm clouds. *Now,* she thought, *let's see if you know what you're about.*

The blue airplane climbed higher and higher above the airport, and with a wag of its dark wings, entered the practice box. Level for an instant, Gallagher pulled up into a sharp zoom climb.

Elena followed the darting shape. The zoom ended in a hammerhead stall. "Watch your line," she said as the slim fuselage wandered a bit through overcontrol. "Watch it . . . watch it . . . good." Gallagher now raced back down straight as the bolt of an arrow.

"Get ready . . ." she said softly. "Now!" As though her words had triggered a reaction at a distance, Gallagher flicked into a rapid inverted spin that ended with the nose exactly on target heading, wings perfectly level. "Very nice," she said. "But can you do it twice?"

Gallagher ran through the entire compulsory program as she watched. *It was good,* she concluded as the end of the sequence came with its knife-edge flight.

But Gallagher, having finished the regular series of figures, now went on beyond them. Elena watched with keen interest. After all, Gallagher would be flying against her at the World Aerobatics Championships. Perhaps he would reveal something.

"What is he doing?" she wondered as the blue plane began a series of rolls, beginning very slowly at first and building with admirable precision and skill in both violence and speed.

First level, then on knife edge, then vertical, then while plummeting earthward, the rolls wound up tighter and tighter, like a figure skater's finale with form blurred by the tremendous rate of rotation. "My God," Elena whispered.

Gallagher recovered inverted and pushed up into an outside loop, still rolling furiously, until in a blink of the eye he stopped suddenly yet surely, finishing the tornadic climb with a final hammerhead stall. Elena's mouth was open. The Sukhoi could roll like no other airplane, but this! She had never seen one turn so fast. She didn't quite believe it was possible, her own eyes notwithstanding.

And there is something else, she thought as the blue plane wagged its wings and left the practice area. *He has the feel. The confidence.* The eye could tell. Except for one slight miscue early in his sequence, each figure had the look, the elusive look of *rightness* that seems like a beautiful Aresti drawing sketched on the sky; it was fierceness and grace combined. *We should never sell them Sukhois,* she thought as she saw Gallagher land. She turned to leave and nearly collided with Slepkin's creature, Zarkich.

"Elena Pasvalys?" he said, the wooden match still in his teeth.

"What do you wish?" she asked with a frown. "Who are you?"

Zarkich looked much older than his age in the low sun. It picked up a badland of lines on his face. "I work with Colonel Slepkin," he said with a small bow that somehow managed to make Elena feel dishonored. "He asks that you meet him before going to dinner with your team."

"I'll be at the hotel."

"So will we," said Zarkich with a strange smile. "At six," Zarkich said with a tiny smirk. He bowed again and left.

Gallagher swept in low over the giant Antonov's nose as he landed, skimming the grass with his wheels so lightly he could barely feel them touch. Bouncing over the turf, he let the Sukhoi roll toward the spot where Frolov stood waiting. He would just beat the storm. He ran the engine up to a shout and pulled the mixture control all the way back. The Vedneyev coughed once and died with a heavy clank of its nine big cylinders. Frolov was waiting for him on the ramp. He was clapping, smiling, though Gallagher couldn't hear it; the roar of the engine still echoed in his ears. He unlocked the canopy and pushed it up, letting the cool wind wash over his sweaty face. A faint roll of thunder shook the shimmering glass of the teardrop canopy.

"Very nice," said Frolov, still clapping. "Very very nice. I think you will be okay." He turned to face the oncoming thunderstorm, then turned back to face Gallagher. "I was watching you. I think there is one big mistake."

"Oh?" said Gallagher as he wearily stood up, putting one leg over the cockpit rail. "What might that be?"

"We should never have sold you a Sukhoi," Frolov replied with a grin. Another roll of thunder issued from the belly of the storm. "You want help tying the plane down? It's going to rain soon."

Gallagher jumped off the wing to the dry grass. "No thanks, Evgeni. It's my job now."

Frolov nodded with understanding in his eyes. The machine was no longer a stranger to the tall American; it was his. "She is all yours," Frolov said with a bow. "Good luck, and remember, two things."

"Russian women and Russian airplanes?"

"No," Frolov said with a quick shake of his head, "when you win a gold medal, remember who built your machine, and"—he smiled—"who taught you to fly it. Deal?"

"Deal," said Gallagher as he fastened first one, then both wings down to the ground with strong nylon ropes. He didn't want *Silky Sue* blowing away in a storm.

"The car will take you back to the hotel when you are ready. Tell the driver when you wish to be picked up in the morning. You won't need me anymore, will you?"

"I guess not."

"Then I will go see what the factory wants me to do next."
Frolov turned to leave.

"Evgeni?" called out Gallagher.

The Sukhoi test pilot stopped and turned. "Yes? What now?"

Gallagher stood up and brushed the dry grass and dust from
where it clung to his sweaty flightsuit. He walked over to where the
Russian stood. "Thanks a heap."

"A heap? What is this 'heap'? It was nothing. Just don't hit
anybody else. Especially not *her*."

"I promise."

Frolov tugged at his ball cap, nodded, and left.

A strong, cool breeze swept over Gallagher, lifting the hairs on
his neck, chilling him after the hot work of flying. Another peal of
thunder, louder and closer now, came from the darkening sky. He
reached into the small baggage compartment hidden in the Sukhoi's
upper fuselage and retrieved his brown duffel bag. The first drops of
rain, big as marbles, began to fall as he closed the Sukhoi's canopy.
A flash of lightning reflected in its rain-spattered surface, and in that
instant, Gallagher saw a figure standing close behind him. He
swung around.

"Good day, Dr. Gallagher."

"You!" he shouted, the word erupting from his mouth. "What
are you doing here?"

"I told you I'd be here to backstop you. How else were you going
to get the dope to the woman unless I gave it to you first?"

"Here?" said Gallagher, glancing around nervously.

"Why not?" Parrum reached into the slash pocket of his running
jacket and handed Gallagher an envelope. "She's in room two ten.
Good luck."

Gallagher glanced at the thin envelope, then looked up. "Then
I'll be finished?"

"Go get 'em, tiger," said Parrum with a very easy smile.

The rain pelted the steel hangar roof over Slepkin's head with the
rattle of buckshot. *So it is true,* he thought. Gallagher was working

for them. But what were they doing? He had the distinct sensation of a multitude of carved wooden blocks falling end for end, tumbling into a frame, and suddenly, there it was: a picture. He didn't like what he saw.

A premonitory twinge of worry announced itself to the KGB man as he stood in the storm-shadowed hangar. In a tinder-dry forest, the slightest smell of smoke was dangerous. And the resulting fire? It would consume not only his charge, Elena Pasvalys. It would consume him as well. He knew the names now, the faces. An American scientist working with the CIA. A Soviet scientist—no, a *Lithuanian*. The outlines were all there, and Slepkin didn't like what was beginning to emerge.

He watched as Parrum stood back from Gallagher and waited, balanced on the balls of his feet as though he expected to run. Slepkin watched closely. Parrum waited, rocking back and forth, and then nodded. Seemingly satisfied with the meeting, he turned on his heel and left, his dark jogging suit merging with the sheets of rain sweeping across the grass. *Something has been decided.*

"Colonel?" Slepkin spun around and saw Kolya Zarkich.

"You walk too softly for an honest man," said Slepkin, although he knew Zarkich had picked up that habit out of raw necessity in a place called the Devil's Nest: Afghanistan.

"The liaison office taped the entire incident," said Zarkich. "We can go review it anytime you wish."

"Good," said Slepkin, wondering what the videotape of Elena's encounter with the American would show. Was it staged? Had information been passed in the confusion? Anything was possible, now that he knew beyond question that Gallagher's presence in Moscow was far from innocent. "Did you speak with Elena?"

"I told her you would see her in her room," said Zarkich in a slow, almost sleepy voice that edged on insolence.

Curtains of rain fell across the open field, but even so, Slepkin could still make out the outline of Gallagher's blue airplane. But Gallagher was gone. His premonition of danger turned at once from a wisp of smoke to a glowing red ember. "Let's go see that tape," he said.

15

Gallagher hurried under the awning jutting out over the Hotel Aeroflot's front door. "Some storm," he said to the doorman sitting on a small, velvet-covered stool. The doorman eyed him briefly and looked away.

Gallagher's green flightsuit was stained black with rain, and traffic out on Leningradskaya Prospekt splashed through the puddles and rivulets. Sharp spikes of yellow lightning stabbed at Moscow's vitals. As he watched, the great TV tower at Ostankino was struck once, again, and then a third time. *Room two ten*, he reminded himself. *I'm going to offer my apologies*. Parrum had come up with a thin excuse for barging in on Elena Pasvalys. Gallagher hoped he would have no reason to use it.

Another barrage of lightning and thunder raked the city. He saw the black Mercedes that had picked him up at the Savoy that morning parked opposite the small Cafe Aist; its driver was probably inside, drinking and waiting to take him back to the hotel. He turned away from the busy street and pushed through the glass doors.

The lobby was hushed, but far from empty. A cluster of figures sat around an ancient television. Some wore the red flightsuits of the Soviet aerobatics team. Most were dressed more casually. A rangy-looking man looked up with an expression of utter boredom, then returned his attention to the television. The high wooden front desk, backed by a warren of message boxes, was deserted. Where was the hotel staff? *And what,* he wondered, *is everybody watching on television?* He caught a fragment of English and stopped, wondering what other American was around. Then he saw the familiar face of the American secretary of state on the small screen. He strained his ears, trying not to draw attention to himself as he adjusted his path to pass close by the television.

". . . together on this issue, perhaps for the first time in half a century," said James Baker. "Together, we will work to make certain that Iraqi aggression will not stand."

Gallagher stopped, placed his duffel on the floor, and pretended to tie a shoe. When he looked back up, the secretary of state had been joined at a wide lectern by Eduard Shevardnadze, the Soviet foreign minister. There was no translation offered of Shevardnadze's reply. The screen dissolved into what was obviously a Russian news program. He stood up.

On the black-and-white screen, an announcer was pointing at a map covered with arrows and lines. He recognized the familiar outline of the Persian Gulf. All the arrows jabbed deep into Kuwait.

Gallagher saw the bank of elevators next to the main desk and headed for them. *Keep watching the tube, comrades,* he thought as he swung the small brown duffel bag as freely as his nerves allowed.

Two faceted glass jewels were mounted on the elevator control panel, the lower one red, the upper one green. He pressed the green button and waited. No lights illuminated and no machinery whirred. He pressed it again. The effect was the same. *Now what?* He glanced nervously at the group huddled around the television. How long would they fail to notice him, a visitor from another planet in their midst?

He pressed the red button, and this time, a series of solid clanks issued from behind the elevator doors. A whine like a distant siren joined the boilermaking thumping. Gallagher's heart jumped to match the elevator's sick beat. He might as well have worn a neon sign that read *intruder.*

"Nyet!" shouted a man from the group gathered at the television.

Gallagher froze, his neck veins bulging. *Here it comes.* He couldn't for his very life remember what Parrum had told him to say. Gallagher slowly turned to see a small, bald man dressed in black pants and white shirt, tie loosened and dangling. He was scowling and pointing. Gallagher followed his outstretched arm. *A door?* The small man motioned again for emphasis just as the thumping and whining from the broken elevator came to a sudden and merciful stop. Gallagher swallowed and walked toward the unmarked door. He felt all the eyes of the television watchers boring into his back as he reached for the greasy knob, turned it, and pulled open the blank door. A whoosh of diesel-scented air rushed by him.

Stairs! The smile on his face was genuine when he turned to the group to thank them. Not one of them was watching him. They all had returned their attention to the battered set. Gallagher stepped into the stairwell and padded upward, his Nikes as silent as moccasins.

As the stairwell door shut, the rangy man sitting by the lobby television stood up, a wooden match tight between his teeth, and left.

Elena placed her diamond necklace on the edge of the sink and opened the shower valve. A jagged bolt of lightning flashed close by, its thunder following an instant later. Rain drummed up on the bathroom window, almost as strong as the water cascading down the shower glass. She caught sight of herself in the mirror.

The face that stared back was shockingly foreign: limp, sweat-plaited hair, bloodshot eyes. She looked drained. When had she last been truly happy? *That first morning after the Stingray test,* she remembered. The whole world had seemed open to her then. And now?

The room soon filled with mist from the shower. She took a brush out of her travel kit and began pulling at her short hair. It was sticky with oil and flecked with dust. The heat from the shower penetrated straight into her tired body. It felt good and soothing, even though it was terribly wasteful.

So what? she thought. Taking her off Stingray was even more wasteful. Elena opened the glass door and reached in, testing the water's heat. *Mmmm.* She took off her terry-cloth bathrobe and stepped under the stream.

The Sukhoi's clear canopy had provided no shade for her neck; it was burned a deep, painful red. The water tingled on the tight skin. She splashed the water onto her face, feeling each protesting muscle slowly give up its cargo of tension and ache. She turned and let the water beat on her naked back, her arms out to prop her up as she rocked back and forth, eyes shut. *I could sleep right here.*

When her internal clock rang its alarm, she tore open a new package of soap and lathered. A stridently floral aroma enveloped her in full industrial strength. She worked the soap over her breasts, rubbing in slow circles, her eyes closed, a smile stretching lazily over her mouth as she teased her nipples firm. *Perhaps,* she thought, *Yuri might be lucky tonight after all.* It had been a very long time. She slid the soap over her flat belly and down a thigh that still trembled from her flight. She soothed it, massaging the tired muscles. She let her hand flow up between her legs, and she gasped at the sudden spark of pleasure. She murmured softly.

In a moment, her hips were rocking in their own rhythm, a flood of warmth rising inside her, reddening her already sunburned neck. She leaned back, feeling the life flow strong within her body. Suddenly, a click came from the unlocked bathroom door, and the echo of the shower's spray changed. Her eyes shot open. Someone was in the room with her! She pushed back into the far corner of the tiled shower stall as a dark form eclipsed the light coming in through the window.

A hand cleared a circle in the misted shower door, and a face appeared. ''Elena?''

Her heart jumped into her throat as she stifled a scream. ''Who?'' she said, incapable of completing the thought or the words. ''Who is there?'' Her neck hairs stood straight out.

"Am I early?" asked Slepkin. "Zarkich said you would be here."

"I . . . I am in the shower!" she spluttered in outrage.

"It's getting late and I need to speak with you. And Elena," he continued, "what soap is that? It smells so much like flowers I thought I was walking in a garden. Is it imported?"

"Get out," she said, her voice barely able to rise above the hiss of the water. She gathered herself. "Get out and close the door behind you."

"As you wish, *Academician,*" he replied, the spike of sarcasm sticking through his words.

She watched as his dark shape receded like a storm cloud. "The door!"

Slepkin chuckled softly as the door clicked shut.

She twisted the shower off. *Pig.* Elena cracked the door open to be sure he was really gone and reached for her robe. She put it on quickly and tied it tightly at her waist. The rain had stopped, but far-off thunder rumbled like a distant artillery duel. She put the big artificial diamond around her neck, burrowing it beneath her robe. "What is it you wanted?" she said through the closed door.

"It is not a matter to shout."

Elena reached for the cold doorknob, breathed in twice to calm herself, then opened the door. Slepkin was sitting on her bed, legs crossed casually. He was fingering the silk of the dress she planned to wear that evening. *Pig!* She put out her hand. "The dress, please. I do not like people toying with my clothes." He held it up, just barely within her reach. She snapped it from his hands. "And I do not like it when they toy with me."

"I do not toy, Elena," Slepkin warned. "Do not make the mistake of thinking so. Do you remember the warning I gave you about contacting the American?"

"So? I only contacted him briefly," she said, holding up a fist. "What more is there to tell?"

"Quite a bit, I'm afraid. I had him followed this afternoon. I was quite correct to take the precaution. Gallagher is working for the American intelligence services."

"He's *what?*" she said, brought away from her fear by disbelief. "A *spy?*" Somehow she could not believe the man she had seen flying this afternoon could be something so low, so poisonous. *And so much like you.*

"Yes, I suppose he is," said Slepkin. "Now, what do you suppose he's doing here?"

Gallagher? A spy? "That's your expertise, Colonel. Not mine."

"There's more. Gallagher is not working alone. His friend is of the old school. A man with dirty, dirty hands." Slepkin held up his own white fingers. "It would be very bad if he ever got his hands on you. You haven't made any further arrangements to see him, or see any stranger here in town, have you?"

"Of course not," she said quickly, turning away and facing the mirror above the dresser, watching his reflection.

He slowly got to his feet and approached her. There was heat in his look, a gnawing hunger that frightened her. She pretended to look for something in the top drawer.

"Why would these two suddenly appear in Moscow, together, and right here?" he said as his voice came closer. "To see you, perhaps? To work some arrangement out?"

She kept her back to him as she opened a small jewelry box and fished for a pair of gold earrings. Her hands were shaking.

"Why indeed? This is what I keep asking myself, and to be honest, I haven't come to a conclusion. What do you think?" Slepkin asked, close.

She clipped on one earring. "I haven't a clue." She smelled his strong cologne, then felt warm breath tickle at the nape of her neck.

"Of course you wouldn't. But I will know before long. I promise you that. Permit me?" he said, reaching around her and taking the other earring from her hand. He brushed the cool gold hoop up the length of her neck, behind her ear, teasing at the folds of skin. "Remember," he said as he fastened it to her, "I am your sword and shield. You can rely on me, Elena, to be very watchful."

She shivered at his touch. "Then why do you sound as though you are warning me?" she asked, her voice quavering against her will.

"Because I am."

She looked down into the small jewelry box again. When she glanced up into the mirror, he was already gone.

She opened the top drawer and pulled out a lacy black bra and matching panties, but all the energy, all the anticipation, of the evening ahead was gone, stolen by Slepkin and what he represented. She wanted to sleep, to escape from him forever, to wake up and find herself back . . . back where? *Home*.

She moved over to the bed and stretched out, flat on her back. The terry robe was damp and cool on her skin. Only the diamond pendant seemed warm. It seemed more alive than she herself felt. *Maybe it is,* she thought, closing her eyes.

Two soft knocks came from the door. Her eyes popped open. Two more knocks sounded. Who was it now? Surely not Slepkin. He wouldn't bother to knock. Yuri? She sighed. She didn't much feel like a plate of meat and a bottle of wine, as he had put it. Not anymore. The doorknob turned, and that, at last, energized her.

She was up and over by the door in two quick, determined steps, her bare foot planted to keep it from opening into the room. Elena had had all the surprises she was willing to endure for the day. First that idiot colliding with her over the airfield, then Slepkin. *This* was the final line no intruder would pass. She grasped the doorknob and stopped its creeping rotation. "Who is it!" she demanded angrily.

Gallagher leaned closer to the peeling veneered door of room 210. His small brown duffel was at his feet, and the envelope Parrum had given him was in his hand. "Elena?" he said again, this time a little louder. Suddenly, the door swung open, fast enough that he almost lost his balance.

"You?" she said.

Gallagher's eyes widened when he saw her in her robe, her dark hair black and shining. He forgot the throbbing in his battered nose as he followed the movement of a bead of water down her neck as it flowed along a fine gold chain before disappearing into her robe. He almost forgot again why he was here. But not quite. "Here," he said, handing her the envelope, allowing his own eyes to linger, to catch on the deep blue of her own. He expected her surprise to melt away into understanding. After all, Parrum had said she would be expecting him. But her face hardened like setting ice.

"Get out," she said, ignoring the envelope.

"It's yours. I mean—"

"Go! Get out!" she repeated. The door began to swing shut.

Gallagher shot his foot out to block it, but too late. In the instant before it slammed shut, he thrust Parrum's envelope into the narrowing slot. He heard the lock slide fast.

I guess that's about it, he thought. *I'm out of here.* He turned and walked down the narrow corridor, his feet silent on the mangy orange carpet. He was done. Whatever good Parrum thought it would do, whatever reason it might be worth $200,000 of Kratos Foundation money, it was done. Now Gallagher could go back to what he knew best: flying, not spying.

He ignored the elevator and walked to the door leading into the stairwell. He hesitated for an instant, his hand on the knob, Elena's face swimming into his memory with a vigorous and independent will. He shook away the image and opened the door. *Done,* he said as he took the stairs down two at a time.

16

"You're certain?" asked Slepkin as he punched the button for the second floor. The elevator doors shut smoothly and quietly, and the cab surged upward from the subbasement level.

"Maybe they're fucking." Zarkich spat into the corner of the elevator and nodded. "There will be tapes to prove it. Do you want to check them first?" The elevator doors opened onto the second floor.

"No," said Slepkin. "I will hear it from her, first." He stepped out into the corridor.

Zarkich chuckled and followed close behind. The wooden match in his mouth was chewed to shreds. He spat it out and magically, seemingly out of thin air, another appeared. He watched the way Slepkin moved, the turn of his head, the quick appraising glances that missed nothing. He didn't need to be told. His 9-mm Makarov was out of its shoulder holster and in his hand, its black muzzle pointed carefully at the ceiling. The sword and shield insignia of the KGB was stamped on its grip. This night might well prove amusing after all.

Slepkin paused before Elena's room, listening. He nodded approvingly as Zarkich took up station to one side, ready, waiting. The muffled sound of movement came from beyond the door, but no voices. As his thin hand formed into a fist, ready to knock,

175

Slepkin had the acute sensation of a stage play about to begin. His nerves seemed to extend right out of his body, his senses supernaturally sensitive. Even the air smelled different, like ozone. The three quick knocks on her door sounded like a cannonade.

Zarkich caught Slepkin's eye and made a movement with his shoulder. *Knock it down?* he mimed.

Slepkin shook his head and pulled out a master key.

"Yes?" said Elena. "Who is it?"

Slepkin knocked again, using the sound to cover the click of the master key in the lock. He felt the tumblers fall as he turned it. *One twist.*

"I said who is—" Elena repeated, but the unlocked door flew open in her face. Her shock was total. Before she knew it, Slepkin was already inside, and Zarkich had shut the door again. She backed away, nearly tripping over her robe, as though wolves had somehow materialized in her room.

"I'm so sorry to bother you again, *Academician* Pasvalys," said Slepkin. "But I have heard terrible, terrible things. They can't be true, can they?" His eyes swept the room, the open door to the bath, Elena's black dress carefully spread out on the bed. "Are we alone, or have you been entertaining visitors?"

"I'm not alone," she said. "You're here with your creature."

Zarkich laughed as he leaned back against her door. It was then that Slepkin saw the envelope sitting in plain sight on top of her dresser. "I see the mail has come," he said, moving toward it.

Elena stepped to block him. She had no idea what was in it, but she had a perfectly clear notion of how it might be used against her.

He walked right up to her, so close he could smell hot fear rising from her scalp. The glint of her diamond pendant flashed up at him from the shadowed valley between her breasts. "Is it private?" he asked. "A love letter, perhaps?"

Her eyes blazed up at him in contempt and defiance. "Would it stop you if it were?" She remembered the letter from her father, so crudely and obviously opened by someone. Who else but Slepkin?

"Not really," said Slepkin as he placed his hands on her shoulders to push her out of the way. "There's no reason to make this difficult." She twisted out of his grasp and stepped back.

"I don't care if you believe me," said Elena. "I know what is true. That's something you will never know."

"Let me tell you what is true, and what is not," said Slepkin. His pale face was flush with anger. "I gave you clear orders. You chose to disobey me. You're just like all your friends in Lithuania. Just like all the damned hooligans trying to take over our country. Well, I may not be able to do much about the rest of them, but I can do something about you. *That* is the truth."

Her eyes blazed back, two needle rays of hate. "Go fuck yourself," she said, crossing her arms over her chest.

Slepkin sighed and nodded to Zarkich.

The tall man was on her in a flash. He yanked her arms behind her back.

"Let me go, you pig!"

Zarkich only chuckled and bent her arms behind her even harder. "It's time we taught her something, don't you think, Colonel?"

"Not yet," said Slepkin as he slit open the envelope and withdrew a single sheet of paper. It was covered with a dense, cursive script.

"Scream," Zarkich whispered in her ear. "I will play the tapes for you later on."

"Enough!" Slepkin ordered. Zarkich ignored him. "Kolya!" Zarkich looked up, and for an instant, Slepkin thought he would be the man's next prey. He saw the fire, the feral glow, slowly ebb from Zarkich's eyes.

Slepkin walked over and bent down until his face was a matter of inches from Elena's own. "It's written in a foreign language. I recognize only an address. Perhaps you could translate it?"

His breath was foul and acid. "You speak English. Make him let me go!"

"It's not English, *Academician*. It's in Lithuanian." Slepkin nodded at Zarkich. The gaunt man yanked her tortured muscles back again, harder this time than the first. "Will you read it for me,

Elena?'' Slepkin asked sweetly, leaning over again until his face was next to hers.

She spat in his eye. "Read it yourself," she said, her voice hoarse with fright.

Slepkin stepped away and dabbed at his eye with a handkerchief. He shook his head sadly. "There's an address on the bottom. Number six Archipova Street. Tell me, Elena, who lives there?" He stepped back a safe distance and nodded to Zarkich. "Let her go."

"But she—"

"Have you forgotten how to obey orders, too? I said, *let her go!*"

Zarkich released her. She wavered, faint.

"You don't look well, Elena. I think you'd better sit down," Slepkin told her. Zarkich shoved her down when she hesitated. "You're in trouble. You can help me figure this out, or you can dig yourself in deeper and deeper until even I cannot save you."

Her jaw tightened as she faced him down.

Slepkin watched as she gathered her robe around her body. He looked at the cryptic message once again. What could this be but treason? What would happen at number six Archipova Street? Would she be there to sell Stingray, or to sell herself? Or would she give them both away? The gibberish above the address might say. He would get it translated at once. "I'm sorry Serpukhov didn't recognize your vast talents. We were too slow, too backward for the likes of you. So now you're out on the open market. That makes you a whore, doesn't it?" He threw the paper aside. It fluttered to the floor.

Elena watched it fall. "You don't even know what you are saying."

"Oh? Don't I?"

"No." She looked up. Her cheeks glistened with tears. "No. Someone—"

"Someone? Who?"

"You already know."

"Say it."

She ground her teeth together, wishing they were sunk into

Slepkin's neck. "It was Gallagher. He planted that paper for you to find. If you were an ape, you'd be smart enough to see it."

"Another Lithuanian scholar, this Gallagher? I just don't understand you." Slepkin's eyes were focused to a place far beyond her room. They were so cold, so cold, yet a pale fire burned in them, an ice fire lit upon a frozen lake that never melted. "You could have taken what was offered you. A position at the Academy. A life in Moscow. A dream for most people. But it wasn't good enough for you, was it?"

Elena shivered, silent.

"No, it wasn't enough. So you struck a deal with Gallagher. You have plotted to exchange information with an American spy. Who knows what else you were planning? Tell me, the American, did you fuck him, too?"

"Don't be an ass. He was here for ten seconds," she said bitterly.

"A quickie," snorted Zarkich.

He stepped close to her and leaned down. "Did you?"

Her words erupted before she could stop them. "You are a *nekulturny* pig."

His palm whipped across the short distance, and the sound of the slap was the loudest thing in all the world. Elena shot to her feet, the urge to flee mixed with the catalyst of fury. She swung to strike him back, but his hand caught hers and gripped it. He smiled as he forced her arm back down, then kept pushing, stepping closer, pushing until the backs of her knees struck the bed and she fell.

"Now you'll learn!" Zarkich crowed.

"Pig!" She coiled her legs to strike, but Slepkin had already moved out of range.

"Listen well, Comrade Pasvalys, *academician* whore," he said as he moved to the door. "You will wait here while we figure out what to do with you. You have disobeyed me, and you have plotted treason. You are worth nothing, less than nothing." He turned to Zarkich. "Keep her here while I call this in and find some idiot who can read this nonsense. Do whatever is necessary, but don't mark her. Is that understood?"

Zarkich smiled and nodded as Slepkin left. He turned to face Elena. *Yes,* he thought, *this night will be a lot of fun.*

Gallagher pushed his way back out onto the street. The air was cool now; the storm had washed away the heat and the humidity. A distant roll of thunder echoed down from the sky, and the late-afternoon sun painted the tops of the receding thundershower a bright gold. The black Mercedes was still parked where he had last seen it, its driver sitting in the front, reading a newspaper. Breathing in a draft of clean, rain-washed air, he walked up to it, tapped on the window, and got in. The heavy door closed like a bank vault and the glass partition separating him from the driver glided down a few inches. "Back to the Hotel Savoy." The driver nodded, the partition raised again, the engine purred, and the big limo pulled out into Leningradskaya Prospekt.

Done, Gallagher said to himself once more as he sat back on the smooth, aromatic hides. He placed the brown duffel bag on his knees. Parrum's envelope had been delivered. He was free to concentrate on flying the Sukhoi to Switzerland, free to wonder how he and *Silky Sue* could win the gold at Yverdon.

The air conditioner in the big Mercedes was blasting directly onto his wet flightsuit. He looked for a window control, but the sidewall was blank. He tapped the glass partition. "Turn it down some, okay?" he asked the driver. The man made no move, gave no hint of understanding. Gallagher leaned forward and rapped on the glass again, harder. "Hey! Can you turn the air conditioner off?"

The partition silently dropped, and George Parrum turned around and smiled, his iron gray hair looking white underneath the black driver's cap. "Did you do it?"

"You get around," said Gallagher. "What happened to the driver?"

"Paid vacation." Parrum adjusted the rearview mirror until it framed Gallagher's face. "I asked you a question. Did she get it?"

"Yes. She got it. I can't guarantee she read it. But she got it." Gallagher sat back and stared at the padded roof. "You know, I'm not cut out for this stuff, George. I just can't lie with a straight face.''

"It comes with practice," said Parrum as he turned left onto the Sadovoye Ring Road. The gray, impervious facades of a hundred different ministries glared down on them as they rolled by. Their tightly fastened windows wept streams of rainwater.

"I just bet it does." Gallagher glanced outside. He turned around, first looking left, then right. "Hey, you turned too soon. The Savoy's the other way."

"We aren't going there, Dr. Gallagher." Parrum glanced up into the mirror. "It wouldn't be prudent just now. In fact, I don't think it would be wise to go back there at all."

"George, I'm finished. I held up my end of the bargain. Take me back there, okay? I've got a long day of flying tomorrow."

"We'll see," said Parrum as he turned off the main avenue. The big buildings disappeared, replaced now by a checkerboard of five-story communal apartments painted in cream, tomato bisque, and dark green. A few old wooden structures stood out like decayed teeth. "I think you'd better leave that particular decision to me."

"What's that supposed to mean?"

"It means we'll wait to be sure it's safe before you go there. There's some risk in everything, Dr. Gallagher. First and foremost, I want to be sure you're not in harm's way."

"Why should I be?"

"Who knows?" Parrum shrugged as he spun the wheel and drove the big Mercedes into a warren of smaller buildings. The five-story flats were the rare ones now; ramshackle wooden structures, all predating the Revolution, predominated. The street became a minefield of potholes. "Trust me," said Parrum as he glanced up into the rearview mirror.

It was as if he had driven off one stage set and onto another. The street hemmed in tighter and tighter. Parrum turned down an even tighter alley, and the sky narrowed to a blue slot.

"Where are we going?" asked Gallagher.

They came to a low, arched tunnel barely wide enough for the Mercedes. Parrum turned into it. The tunnel opened up to a small, enclosed plaza, walled in on all four sides by an ancient three-story wooden building. Ornate scrollwork hung half-nailed from the walls, the wood rotted with moisture and sheer age; peeling green paint revealed a layer of bloodred beneath; the red opened like sores to yellow. Some of the windows were boarded over; some stared down blank as skull sockets, their glass long removed. An applied grid of iron fire escapes seemed to hold the walls erect. The ruins of an old fountain occupied the center. Sunflowers sprouted from the cracked stone, and ravens argued over the contents of a toppled trash bin. "Here," said Parrum.

Slepkin made his way back to the subbasement complex of rooms where the Hotel Aeroflot's elaborate listening gear was monitored. A bank of German tape machines slowly turned, stopping and starting in response to the thousands of microphones embedded in the building's structure. He picked up a telephone and began to dial, but then he hesitated. This situation demanded the proper framing.

On the one hand, his own charge had been in touch with someone working for the opposition. It could easily be seen as his own failure. On the other hand, it was hard enough these days to convince the Committee's foes in Moscow that there *was* an opposition. Suddenly, there it was. The picture snapped into sharp focus for Slepkin. *Of course,* he thought, and dialed his contact officer's weekend number.

A sudden click made him jump. "Vadim? Slepkin here. . . . Yes. I'm in Moscow. Remember the warning you gave me?" Slepkin explained, and a flood of words poured out of the earphone.

"No, I have an even better idea." Slepkin paused, waiting for the drama to reach the correct level before continuing. "How would you like them *both?*" The phone went silent, and then his case officer slowly began to chuckle.

"So what's the deal?" asked Gallagher as he sat down on the battered sofa. It was the one piece of furniture in the otherwise bare apartment. "You said I'd be finished when I handed her the envelope."

"You were." Parrum's voice echoed from the walls.

"Then why did you bring me here?"

"It's just as I said," Parrum replied as he quickly checked the other rooms, then unlocked the painted-over window that led out to the fire escape. He was carrying a small canvas satchel. "I want to be sure you're at no risk. When she comes over, the opposition isn't going to be happy. I want you clear of any possible repercussions."

"When is she coming over?" said Gallagher, a note of alarm creeping in. Could Parrum have arranged for her to defect while he was still in Moscow? *He wouldn't be that dumb.*

"Tonight," said Parrum distractedly.

"Tonight?"

Parrum looked up as though a gnat were circling his head. "Yes, Dr. Gallagher. Tonight. It wasn't supposed to happen this fast, but there's the matter of a war breaking out down in Iraq. Moscow's going schizo over it. The hardliners want to help out their old Arab buddies. The rest want to parlay Russ—I mean, Soviet neutrality for a few megabucks from the West. It's a chaos I can use, but it won't last forever."

"I'm glad it's all worked out so well for you, George, but how do I get to Switzerland? In fact, how the hell do I get out of the country at all?"

"We're working it out right now. It's safer that you don't know all the details. Operational security is my number one concern."

"With a big Mercedes parked outside? You don't think that will draw a crowd?"

Parrum smiled and crooked his finger for Gallagher to come to the window.

"What?" asked Gallagher as he got back up and looked down into the small cobbled plaza below. The limo was already gone.

"I plan ahead, Dr. Gallagher. That's why you'll just have to trust me. It's better that you wait here for the moment." Parrum opened up the canvas bag and withdrew a fifteen-shot Beretta 92F, a large, wicked-looking automatic. "Don't get yourself worked up. This will all resolve itself long before you're due in Switzerland."

Gallagher eyed the heavy handgun. "Hey, wait a minute, George. I'm out of my depth, here, okay? *And what is that goddamned thing for?*"

"My old age. There's a saying, Dr. Gallagher." Parrum checked the fit of the staggered magazine in the 9-mm's grip. "In for an inch, in for a mile." He reached down and pulled out a loaf of black bread and a wedge of cheese from the small sack. "Hungry?"

Gallagher eyed the weapon. "Not anymore."

Two quick raps on her door made Elena jump to her feet and stand behind the bed. She wore the black silk dress she had prepared for her night with Yuri, but one of the straps had been hastily tied where Zarkich had torn it. Her shoulders ached as though she had been left to hang by her wrists for days. One of her eyes was puffed out from where Zurich had playfully struck her, not a true punch, just a taste of what he had in mind for later.

The door pushed open. Slepkin was back. "I see you are dressed." Then he noticed the angry red bruise. He turned to Zarkich. "I told you not to mark her."

Zarkich stood silently by the door with his arms folded across his chest. He shrugged.

Elena's breathing notched another step faster. "I will see you both arrested for this," she vowed. "You can't do this anymore. Not to me, not to anyone. Those days are over."

"What I can or cannot do is no longer your concern. For now, you will simply do as you are told. We must move quickly. Moscow is interested in this. We will all do as Moscow wishes." Slepkin went to the room's small closet and pulled out the clothes she had hung there, dropping them in a heap until he found Elena's summer-weight poplin flying jacket. He tossed it at her. "Put it on."

She let it fall and glared back.

Slepkin toed the jacket at her with his foot. "Let me offer you one final courtesy. Gallagher's little note can mean almost anything. He might have something to sell, he might be acting on his own for other reasons. He might also be setting a trap, and this, Dr. Pasvalys, is an unacceptable option. The first rule in my business is to never play the opponent's game. We will all take a close look at number six Archipova tonight. You will make contact on *my* terms, not his. Your cooperation," he said with a smile, "is not a matter for debate. You are lucky I convinced the center not to simply bring you in for a debriefing."

"Gallagher planted those papers!" she shouted.

"I am sorry, Elena. Truly." Slepkin nodded. The wooden match in Zarkich's mouth twitched like a beetle's antenna. He stepped up and pulled her arms back hard. She opened her mouth to scream, but Slepkin silenced her by pinching her lips shut. With his other hand, he closed Elena's flaring nostrils. She couldn't breathe. "You see? There is nothing that I cannot control. Nothing. Remember that as your first lesson tonight."

Her chest pounded as her lungs demanded air, and a roaring sound filled her ears as her face turned first red, then purple. A silent scream echoed in her throat, but a thought burned clear and hot: *I will kill you for this.*

"Do we have an understanding, Comrade Pasvalys? Will you now do as you are told?"

She nodded fast, her ears roaring.

He let her go and she gasped a lungful of air. "Let us all go pay your Mr. Gallagher a visit, shall we?" He held out her flying jacket.

She snatched it. *I will kill you for this,* she vowed.

The bottle of Armenian brandy Yuri carried was a favorite of Elena's. How long had it been since he had last shared one with her? He tried to remember as he walked down the hotel corridor. He remembered her apartment in Serpukhov, a small, sunny place that always gave him claustrophobia. He was always making her angry, stepping on things, knocking over tables. She was always so fastidious, so orderly. It made him feel like a creature battling its way through a delicate spiderweb. *Don't touch this! Don't sit there!*

One morning—it was to be their last—he had heaved himself from bed and had stepped on her shoes. How could he know she had slipped her last pair of sunglasses into them the night before? He could still hear the crunch.

He walked up to room 210 and straightened his uniform tie, making sure both it and his crimson tunic were spotless. He raised his fist to knock, but something made him pause, a tickle of warning across the heavy matted hair on his arm. Like most aviators, he had come to trust the subtle warnings his body provided, even if his brain could not name them. He pressed his ear against the door, listening. He heard only the soft whoosh of the hotel's air-conditioning system.

"Elena?" he said, then knocked, putting his ear to the thin door. "Are you ready?" He knocked again. There was still no answer, no soft padding of feet from beyond. Was she playing games again? Elena loved to play games. A sudden thought made him bite his lower lip in worry. *Has she forgotten?*

He checked his watch. He was a little late, but not much. Where was she? "Elena?" he said again, and this time he reached down and turned the knob. To his amazement, the door swung open. "Are you here, Squirt?" he called softly. He surveyed the room.

Clothes were strewn across the floor; a table was lying on its side. The bed was rumpled and half-undone; a terry-cloth robe lay on the carpet, its belt dangling from the bathroom doorknob. The telephone had been ripped from the wall, not that it worked anyway, but still . . . He saw the bathroom door ajar and walked in. "Elena?" he called out, feeling his worry blossom into alarm. There was no answer. He saw the neat row of shampoos and creams along the sink. The scent of Elena's favorite shampoo traveled up his nostrils, evoking his fondest memories. This was her room all right. Something was very wrong.

A low growl came to his throat as he stood the bedside table back on its legs and left the room, closing the door quietly behind him, his brow knitted. Gripping the bottle of Armenian brandy like a club, he marched out into the hallway, his polished boots flashing faster and faster. By the time he got to the stairs to the lobby, Yuri was in a dead run.

The front desk was manned by a bored clerk who sat, leaning back, reading yesterday's *Pravda*. He didn't even glance up as Yuri stormed up and smashed his fist down on the bell.

"Hey, you," he said to the clerk. "Where is Elena Pasvalys?"

The clerk slowly looked up, folded his paper, slid it into a drawer, and stood up. "Who?" he asked, as though Yuri had whispered her name and not shouted it loud enough to be heard across Leningradskaya Prospekt.

Yuri smiled and leaned over the desk, pursing his lips as though he were about to whisper. When the clerk leaned in close, he bellowed her name. *"Elena Pasvalys!"*

The clerk's ears flattened against the blast. "All right! All right! I will check." He licked his finger and ran down a scrawled list.

"What? What is it?" Yuri demanded.

The clerk took out a pair of glasses, polishing them on the tail of his shirt, then put them on. "Room two ten," he said, then sat back down.

Yuri's fist on the desktop made the bell leap into the air. *"I know that!"* he roared. "I want to know where she is! Speak!"

The clerk looked at him haughtily. "How should I know where anyone is? What am I? The KGB?"

"Did you see her go by? Hear anything? The room looks like it was taken apart piece by piece!"

"Renovations are ongoing." The clerk shrugged and pulled out his *Pravda*. It was already yellowed.

"Shit," said Yuri to no one in particular and everyone in general. He spun on his bootheel and marched back outside.

The evening sky was still milky white, but the first stars were already out, studding the sky like pearls against satin. Yuri stood for a moment, listening to the distant rumble of thunder, the swishing of traffic out on Leningradskaya Prospekt. Where could she be? He remembered her sitting under the wing of her broken Sukhoi. Could that be where she was? She had seemed so despondent. Could she have taken apart her own room in a fit? It made a certain kind of sense, the kind that appeals when there is no other. He turned on his heel and marched back toward the hidden airstrip behind the hotel.

The tall tail of his own Antonov rose like a giant shark fin at the far end of the runway. It looked like a massive metal sculpture, its aluminum glinting brightly against the dark waters of the Moskva. The lush wet-green smell rose as he pounded his way across the grassy airstrip. There were lights on at the Sukhoi hangar, at least. *We shall see,* he said to himself as he hurried.

The hangar door was still cracked open; not wide enough for his frame, but wide enough for him to set his shoulder to. The doors squealed as he shoved them open. The interior of the hangar was bathed in the soft glow of a few night-lights. Elena's Sukhoi was where he had last seen it, its broken wheel propped up by a wooden sawhorse. "Elena?" he called out, his voice echoing from the rafters. A bird chirped in sleepy surprise. "Elena?" he called out again.

Where is she? he wondered as he walked up to her Sukhoi. The place was deserted. He looked around. *Maybe she is trying to avoid me after all,* he thought with a shrug. He recalled their last times together. He was always saying the wrong thing somehow. Couldn't she tell what he thought of her?

Maybe not. He sat down under the Sukhoi's wing, using its intact landing gear as a backrest. The bottle of brandy seemed to open by itself. He unknotted his tie and relieved the top button of his overly tight shirt.

Maybe she really doesn't want to see me at all, he thought as he leaned back and took a long pull from the bottle.

17

**Midnight,
4 August 1990**

Eisley felt the catapult shuttle go into tension as a cloud of steam blasted back across *Kennedy*'s flight deck, driven by her thirty-knot rush through the night. A yellow light burned high on the carrier's island. When it turned green, they would be cleared to launch. In three seconds, fifty-five thousand pounds of fighter would be accelerated to almost two hundred knots, and Operation Deep Canyon, the Dahr Nema strike, would be under way at last. The lights from his instrument panel mingled with the stars dusting his canopy. They were brilliant and close in the predawn dark. "Ready back there, BB?"

"What do you think?" said Baxter as he cradled the stuffed animal between his legs. When they were airborne, he would put the orange cat back on its Velcro throne atop the instrument panel.

"Me? I think it's gonna be a hot time at the oasis tonight." His wings carried a deadly mix of Sparrow and Sidewinder air-to-air missiles; his belly stations held the ultra-long-range Phoenix.

Eisley swung his controls through their maximum motion, satisfying himself that all was as it had to be. "Okay, Bax. It's time to aviate." He shoved the F-14's throttles into full military power, then around the safety detent into afterburner. Two cones of orange fire shot aft against the jet blast deflector. *Ready.* He thumbed on his red anticollision beacon and saluted the black space between the glowing wands held up by the catapult officer. He pushed his helmet back into his headrest and gripped the throttle guards, waiting, waiting. *Any second.* The light was still yellow as the Tomcat's engines screamed, its nose gear compressed, ready for the powerful stroke.

"I hate night shots," said Baxter. He glanced up at the island structure. Why was the light still yellow? But as he watched, it turned, not green, but red. "Hey! Check out Vulture's Row!"

"What the fuck?" said Eisley. He looked over at the launch officer. "He wants us to throttle back!" The wands were now crossed as the cat officer stepped directly in front of Eisley's Tomcat. "I guess he means it." There was no way to launch without killing him. Eisley pulled his throttles out of reheat, but kept them at full military power.

"Cutlass two zero two," came the voice from PriFly, "throttle back and taxi forward to parking." The deck crew was already motioning him up toward the bow parking area.

"What is the delay?" asked Eisley. He had trained for this moment for years. He was pumped up for a catapult shot and a night strike against a real enemy. What was with this parking crap?

"Taxi forward, two zero two," a different voice came back. "And do it now."

"Was that the CAG?" said Baxter.

"Jesus," said Eisley as he pulled the throttles all the way back to idle. He felt the shuttle disconnect from his nosewheel. He brought his wings back from fully extended to oversweep and blipped his throttles a touch forward. The fighter bounced over the catapult slot toward *Kennedy*'s darkened bow.

Ten minutes later, trailing their communications cables, oxygen hoses, and G-suit straps, Eisley and Baxter stomped into the 0-2 level ready room. A few pilots were already there; most were still up on the flight deck parking their planes. Eisley saw Cotton Mather, his usual wingman. Mather had been scheduled to fly one of the spare fighters in case of an abort. "What the fuck is going on?" he asked him.

"Beats the shit out of me." Cotton shrugged. "You want the truth, you have to wait. All I have is the scuttlebutt."

Eisley flopped down into a padded chair. The thrum of the carrier's screws set his teeth on edge. "And that is?"

Mather leaned close and whispered. "Someone up in CIC says the spooks spotted a bird on the pad, ready to go." He checked his watch. "The CAG's supposed to come and deliver the gospel any minute."

"Are you shitting me, shipmate? You mean to say we waited too long?" said Eisley as more pilots drifted in, each with the same look of puzzlement laced with disgust. "We cut fucking grooves in the ocean, waiting for the word to go, and now it's too late?"

"Sounds like it to me," said Mather. "I guess they snookered us. Now, they see a strike inbound, they push the button, and . . ."

Reynard marched in, his face red with fury.

"Attention on deck!" cried Baxter as the pilots and RIOs jumped to their feet.

"Be seated," said Reynard. He was holding a small piece of paper in his hand. The tension made the tendons stand out, ready to snap like a trap. "I'll make this quick. At twenty-one hundred hours Washington time, the Iraqi ambassador Mohammed Al-Masshad delivered the following to our friends at the State Department." Reynard held out the paper as though it were an already-used square of toilet tissue. " 'The Revolutionary Council of the Government of Iraq demands the removal of all foreign forces now in the Persian Gulf by midnight of five August.' "

"Shee-it," whispered Baxter.

" 'Any attack against Iraqi territory, or Iraqi citizens, *anywhere in the world*,' " Reynard continued, " 'will be considered just cause for direct retaliation against the homelands of the attacking forces.' " Reynard stopped reading and looked up. "It goes on, but I think you get the idea."

"Christ," said Eisley, "that little fuck is threatening to hit the United States? Why don't we just lob a nuke down his throat first?" Eisley had seen the rows of cruise missile warheads down in *JFK*'s special armory. "I say we map 'em and zap 'em." The fighter jocks shouted their agreement.

"Quiet!" Reynard snapped, clearly under a great deal of strain himself. "I'll tell you why, Lieutenant. Because that little fuck you refer to has a missile all his own." Reynard folded up the paper and left without another word.

**Midnight,
4 August 1990**

"Wait for me here," said Parrum as he changed from his driver's uniform into a cloth cap and a midnight blue worker's smock.

"Do I have a choice?" Gallagher replied.

Parrum smiled. "Cynicism is a luxury, Dr. Gallagher," was Parrum's only reply. He left the bread and cheese for him and taking only the bulging canvas satchel, left Gallagher sitting alone in the room. *Judas goat,* he thought as he walked down the rickety wooden stairs to the flat's tiny vestibule. Gallagher would be the bait; he would spring the trap. When it was done, everything would be different. Enstrom would have his prize, and he, Parrum, would feel the stamp of approval on a lifetime of quiet work that some-times, by necessity, had turned dirty. Kratos Foundation would know what to do with the information inside Elena Pasvalys's head. What had Enstrom told him? *Extremism in the defense of liberty is no vice.* Parrum could get along with that real well.

The wooden steps were uneven, dropping first a few inches, then a great many, then a few. Number six Archipova was an old building, one of the few in the last remaining pocket of similar structures in what had once been Moscow's Jewish ghetto. He came to the bottom and stepped out into the walled courtyard. *Good,* he thought. *It's dark enough to get the show going.* The smell of cooked cabbage wafted down as he stood there, eyeing the dark archway that opened out onto Archipova Street. The sounds of the city were muffled by the enclosing walls of the tenements. Overhead, the stars peeked by billows of clouds that glowed a radioactive orange from Moscow's streetlights.

Parrum crossed the courtyard and came to the archway, listening, resting his hands on the greasy stones still slick with rain and warm from the day. The hidden courtyard was guarded by an iron gate that now, several hundred years and several empires removed from its manufacture, no longer budged from the rusted and open position.

Perfect. He nodded. It was an admirable place for a safe house. One main entry, but a great many exits. It was, in a way, like the planetarium he had used to shake his followers a few days back, except that the stars overhead were real. He turned around. A few lights were scattered across the tenement walls. The lights of number six showed through around the edge of the painted-over window. The tenements had black iron fire escapes grafted to their faces like poorly sewn stitches. Most were clogged with chairs and stools where a person could escape the heat and enjoy an evening breeze. A radio was playing, and the tinny music echoed in the walled court.

He walked back to the front wall of number six Archipova. A ladder was set loosely into the crumbling mortar. It led to the fire escape perched just outside the window of the apartment where Gallagher waited. A jumble of old, broken furniture was stored out on the metal landing above. It would make the perfect assassin's perch. Parrum shook it slightly, hearing the creak of old metal. A fall of brick dust cascaded down. Easing his weight onto the ladder, he began to climb. *Christ,* he thought as he felt the ladder sway, *I'm getting too old for this crap.* He reached the landing outside the window of number six. For some reason, his thoughts turned to Enstrom once again. It felt good, damned good, to work for someone who knew his way around the real world for a change.

He squatted down behind a broken bookcase, hidden from view from the courtyard below. He opened the canvas satchel and withdrew the Beretta. Fifteen brass pearls gleamed from the magazine's telltales. In the satchel were three rounds of a different design: powerful Pentatholite darts. But they were for something far more important than simple killing.

He slipped the magazine from the Beretta and began threading one of the dart heads onto the end of the barrel. When he was finished, he held it up. He could see the stars reflected on its smooth, machined surface. As he settled himself in for the wait, he wondered how often history had been bent around the barrel of a gun. Presidents, dictators, wicked men, wise men. History always necked down to a point, a fulcrum. He gripped the Pentatholite-equipped Beretta. This was Parrum's fulcrum. One good man. One good weapon. The right time and place. What more was necessary?

"Right here will be fine," said Van Zandt Wilkerson. The Moscow station chief had the cabdriver stop at the entrance to Khistoprudni Park. He paid in the only currency the local cabbies accepted these days, American dollars, and got out.

Despite the hour, couples still walked arm and arm around the broad oval of the model-boat basin that formed the focus of the vest-pocket park. Bright orange lights bathed the scene in a light nearly Mediterranean in intensity. Boats of every description scooted along the dark waters under radio command of their captains. Low gray warships busied themselves by cutting wakes for the sailboats to contend with. The temperature was cool, the air fresh from the afternoon's storm.

If winter was Moscow's prettiest season, then night was its best time. The dark shadows clothed the shabbiness, the thinness, nearly as well as snow. It was possible for Wilkerson to watch the evening activities around the boat basin and imagine himself almost anywhere.

As he strolled casually around the perimeter, watching for a tail, he saw a square-rigged Roman trireme accosted by a lurking U-boat. A fireboat spouted a stream of brackish water into the air; the droplets caught, hanging like diamonds before they fell back to the murk. All to the musical accompaniment of a waltz that tinkled down from speakers mounted in the limbs of trees. It seemed an apt chaotic vision for the last days of a shattered empire. When he was sure he had not been followed, he cut across the fragrant green grass to a second, older gate, one that had clearly not been used, other than by vandals, for a long, long time.

Beyond the corroded iron lay a jumble of headstones, gray as fossil bones against the shadowed ground. Most were broken. Spray paint daubed everything that still stood upright. It was the old Jewish cemetery, a small plot crowded with stone upon stone until it was nearly impossible to walk between graves. Wilkerson picked his way, listening as the waltz grew tinnier and more distant. On the far side of the cemetery, a broken gate hung lopsided by a single hinge. On the far side was Archipova Street.

His leather-soled shoes were impossibly loud as he walked on Archipova's cobblestones. The neighborhood was strangely quiet, as though its inhabitants had closed up like barnacles against a falling tide. Half the streetlights that hung over the center of the narrow street were out, and the gloomy aura invaded his mood.

It was far too quiet a place for a snatch. That's what this was shaping up to be. A series of inquiries back to Langley had yielded the full dossier on George Parrum, and a great deal of information that didn't appear in his personnel jacket. The man had *rogue* written all over him. He stopped and bent over to tie his shoe, catching an innocent look back. *Good.*

The address sign was missing, but Wilkerson knew the route. He turned into what seemed a mere break in the solid row of prewar flats. Dark as the way had been, the alley leading down to number six Archipova was darker still; not even the pale wash of city light that illuminated the night sky was of much use; the narrow alley was walled in like a dry creek through sheer cliffs.

The slate sidewalk was slightly lighter than the cobbled street. It gave Wilkerson just enough of a cue to keep him from stepping off the curb. It was well that he knew the way. He paused and turned again. There was still no tail.

They alley turned a sharp bend, so sharp that even the tiny Ladas could not pass two abreast. It was, Wilkerson decided, an excellent place for a trap if someone had it in his mind to set one.

He examined the hanging ironmongery of the fire escapes for a trail watcher. The night was warm enough to drive the people from their rooms, but the escapes were oddly empty. He thought he knew why. Jews had centuries of experience when it came to tragedy. No doubt their inner senses detected the onrush of another wave from the black night. They knew the turning of history would bring back the ancient hatreds once again. Why else would thousands of them flee each month, moving to the bull's-eye, the ground zero of the new war? Hadn't Saddam Hussein said as much himself by vowing to "burn down half of Israel" if she interfered?

Not that the situation was any better right here. Gorbachev was losing his grip; the Army and the KGB were reestablishing their own. The ruin of an empire demanded a scapegoat, and the people of Archipova Street had no doubts over who it would be this time. Who had it always been?

The alley twisted once and then arrowed straight toward the block of buildings that finally put an end to its serpentine course. He walked through the short tunnel and emerged into a private court. A light glowed through the painted-over window of number six. "Bingo," he said softly. He had almost reached the dry fountain at the center of the courtyard when he heard the sound of a car approaching from behind. He crouched behind a broken stone figurine as headlights swept across the entrance to the tunnel. *Busy night,* he said to himself, wondering whether the lights belonged to Parrum, his target, or someone less welcome.

Suddenly, like two supernovas bursting to life in the center of the dark tunnel, a pair of headlights appeared. They grew brighter as the car cautiously approached, then went out as the nose of the car edged into the courtyard. Parrum, target, or someone less welcome? He turned and saw the light still on at number six. Wilkerson, and whoever was up in that flat, would shortly find out.

18

**Early Saturday Morning,
4 August 1990**

Zarkich rolled the Chaika's passenger window down and took a quick sniff. "I smell Jews."

"Patience, Kolya," said Slepkin.

The rows of prewar flats crowded close to the cobblestones, nearly overhanging the street as it grew more narrow and twisted. Slepkin swung the wheel and braked to a stop. "Get out the map," he told Zarkich. "I think we have passed it."

They had stopped across from the ancient Jewish cemetery. He looked up and saw, down the slight hill, the lights of Khistoprudni Park. He folded the map open, shifted into first, and turned around in the narrow street.

They slowed as they hunted for the narrow entrance to number six Archipova. Slepkin saw a cleft in the wall of tenements. *Could that be it?* It was narrow and foreboding, and it activated his professional dislike of confining spaces.

Zarkich saw what Slepkin was eyeing. "I do not like it. It is not a good place."

"You don't need to like it, Kolya," said Slepkin. "All that is required is that a certain Mr. Parrum finds it to his liking." He doused the headlights and nosed the Chaika into the darkness.

■　　■　　■

Gallagher stretched out on the battered sofa, the one piece of furniture in the otherwise bare room. *Idiot,* he told himself. *Might as well trust a snake.* He had expected George Parrum to lie, of course. Just not to him. He should have taken Sara Avilar's advice and thought it out. *Too late.*

One thing he knew to be certain: there was a lot of real estate between him and his passport back at the Savoy. He thought of the dark blue Sukhoi with the number 8 on her tail. His. He looked up at the cracked plaster hanging from the ceiling. Was Elena Pasvalys's defection a lie, too? And if she showed up tonight, and Parrum made good his plan to help her out, then what would face him tomorrow at Moscow Central? He doubted whether there would be much clapping this time around. And what could Frolov say? Wasn't he betraying his new friend?

A faint sound from outside made him stop, cock his head, and listen. He checked his watch. It was after midnight. *About time,* he thought. *Let's get this show on the road.*

Slepkin slowly pushed open the front door and saw a row of old mailboxes, each with a brass nameplate corroded a dark green. He wrinkled his nose at the sour smell of cooking mixed with dust and age. Number six Archipova, he saw, was the second-level flat.

He used one hand to hold Elena, the other wrapped firmly around his Makarov. The inner hall was empty. He nodded for Zarkich to move ahead.

Zarkich held his own automatic at the ready and deployed inside, peering up the stairs at the cluster of four naked bulbs burning four floors up. He gave the all clear and walked silently down the stairs to the vestibule. A new wooden match was in his teeth.

"All right," Slepkin whispered to Elena. "We are nearly done. The sooner we see if your friends are here, the sooner we can start forgetting that any of this has happened. If you cooperate, you may yet be saved."

She turned to Slepkin. When she spoke, even she could hear the desperation in her voice. "Please. This is wrong. I have never heard of this place before. This has all been done to ruin me."

"Quiet," Slepkin said between his teeth. Catching such a one as Parrum would be a very great prize indeed, especially these days. Slepkin knew that opportunities such as this didn't come round very often. "Up you go," he said.

She took another step and Slepkin closed the outer door quietly. "Stay here and wait," he told Zarkich as he pushed Elena by her shoulder toward the first step.

Zarkich sneered in reply, though Slepkin realized he was merely chewing the wooden match in anticipation. "Up," Slepkin told her.

She faltered and felt Slepkin's hands push under the thin cotton jacket she wore. "Up," he whispered.

She took another step. *I will kill you for this,* she thought. She felt dirtied by the smooth hands urging her upward. "Come on, come on," Slepkin said impatiently. Suddenly, a light came on up above on the third level. Slepkin froze as the sound of slippered feet scuffed to the edge of the railing. An old man leaned over the railing and peered down, his face marked by sleep.

"Who is it?" he demanded. "I'll call the militia! Who is there?"

"Go back inside!" Slepkin spat. He nodded, and Zarkich was up the stairs in a flash. The old man was shoved back into his flat without explanation.

"Go watch the front door," Slepkin ordered. *If that old fool has blown this . . .* Slepkin seethed as he climbed the stairs behind Elena. How could it not? But no battle plan survives the first moments of combat. Now he would have to rely on speed. He shoved Elena the last few steps and up to the door to number six.

Slepkin let go of her and stood to one side, hidden from view to anyone opening the door. He motioned for her to knock.

She raised an arm and rapped weakly. Her racing pulse throbbed in her neck. Whoever this Parrum was, he was about to regret ever coming to Moscow. And Gallagher! He had started all of this with his damned envelope! She eyed Slepkin. *No,* she corrected herself, *he didn't start it. He only ended it.* The veins in her temples bulged to bursting. She was about to knock again when she heard the scuffle of feet from beyond the door. A lock snapped, a chain rattled, and the door swung wide.

Jesus! "Elena! I mean, Dr. Pasvalys!" said Gallagher. "I was beginning to think . . ." he began, but then he stopped. "What's wrong?" he asked when he saw her expression. Then he saw her bruises, her puffy face, the red splotches. "Christ! What happened? Was there some kind of—"

Suddenly, Slepkin stepped into the doorway, his Makarov leveled at Gallagher's chest. A smile of absolute triumph flashed across his face like a neon sign.

"Who . . ." said Gallagher, but the weapon answered his question before it could be asked.

"Good night, Dr. Gallagher," said Slepkin, his English unrefined but serviceable. "I hope you are enjoying Moscow." He motioned for him to step back into the apartment.

"Easy, friend," said Gallagher, his eyes glued to the evil piece of steel in Slepkin's hand. "Take it easy. You're making a hell of a mistake. I'm an American with—"

"I do not care what you say you are, Dr. Gallagher. I know," said Slepkin. "I know more than that, too. I know who else has come here. I know why you and this"—his lip curled when he regarded Elena—"this woman have secretly met."

"We have done nothing!" Elena shouted.

"Then I have caught you in time." Slepkin kept advancing, the black Makarov an accusing finger pointed at Gallagher's heart.

"Great. Maybe you can tell me what this is all about then," said Gallagher as he backed away from the muzzle. What was going on? Why had Elena brought the police? And where the fuck was George Parrum?

Parrum crouched on the iron fire escape and watched Gallagher back away from the open door. *Good boy,* he thought. *Just play it dumb.* Was this all the force the opposition could bring to bear?

Things must be far more tenuous than even he had allowed himself to believe. The window, opened only far enough to admit the Pentatholite dart head, let a whiff of air pass as the pressures within the flat changed with the closing door. He checked to see that the dart was fully threaded onto the gun barrel. It made the Beretta a single-shot weapon. One shot against two opponents. The dart would administer a fast-acting sedative that would guarantee a minimum of thirty minutes of sleep. It would do. He would make it work. He was a professional.

He thumbed the safety off the Beretta 92F and watched as Gallagher was backed up toward the couch by the man with the gun. He steadied the Pentatholite head on the windowsill as Elena stepped farther into the room. The thin man in the loose suit was keeping his body behind hers, which meant he wasn't so dumb, not that it would make any difference in a few seconds. The dart ejector would fire its crushable nylon syringe across the small space with adequate accuracy. Smart or dumb, he would be out of the order of battle in seconds. Professional or not, the target was going down.

Come on, he urged Elena's companion. *Let's get this moving!* There was a car waiting, the black Mercedes, for a run to the Baltic Sea. Who would stop it? The police would salute it. At the Riga docks, she would be put aboard a trawler bound for blue water. After that, borders were no longer an issue.

Parrum's pistol followed Slepkin. His finger tightened on the trigger, loosened, then tightened as Slepkin moved. He could handle her. It was the 9-mm unfriendliness in the opposition's hands that now had Parrum's full attention. It would be far easier to kill him, but that would hardly leave the right message behind, would it?

Elena moved slightly and Slepkin's shoulder became briefly exposed. Parrum centered the barrel, waiting for a larger slice of chest to show. Parrum wanted the man alive, but down. *Almost . . . almost . . . There!*

He exhaled, the barrel pointing at Slepkin's chest, when the sound of the front door opening below stopped his white-tensed finger. Parrum looked down at the dim pool of light shed at the entry. *Wilkerson?* Where in God's creation had *he* come from? Suddenly, the sound of a violent scuffle came from the vestibule.

Slepkin heard the sound as well and spun, dashing out the door of number six, into the hallway beyond.

Parrum's mind raced through the possible permutations of his own actions like a kaleidoscope shifting, shifting, shifting. This was why a man on the ground was superior to the most exotic of "technical means." A man could adapt, a man could accommodate. He swung the Beretta away from Slepkin's back. Elena hesitated an instant too long.

Parrum centered the sighting pip on Elena's thigh. He squeezed the trigger. There was a sharp, electric spit of the exploding cordite accelerant.

The heavy Pentatholite attachment made the Beretta's buck imbalanced, but the powerful chemical dart found its target with ruthless precision. Even as Parrum was shoving the magazine of live rounds into the handle and screwing in the silencer in the dart head's place, Elena was going down.

With fifteen brass rounds gleaming through the 92F's telltales, he heaved the window open and stepped forward to collect his prize.

Zarkich laughed as he squeezed the breath from Wilkerson's lungs with one arm, the other tight around the CIA station chief's neck. Like a boa, he squeezed, first chest, then neck, chest then neck; each incremental pressure was greater than the last, constricting his windpipe to the vanishing point until there was nothing in all the world for Wilkerson to breathe. Nothing. Zarkich himself was lost in a killing trance. He did not hear the scuffle of feet from above as Slepkin rushed to the banister, much less the considerably fainter sound from the third-floor balcony. He squeezed again, relishing the exquisite shade of purple suffusing Wilkerson's face.

It was the *bagpipe,* a measure Zarkich had learned in the Osnaz, the KGB's Special Forces, for extracting confessions. "Bastard," hissed Zarkich, and he ratcheted his grip another notch tighter. Who cared who he was? It was enough to feel him die.

Slepkin turned his back on Gallagher and Elena and pounded to the banister. "Zarkich!" he shouted. *"Nyet! Poost on valeet! Nyet!"*

The gasping sounds below turned to a dry rattle as Zarkich's bagpipe pushed out its last reserve of air.

Slepkin shouted again. Zarkich ignored him. More noise and someone—perhaps that old fool upstairs—would call the blasted city militia! "Zarkich! Drop!" He toyed with the idea of shooting them both. His Makarov was there in his hand, awaiting its marching orders.

Then a sound so small that only his reflexes noted it came from behind him. His instinct knew before his analytical mind caught up that he had made a foolish, and very possibly fatal, mistake. Before he could turn, a different voice spoke. *"Haroshaya eedyeya,"* said the new voice. "Drop it. *Myedlenna."*

Slepkin spun to face George Parrum and a silenced Beretta aimed at his eyes, the silencer a perfect, black *0.*

Slepkin's pistol hand twitched for an instant, then eased the Makarov down to the floor. *Zarkich!* he seethed. *I should have shot him while I could!*

Parrum motioned for him to move away from the weapon. He stood back up and saw Parrum's smile in the hallway gloom. He saw that smile flicker in doubt, then surprise. Slepkin wavered, feeling the seductive whisper of escape in Parrum's diverted expression.

"Jesus!" Parrum watched as a heavy white object hurtled down behind Slepkin toward the vestibule below. It was an object so familiar, yet so completely out of place, that Parrum could not erase the look of wonder the flying toilet tank lid had painted on his face. The heavy old artifact landed with a wet thud below, sounding for all the world like a watermelon dropped from on high. The thud instantly resolved with an almost musical crack as the lid disintegrated into jagged shards. He looked up and only caught the edge of a tattered bathrobe retreating into the shadows. A door slammed shut.

Slepkin's thighs tensed, his arm ready to strike. But Parrum's hand, and the Beretta, remained firm. The sounds of struggle and slow strangulation from below had stopped.

"Brasai aroozhie!" Parrum ordered.

Slepkin winced. "My English is better than your Russian, Mr. Parrum," he said, though he turned just the same. He saw the surprise on Parrum's face. "Yes. I know who you are."

"Fine. Then put your hands together on the railing," Parrum said as he pulled a handful of heavy nylon ties from his pocket. "Your wrists together, please. Now," said Parrum, "let's make it even. Who are you?" When Slepkin remained silent, he pulled the thick bands tight, then tighter until the Russian's pale hands turned bright red.

"You are in a great deal of trouble," he said with a wince. He was able to glance down the stairwell. Zarkich's shoes could just be seen. There was shattered white ceramic everywhere. Parrum drew the ties even tighter. "This is Moscow. Not your own Washington. This is my ground, and you would do well to remember this."

"Oh, I doubt I'll forget tonight. Not for a long, long time," Parrum said as he patted him down. He found Slepkin's wallet and flipped it open. The red-edged KGB identity card was impossible to miss. "Your credentials don't seem up to date, Colonel Slepkin. They say you belong someplace called Serpukhov if I read this right. What happened? Lose your way? Hell of a dark night out there."

"You are making a very large mistake."

"Not by the looks of things."

"Parrum?" came a voice from behind. "George? You shot her! What in the name of God is happening with—"

"Stay with the woman," he ordered Gallagher, his attentions still focused on Slepkin. Parrum slipped the nylon ties around Slepkin's ankles and pulled them tight to the railing. "I suppose you'd say that wraps it up." He picked up the Makarov, safetied it, and thrust it into his pocket. Only then did he look behind to see Gallagher crouched over Elena's body.

It was then that Wilkerson came staggering up the stairs, his face still beet red, a raw bruise around his neck. Jagged pieces of white ceramic covered his dark suit jacket. He was still wheezing when he came up to the second-floor landing. Parrum looked down beyond him. Even in the dim light of the hallway, the extravagant halo of gore and broken ceramic that surrounded Zarkich's ruined head told Parrum all he needed to know. Zarkich's legs were splayed in a manner no living man could duplicate, not even the most limber of acrobats, the most clever of magicians. He shook his head as Wilkerson tried to breathe through his swollen windpipe.

"You have a hell of a sense of timing," said Parrum.

Wilkerson squinted, trying to force his eyes to focus.

"You people never know when to keep your fingers out of a real operation," Parrum continued as he snapped the load of rounds out of the Beretta and began threading on another Pentatholite head. "You think you can do your job by writing memos. Covering your asses. Well, sometimes you can"—he gave the dart head a final twist—"and sometimes you can't."

"What . . ." Wilkerson wheezed, "what is this . . ." He stopped when he saw the Pentatholite rise level with his chest. "No," he said, backing away from Parrum. He came to the edge of the landing and stopped. "You can't . . . I . . . I order . . ."

"You can't order me to do squat," said Parrum. "Not anymore."

"You can't . . . do this!" Wilkerson croaked.

"Watch me." The Pentatholite spit, the Beretta bucked back, and the powerful dart buried itself into Wilkerson's stomach. Wilkerson was down before the look of astonishment left his face.

Slepkin's muscles had tensed to deflect the bullet he was sure had been fired at him. When the sharp spit of the shot died away, he opened his eyes in surprise at finding the dim world of a Moscow tenement hall still before him. "You will make a great error if you take Academician Pasvalys. Your own people will hunt you down!

Haven't you heard? You need us now. We cooperate.''

"I'll be sure to look for you at the company picnic," Parrum said, chuckling.

"No effort will be spared to retrieve her."

"Thanks for the warning," said Parrum as he checked the security of Slepkin's bonds. "But I think I'll have to leave that decision in her hands. After all," he lied, "I'm only helping her get what she said she wanted. She planned this whole thing. Not us."

That whore, Slepkin thought. He forced himself back under control. "I . . . I do not follow you."

Parrum took an especially long tie and wrapped it around Slepkin's neck. He fed it through the railing and cinched it tight.

"No," Parrum replied. "That's right. You don't." He chuckled and turned away at last to face the apartment. "Okay, Doc," he called in, "let's help the little lady out."

There was no answer from within. He sighed. He expected to have to deal with Gallagher at some time, but right here and right now didn't qualify as prime time. "Dr. Gallagher?" he said. Still there was no answer. He turned back to Slepkin. "Don't go anywhere," he said with a smirk.

Slepkin kept his face utterly blank as Parrum left him trussed up to the railing.

"Gallagher?" Parrum stepped inside the apartment. The room was empty. Gallagher and Elena were gone. "God damn you." He rushed to the communicating room. *Empty.* Even as he ran to the window leading out to the fire escape, he knew deep in his gut what he would see.

He threw the wooden sash open just as the engine in Slepkin's Chaika roared to life, and then, in a squeal of tires and a flash of headlights, it dove into the dark tunnel leading out onto Archipova Street. "God damn you," said Parrum again. "God damn you."

19

Saturday Morning,
4 August 1990

Gallagher didn't look back as he gunned the Chaika through the tunnel and out onto the narrow alley that led to Archipova Street. Would Parrum follow? Would the man who had held a gun to his chest get word to his superiors? Was every cop in Moscow looking for him right this instant? *Forget it.* All that would come later. This was now.

He pressed his foot hard against the accelerator as though he knew where he and Elena were headed; as though he had a clear destination in mind. He didn't. Other than that he was leaving both Parrum and Slepkin behind, he didn't have a clue. It was instinct, a reaction to Parrum's lies, to the bruises on Elena's face, to the horrible instant when he was sure Parrum had shot and killed her.

He swung around a tight bend in the alley and immediately felt the tires lose their grip and begin to slide on the slick paving stones. Slepkin's car fishtailed, striking a row of bins with a clatter and crunch of thin metal. Lights came on from above. He slammed the shifter into first and moved off once more, slowing only long enough to glance back at Elena. She was still stretched out the length of the rear seat. He heard her moan softly, still under the spell of the Pentatholite dart.

He revved the Chaika's powerful engine and shifted up into second gear. Ahead, the alley opened up onto Archipova Street, and a pale orange glow cast by a burning lamp illuminated the scene. As he came to the juncture, Gallagher stomped on the brake pedal. It went straight to the floor, hardly slowing them at all. *Oh, shit.*

They shot out onto Archipova like a battered pellet from the gun barrel of the alley. The heavy Chaika kept on going. It bounced over the crown, over the concrete divider. For a brief moment, all four wheels were aloft, and once more Gallagher was a pilot.

He downshifted as they landed hard on the other side of the divide. A brief indignant shriek erupted from the transmission, but the solid Russian gearing held. They slowed, back in control. Gallagher swung back across the divider and turned north. *Now what?* He was in the center of Moscow, in the middle of the Soviet Union. If the police weren't after him already, they shortly would be. Even if he knew where to go, to hide, he didn't know how to get there.

He pulled over and ground the weak brakes until they snubbed the heavy car to a stop. The motor surged as Gallagher's brain raced ahead. His thoughts flew by so fast he could scarcely identify them. *The Embassy?* he wondered. Where the hell was it, anyway? He could hardly pull over in a battered official's car and ask the first policeman, could he? He turned to see Elena again. No, he'd wind up ice fishing before he ever saw the American Embassy.

The Savoy? His passport was there, and thus his passage out of the country. But wouldn't they be there, waiting for him? He willed his thoughts to slow just as he would before flying a complicated series of aerobatic figures. The dim outline of a plan rose through his panic. *I wonder.* Then, as if by its own volition, his hand engaged the shifter. He swung the thick steering wheel, and the Chaika pulled away from the curb.

As the darkness of a deserted park appeared dead ahead, Gallagher realized he *did* have a destination. Like a sheltered cove, it was the one place he and every other aviator could call home, regardless of the city, the nation; the image of a bright orange wind sock swam up from his memory, bright orange waving against green grass.

No one stopped the official car. Bending his course north by west, he came to the huge expanse of Leningradskaya Prospekt. Turning west, he shifted the Chaika into high gear. He didn't slow until he saw the blue sign of the Aeroflot Hotel appear ahead. Behind it was his refuge, his harbor; Moscow Central airfield.

A red Moskvitch with the insignia of the Special Mobile Division painted on its door clattered like a cheap toy through the tunnel leading into the enclosed courtyard. It stopped in front of the doorway to number six, its blue strobe winking.

"Wait for me here," People's Militiaman Arkady Gorin told his partner. *What a fucking night.* Half of Moscow was holding the other half by the throat. Gorin had been a Red Army sergeant for years without seeing as much combat as he had seen in Moscow over the last four months.

It was a cool night, but sweat dripped from the ends of Gorin's droopy mustache. The pale light made his already waxy features seem ready to melt. The blue strobe flashed across the courtyard's walls as he walked up to the door leading into number six Archipova. Someone had called 02, Moscow's emergency number. A fight, they said. So what was new? He squared his beefy shoulders, swiped off the sweat with the cuff of his hot leather jacket, and knocked on the door. He checked his watch as he waited. The imitation gold sparkled with the blue light of the police strobe. He knocked again.

He was about to push it open when something made him pause, to wonder whether perhaps this was something more real than normal, more real and more dangerous. He unsnapped the cover to his sidearm. With the toe of his boot, he pushed the door open.

Mother of God, he swore. He didn't need to bother feeling for a pulse; the man sprawled within was dead. The murder weapon was just as obvious. The white fragments of a ceramic toilet lid were scattered everywhere. Gorin looked up into the dim stairwell, then back down. The matted blood, the pulpy softness to the crown of the head, the impossible angle of the corpse's legs, told Gorin all he needed to know. He slipped his pistol out and carefully eased his way inside, stepping around Zarkich's body. A fan of wooden matches had been sprayed across the dirty tile floor. Had someone thought of setting a fire to erase the evidence of murder?

He looked up the dim stairs. From the fragments all around him on the floor, he knew that his black jackboots were crunching ceramic, but it sounded altogether too much like shattered bone. *This is going to be a very long night,* he thought as he climbed the stairs.

He found a second body sprawled on the landing, and tied to the railing, mad as a bottled demon, he found Slepkin.

"It took you fools long enough. Release me!" Slepkin's usually loose face had the tight, stretched look of a balloon about to explode. "Did Teplyystan send you?" he asked, referring to KGB headquarters.

"No," said Gorin. Was this a Mafia murder? A falling out of drug smugglers? Pimps? Everyone was in business for himself these days. Anything was possible in this dingy little corner of the old Jewish section of town. "Your name?"

Slepkin seethed. "The pertinent initials are simple, comrade. Even for a turnip-headed militiaman! They are K . . . G . . . B."

"Your name and branch," Gorin demanded, unconvinced. What would the fancy-pants KGB be up to in this place?

Slepkin clamped his jaw and spat his name through his teeth. "Slepkin. Col. Nikolai Slepkin. Ninth Directorate, chief of security at . . . at a place I will not tell the likes of an ignorant farm boy two sizes too big for his leather jacket!"

"Who is this one?" Gorin nodded at Wilkerson.

"How the devil should I know? He isn't dead. Just tranquilized. You'll find the dart someplace around him."

"Dart?" These were deep waters for a militiaman. Gorin turned to face the open door of the apartment. "Anybody inside?"

"Not anymore," said Slepkin angrily. He had heard the sound of his Chaika revving up down below, and he rather doubted George

Parrum had waited around for the next available ride. "They took my car. We have to stop them."

"Keep your shirt on." Gorin kept his weapon covering Slepkin. He eyed the empty interior of the apartment and turned his attentions back to the body sprawled next to Slepkin on the landing. *And who are you?* he wondered as he opened Wilkerson's suit jacket, noting its fine wool as evidence pointing outside the borders of the USSR. That meant it could be Mafia, or KGB. Either one was equally likely.

Oh! he pulled his hand away when he felt the heartbeat. *This one is alive!* He removed the thin wallet, noticing a tiny pinprick of blood on the man's shirt, and flipped it open. The words *United States* were printed on the plastic Embassy ID card. What a night! A call on 02 coming at the end of his shift; a man with his head caved in by a toilet cover; a drugged American diplomat. And one Russian left alive who claimed . . .

"Well?" Slepkin demanded. "Are you quite finished?"

"All right." Gorin gave in to the obvious. He reached for his pocketknife and sliced the nylon ties at Slepkin's neck.

Slepkin held up his wrists. "The hands. Be quick or you will wish you had been." The knife snicked the ties and Slepkin rubbed life back into his cold, cramped hands. "Once more," he ordered, and the officer cut the final tie wraps securing his ankles. "Very well," he said darkly. "You *may* survive if your bumbling has not cost us. I don't suppose there is a radio in your car? Did anyone see the criminals responsible for all of this? They left in my Chaika."

"There is a radio," Gorin said, helping Slepkin to his feet. "But there is nothing down in the courtyard."

"Very well then," said Slepkin, making an exaggerated move to straighten his tie. "We must act quickly. Give the GAI the alarm to seal off the roads to the countryside." The GAI was Moscow's ubiquitous traffic police. "They must know all the best places."

"Colonel Slepkin, an American diplomat has been shot. That places us in a very different—"

"Not shot, fool. Darted. I told you as much. . . ." But then he stopped. "An American diplomat? Let's see what we have in our net." He was feeling better by the second. Issuing commands had a medicinal effect on Slepkin.

He read Wilkerson's Embassy ID. "Bait. But take him in all the same." Slepkin pocketed Wilkerson's papers. "You did not see these. As far as you know, he is an unknown suspect accused of murdering my partner."

"The one below is also KGB?" asked Gorin. By now he was willing to believe anything if it meant Slepkin would take responsibility.

"Was," Slepkin replied disgustedly. "What is important is that we stop them from stealing . . ." He narrowed his eyes. "You said your car has a radio?"

"Yes." Gorin nodded. "What has been stolen?"

"Not what," said Slepkin. "Who." Where would Parrum go with Elena? How would she plan an escape? The American Embassy? *Possibly*. It was not that far away. They would be there already. A sudden thought chilled him. *Gallagher!* The pieces suddenly fell together in his mind. Gallagher was a *pilot*. All color drained from his face as he looked at Gorin.

"Shall I take you out to Teplyystan?" asked the militiaman, referring to the new KGB headquarters outside Moscow.

"No. Contact the GAI. Have them set up roadblocks out of the city. And get me to the Lubyanka as fast as you can."

"Oh, yes." Yuri rolled over and hugged Elena tight to his massive chest. Her firm body possessed just the right amount of softness against him, like a small ball gripped by a powerful hand. "Yesss. . . ."

He smelled her perfume, a deep, rich scent of . . . he stopped and sniffed. Rubber? His eyes popped open. He blinked. "What?" There was no way to mistake the floor of the Sukhoi hangar for a bedroom, any more than the tire he was hugging, the unbroken landing gear of Elena's Sukhoi, could be mistaken for Elena herself.

He scowled and smacked his lips, trying to clear the awful aftertaste left by an entire bottle of Armenian brandy. The bottle lay like a guillotined soldier, a trickle of red fluid issuing from its open neck.

"Acch." He sat up, his head spinning. What time was it? He shoved back his uniform sleeve. The elaborate aviator's chronograph said he had spent the last five hours on the cool concrete floor. "Acch." He focused his eyes, first one, then the other. The hangar seemed to pitch and heave like the deck of a ship at sea. He wrinkled his nose and gagged back the acid bile in his throat. *Women!* he thought. They didn't even have to be around. They could torture you by remote control. He staggered to his feet, leaning on the wing of Elena's Sukhoi. "Too bad, Squirt," he said with a belch of impure alcohol. "You missed the party." He tugged his tie back into some semblance of order, buttoned his jacket, and with a cursory swipe at the dust on his pants, he weaved his way toward the partially open hangar door.

Gallagher turned onto the small access road leading to the airfield, bypassing the Hotel Aeroflot. The big white moon of the Metro sign flashed by. Except for a few drunks lingering by the stairs leading down to the subway, Leningradskaya Prospekt was deserted. He swung the Chaika around a bend and doused the headlights. Dead ahead, square in his path, was a red light shining over a security gate. A small white light glowed from the guard booth's shack.

Once the guard had saluted Gallagher. That was in the black Mercedes. Now Gallagher was in a stolen police car in the middle of the night, with Elena still under the influence of the powerful Pentatholite sedative. What would he do now? He heard her murmur again.

Gallagher slowed and pulled to one side. He reached back and gently jostled her. "Elena?" he whispered.

"Ummm," she replied, her eyes slitted open. *"Gdye . . . Gdye ya . . ."* Her eyes blinked once, again, and closed. "Ummm."

"Great." He looked once more at the guard booth. What would

he say? Indeed, what would he do even if he managed to get through? The airport was a fine place to visit; he had no illusions about its being a wise place to remain. They would be all over this place eventually. But what now?

The rattle of a chain snapped him back to the present. *What's happening?* As he watched, the gate ahead began to roll open. A flashlight blinked on in the guard booth and the door cracked open. Gallagher heard the guard's challenge. After two missed beats of his heart, he realized the guard was talking to someone else.

The guard had been busy reading a copy of the new Polish *Playboy* when the dim night-lights burning across the runway at the Sukhoi hangar flickered. He glanced up and saw that it wasn't another power failure; a man was walking, or trying to walk, across the grass airfield. He hid the magazine—old habits were hard to change—picked up his flashlight, and snapped it on. When he popped open the wooden door, he heard singing. *Singing?* He hit the button to roll open the gate. "Who is there?" he challenged as the rattling chain pulled the gate wide.

The singing stopped. "Who wants to know?" came the insouciant reply.

A drunk, thought the guard with a shake of his head. The Sukhoi workers were always drinking after work; sometimes *during* work. They would fall dead to the world like flies caught in a frost and wake up at all hours, usually on his shift. Didn't they know he had to log the names of everyone passing through during his duty? On the other hand, they usually brought him something to while away the empty hours till dawn. The weaving dark shape stepped into the dim pool of light issuing from the guard booth.

"Women," said Yuri as he stumbled through the gate.

"Halt!" the guard shouted, and stepped out. He flashed his lamp in Yuri's face. "Drinking, is it?"

"Mind your own fucking business," Yuri replied wearily, waving away the bright light that was blinding him.

The guard kept it focused square into his eyes. "Your name!" he demanded. He hadn't caught a good one in months. And an officer! "What is your name?"

"Gorbachev," Yuri answered with a snort. "But you can call me Misha. Now get that fucking light away from my face or I'll make you eat it." He started walking again.

"I said to halt! You are in a forbidden area. I will have to make a report." Suddenly, a dark mass eclipsed the lights of the runway, blotted out the stars.

"Then I will give you something worth reporting," growled Yuri. He grabbed the guard by his jacket. The flashlight tumbled. Something whistled in the air like an approaching artillery shell.

The next thing the guard knew, the stars came out once more, swirling galaxies, entire universes of flashing, twinkling stars.

"Toothpicks." Yuri stumbled through the gate and weaved his way down the road toward the hotel. He came to a parked car, a black Chaika. *Who would leave a car parked out here?* he wondered groggily. "Fucking VIP," he muttered. Propping himself up with one hand, he unbuttoned his fly and urinated on its tire. "Fucking poison. I swear I'll never—"

Suddenly, the engine roared to life and the headlights came on. In the reflected glow, Yuri saw Gallagher in the front seat. But that was not significant. He didn't know him.

The woman lying flat in the back was another matter entirely.

"Elena?" The Chaika roared off toward the open gate to the airfield. "Elena?" He pivoted to follow the speeding car. His mouth open, his boots splashed, Yuri watched it go. "Hey!" he shouted. "Hey!"

The two militiamen drove straight for Dzerzhinsky Square, the wheezy little Moskvitch seemingly propelled as much by blue oil fumes as its small engine. "Get those lazy bastards at GAI moving!" said Slepkin as he jumped out. The blue strobe flashed across a high, dark wall of a building, as sheer and as black as a curling breaker rushing out of the night.

Militiaman Arkady Gorin watched the wiry figure run for the

ornate building that stood guard over the square. "KGB," he said to his partner, and reached for the radio. "Mobile unit four," he transmitted back to his station.

"Go ahead, four," came a sleepy reply.

"You'd better get a pencil," said Gorin. "You'll never believe this one."

Slepkin pounded up the stairs of the old, prewar insurance firm that had been, for most of its life, the very nexus of the Soviet police state: Lubyanka Prison. The former headquarters of the Committee for State Security, it had been displaced when the KGB moved into a more commodious, and far less ominous, campus out in a placid Moscow suburb. It still served as the Committee's in-town head-quarters.

It took ten minutes of waiting on the telephone to rouse the Hotel Aeroflot's security detail. It took another five to get the night-duty reaction team from the Seventh Directorate moving in from Tep-lyystan. As he waited for the two black-jacketed "action" men from Seventh, Slepkin confirmed that the Moscow Traffic Police, the GAI, were looking for his car and its occupants. All roads from the city had been sealed, even the ferry terminals.

A half hour after his arrival, two men appeared at the door to the office he had commandeered. "You took long enough," he said to them. "Let's go."

Even by daylight, the men from the KGB's Seventh Directorate tended to look alike. Their matching leather coats exaggerated this effect, as did their matching, pallid faces, each puffy with sleep. As they ran down the stone stairs toward the street, Slepkin decided that the first would be Dragunov, named for the powerful sniper rifle he carried cradled in his arms; the second would be Rockets, for the RPG-7 he had thoughtfully brought along. The steel tube of the antitank weapon was placed in the trunk, along with a brace of bowling-pin-shaped rockets.

Thirty-five minutes after Slepkin had arrived, Rockets brought to life the powerful motor of their vehicle. Dragunov was in the front right seat. Slepkin sat in the back. They were driving an Interceptor, a specially modified Volga sedan. The car had a big Chaika engine up front, ballast in the back, and was built to outpace anything on the road.

"So where are they?" asked Dragunov as he snapped the big nightsight onto the sniper rifle.

"Moscow Central airfield," Slepkin ordered.

20

Saturday Morning, 4 August 1990

This had better be it, thought Parrum as he pulled the black Mercedes into the far back of the hotel parking lot. The lights of the Hotel Aeroflot didn't reach this far, and the car blended perfectly with the night. *This had goddamned better be it.* Parrum was on the thinnest of edges, and it all came down to this one place, this one time. Either Gallagher had run to ground here, or everything, the entire operation, was burned. He remembered that Wilkerson had told him as he handed over the keys to number six Archipova. *If you start smoking,* the station chief had said with that superior smirk Parrum found so irritating, *don't come here yelling fire.*

Smart-ass. He hoped the locals would wonder why an official from the Embassy was fast asleep on the second-floor landing of number six Archipova. He hoped they would wonder good and long. *Chew slowly, comrades,* he thought with an evil smile. He put the thought away for later. There was business to be taken care of, and its name was Gallagher.

Parrum had stopped by the Hotel Savoy first; no one had seen Gallagher. Then the American Embassy. All the lights were out on its ten-story facade, and the militiamen posted at the front steps were in their boxes, asleep. A moment of alarm jangled Parrum's nerves. *If that damned fool took to the roads,* he thought, but then he shook his head. His gut had never steered him wrong. Gallagher was a pilot. He looked back across the darkened airfield. Where else would a pilot go?

He pulled out a pair of binoculars. From where he had parked, he had a direct view through the chain-link fence out onto the dark rectangle of grass that was Moscow Central airfield. Faint blue edge lights showed its outline. At the far end of the field, the tall fin of the enormous Antonov transport poked up higher than the surrounding apartment buildings.

Closer in, directly across the field, a band of illumination showed through the doors to the Sukhoi hangar. But as he watched it, it seemed to grow thinner, waning like a sliver moon. Someone was closing those doors!

He focused on the partially open doors. *There.* The taillights of a car showed in the instant before the doors closed. It was Slepkin's Chaika all right! But he had seen something else, too; a quick, almost subliminal flash of motion just before the light winked out. *Got you,* he said to himself. A figure had passed through the beam of light and was gone, but Parrum knew that profile all too well.

He pulled out the Beretta 92F. There would be no more mistakes of trust; there was no time, no room, for errors now. Gallagher was going to get a fast lesson in following orders.

He checked that the gun's magazine held a full load. Fifteen rounds gleamed from the magazine's telltales. He put it down on the seat, reached up, and disconnected the dome light by crushing the bulb in his fingers. With the 92F in a cool, firm grip, he quietly opened the Mercedes's door and slid out of his seat. Parrum edged his way toward the perimeter fence. *It all comes down to one sharp point,* he thought as he climbed over the top.

The four cardinal elements of an officer's universe were observation, competence, stealth, and force. The first three had been employed to no effect. It was time for the last.

Yuri came to the hangar doors just as the motor that was closing them ceased its whine. "Shit," he cursed as he tried to pry open the doors with his fingers. He put his shoulder to them. They shook but would not open. He briefly considered leaving this place and Elena Pasvalys behind. Why should he go to any trouble, anyway? She had been stretched out on the backseat of that Chaika like some incautious village girl after a squadron party. Was that it? Had the mess in her room been a party, a party that he, Col. Yuri Komarov, captain of the largest airplane in all the world, had not been invited to? *No. Not Elena.* He growled and kicked the door. "Open up!" he shouted, and lunged again.

Gallagher froze. "Christ." Someone had seen them after all! He threw the hook that locked both hangar doors together as another powerful lunge slammed against the metal. The boom echoed through the hangar, followed by another shout. He looked up at the scattered night-lights. Their yellow beams reflected off the crimson skin of Elena's damaged Sukhoi. The black Chaika sat like a frozen, three-dimensional shadow. A third impact nearly threw the heavy hangar doors off their rails. The silence that followed energized him. *Lock the other goddamned doors!* Leaving Elena behind, he ran for the back of the big hangar.

The main work area was surrounded by smaller, glassed-in workshops. A corridor ran straight back to the other end, offices springing off to either side. Another thump, another curse. Pigeons fluttered through the rafters, their sleep disturbed by the commotion below.

Gallagher came to an outside door and grabbed the knob, checking that it was locked. He hurried through a designer's area, tables mounded with blueprints and the air stinging with copying ammonia. Its door was also locked. The offices wouldn't have outside entrances. The main door at the far back of the hangar was last. Gallagher ran for it like a sprinter off the block. A stippled glass pane let through the weak glow of a small night-light over the doorway. As he reached for the knob, a looming black shadow suddenly blotted out the feeble light. The door burst open in his face, its swing pinning Gallagher against the wall.

"Elena!" shouted Yuri as he rumbled in, oblivious to Gallagher's presence behind the glass. "Elena Pasvalys!" Her name echoed over and over through the arched hangar as Yuri stomped in, his head swiveling with the slow, implacable motion of a tank turret. "Hey, Squirt! Where are you?"

Gallagher watched as he marched down the corridor and out onto the main hangar floor. He let out his breath with a gasp. It was over. He had been found. He could run for it! He *should* run for it! He heard the Chaika's car door squeak open. Elena's face came back to him, her light body in his arms as he brought her out from number six Archipova, away from Parrum, away from the others who had beaten her. Away from the red-haired man with the gun. *Run!* his every sense shouted. His thigh muscles tingled with energy, ready. *No.* Slowly, his Nikes silent on the concrete floor, he made his way back toward Elena.

"Hey," said Yuri, shaking Elena by the shoulder, "wake up! It's me! Where've you been?" He noticed Gallagher's duffel bag behind her head.

"Ummm," she replied, her eyes still closed. "*Bayushki, bayu* . . ." She rolled off the duffel and nearly fell into the Chaika's footwell.

Yuri pushed her back. "Forget the lullabies." Yuri shook her again. "What's wrong with you, Elena? Drunk?" He leaned down and placed his face next to hers and sniffed. No, there was no smell of booze. So what was wrong with her? *What is this?* he thought when he noticed her bruised face. He touched her neck and felt the slow, thudding pump of her heart. *So slow!* He ran his palm down her puffy cheek, feeling the heat rise from the ugly red splotches. Then he noticed her torn dress. *This* was no party. Someone had beaten his Elena! *Beaten!* Yuri clenched his teeth, but it didn't stop the growl from seeping by. "Elena," he whispered, his face still close to hers, "come on. Wake up. Who did this to you? Who did this? Tell me and I will—"

"She's okay," said Gallagher. "It's just . . ."

Yuri stood up fast, slamming his head against the roof of the

Chaika. The car lifted off its suspension, but Yuri didn't seem to notice. *This* was the one he had seen driving the car! He balled his fist and moved in on Gallagher. "You skinny little bastard!" he shouted. "You want to hit someone? Eh?" He lazily swiped the air as Gallagher danced back. "You want to fight? You like that?" Another slow swing described an arc through the air. "Well? Let's see you fight, toothpick! Or do you only hit girls?" Yuri put both his hands in the air, inviting Gallagher to do his worst. "Hit me!"

"Listen to me!" said Gallagher. "I'm only trying to—"

"English?" said Yuri, only now realizing that Gallagher was a foreigner. "I hate English!" he roared. "You fuck boys and hit girls, is that it, English? *Hit me!*" Suddenly, Yuri's eyebrows knitted together.

Gallagher saw the blow coming and snapped his head back as a massive fist whistled by close enough for him to feel its wake. "I didn't hit anybody!" he shouted as he ran for cover on the far side of the Chaika, keeping the car between him and this menacing creature. "You don't understand!"

"No? Then tell me close. Stand still!" Yuri commanded as he jumped onto the Chaika's hood. The metal dished in as he pounded onto the car's roof after Gallagher. "What's wrong, English? Afraid to hit boys?" He waved his fist at Gallagher. "I will send you home tonight all by myself!"

"I didn't hit her!"

"You lie." Yuri's eyebrows knitted together again.

This time Gallagher didn't wait. He sprang back behind the wing of Elena's Sukhoi as Yuri pounced. The big man landed heavily, his eyes never wavering from Gallagher as though they were gyro-stabilized. How could anyone that big move so fast, so light? "Listen to me!" he shouted as Yuri moved back into range. "I didn't hit her! I took her away from the ones who—" He backed away as Yuri kept coming. His shoe struck the extended foot of a wing jack. He scrambled for a handhold as he fell, but his hand just slid along the ultrasmooth surface of Elena's wing. His head struck the concrete floor, dazzling him for an instant. Then, the high yellow night-lights were blotted out by the solid overcast of Col. Yuri Komarov.

"I wonder. How shall I do this?" said Yuri, his fist to his chin. "Piece by piece, or maybe just flatten you? It would be cheap to mail you home in a letter, yes?"

Gallagher tried to scramble under Elena's Sukhoi, but Yuri simply pinned him to the ground with a boot to his chest. "How many ribs has the English?" he asked. "Let me see if I remember my counting lessons. I start with one."

The pressure on Gallagher's chest suddenly doubled. He heard a whoosh and a creak as the air was driven from his chest. A knifeblade of pain cut straight through him, slicing off all feeling below the mass bearing down on him. He clutched at Yuri's ankle, but it was solid as a foundation pier. Gallagher felt the rib loosening, letting go, getting ready to shatter. Gallagher's vision began to tunnel, dark edges creeping in, his head ready to burst, the roar of surf loud in his ears.

A faint sound like a distant birdcall filtered into Gallagher's ears. "Yuri . . ." The pressure paused. The voice came again, stronger this time. "Yuri."

Yuri swung his head. Elena was sitting up in the backseat of the Chaika! "Elena!"

"No . . ." she said, her head swaying, her arms propping her upright. Her eyes wandered eccentric orbits, the world shifting around and around like a kaleidoscope. "No . . ."

"Wait and I will be right there! First there is a little bug I must crush. Where was I? Oh, yes. One." The boot ground down onto Gallagher's rib cage.

"Yuri," she said again, her head bobbing as though it teetered on a tiny balance, "don't. He's . . . he's not . . . he didn't . . . do this."

"Eh?" Yuri looked up. "What?"

Elena closed her eyes. It made speaking easier. "It was the other, not him. Don't . . ."

"You mean this little twig didn't beat you up? Then why were you with him?" The pressure on Gallagher's chest eased.

"I . . . I don't remember. I can't think, damn it!" She swung her head, her eyes still closed, then sat back up. Each breath of clean air seemed to drive away the heavy, rancid fog that clouded her brain. She opened her eyes again, and this time, she brought them both into focus. "Yuri, it was Slepkin, not him." She paused and licked her dry lips. "It was Slepkin, it was his . . . it was Zarkich and . . . Let Gallagher go."

"Gallagher?" Yuri took another few tons of pressure off Gallagher's chest. "The English is Gallagher?"

"American," she said as a sudden wave of nausea rose up her throat. She leaned down and put her head between her knees.

Gallagher heard his name. How many ribs did he have? Wouldn't it be just as easy to break them all at once? How could he get the message across that it would be all right to break them all at once? If he was really lucky, one would puncture a lung, or better yet, his heart. But then the weight was gone. Gone! *Am I dead?* he wondered. His brain commanded his lungs to breathe. *Not dead.*

With a rattling gasp, Gallagher sucked in air. It scorched his chest as it filled up his lungs. The next was easier.

"Elena," said Yuri as he leaned down. She had her head in her hands. "Are you sure? Are you all right? Who is this Slepkin?"

"*Stukach,*" she whispered, her head still between her knees. "KGB."

"Them? Those goons beat you up? Why?"

Elena looked up. Her face was streaked with tears. "Yuri, don't . . . don't . . ."

"Don't what?" he asked, moving closer.

"Don't let them get me. Please. Promise that you won't let . . ."

"Quiet." He cradled her, patting her sweaty hair. "Don't worry, Squirt. You're safe with me. I won't let them even *think* of you. You're safe, understand? Safe."

She looked up, her blue eyes brimming. Elena shook her head.

"No? What is no?" asked Yuri.

She looked over at Gallagher as he slowly gathered his legs to stand.

Yuri followed her gaze. "Hey. Sorry, English," he said as

Gallagher staggered to his feet. "I thought you hit my friend. I am sorry. Okay? Sorry, yes?"

Gallagher nodded and held his hand up as though it had been a simple misunderstanding over a parking space.

Yuri turned back to Elena. She had her hand across her face. Sweat began to bead at her brow. Her skin was hot and flushed. "What is it, Elena? What's wrong now?"

"I . . . " she began, then stopped, shaking her head. "I can't stay here." She looked up at him, and something of the old fire was in her eyes. "Yuri, I can't stay here."

"No problem." Yuri nodded. "I'll carry you back to the hotel. You need to change your clothes anyway, yes?"

Elena looked down at the tears in her black silk dress. It was ruined.

"A little rest, a little food, some wine, and by—"

"No," she interrupted him. "I can't stay in Moscow. They'll come for me. I have to get out."

"Get out? Where? Ah. Of course!" He snapped his fingers. "You want to go back to Serpukhov. Where better to rest than in your own place? We'll take this car. You'll be asleep in your own bed in no time, and then we can—"

"No," she interrupted again.

"What is this with all the nos?" Yuri asked, frustrated. "No this, no that. What is so wrong?" What was Elena saying?

She looked at Gallagher. "Why did you do this?" she asked him in English. "Why have you ruined me?"

"Ruined?" he said as he walked up to the Chaika and pulled out his brown duffel. He unzipped it and drew out his spare flightsuit. "That's a joke, right? Here," he said, handing the green one-piece outfit to her, "you can wear this until you get some new clothes. It's a mite big, but you can fold it up some."

She didn't make a move to take the garment. "Why did you come, Gallagher? Why did you make it so I had no place to go?"

"Whoa, I came here so you *would* have a place to go. That's what defecting is all—"

"Defecting?" she said, her voice nearly normal, her eyes clear and hot. *"Defecting?"*

Yuri misunderstood. "He wants to live *here?"*

"When I heard you wanted to come out, I thought, well, I mean," Gallagher stammered, "it isn't exactly my line of work, right? But I thought I could help. It seemed like the right time, the right place and all. I thought I could help you get out and do the world a real favor." He folded the flightsuit over his arm.

"Me? You think *I* want to defect? Are you *insane?"*

Gallagher smiled and formed a ready answer. It didn't make it by his throat. *Oh, my God,* he thought, a hammer of truth striking him like one of Yuri's fists. *Oh, my God.*

The Volga Interceptor skidded as it swung off Leningradskaya Prospekt and onto Aeroport Road. "What makes you think they're here?" asked the RPG man as he roared up the access road, passing the hotel and the small parking lot at its rear.

"My nose," said Slepkin.

They blasted through a gap between two old hangars toward the security gate. The Interceptor's headlights pinned the guard booth in its glare. A man was sitting on the ground, feeling around for something.

"Who is that?" asked the one with the Dragunov sniper rifle.

"Some old fart of a pensioner drinking through guard duty," muttered Rockets as he brought the powerful car to a stop.

The guard looked into the high beams, squinting as the two Seventh Directorate men got out. Dragunov centered the man's forehead in his starscope as Rockets hovered near him menacingly.

"Hey!" the guard protested. "Who do you think you are? Where are my damned glasses anyway. . . ."

"Up, old man," said Rockets. "Or else we'll pension you right here and now." The Seventh Directorate man hauled back and kicked him with the pointy toe of his boot.

"Ow! Help! Hooligans!" the guard shouted. Rockets kicked him again. "Ow!"

"Who did this to you?" asked Slepkin as he eyed the quiet airfield.

"What is the world coming to?" said the guard as Rockets yanked him to his feet. "No respect for the law. No respect for—"

"We *are* the law," said Slepkin. "Once more, and then you come back to the Lubyanka for questioning. Who came this way?"

"Lubyanka?" The guard's eyes went wide and white as two full moons. "KGB, is it? About time you got here. I fought them off, I did! A whole gang of them! But one came up behind and—"

"The truth," said Slepkin. Rockets grabbed the guard's loose stomach flesh and began to twist.

"Ow! Hey! All right! All right!"

Rockets gave the guard another vicious twist, then let go.

"Well?" asked Slepkin.

"It was a soldier. An *officer.*" Rockets grabbed his flesh again. "No! I mean it! As God bears witness! It was an Air Force officer. He'd been drinking. He came from over there." The guard pointed at the Sukhoi hangar. Dim yellow lights showed through its upper windows. It was dead quiet. "When I tried to stop him, he hit me. Now where are my damned glasses?"

"I think I see them," said Rockets as he ground his boot on them. The lenses crunched; he held up the bent frames. "Here you go."

"Movement," said the man with the SVD Dragunov. The sniper rifle was in his arms as he peered out across the darkened airstrip. He chambered one of the 7.62-mm rounds with a soft, well-oiled click.

"Are you sure there's just one?" said Slepkin.

"One. He's low-crawling." The rifle tracked slowly, following the furtive figure moving toward the Sukhoi hangar.

"Crawling? He's just drunk!" the guard crowed. "You see! I was telling—"

"Let's go find out who it is," Slepkin said as he got back into the Volga Interceptor. They moved off, leaving the puzzled and somewhat dazed guard behind. The headlights swept the airfield, splashing across the Sukhoi hangar. *If someone is in there . . .* thought

Slepkin. He leaned forward and tapped Rockets on the shoulder. "We'll use the starscope. Kill the lights." The brilliant beams went out as they gunned across the grass strip.

"Running," said Dragunov as he peered into the starscope, the muzzle pointed out the open window.

"Shoot him," said Slepkin. The Interceptor surged ahead. "Not to kill. I want him talking."

The play of lights flashed through the hangar rafters, then went out. "Someone is here," said Yuri, but Elena didn't pay him any attention. Still groggy with the aftereffects of the Pentatholite dart, she nevertheless looked ready to leap up from the backseat of the Chaika and bite Gallagher in two.

Gallagher saw the lights in the corner of his eye. He glanced up, then back down at Elena. "I'm sorry, Elena," he said at last. "I didn't know. I was told—"

"You were told a lie! What did you expect, you idiot?" she said, her jaw lined with tensed muscles. "What are you, a puppy dog? Sit! Roll over! Can't you think for yourself? It was *obvious.*"

"Maybe to you. I thought—"

"Elena," said Yuri, "perhaps we should continue this someplace else? Someone has just come through the gates." He turned to face the locked hangar door. They wouldn't be coming in *that* way. He looked down the corridor to the open glass door he had used. Then what? His eyebrows arched as he chewed on an idea. *Perhaps.*

"I'm sorry," said Gallagher again. He offered her the flightsuit again.

This time she took it. *"You're sorry!"* she shouted as she got to her feet. "What good will that do now?" She kicked off her shoes and without the slightest bow to modesty, yanked the torn black dress over her head and threw it aside.

The huge diamond crystal hanging from its chain telegraphed a brilliant spark of light that seemed to bore right into Gallagher's brain. One milky thigh was bruised a deep purple where the Pentatholite dart had bitten.

"Hey, English," Yuri warned, and Gallagher looked away.

"Tell me!" she demanded as she stepped into Gallagher's green flightsuit. "What good is that now!"

Gallagher, standing with his back to her, heard the zipper zip. "I don't know," he said. "I . . . I did my best with what I thought I knew was true. I took you away from them, didn't I?"

"You should have killed me when you had the chance. Over the airfield. It would have been quicker. Better."

"Elena," said Yuri, taking her firmly by the shoulder, "no more talk of killing, okay? We are going. Now."

"Going? Where?"

"Where it's safe. Trust me, Squirt." Yuri strained, listening for the sound of the car he knew was closing in outside. He looked over at Gallagher. "Okay, English, you can turn around now."

Gallagher turned and saw Elena swathed in the tentlike volume of his green flightsuit. A bright red patch over her breast read *Texas Twistoff*. She had rolled up the legs and the arms, and the chest zipper went all the way to her chin.

"Don't tell them you saw us," said Yuri as he guided her away. "Forgive and forget, okay?"

"Where are you going?" asked Gallagher.

"Yuri!" said Elena as she lost her balance.

He swept her up as though she were weightless. "You're safe." Yuri flung her over his broad shoulder. "Let the goons spend some time with him," he said to her.

"But . . ."

"So long, English!" he called over his shoulder as he ran across the hangar, leaving Gallagher behind. Elena raised her head, and as they made for the back door, she said something to Yuri. He stopped and shook his head vigorously, then she spoke again, too quiet for Gallagher to hear. Yuri shrugged and turned. "Hey, English!" he called out. "Come with us."

George Parrum has seen the Interceptor pause at the main gate to the field and immediately dropped flat to the grass, slithering through the stubble toward the Sukhoi hangar. *Stay busy, comrades,* he wished as he moved along tight to the ground. Silent or fast? It was a toss-up. He chose something halfway between the two. The dark facade of the hangar was close when the lights began to move once again, the sound of the Interceptor's engine roaring as it approached. He gave up on stealth, stood up, and made a run for the shelter of the hangar. The lights swept over his head, then went out. That was a very bad sign. It meant they were equipped for night fighting.

He dove behind a line of empty fuel drums, and in the same instant, a solid shot smashed through the steel, dishing in the barrel with a tremendous clang. Only then did the crack of the rifle sting Parrum's ears. A deep furrow of earth ended at the edge of the hangar's concrete slab, not a foot from Parrum. *Christ!* He scrambled down the line of drums until he got to the last. The Beretta in his hand felt good, but it didn't shorten the ten-foot gap between him and the corner of the hangar. He could hear the Volga's engine come nearer. *One driver, one shooter. Maybe more.* They could see him; he could not return the courtesy. George Parrum's career seemed close to a logical, if premature, end. *Focus!*

His knee brushed against a length of pipe. It wasn't much, but it was all that lady luck was good for. He grabbed it in his left hand and slowly pushed it down the row of drums. Levering it against one of the hangar door stanchions, he raised the pipe until it tapped the farthest drum. He breathed heavily, sucking in air, bunching his muscles, praying that his body would forget its age and remember that life was far too sweet to abandon. He thumbed the Beretta's safety off. He would have one chance. Maybe. He swung the pipe away from the barrel and brought it back in a vicious swing.

The steel boomed as the barrel began to topple. As it fell, Parrum leaped up from behind cover. The Dragunov fired. Parrum didn't even hear the shot. He centered the silenced Beretta on the yellow muzzle flash and snapped off three quick rounds. As a near-miss sparked off the roof of the Volga Interceptor, Parrum turned and ran for the edge of the hangar. Voices shouted from the darkness.

Eight feet to the corner. Five. One. He could hardly believe it when he reached the alley between the hangars. Parrum turned the corner. His feet pounded the grass like engine pistons running wild; his heart shed its years, remembering only the old feeling of invincibility that had melted away so long ago. What if he was trapped in the middle of Moscow, his way out of the country compromised? What if his carefully crafted design had been wrecked by Gallagher, by an amateur? A man, a *professional,* capable of focus, could adapt. *And win,* he silently added as he ran along the rear wall. *And win.*

21

**Saturday Morning,
4 August 1990**

Yuri led the way toward the huge Antonov transport, keeping close by the shadows of the empty, dark hangars. Their shoes were soaked with rain and dew, leaving a dark, clear trail for anyone to follow. The smell of the river Moskva rose with the fog from the marshes at the end of the short runway. "Don't worry, Squirt," Yuri said to Elena as he carried her. "We can think this over. There's always a way, yes?" She was still over his broad shoulders, with Gallagher a few steps behind. "When we get to . . ." He stopped, the first shot freezing him in place; the second, coming a few seconds later, spurred him into a gallop. The rattle of toppling steel drums echoed across the dewy grass.

Gallagher looked back toward the Sukhoi hangar. Who is it? Parrum or the ones who had beaten Elena? When he turned back, Yuri was a good distance away. The big man, for all his bulk, could really move. Gallagher dug in his Nikes and took off after them.

The fuselage of the AN-124 loomed like a steel cliff against the bright stars; its huge drooping wings blotted out the sky. Four enormous engines, each the diameter of a typical airliner's body, hung from those wings, and the entire affair rested on fourteen sets of big low-pressure tires. Gallagher was in awe, but not because of the scale of the beast. How in hell had Yuri landed it on a two-thousand-meter grass strip? *He* had almost missed the field in the tiny Sukhoi! The thought of the blue plane he had only just come to know made him glance across to the far side of the field. There, sleeping under the stars, was *Silky Sue*. Would he ever feel her again?

"Hey, English!" Yuri called from beneath the tail. A boarding ramp had been wheeled up to the metal skin, and a dim red light glowed through the open hatch at its top. "Follow me," he said as he bounded up. The stairs shook under his boots.

Gallagher followed him up. He looked down from the high vantage and saw the sparking blue strobe of a police car arrive at the far end of the airfield. An instant later, a second strobe joined the first. A warm breeze laden with the stink of mud and rotting bracken rose from the river. He glanced up. The stars were the same stars that rode the dry, clear skies above Lawrence Livermore. The same constellations, the same band of the Milky Way. How could everything here be so much the same, yet so different, so foreign, so dangerous? Parrum's face came to him as he watched the firefly streak of a meteorite.

"English! Inside," Yuri ordered him impatiently.

Gallagher turned and stepped into the AN-124. Once Gallagher was in, Yuri closed the heavy pressure-tight door and dogged it with a twist of a massive bar. "This way." Yuri walked forward in the dark and snapped on another red light. Gallagher found it even harder now to imagine that this object was meant to fly. *Jesus!* The Russians sure built them to Texas scale! The Antonov looked like a railroad tunnel bored through solid rock, the curved roof lost in shadow high overhead.

Four Sukhoi 26s, their bright crimson paint dark in the dim light, were chained down to the metal deck up ahead.

To the rear, a larger SU-29, the two-place version of the nimble aerobat flown by the team trainer, Kashum, sat ready to roll out at Switzerland. It looked like something the Antonov had swallowed for an appetizer. Gallagher sniffed the air. Was that gasoline he smelled? Then he saw the big cylindrical tank lashed to the deck. A small puddle had formed beneath it! It was dripping! He put his hand to the cold metal. The tank was indeed filled with fuel, but the dripping was just condensation from Moscow's inescapable humidity.

Yuri motioned for them all to follow him forward to the cockpit. They took a set of wide stairs up from the lower cargo hold into a passenger deck roughly equal to that of any large airliner. Beyond the rows of seats was a sleeping-berth compartment, and ahead of this was a gleaming stainless steel galley, fit to feed a small hotel. Gallagher walked by rows of steel bunks, banks of toilets, the radio cubicle, and just before the final door to the cockpit, the side-facing engineer's station. It wasn't like anything built in the West in the last twenty years. A blizzard of dials and gauges glinted down from above the engineer's seat. How could anyone keep track of all that?

Yuri settled into the front left seat. Gallagher noticed that the blue-painted instrument panel was also crude by Western standards; all the instruments were round-faced and mechanical. Not a CRT anywhere. A museum piece that happened to be brand-new, the Antonov reeked of brute force. For the first time in what seemed like ages, he remembered the Prototype, the optical-image processor he had built back at the Lab. What could the Russians do if they ever joined brute force with sophistication?

"Yuri," said Elena. "I have decided. I have complicated too many things for one night. There is no reason for you to become involved. Your career must not be endangered." Her voice sounded completely normal. Only a lingering nausea and an occasional tic of her eyelid betrayed the last of the sleeping venom in her veins. Her bare feet were tucked beneath her in the copilot's seat.

"No?" Yuri seemed disappointed. "You think I would let that KGB worm harm you?" He looked out the flat expanse of his side window. "Huh?" He had seen the blue police strobes.

She touched his arm. "I know you would protect me. But there is still time for you to stay clear." She saw the streak of blue light outside. "Let me go talk to them."

"Hey, Squirt." He patted her hand. "I made you a promise. You said, 'Don't let them get me,' remember?"

"But that was before—"

"Hush. I can take care of myself. The real question, Elena, is what can be done for you. For years, I have been trying to discover that secret. And now look at all your troubles. I tell you this: if I have to fly you there myself, I will see you safe from the goons who beat you. I gave my word. The world is crazy, Elena, but my word stands.''

"I wish there were a safe place, Yuri. But if there is, I don't know how to find it. Not anymore." Elena knew he would carry her to Zanzibar if she asked. But now it was a matter of his life, too. Not just hers. That was too high a price to pay. "Look, Yuri. Times have changed. They're not all like Slepkin. Someplace there is one who will listen to reason. I know—''

"What do you know?" said Yuri, shaking his head. "You shouldn't believe everything you read. Things are so different? Hah. They are worse.''

Gallagher watched as the blue strobe of a police car nosed along the trail they had left in the wet grass. He remembered how it felt when he was first learning to play chess; the moves narrowing one by one, safe territory suddenly rendered fatal. The angle of his opponent's attack throwing lines of invisible force across his positions like a net, until there was but one corner, one square, left to occupy. Was that what Parrum had done to him? Was that his plan for Elena Pasvalys? He glanced at the sparking blue light. He was fresh out of moves.

"Someone will listen to reason," she said again.

"Excuse me, Elena," Yuri said. "Maybe they would listen to a mere pilot, but not you. Not with everything that is stuffed inside your head. Even I know that much.''

"Just the same," she said, "I think I should go and talk with them.''

What are they saying? Gallagher wondered. "What's going on?" he asked Elena.

"I was saying to him I should go talk with them. I have brought troubles to enough people. Or shall I say, *you* have.''

"The last guy I saw you with didn't seem too interested in chatting.''

Slepkin. She scowled. "You and your schemes. Your envelopes.

Your dirty secrets. You did this to me. Why should Yuri pay a price? Why should *I?*''

"I didn't know," said Gallagher. But she was right. He had played a part in this. Didn't he owe her a way out? He glanced outside. What he saw made him draw in his breath. A pack of police cars were heading straight down the field, away from the Sukhoi hangar. They were heading straight for the Antonov.

Elena closed her eyes as the image of Slepkin's thin smile came back. A wave of nausea rose up her throat.

"Elena! Are you all right?" asked Yuri. "Look, I promise you. There will be a safe . . ."

Gallagher tapped him on his shoulder. It had the same muscular firmness as a bulldog's flanks. "Look out the window."

"What? Oh." Yuri observed with a disdainful eye the police cars gathered around the Antonov like minnows around a whale. *Toys,* he thought. Still, he knew it would not be long now. "Elena," he said, "it is time to do something." He reached overhead, snapped on the ground power switch, and activated the hydraulic accumulators to lock all the Antonov's various hatches and doors. "The more I think of it, the more I dislike Moscow. Such a big, dirty city. So dangerous. I never liked it."

"What are you suggesting?" Far below the behemoth's silver nose, Elena saw men running, fanning out across the grass. Once again a jangle of fear coursed through her. Slepkin had been a pig before; what would he do now?

"That we go elsewhere."

"You mean . . ."

"Yes, of course," said Yuri. "Why not?"

Parrum watched from behind a pile of scrap aluminum, silent, scarcely breathing as the militiaman played his flashlight across the corrugated wall of the old hangar, searching in a desultory fashion. *Idiot,* he thought. His eyes would be ruined for the dark. But not Parrum's. He waited as the man's boots scuffed noisily by, and then, slowly, he raised himself from behind the scrap pile and stepped out into the alley. His shoe caught on a jagged piece of aluminum. He felt the tug before it made a sound. *Damn!* He pushed his shoe back, then forward, but it was still caught. The militiaman was already fifteen paces away.

Parrum hadn't planned to kill; it was always better to avoid that. But a piece of metal no bigger than a plate had doomed the unknown man. Balanced on one foot, Parrum raised the silenced Beretta, centered it on the militiaman's back, slightly up and to the left, and squeezed the trigger.

A minute later, with the man's legs still walking in death, twitching, Parrum left the body hidden behind the scrap pile. He switched the flashlight off. The man's cap and his jacket wouldn't pass close scrutiny on him, but it was dark, and he had been quick to pull the jacket away from the pooling blood. They would have to do.

"Yuri!" shouted Elena when she realized he was serious.

"Hush! Did I not promise?"

"You can't do this!"

"You always say no too quickly, Elena," said Yuri as he glanced out at the runway. Police cars, at least a dozen of them now, were strung across the grass like blue diamonds against velvet. "Listen to me, Elena. If they have you in their hands, you have nothing. If they want you, you have far more to bargain with."

"What's he saying?" asked Gallagher. "What's he suggesting?" Elena and Yuri turned. Neither one answered.

The sudden banging on the Antonov's cabin door ended the silence.

"Mice," said Yuri with disdain. "Let them bang. They will break their hands. Elena, you must leave this place, yes? Unless you want to swim in the Moskva, I have the only way. Now, where shall I take you in my magic carpet? London? Paris? You name it."

"But Yuri," said Elena, "look at the runway. They have blocked it completely."

"Blocked?" Yuri laughed. "You think because they drive their little toys onto the runway that we are blocked?" The banging at the hatch grew louder. "Do not be concerned. It would take a cutting torch to get in. I have bypassed the safety releases. They would have to blow us out." His smile darkened. Would they do that? He reached up to the lighting subpanel and switched on the cockpit lights.

"What are you doing?" Elena said, a rising panic in her tone. They would be visible from the ground, all of them!

"Hush, I must see." Yuri flipped through the thick operating handbook and stopped at a well-thumbed section marked *Prestart checklist*.

A snapping insect whine came from the sloping windshield. There was a spiderweb of cracks where a small-caliber bullet had deflected off the heavy glass.

"You see?" Yuri said. "Bulletproof!" Another crack suddenly appeared in the side glass. "Go back to bed!" He chuckled as his fingers found their way through the beginning steps of the start-up procedure.

"Jesus!" Gallagher watched as Yuri advanced all four throttle levers from cutoff to start position. The row of yellow knobs made even Yuri's fingers stretch.

Elena saw it, too. "Yuri!" But the pilot waved her away. A heavy clang sounded from the cabin door. Even Yuri looked up. "Acch," he said, and returned to his checklist. A thud came from below their feet as someone tried the nosewheel well hatch. "They cannot get in that way, either."

Yuri brought on power from the batteries. The instrument panel came alive. His finger jabbed the autostart for the number one auxiliary power unit. He looked up as the whine of the 60-kw APU became a hiss. "Good." He pressed the autostart button on the number one outboard engine. The fire took hold in the guts of the huge Lotarev turbofan. "Good start on one," he said as the igniters tick-tick-ticked the second engine into a sudden roar. "A good start on two." His finger had already jabbed the third engine to life.

"They're in the airplane!" came the excited voice over the walkie-talkie.

"Then they're finished," said Slepkin to the two Seventh Directorate wet men. The radio in the Volga Interceptor blatted. "I want a status . . ." He stopped as the penetrating scream of a jet engine cut through the night. *My God!* They wouldn't dare! Suddenly, the scream became a low rumble, and then a second engine joined the thunderous chorus, then a third, and finally the last. He looked over at the Seventh Directorate man with the sniper rifle, Dragunov. "Get in the car," he ordered the two men. "We've got to stop them."

"Colonel?" said Rockets as he lifted the trunk lid. He nodded inside.

A long brown tube was there. Four small spindle-shaped rockets lay next to it. It was an RPG-7, a light antiarmor weapon. Slepkin regarded the device for a moment, then nodded. "Very well. Bring it out."

Spitting wet grass from its tires, the Volga gunned down the runway, slewing to a stop fifty feet in front of the Antonov's nose. Its engines shook the ground with their thunder.

"Movement in the cockpit!" said Dragunov as he peered through his starscope. "I count two. No! Three!"

Slepkin smiled and nodded. "Stop them."

Yuri saw the car blocking the way and laughed. He advanced the throttle of his right outboard engine. The huge transport rocked once, then began to inch forward, its long wing sweeping around as they turned. The boarding ramp tilted and toppled with a crash and a clatter. Huge tires rolled over the wreckage, flattening it.

Gallagher watched, his eyes wide. *Six thousand feet of turf!* How could this titanium mountain be coaxed into the air? And what was he doing inside it? "Where are we—" he began, but the sudden crash of a high-velocity bullet through the cockpit silenced him. Yuri covered Elena with his body as glass sparkled and twisted in slow motion as it hung, suspended in the red cockpit lights like a cloud of tiny rubies. The crack of the rifle flooded through the smashed side window. Yuri sat back up in his seat. Gallagher grabbed Elena's head and shoved it below the window line. Her flightsuit was covered in tiny slivers of glass. "Get down!"

"Yuri!" Elena screamed as she twisted out of Gallagher's grasp. "You're cut!"

Yuri shoved all four throttles forward and the Antonov began to roll in earnest. He wiped away a smear of blood from his face. "What, this? I do worse when I shave," he said with a smile. He reached up and snapped off the cockpit lights with his left hand. The right remained gripped around the power levers. "Elena," he said as they bore down on Slepkin's car, "Elena. Listen to me. I want you to go back. To go and unchain one of those little toy airplanes in the back. You know how to fly them, yes?" He saw three figures scramble into the car and move it as the monstrous plane came at them. *Good.* A shiver went through his powerful body as though a winter gust had somehow found its way into the Moscow summer's night.

"Why? What for? What—"

"Do as I say!" he roared. "There is fuel in a tank right next to them. Fill the one farthest aft. Be ready when I tell you. Get the engine started and be ready!"

"But—"

"What's he saying?"

"He wants me to fly away in one of the Sukhois in the back!"

"Fly?" said Gallagher. "You mean, one of the—"

"Both of you!" Yuri commanded as he steered them out into the middle of the grass and paused, the nose of the huge airplane pointed straight down the dark rectangle of runway.

"Yuri," she said, pleading, tugging at his tunic. "I can't let you . . ." She stopped, then held up her hand to her face. "Oh, my God," she whispered.

Her hand was covered in Yuri's slick, warm blood.

"You're—" Gallagher began, but Yuri waved him silent.

"Nobody lets me," Yuri said, his fist spanning the four yellow throttles. "I make my own mind up, Elena. My word. I do this for my word, and for you." He advanced all four levers to takeoff power, his boots jammed down hard on the brakes. The Lotarevs built up into their powerful moan. He glanced over at Elena. She was still looking at her hand, her lips moving, no words coming out. He reached over and cuffed her. "Do as I say!" he shouted over the roar of the engines. He looked back at Gallagher. "Take her! Keep her safe, English! Promise!"

Gallagher stood up from the engineer's seat. A second high-power slug came crashing through the other side window. He grabbed Elena by the arm and pulled her away from the gaping sockets filled with jagged glass.

"Go!" yelled Yuri as he released the brakes. The Antonov began to roll.

Parrum watched in disbelief as the big jet moved out and lined up on the grass runway. Someone shouted. He turned and saw a militia-man motioning for him to follow. He nodded and ran the opposite way, deep into the center of the unlit expanse of grass. The Antonov sat at the far end like a bull ready for the charge. A million moves played through him as he heard the scream of its engines become a low roar that resonated in his chest. The ground beneath his feet trembled; the air itself vibrated with the raw energy building up to a thunderstorm of power at the end of the runway.

The world would have been a better place with Elena working at the Lab. It wasn't going to happen, now. The world would be a worse place with Gallagher in the hands of the opposition. He slipped the Beretta from his pocket and checked the magazine. There were thirteen rounds left. Lucky thirteen. Gallagher in the hands of the other side? He shook his head. No, that wasn't going to happen, either.

Elena grabbed a handhold as the big jet swerved. The drug was still in her, and she began to topple.

Gallagher caught her as she started to fall. She looked up at him, her eyes pooled with tears. She held up her reddened hand to his face. There was no need to speak. What had he done? *Parrum.* The very word summoned an anger powerful enough to overcome his mounting guilt. "Come on," he said as he held her. "I'll fuel it. You get it ready. We'll work the rest out later."

Kashum's two-place SU-29 trainer was lashed down to the cargo deck just ahead of the long, sloping loading ramp at the transport's tail. Elena pulled the canopy cover off and threw it aside as Gallagher yanked the coiled fuel hose from under the storage tank and opened the Sukhoi's wing tank. With a twist of a valve, a gusher of aviation fuel spilled forth.

"Gallagher," said Elena as she watched him fill the first tank and start on the second, "there isn't much time. I will not follow you. Do you understand? I will not defect. I will fly us. Not you. Otherwise you can go—"

"Do what you want," he said as the fuel splashed over the filler neck. He threaded the cap back on tight. "If you think you can stay awake, you fly us."

The Antonov suddenly lurched and bounced; a crunching sound came from its wheels. Elena bent down to unchain the Sukhoi's wing, but fell to her knees as the jet picked up speed.

Gallagher was over in a flash, helping her to her feet. The titanium cargo deck thrummed as the big jet rolled. He held her there for a moment, his eyes locked with hers. "My word's as good as your friend's," he said. "I got you into this. By God, I'll get you out."

"I'm all right," she said, twisting away. She worked the chain loose. The clamp fell to the deck with a loud clang. "I have flown these airplanes for years. I can fly it one more time."

Gallagher looked up as a screeching, tearing sound of yielding metal came from someplace far forward. The Antonov seemed to lose momentum, then pick up the pace once more.

Elena looked at him from the other side of the Sukhoi. *Am I really this crazy?* she wondered.

Gallagher reached over and unlocked the long bubble canopy and threw it back. "Well?" he said.

The Antonov rocked as it rolled down the runway. Here, deep in its guts, Gallagher had no way to know where they were heading, what they were doing. The rumble of the main wheels and the scream of the engines told him one thing without doubt: the Antonov was picking up steam.

Elena tried to stand up on the SU-29's wing, but she kept slipping, falling, her bare feet finding no hold on the wing's smooth surface. Gallagher stepped across the cockpit and gently pulled her in, placing her lightly into the rear seat. "Strap in," he said as he stood on the plane's forward seat.

Gallagher looked about the shaking, roaring cargo hold for an answer. He couldn't even think for the noise. It was like a boiler factory. A red beacon began to flash above the field, sweeping them with its bloody light like a hellish lighthouse. He turned and saw Elena looking up at him. The red warning light flashed across her face, then went dark, then light again. "Sit," she commanded. "Yuri would be . . ." She stopped. "Just sit."

Gallagher settled into the front cockpit and pulled his shoulder straps down, locking them tight into the belt block.

Elena snapped on the SU-29's master switch, and the small instrument panel came alive. "Clear prop!" Elena called. The Vedneyev's compressed-air starter whooshed. The metal blades spun once, twice, three times, and in a puff of blue smoke that was instantly gagging in the confines of the cargo hold, the radial added its chesty roar to the jet's high scream.

Yuri stomped on the rudder pedal to avoid a head-on impact with the police car below him. Instead, the Antonov clipped it with the sharp prow of the left nose-gear door, sending a small quiver through the transport, shoving the puny car aside. He looked out ahead. Some fool was waving a light for him to stop!

He laughed a deep, rumbling laugh, but a sudden jab of icy

pressure strangled it off. His body felt cold, his throat swollen. He coughed and spat a gob of blood onto the plane's titanium deck. *Lungs,* he thought sadly. He felt the ship tremble beneath his hands as he guided it down the runway. The beat of its engines was his own heart; its tough hide his own skin. He caressed the four throttles, feeling the living force rise from them into his own body. He laughed again as he shoved them to the stops. As the Lotarevs spooled into their furious shout, the man down below did the wise thing: he dropped the light and ran for his life. The first runway distance marker went by. *One thousand.* Half the field was behind him.

Another man appeared, out in front of them, close! Yuri laughed once more. He would be flattened if he did not run!

But this one did not run. For the briefest flicker, Yuri's eyes, seventy feet in the air and galloping along at fifty knots, locked with George Parrum's. Parrum held a pistol in his hand. Yuri laughed. *More pop guns!* A staccato of rapid-fire flashes lit Parrum's face, and then the lumbering Antonov swept by him. *Ant,* thought Yuri. *Now,* he thought as the first line of police cars loomed ahead, *we shall see how well you are built.*

He steered the double nosewheels to pass between the flash of two blue strobe lights. The nose swept through the gap, the wheels of the left main gear smashing into metal like a runaway freight train, exploding the little impudent Moskvitches into instant scrap. "Hah!" he shouted as he brought the power back. There was no reason to mistreat the engines, after all, and there was certainly no way he could take off. Yuri, commanding the two-hundred-ton plow, was simply sweeping the runway free of vermin.

Suddenly, an alarm buzzer went off back at the engineer's station. A light flashed on Yuri's overhead panel, illuminating a big button labeled *FIRE.* Something was not well in the left outermost engine. Yuri pulled its throttle back and shut off its fuel flow, then punched the first fire-bottle release. A flood of halon gas filled the Lotarev and the fire alarm winked dark.

"Hah!" Yuri bellowed, and reached over to the cargo-ramp

control panel. A warning buzzer sounded, and Yuri slapped the safety disarm off like a bothersome mosquito. Rumbling down the runway at almost flying speed, he shoved the big metal handle down. Two hundred and thirty feet behind him, two enormous clamshell doors began to open under the high tail.

But everything was not all right. The fire alarm button glowed again. Yuri punched the second halon-bottle release. The light, this time, did not go out.

22

"Two hits in the cockpit!" said Dragunov as the Volga slewed to a stop just beyond the edge of the runway. The Antonov's wing whizzed by overhead as it roared down the grass strip. "I'm sure of two!"

"It hasn't slowed them, has it?" Slepkin observed sourly.

A loud clamor and crash drew all eyes to the lumbering Antonov.

The jet had broken through the first line of militia cars and was bearing down on the second. "You! Drive!" he ordered the marksman. Rockets slid over into the passenger seat, training the RPG out the window. The spindle-shaped missile gleamed a dull silver. "Let's go." Dragunov gunned the powerful engine and the Volga Interceptor leaped forward. Fifty, eighty, a hundred kilometers an hour showed on its round speedometer. At almost one hundred and thirty, they began to catch up. At one hundred and eighty, they were closing in rapidly with the four giant orange cones of flames blasting aft from the transport's engines.

Slepkin's window shook with the thunder of the AN-124's engines as he pressed against the glass to watch. The stink of hot kerosene filled the air. The big jet swerved off the runway, narrowly missing a militia van.

Slepkin shook his head. He should have anticipated this moment; Elena Pasvalys was a rebel. It was in her very blood. There was only one end for such a naturally disloyal personality, no matter how lovely she might be. It was a shame, of course; she might die without having learned submission. But Slepkin was not about to take any more chances this night. He saw Rockets heft the RPG and level it at the Antonov. "Aim for the wing!" he shouted over the Volga's roaring engine. "Only the wing!" The man smiled as though his professionalism had been foolishly called into question.

A wrecked police car flashed by, then another. They swerved, brakes locked, tires digging long, looping furrows into the grass. Slepkin grabbed on to the back of the front seat as they skidded through the incredible mess the Antonov had left behind. Far down the runway, the jet was still moving, well beyond the second blockade, but it was not moving so fast, not nearly fast enough to launch itself into the air. What was it doing? It was far too slow to take off!

The Volga dodged a piece of airplane shed in the abortive takeoff run, and as the headlights swept the runway's edge, Slepkin saw a figure dash from the glare. *Stupid turnip of a militia . . .* he stopped, mouth hanging open. Only a slash of dark blue, the figure's details were nonetheless burned into Slepkin's memory with perfect, shamed clarity. "Stop!"

The driver shot him a glance. "Colonel?"

"Stop!" The Interceptor swung sideways as Dragunov brought them to a panic stop. Slepkin slipped his borrowed Makarov's safety off and leaped from the Volga. He pounded its roof with the butt of his pistol. "Stop that aircraft. If you can, bring them out alive. But do what is necessary."

Slepkin had made one mistake this night by turning his back on George Parrum. As the Interceptor roared off in hot pursuit of the slowing transport, he swore he would not make that same mistake again.

The end of the runway was looming directly off the Antonov's nose. Yuri deployed the thrust reversers and applied maximum power. It was well he was strapped in. The jet slowed with a sudden and violent lurch that threw him forward against the belts. The Antonov bucked and snorted. The green light indicating the aft cargo doors were open burned bright on his panel. The cold, numb area that surrounded the hole made by the tumbling rifle bullet had grown; his whole left side seemed remote, floating apart, not attached to him at all. He was having trouble breathing as his burst lung began to fill. The transport seemed far more vibrant, more alive. But it, too, was living on borrowed time.

The two big cargo doors in the tail were spread wide like sails to the wind. Only one thing was left now. Yuri raised the switch guard and stabbed the button to lower the loading ramp. The cockpit lights dimmed as power was fed to the heavy motors.

Still rolling at thirty knots, the heavy ramp, built to feel the treads of main battle tanks, obediently dropped to the ground. When it touched the runway, a fountain of grass and dirt sprayed up as the metal plowed a deep furrow. Yuri checked the airspeed indicator. It was already dead. There was another line of blue sparks ahead, more militia. But he would have no need to break through it. The runway behind them was all that counted now. With a growl of hot brake discs, Yuri wrestled the half-million-pound jet to a stop. He pulled all the yellow throttles back to cut off and looked up.

The engine-fire annunciator was still flashing. He was not the only one with a mortal wound; the outboard left engine was in trouble. Yuri watched as the interstage turbine temperature climbed through the red danger zone and pegged. He listened in the sudden silence of the shut-down jets and smiled. He could hear the alien rumble of a radial piston engine bellowing in the cargo hold. With an engine fire gnawing at the Antonov's vitals, it was time to go. He turned to the bank of jump seats behind him. There he saw Elena Pasvalys, not as she was, but as she had been when they first met. A shy, blue-eyed girl who was a wizard at math, who was willing to be shown the beauty of flight.

"Elena," he said as though she stood next to him. "You see? I am a man of my word." Her shimmering form leaned down to kiss his forehead. "Ah. Was that so terrible?" he said. "Why did it take all these years?'' She smiled her secretive smile, and as smoke began to drift into the cockpit, she evaporated.

The engine note from the cargo hold changed. He cocked his head and listened as the roar became deep and determined. A slight vibration fed up from the hold as the Sukhoi began to roll. *Good luck to you,* he wished. *Good luck to you, my love.*

''Ready?'' Elena shouted over the howl of the Vedneyev. Gallagher sat up front, Elena in the command position behind. His feet were pressed hard on the brakes as the Antonov lurched, slowing to a stop. It was like taking off in a tunnel. The world beyond his windshield was a tube that ended in a black circle, and in that circle sparked the blue strobes of the militia.

''Gallagher! Release the brakes!'' She loosened her shoulder straps, leaned forward, and slapped him hard.

In surprise, Gallagher took his feet from the brake pedals. Elena shoved the throttle all the way forward. The Vedneyev rumbled with a strange echo, its voice reflected off the metal sides of the cargo hold.

The small plane tipped toward the sloping ramp like a ski jumper on an irreversible leap. They skittered over the lip and hurtled down, swerving right, then overcontrolling to the left. Elena steered them back to the center of the ramp. With a heavy thud, they bounced out onto the torn-up grass runway. The Sukhoi's wheels spun up as the red plane struggled to reach flying speed.

Now. Elena fed a little forward pressure on the stick. The tail came up. Directly ahead of them, the blue strobes of the police seemed like stars on the horizon. Suddenly, two headlights, close and dead ahead, switched on.

''Look out!'' Gallagher yelled. ''Get this thing flying!''

''Not yet, not yet . . .'' she said, her face a mask of concentration. To pull it off too soon would mean a mushing, vulnerable stagger above the heads of the men in that car ahead; perhaps a stall and a crash.

Gallagher stared at the onrushing car. If they didn't break ground quickly, the whole exercise was going to end right then and there. The car was close now, and even as he watched, it skidded sideways and stopped directly across the path of their takeoff run. "Elena!"

The Sukhoi was getting light on its feet, dancing, skipping over the runway. She tugged back on the stick and felt the nose rise, but the tail sagged back to the dirt. "Not yet, not yet," she said, pushing the throttle even though there was no place for it to go. She looked by Gallagher's head and saw they would never make it into the air before reaching the car.

The two lights became a car became two men became a man with a weapon as the scene ballooned in Gallagher's windshield. "Elena! Look—" Gallagher shouted. The two men dived to either side. There was no way. He closed his eyes against the crash.

Elena yanked the stick back and the Sukhoi staggered a few feet aloft, then, with equal vigor, she shoved it forward. The plane struck hard on its wheels and then bounced, high and soaring, not flying except in the manner of a rubber ball, over the car roof and down to the runway beyond.

The tail came up again, firm and confident, and Elena pulled back. The Sukhoi levitated, its wheels a foot above the runway. Flying. Gallagher shot a glance at the airspeed indicator, saw the needle rising smoothly up through 110, then 120 kilometers to the hour. At 150, Elena pulled straight up into a vertical climb. Gallagher's words came without a single thought to filter them. "God damn!" he shouted. "God damn!" They shot up and Elena rolled, then pushed the nose back down so that they were now headed in the opposite direction from the takeoff run, a thousand feet above the dazzling nighttime galaxy of Moscow.

Parrum knew his slugs had struck pay dirt as the Antonov had come straight at him. Standing in its way like a man defying a tidal wave, he saw the first rounds strike the open maw of the outboard engine's fan, sending sparks flying as the bullets shattered the carefully shaped compressor blades. With luck, those blades would be sucked down deep into the engine's vitals where they would begin a cascade of destruction. But Parrum was not in the mood for luck. As the huge plane came at him, he placed his last shots into the nearby wings, where, he knew, the fuel would be.

He succeeded far more than he knew. His first five rounds cracked off three of the big fan blades. Two flew out into the containing shroud and struck, bouncing back and down the fiery throat where they tore at the Lotarev's compressor sections. The third penetrated the shroud like a lance and opened up a shower of jet fuel from the wing tank. Parrum's last five shots were wasted. There was nothing on earth that would stop the Antonov from burning.

Parrum had flung himself down, flattened to the runway, as the huge wing swept over him, the thrust of the roaring engines deafening, the heat of the jet blast enough to blow off his stolen militia cap and singe his neck. He had felt the rumble of the wheels in the very earth. He had opened his eyes and seen what he had hoped to find; the engine he had ruined trailed a billowing stream of white vapor, and drops of pure fire sprayed aft. The Antonov hurtled unconcerned toward its doom.

Focus, he thought. It was all it took. The sound of another engine made him sit up. He saw the twin headlight eyes of a car speeding down the runway. He rolled to his feet and ran for the weeds off the edge. The black Mercedes was just beyond a simple barrier of metal links; nothing compared with the hurdles he had already jumped this night. A muffled boom came from the burning jet transport. *So long, Doc,* he thought at the rising ball of orange fire. *Both of you.*

But the car was turning his way. The lights swept over him. There was no chance he had been missed! Parrum took off at ninety degrees, then dodged another ninety. Had they seen him? The car was stopping.

Parrum ran straight for the perimeter fence. There was no time left for subtlety. He heard the car start up and move off once again in the direction of the crippled transport.

Then, George Parrum made a mistake. He stopped and turned, his body a dark shape against the lights of the Aeroflot Hotel parking area.

A flash of yellow cordite and a tremendous blow to his side came at exactly the same instant. Only as he spun to the ground did the snapping whine of the shot follow, then a second.

He kept on rolling as he hit, the pain in his side like a pocketful of white-hot coals. He staggered into a crouch and yanked the empty magazine out of the Beretta and shoved in a new one; his last. His head felt hot and sticky as the shock flooded his system. *No!* He commanded his body to obey. Parrum wanted, needed *focus.*

He listened for running feet. There was no sound except the roar of the Antonov as a series of heavy concussions rocked it. Low to the ground, he half-walked, half-crawled once more toward the fence, still twenty feet away.

Parrum stopped, his breathing becoming labored. He looked at the fence. *Ten feet.* He started to crawl once more. He smelled the sweetness of wet earth and new grass beckoning.

Parrum heard the shot. He assumed it was a miss, but when his right leg refused to move, he looked back and saw his bootheel dangling from the sole, and a dull, powerful ache was spreading up his calf. Parrum pulled himself around to face his tormentor. To his complete shock, the blacked-out figure of a man stood not five feet behind him, tall against the stars.

"What a surprise," Slepkin said with a laugh. He held the empty clip from Parrum's gun in his other hand. "I believe you left this?" He tossed it at Parrum. "I hope I have not kept you waiting long, but I was rather tied up this evening."

Can he see my gun? The Beretta had a full clip in it. *The cocky bastard thinks I'm out of rounds!* Parrum shifted his legs to allow him to bring the Beretta slowly to bear.

But Slepkin was no longer a believer in luck. He shook his head and shot Parrum in the other heel with a sharp crack of thunder followed by a cloudburst of unbelievable pain. A thousand needle-teeth clamped around Parrum's ankle and slowly, slowly gnawed it to the bone. Parrum felt the scream rise, fought it, fought it, but it pried open his teeth and blasted into the night.

"I would suggest that you not make me jump again. I would not wish to lose such a prize to a mere reflex." Slepkin knew a dozen such places on the body that would hurt beyond measure but would not kill. And he had plenty of time for exploration.

Parrum looked up through a red-rimmed haze of agony and thought one, burning thought brighter than even the boiling lava that now coursed through his nerves: *you lose, bastard.* He watched, motionless, waiting as Slepkin chuckled once more. Except for a distant howl of a police siren, there was very little sound. The Antonov's jets were silent.

"You see?" Slepkin said, triumph in his voice. "She is mine after all." He laughed. "And your own Gallagher. And you, my friend, you did it for us!" It was very, very amusing. "I suppose it is true. The American agencies are not what they used to be."

"What . . ." Parrum bit down on his lip hard to clear his mind. "What are you saying?" He groaned, rolling slightly to expose the Beretta.

"Only that your people and mine had reached—how is it said?— a certain understanding. But I see that no longer holds. You are playing a very old game, Parrum. And you have lost."

Parrum moved again. "Go fuck yourself." *Almost.*

"I think not." Slepkin stepped back suddenly, his head turning slightly to place his ear in a direct line with the burning Antonov. There was a new sound, and he desperately wished to look, to see what made it. It was the unmistakable roar of a radial engine.

Parrum weighed the moment. *Not yet . . .*

Slepkin shot a look in the direction of the Antonov. "No!" he yelled. The Antonov was now burning vigorously, the wing gushing flames in a brilliant orange geyser. Against the fire's light he had seen the darting shape of a Sukhoi in its takeoff run. "No!"

Slepkin's shout pulled Parrum back from the clay cold that reached for his heart. *You lose,* he thought, and the words echoed down a long, empty chamber inside him. *You lose.* His hands shaking, the Beretta heavy as a barbell in his grip, George Parrum centered the 92F on Slepkin's spine.

Slepkin spun around, his own senses screaming subliminal warning just as Parrum squeezed off two shots. The impact lifted the Russian clear of the ground, his arms windmilling, frantic. He rose, rose into the air as Parrum watched, his arms beating like wings, as though he meant to give the Sukhoi chase by the force of his will. Then he fell. One leg snapped under his weight as he struck.

You lose, Parrum said as Slepkin lay heaped on the ground. *You lose.* He turned, the pain now nearly gone. He commanded his limbs to make the motions to bring him the last few feet to the fence.

Like a blinded creature feeling its way, Parrum crawled the short distance and shoved his head against the fence. He hauled himself upright, and a fresh boil of pain spilled in his guts. He grabbed another handful of fence and pulled again, his limbs now thinking for themselves, taking the one, single motion they were competent to effect and repeating it again and again.

The human body is capable of amazing feats. They found George Parrum halfway over the top, his thick body folded in half, in the gray dawn light of the new day.

Col. Nikolai Slepkin was not two feet below, his blue fingers closed around the wire mesh.

Yuri could feel the heat of the fire through the skin of the burning jet. He touched the metal and quickly drew his hand away. The captain of a sinking ship, he staggered back through the darkened corridors, through the passenger deck toward the empty cargo hold. He could smell not only the stink of burning kerosene, but the oily vapor from the Sukhoi. He opened the door to the cargo deck, and the heat and smoke blew up in his face. He slammed it shut.

Smoke tendrils curled along the floor like black vipers as he made his way forward again. The latch was hot to the touch when he reached for it and swung it wide.

It was like staring into a furnace. The cockpit was irradiated with brilliant firelight as rivers of jet fuel burned along the runway, flaring up into boils of yellow and purple. A series of sharp, cracking explosions rocked the jet, and suddenly it sagged, listing sharply to the left, the main-gear tires vaporized. Yuri took a look out through the empty window frame and decided that it was no place for him.

It left only one direction, and that, he knew, could only be temporary.

Using the one hand that still obeyed his command, Yuri gritted his teeth against the painful heat of the handle and yanked the ceiling-hatch door open. Immediately, a draft pulled in clouds of choking, acid smoke from the fuselage. With an iron grip on the rim of the hatch, he hauled his weight single-handed up through the roof. A moment later, he was standing, feet astride the tilted, curving body of the Antonov, surveying the fire below.

He saw a car pull up outside the circumference of flames. Two men got out, shielding their faces from the heat.

Yuri held up his arm to block the intense smoke that billowed by him and watched as one shouldered what he knew to be a rocket-propelled antitank weapon. "Hey, you!" he bellowed, his voice a snap of dry grass in a forest inferno. *"You!"*

The man crouched down on a knee and leveled the tube at his jet. "No!" Yuri reached down and yanked a heavy blade antenna out by its wire roots, and in a fury that did not recognize futility, he whipped it at them, his fire-lit face a rage of defiance. *"No!"* A sheet of orange flame drew itself like a curtain behind him, a backdrop against which he raised the fist of Thor against the two puny creatures below.

The RPG flared white as it fired its charge into the dying Antonov. "Hah!" At first there was nothing, no reaction. "HAH!" Then, as the warhead's detonation sprayed tons of fuel into atomized vapor, a shattering explosion blasted into the red Moscow sky.

At the flash of light, Elena reefed the Sukhoi into a tight turn back toward Moscow Central. "Yuri!"

"Jesus," Gallagher said quietly as a mushroom cloud blasted skyward. "Oh, God," he whispered. Everything he'd touched had become so much smoke and ash. He watched the dancing fire and had, for a flicker of an instant, the impulse to grab the control stick and point the Sukhoi at its heart.

"Take it," Elena said. "Please. Take it." He felt the control stick go limp in his hands.

Gallagher pushed his feet into the stirrups on the rudder pedals and gently rolled the plane away from the inferno. He glanced in the small mirror mounted on the canopy and saw Elena's head resting on the Plexiglas, her hair tinged with the flickering light of the distant flames. "Where do we go now?" he asked.

She caught him looking at her in the mirror, but still she did not move, not even as her tears flowed down the vibrating canopy glass in a rain impervious to the steady 150-knot slipstream a quarter inch beyond. There was only one name for the place she wished to be; the place was called home.

"Well?" he asked again.

"Fly two hundred and sixty degrees magnetic." Her throat swelled as she spoke. "Three hours. Six hundred kilometers."

Gallagher banked the Sukhoi west, the lights of the Leningrad highway petering out into the darkness of the countryside. "Where does that take us?"

"Lithuania," she replied. *Home.*

23

Sunrise,
4 August 1990

Gallagher pushed the stick forward again. He had been microsleeping, fighting to raise the irresistible weight of his eyelids high enough to see the instrument panel. The Sukhoi had climbed to nearly two hundred meters above the gently rolling terrain below. That was a good way to show up on someone's radar, and he was sure that the scopes would be manned and operating this morning.

He scanned the pearly gray sky. Except for the brilliant hanging diamond of a star directly behind him, the world seemed utterly empty, an uninhabited planet scrolling by beneath his crimson wings. He watched the needle on the altimeter fall, leveling out at fifty meters. He reached down and opened a side vent. A cold, wet jet of air blasted by his knee. *Fifty meters.* This was how the German who had landed in Red Square had done it. Of course, Gallagher knew they had made some changes after Mathias Rust played his prank on Moscow's vaunted air defenses. *Why'd he land there, and not at Moscow Central?* he wondered, his mind mired and functioning from within a tar pit of fatigue.

He checked his watch as the northern sun, still below the horizon, cast bright red rays across the gray sky. As the light intensified, he saw the mounded islands of fog directly ahead, each sitting over its own small lake. The land below looked a great deal like Wisconsin: low hills, a carpet of trees, and a skein of streams meandering from lake to lake. It was a gentle, appealing country. Was it Lithuania? The two largest hillocks of fog drew near.

Gallagher banked the Sukhoi between the soft, cool clouds. Ahead, the islands coalesced into a peninsula; beyond them, a continent. *Can't fly through that,* he decided, letting the nose rise slightly. The Sukhoi slowly climbed.

He stared at his Air King again. For some reason, the simple sweep of its hands had become strange and unreadable. He forced his eyes to focus. *Four-ten.* They had been aloft now for over four hours. How much fuel did the two-place Sukhoi hold? He recalled splashing its tanks full as the Antonov had rolled down the grass. Were they full? He had no fuel gauges in the front cockpit, and for some reason he could not explain, he couldn't bring himself to wake Elena. He glanced up in the canopy mirror. She was still asleep.

A thin, wispy thread of fog snaked by the windshield. Gallagher banked as it thickened, climbing slightly to stay above it, until the glaciated landscape below was almost entirely hidden. One elongated hole framed the dark blue waters of a river. *I wonder which one it is?* he thought. He toyed with the notion of following it; it would surely lead him to the coast, to the Baltic Sea. *And a big town with a big radar, too.* He held on to his heading with grim determination. The river disappeared behind his tail.

The fog solidified into a dense undercast that stretched from horizon to horizon. Only back to the east was there any clear air, and that was not a direction that Gallagher found attractive. How far could he fly westbound? Suppose he flew out over the ocean and didn't know it?

"Gallagher?" He looked up in the mirror and saw that Elena was now awake. "Where are we?"

"I'm not exactly sure. I've been holding a compass heading, but other than that . . ."

"We've got to land. There's no fuel." She squinted at her fuel gauges. Both needles rested deep in the yellow caution zones.

"Like where?" He looked outside at the fog-covered ground. He wagged the wings, listening for the slosh of gasoline, but all he could hear was the steady thrum of the Vedneyev and the whisper of air streaming by. "What's it showing?"

"Another minute, perhaps another five." Elena's voice sounded empty, hollow, as though the words fell down a long tube before reaching Gallagher. "How long have I been asleep?"

"Four hours plus or minus."

She nodded. "Bravo, Dr. Gallagher."

"Wyn."

She shook her head. It didn't matter anymore. "Bravo, Wyn. You have flown us to our graves. Did you see anything through the fog?"

"A big river. It was flowing northwest. About twenty miles back."

"The Daugava. It's near the Lithuanian border. I'm already home." There was a strange note of resignation in her voice; she had seen too much, hurt too much. The future seemed as gray as the dense blanket of fog below them. "At least I'll die in Lithuania," she said with a sigh.

"I'm glad you think we're in good . . ." He stopped when the Sukhoi's engine stumbled. Gallagher hit the wobble pump. The Vedneyev steadied, but its reassuring rumble was broken into spits and belches of flame from its exhaust stack. Gallagher yawed the plane to dislodge whatever fuel was left in the wing tanks. "Oh, shit."

"Gall—" she began, but then corrected herself. "Wyn. You're a good man. I'm sorry."

"For what?" he said, his voice rising almost an octave. He banked the Sukhoi around, hoping against hope to find a break in the undercast.

"For everything. For hitting you. For their betraying you . . . just for everything."

"Save it." The engine surged. "I don't know about you," he said, utterly awake now, "but I didn't come all this way to give up." He swung around back to the east, but the division between clear air and cloud was impossibly far.

Elena had trained in Sukhois for years, but never once had she landed one blind. The fog probably went all the way to the ground; they would see a dark flash of earth and then it would be over. Done. She put her head back against the seat cushion. The sky was a milky blue overhead. It wasn't the worst thing to see before she died, was it? "It's better this way," she said to herself. "You and I," she went on as they spiraled, "we push the world from its perch with what we know. With what's in our heads. But the world pushes back. The world is balanced after—"

"I don't know about you," he interrupted. "but I'm landing this sucker."

"You've never learned to give up when it's too . . ." She stopped when the engine stumbled, this time for good.

The Vedneyev had drawn its last drops from the fuselage tank and stopped cold, the only sound the clanking of dead pistons driven by the windmilling prop. Gallagher's fingers tingled on the stick, the engine vibrations living on in their memory. It was like a cue, a message from the machine reminding him that it was now all up to him. Gallagher pulled the nose up hard.

"What are you doing?" she shouted. Was he going to spin them in?

"You may know how to take this bastard off," he said as he leveled at a lower speed, "but when it comes to not giving up, I'm the local expert." Gallagher banked, all his fatigue whitewashed out in the jolt of adrenaline, circling gently, looking down into the fog for a hint of a landing spot. A snake of doubt coiled in his gut. *Maybe she's right. Maybe I'm all hat and no cattle.*

He glanced up as an orange crescent of burning sun eased over the eastern horizon. The brilliant star—or was it a planet?—was still there, beckoning him with its diamond light. He pushed over into a shallow dive. The speed built up immediately. Gallagher knew he was now throwing away something precious, burning up his capital like a madman tossing bills into a fireplace. Once given up, there would be no way to take back their speed.

"I forgive you, Wyn," Elena whispered as the dense white mists rose toward them.

"No!" He corrected left as the white fogbank filled the windshield, and suddenly they were within its damp, cool belly. He held on to his heading, watching the accusing altimeter unwind. The hands dropped through a hundred meters, ninety, eighty. At just under forty meters, a dark building suddenly appeared out of the mists and shot by them. Ahead, a small lake was tinted the color of mercury by the filtered light. A tiny beach rimmed its far shore, backed up by stands of trees. Gallagher froze the view in his mind as they flashed over the still waters, far too fast to land.

With his last irreplaceable reserve of speed, Gallagher pulled the Sukhoi up, up, up, bursting through the low fog like a surfacing submarine and into the clear air above. The stick shuddered as the Sukhoi neared the stall. At the right moment, the irreplaceably correct instant, Gallagher kicked right rudder and the plane pivoted neatly in a hammerhead stall. The windshield now pointed straight down at the fog-covered ground.

Gallagher banked to align the featureless fog with his memory of the land beneath it. He leveled the wings and sank down toward the billowing cloud tops.

"You cannot!"

"I sure hope you're wrong." The top of the fogbank looked so solid, Gallagher was tempted to land on it, but the Sukhoi plunged through the surface without the slightest hesitation.

Once more the wet, gray wool surrounded them. Gallagher could smell the water below, close by. Down through eighty meters, the fog began to tear open, strips blasting by the canopy as he descended. A quick view of the lake flashed before him, closed over, then opened again. Like it or not, the Sukhoi was on final approach. The tiny strip of beach was dead ahead, the tall spikes of birch trees poking their heads into the fog just beyond.

He held the plane in a steep slip to bleed off the speed and the altitude as the dark waters rose up. A rattle of spray splashed up as his wheels skimmed the lake. He pulled up slightly, holding the plane steady, steady, as the beach seemed to crawl closer. *Just a little more!*

The trees were a wall not fifty feet away; suddenly, sand flashed inches beneath his wheels. He kicked them around in a tight bank that used all the remainder of his precious energy. The landing gear dug in an instant later.

The small wheels rumbled as they bounced over the sand. The soft surface tugged at them, slowing, slowing them, braking them to a fast walk, then a slow one, and then, finally, they were stopped. The world still seemed to move, but that was just an illusion. The deserted, fog-shrouded beach was absolutely still. There was not the slightest sound.

He looked out through the clear bubble of the canopy and there was nothing, no evidence a world greater than this existed; no Pitts Specials falling from the sky, no betrayals, no lies. Just peace; peace, the shifting, swirling vapors of morning fog, and the silence of a small lake in central Lithuania at dawn. Gallagher reached over his head, unlocked the canopy, and threw it open. The sound of wind came down from the invisible treetops; the cry of a gull drifted across the water.

Elena sat back against the headrest and breathed in the rich smells of the nearby forest, which, magnified by the damp fog, were so sweet, so overwhelming, so very much like home. Elena looked away as Gallagher freed himself from the seat harness and slowly, stiffly stood up in the cockpit, bracing his hands on the windshield. He turned and looked down the two parallel lines the Sukhoi had scribed in the sand in its landing roll. "Elena, there was some kind of building back there. We should go check it out."

"What?" She looked up as though from a dream. "What did you say?"

"Come on." He held his hand out. "You can't sit in that hole all morning. We need to find out where we are. Get some gas maybe. But first, let's wheel this thing back into the trees, okay? Just in case."

Elena looked up, her eyes red with weariness. She looked so small, so vulnerable and childlike. "You don't know when it is over, do you?"

"It ain't over till it's over. After all, out of all the miserable places to land, we were handed this one on a platter. Things are looking up.'' He stopped, cocking his head to one side.

At first it was just a whisper, a faint trembling in the air. It grew into the definitive *whop whop whop* of a heavy helicopter.

''Come on!'' he shouted, pulling her up from the Sukhoi's rear seat. Gallagher felt her hand tremble in his grasp. ''Let's get this thing pushed back into the trees.'' The sound of the rotor blades was cut by the high whine of a jet engine.

''They can't see us any more than we can see them,'' she answered.

''What are you willing to bet? Your life?''

She staggered off the Sukhoi's wing, her bare toes curling into the gravelly sand.

Gallagher made his way to the far wing and began to push. She bent her strength to the task, and together, they pushed the feather-light Sukhoi back into the trees until its wings touched birch bark. It wouldn't be hard to spot from close by, but it would be proof against a quick glance. Gallagher noticed a myriad of tiny hoof marks, cloven hoof marks, pressed into the sand. *Sheep?*

''They're going away,'' she said.

He stood there, listening. The helicopter's sound was fading.

It was getting noticeably brighter, the gray beginning to grow white with the new sun. The patches on Elena's borrowed flightsuit glowed. *Red Deer. Texas Twistoff. Fond du Lac.* Her slim body swam in the folds of green fabric. ''Do you think they were looking for us?'' she asked.

''Who knows?'' Gallagher looked down the tracks left by their landing. ''Let's be safe, okay? This fog's burning off.''

They walked through the cool, damp sand away from the Sukhoi. The beach seemed to be from another geologic era, empty, quiet. He smoothed the wheel marks as they made their way toward the small building he had seen in a flash from the air. It couldn't have been very long, but the masking fog made it seem like a walk off the ends of the earth itself.

They came to a dilapidated ruin of a boat shed. Boards were

missing from its sides, though the roof seemed intact. It was empty now, taken over by some farmer and used as an animal shelter. The fresh, alive smell of new hay came from within.

Gallagher lifted a splintered beam off its hook and swung it wide. The adrenaline was wearing off, and the sleep his body demanded could no longer be denied. He walked into the fragrant interior, feeling his way in the dark, his hands out in front to guard against hitting something invisible. His feet plowed into a loose pile of hay. He dropped to his knees and fell deep into the hay mound.

Elena waited by the crude gate, listening to the rustle of straw, feeling the events of the last days weigh like a stack of pig-iron ingots in her arms. She couldn't carry them forever. "May . . . may I join you?" she asked hesitantly. "Of course, if you would rather—"

"Please, come."

She homed in on his breathing, felt the pile of hay at her feet, and gently lowered herself into its comforting softness. She turned to face Gallagher, his body a darker outline against the hay.

"Did you really mean what you said? When we were landing? About forgiving me?"

"Hold me," she said. "Just that. Hold me."

Gallagher reached out and felt Elena's arms reaching for him. Intertwined in the sweet stillness of the ramshackle boat shed, they dropped into a sleep too deep for even the voices of ghosts to be heard.

The fire burned well into the morning, streaks of blackened grass extending from the monumental ruin that had once been the largest airplane in the world. Stainless steel tubing poked into the sky at odd angles. Pools of aluminum jelled in the blackened turf; titanium rivulets froze to glaciers. A funereal pall hung above Moscow Central airfield, trapped by the buildings on three sides. Four blackened cylinders that had once been powerful Lotarev turbofans lay scattered where the wings had dropped them.

"What a mess," said Gen. Lt. I. M. Tretyak as he surveyed the scene, keeping a safe distance from the shimmering hulk. He scratched the deep cleft in his chin. It was his early-warning antenna, he liked to tell his staff; they called it the viper's pit. A belt radio kept him in touch with the far-flung net of early-warning radars and interceptor squadrons under his command. The radio was ominously quiet. "Maybe we'll be lucky."

"I don't believe in luck," said Gen. Boris Gromov, ultra conservative member of the Congress of People's Deputies. He dropped his field glasses. "I don't suppose we'll find them in there."

"The investigators from VTA will be here any moment," said Tretyak, referring to the Soviet military airlift command. "I held off everyone else on their account. Meanwhile, we've gone through the cockpit area. Only the one."

"The drunken pilot. So much for your luck," said Gromov. A hero of the Afghan War, he was a member of a small but strengthening coalition of Army leaders and KGB officers who sought to reverse the tide of chaos unleashed by the fools in the Kremlin they called the Informals.

"We won't know for certain until we sift through the rest of the wreckage, but there was the eyewitness report of—"

"Yes, I know. What about your radars? Nothing?"

"Nothing yet, General. It's a very small target." Tretyak shrugged as he checked his watch. "There are helicopters up between here and the borders. Their maximum radius is eight hundred kilometers. I've put young Kolchenoveniy in charge."

"He's reliable, but that's a great deal of territory," said Gromov. "Have you given the colonel enough men and equipment?"

"Seventy-sixth Air Assault," Tretyak said with a nod. "They have hundreds of helicopters out looking. But in any event, she is on the ground now someplace. Their fuel—"

"Someplace," Gromov said with a scowl. "Has Marshal Yazov been informed?"

"Of course."

"Good. I hate to think of what those idiots would do if they knew of . . ." He was about to say "Stingray," but held his tongue. Some secrets were far too important to share with the likes of the wreckers in the Kremlin. Gromov gritted his teeth and scowled. "They've thrown away everything we have fought for, Ivan Moiseivich," he said at last.

"True."

"Our soldiers sell their uniforms to the Germans. The Pact is gone. And now look how we hand them Iraq, our oldest ally in a very difficult part of the world. Thrown away like garbage."

"Shameful." Tretyak nodded.

"They've taken an empire and turned it into a whorehouse. The West must think we're savages. We'll sell them St. Basil's for a boatload of trinkets." Gromov placed the glasses to his eyes again and swept them across the smoldering hulk. "Pray that she is in there someplace, Ivan Moiseivich. Pray your young colonel does his job."

"We'll find them."

"I hope so. Because what that woman knows," Gromov said, staring at the smoking hulk of the Antonov, "is far better burned than given away."

Heat. Gallagher's face felt as though it were on fire, and in his dream he saw the leaping flames of the burning Antonov blowing skyward. Gallagher's heart beat fast. Yuri's face was wreathed in fire, then Parrum's face was formed by a swirling knot of burning gas. Parrum held up the black weapon to Yuri's head. His trigger finger curled. "No!" Parrum smiled and handed the Beretta to Gallagher. Its steel singed his flesh, smoking like a cattle brand. Gallagher had killed him as sure as pointing a gun at his head and pulling the trigger! "NO!" he shouted from the bottom of his dream. "NO!"

Elena put her hand over Gallagher's mouth as his eyes popped wide and white in fear. She was close beside him, her face golden in a pool of brilliant sun streaming through the glassless window on the boat shed's east wall. "It's all right. Be still. It's all right."

Gallagher looked up at her as she fingered his sweaty hair from his face.

He felt his heart gradually slow. "I dreamed . . ." he began, "the crash, the fire . . ." but then stopped, watching the play of light across her face, the touch of her fingers. "Have you been awake for long?"

"Not very." She turned and looked over the swinging gate that served to bar the boat shed's front door. "The fog burned away. I haven't heard any more helicopters. Maybe you can find some gasoline. You'll need to fill the tanks to the top."

"Me?" He sat up on his elbows. "What about you?"

"What about me? You're three hours' flight time from Sweden. I'm home. I told you last night. I won't come with you."

Gallagher breathed in deeply, calming his heart from the dream. "How can you stay? I thought that with everything, you know, that happened, that you might . . ."

"Change my mind?" She smiled sadly. "If only it were that easy."

"It can be."

"It isn't. You know what happened with me, with my project?"

"It was Parrum. I'm sorry I ever—"

"No." She put her fingers to his lips. "Don't blame yourself. It has nothing to do with you. I was already finished. The liars threw me out. Just as everything was coming together. Why?" She smiled. "They worried I might not be loyal enough to keep my mouth shut after everything I worked for was buried. It happened before you ever came to Moscow. Forgive yourself. I do."

"Then I didn't—"

"No. You were played for a fool. I was too, in my own way." She gathered a fistful of sweet hay and held it to her nose. "Secrets breed fools and liars," she said. "We were both taken in. We believed them, and then, when we saw it was all a lie, it was too late. Words are just tools to them. Nothing is true. They set up their little boxes, their traps, and herd us from one to the next."

"Unless you cut across. Play across the grain." The image of the chessboard came back to Gallagher, its invisible, shimmering lines of force, its angles of attack.

"The nail who holds his head high feels the hammer. There's no room for truth, Wyn. Only obedience."

"No. One thing's true: I promised to keep you safe," he said seriously. He saw her face chill at the memory of Yuri's vow. "He was a real good friend of yours, Elena. I mean to keep my word, too. I can't let you stay behind."

"I won't go with you."

"But—"

"But nothing. Listen. I do have a suggestion." She looked at him hesitantly. It was the only way for them both. Could he be made to see it?

"What's there to say? They'll toss you in jail if you go back," he said. "You'll never be allowed to work on anything real again."

"Will you listen to me?"

"What kind of suggestion?"

"I know what you do at Lawrence Livermore. Oh," she said with a wave, "not as much as you seem to know of me. But enough to know that each of us has a piece, a necessary piece, of something very big, something very important. Something the world needs. *All* the world. Not just the liars in America, or the liars right here. You know what I mean."

"Parrum showed me pictures of the Bear."

"Bear? Oh. You mean the Tupolev. Yes. But it isn't complete. It's just a prototype. A crude one at that. There's no intelligence behind it." Her eyes seemed to bore into Gallagher's. "You can provide that, can't you?"

"A prototype?" The word roused Gallagher's memory of the slim gold cylinder back at Lawrence Livermore. The PALS Prototype.

"Listen to me, Wyn. I have made the gun. Your computer. I know it's the gunsight. Missiles are ready to fly everywhere you look. We can stop them. Not alone. But together."

"Together? You want me to come work with *you?* Where? In jail?"

She laughed. ''Don't be crazy.'' Her smile faded. ''And don't be naive. What chance will you have back at your lab, after this? Who will trust you? You have been in contact with dangerous people from the other side. The enemy.''

''They won't have to say it. I got defunded. I'm out, too.''

''Then it is the same. We are both no longer worthy of the trust of liars. A fine condition, don't you think?''

It was true. Gallagher sighed.

''But there is a way,'' She shifted down, close to him, her voice almost a whisper. ''I propose an exchange. I will give you my work, you give me yours. Each of us has a ticket to take home, to pay our way back. Both of us. Who loses but the liars?''

He gazed into her smooth face. ''You're serious, aren't you?''

''Very.''

A square of golden sunlight beamed in, catching in her eyes. Was this all a setup, from the very start? To hand over his optical-image recognition system, in exchange for what? Or was it real, was she right?

''What are you looking at?'' she asked.

His eyes refocused. ''You.''

''What's wrong? Have I shocked you?''

''Not at all. I was just thinking. I don't know. I spent five years on the—''

''And I have not given my life to my work?'' she interrupted.

''No, it's just that I got into this mess by trusting a guy I should have seen right through.'' He shook his head. ''Now you want me to hand over something, to trust a person I never—''

''For the same reason I should trust you, a dangerous spy.'' She laughed. ''Wyn, either we work our way out of the little boxes they've made for us, or else we die inside them. It's a chance. I think we should take it. Together.''

''But how do I know you'll give me the real McCoy?''

''McCoy?''

''The truth.''

''I won't give. But I will trade.'' She smiled. ''I have something to show you.'' She reached for the zipper of her flightsuit.

Gallagher sucked in his breath as she drew it down, but his eyes were caught by the sparkling dazzle of a huge crystal hanging between her breasts.

"This is what I offer." She held the artificial diamond up for the light to strike. It flashed reds, blues, greens, like the morning star Gallagher had steered by, like the blue of Elena's eyes.

He held out his hand and touched its faceted surface. It was warm with her body. "What is it?"

"Diamond, of course."

"*Diamond?* Is it real?"

She closed his hand over it. "Very. I should know. I made it."

"You *made* it?" He searched her face, but she wasn't lying.

"This is nothing. There's another one the size of a soccer ball. It's at the heart of something called . . ." She stopped, searching for the right word. "Stingray. That is the McCoy. The beam device. Stingray."

Together. Gun and gunsight. The world. These words flashed in Gallagher's mind as he watched the sun deepen on her face. *Together.* Gallagher edged closer to her and leaned down, his face a foot from hers.

Her eyes held his. At first it was a contest. Who would blink? Then it was something more, something sudden and wild. "What?" she asked, her voice husky.

"Would you ever kiss a dangerous spy?"

"You? Dangerous?" Her neck flushed red and her breath caught. "Never," she said, but her eyes said otherwise.

"That's what I thought." He took her face in his hand and pulled her to him. He felt her heart beat against his chest. Her kiss became stronger, faster, more frantic, as though Gallagher were her last connection to the world and she could not let it go, not for an instant. Finally, he was the one to pull back.

"Wow," he said. "You sure kiss good for a chemist."

"A physical chemist," she corrected. She pulled away from him and sat up. "You know this is impossible. It's a trick. Danger does this to us, it's not our minds. We are both too smart. Let's leave it as a technical exchange."

"Elena, I don't ever want to get that smart."

Her pulse raced despite her best efforts. "You are suggesting a deeper collaboration?"

"I sure hope so." He reached over and pulled her to him again. The kiss was longer, deeper than the last. He felt the heat rise from her body, a warm, woman smell from the open neck of her flightsuit.

Her breath was coming fast now, and when he reached inside her flightsuit to touch her breasts, he could feel her heart hammering away within her ribs. Her eyes were closed as he stroked her.

Why do I want this? she wondered. *This man has changed everything!* Her thought stopped right there. *Perhaps that is the good news,* she realized. *Perhaps that is the very best thing of all.* Love was always the first step. Isn't that what all the wise men said?

"Elena," he whispered, "where did you go?"

"Home." She stood up and drew the zipper of her flightsuit all the way down. She stepped out of it, carefully hanging it on a wooden peg as though she feared to get it dirty. The bruise on her thigh from Parrum's dart was lost in the shadows. She reached behind her back and unhooked the black bra she had meant for Yuri to see.

God! he thought as her small, firm breasts caught the yellow sun, their stiffening nipples the color and shape of ripe, bursting raspberries.

"You are next, spy. We will seal our bargain."

He was out of his clothes in a flash. Gallagher took her into his arms, skin to warm skin, her body starting somewhere above his ankles and ending with her lips against his. He wanted Elena. The hunger in him demanded her. Now.

"No," she said. "Wait." She pushed him back down against the hay, swung her legs over his, and straddled him. Elena closed her eyes as she slowly lowered herself onto him, enveloping Gallagher's body and spirit like hot liquid amber. She let him fill her, a small cry escaping from her throat as he reached the very end of her.

At first they could not find their rhythm. Then he felt his hunger become her hunger, become a force that drew them both into its powerful beating center. Action and reaction, sight and sense. Their lovemaking dissolved their skins and their histories.

She threw her arms up and held on to a wooden beam as she rode him, her cries now coming with every breath. At the last instant, Gallagher took both her hands and held them. "Look at me!" Her eyes were still shut. *"Look at me!"*

She opened them. They glowed like two sapphires as the first flash sparked through her. She threw her head back and cried out as each wave carried her further and further away. First a cry of joy, then of relief, of sadness, finally of loss.

"God," he said as her sweat trickled down and mingled with his. "I don't want to hold out from you. I want to give it all to you, do you understand? No secrets. Everything."

She gently closed his eyes and slipped the diamond from her neck. "Rest," she said. "Rest. We both have a long way to go before we are home."

"You have to come with me. I can't leave you here."

"Rest." She pressed the bright jewel with the integrated circuit at its heart into his hand.

24

**Saturday Afternoon,
4 August 1990**

"I guess it's time," said Gallagher. It had been several hours since the last helicopter beat its way through the bright sky.

"If you plan to land before dark," said Elena. "You should have no trouble crossing over. West will take you to Sweden. Northwest to Finland. And—"

"I know where I'm headed," said Gallagher. "Why won't you come with me?"

"You have plenty of fuel, don't you?" she persisted.

"Thanks to your uncle."

"He was only making a joke." The farmer who used the boat shed had come by at midday, a noisy gaggle of black-faced sheep spread before him. At first he took them for Russians. But when Elena spoke her native tongue, and his, the man's scowl evaporated. When she told him her name, and a little of her story, his face became set with outrage. *Pasvalys? I know your uncle, don't I? How can I help?*

Where were they? Elena asked him. *A hundred kilometers north of Vilnius, little Utena is just over there.* Fuel? *No problem.* He had disappeared with his sheep and returned an hour later, his tractor towing a large steel tank. It wasn't aviation grade, but the Sukhoi wouldn't know the difference. Pay? *Never!* Elena was expected for dinner. *Don't say no!*

They sat in the shade of a stand of birch, the afternoon sun glinting into their eyes. Elena held an annotated diagram in her hands; Gallagher had the diamond hung around his neck.

"Fly west," she said, "right into the sun. You'll come to Kursky Zaliv. It's a big enclosed bay just before the Baltic. A barrier island. Just sand, weeds. Nobody lives there except a few fishermen. From there it's all water."

"We can both go," he said for what seemed like the hundredth time.

"Keep going west," she said, her voice catching, "then turn south. It's a long way out across the Baltic to Bornholm Island, maybe three hundred kilometers—"

"Come with me."

"If you miss the island, you'll hit Sweden. You've got enough fuel. You should be safe. I know the Sukhoi will take you there. Just don't fall asleep and splash. The water is very cold."

"Come with me, Elena," he said, taking her by the shoulders. "Come with me."

A tear crept out from the corner of her eye. "Wyn, the most important thing for any of us to know is where our home is." She ground her bare foot into the sand. "This is my home. This is where everything starts, where it ends. You need to find your own." She wiped her eye dry. "Maybe I'll see you in Switzerland next week. At the aerobatics championships. If they believe this," she said, holding up the schematic to Gallagher's optical processor.

"And if they believe this." Gallagher reached into the neck of his flightsuit and pulled out the sparkling diamond. It cast bright flecks of pure sun across her face. He took her in his arms, their shadows cast long by the low sun.

"It's time," she said, breaking away. "Let's push the plane out."

Together, they rolled the red Sukhoi 29 out to the far end of the beach, its nose pointing into the west wind. Gallagher stepped up and settled into the rear cockpit. He looked down to fasten the shoulder harness, and when he looked back up, Elena was halfway to the trees, walking steadily in the direction of Utena. "Elena!"

She stopped. "See you in Switzerland!" she said, waving, and then turned her back on him. She disappeared among the birches.

Elena heard the radial engine cough to life, heard the roar of its takeoff. She eased from behind a fallen tree as the Sukhoi angled its wings, low to the earth, heading due west. Its red wings melted quickly into the crimson sunset.

She took out the detailed sketch of his optical processor. They had started something together. They had jumped the walls placed in their way by men who thought they owned the universe. But they didn't. The diamond device was Elena's; this computer was Gallagher's. These came from *their* minds. It would be up to *them* to say how their creations would be used. They each had chosen peace over war, cooperation over mindless competition. They had chosen to work together.

No more secrets, she thought as she began walking toward the village. *No more secrets.*

Sunday Morning, 5 August 1990

Foreign Minister Eduard Shevardnadze stood at his office window, looking down as the long black embassy car pulled away. Would this be the opening shot? The *causa belli* for the old ghosts to rally round their tattered flag? He knew the Army and his old employer the KGB were waiting, watching for the right moment to move against *perestroika* and *glasnost*. Would this be it? He let the curtain fall shut and turned to his aide. "Get me Yazov," he said.

"The marshal's at Zavidovo this weekend, sir. I think—"

"Now."

The gruff bark of Defense Minister Yazov came over the desktop speaker a few moments later.

"Dmitri Timofeyovich," said Shevardnadze, "I have just had a very interesting briefing. It covered one of our newest technological triumphs. One, I must admit, I had not heard of before. A very great secret, no doubt."

"Oh? What was it?" said Yazov.

"A device code-named Stingray."

The phone went silent, then Yazov spoke. "Stingray, is it? Never heard of it."

"Precisely what I said to him. Of course, who am I to keep track of all the things you do in your underworld?"

"Who briefed you on this so-called secret?"

Shevardnadze paused, imagining the expression that would shortly sweep Yazov's face. "A gentleman named James Baker," he said at last.

"Who?"

"The American secretary of state."

"I know who he is! How the hell did—" Yazov clamped his mouth shut.

"There's more. You see, it seems they not only know more about this Stingray than I do," Shevardnadze said, "but they would like to borrow it."

"Borrow it! Why the devil would . . ."

"You will recall the unpleasantness taking place in Southwest Asia just now?" Shevardnadze looked at his watch. "Iraq gave them until noon today to pull back their aircraft carriers. That will explain the reason Mr. Baker saw fit to phone me this morning. You see, they want to borrow Stingray tonight."

"Impossible!"

"No," Shevardnadze corrected, "it's not impossible at all. You recall the arrangement we're working out for food credits? The winter's not very far off, Marshal Yazov. I'm sure you wouldn't want anything to come in the way of feeding the people this winter, would you?"

"But—"

"Do it," said Shevardnadze, and hung up. *What,* he wondered as he sat alone in his office, *will this cost us?*

He found out a month later.

On 9 September, thirty IL-76 troop transports showed up unannounced on the Moscow radar screens. Their pilots informed the startled air traffic controllers that they carried food to feed children displaced by the disaster at Chernobyl. They landed at small airfields around the perimeter of the capital. Three landed at Moscow Central, where the hulk of the burned Antonov had been pushed into an unused hangar. When their ramps dropped to the ground, a full regiment of the Seventy-sixth Air Assault Division, dressed in full battle gear and armed with live ammunition, poured out. Their commander was Colonel Kolchenoveniy.

They were joined by an armored column of the Vitebsk VDK (Air Assault) Regiment. These forces took immediate control of strategic points within Moscow, throwing up secure perimeters around their airfields and the weekend dachas of STAVKA, the Soviet High Command, at Ordintsovo. After an outcry in the newly unfettered press, the exercise ended on 13 September.

As a demonstration of power, it worked.

On 20 December, Foreign Minister Eduard Shevardnadze, coarchitect of *glasnost* and *perestroika,* resigned his position, warning a stunned Congress of People's Deputies of an imminent military dictatorship.

On 14 January, Bloody Sunday, paratroops in tanks rolled down Cosmonaut Avenue in Vilnius, Lithuania. Fourteen people were killed and many more wounded as troops from Seventy-sixth Air Assault seized the city in a show of brutal force.

Action had spawned reaction; pieces had been moved and lost. Angles of attack spanned and clashed across a checkered board. Only the finish, the endgame, remained to be played.

"Rock and roll!" said Eisley as he watched the last of the Dahr Nema strike force, a heavily laden A-6, burn down the *Kennedy*'s bow catapult and claw its way into the sky. *And about time!*

The Intruder banked south and disappeared into the dusk. A second later, the Tomcat piloted by Eisley's wingman roared off the waist cat. Eisley's plane would be next. Catapult steam billowed orange; flames blasted aft from wide-open jet nozzles. A click sounded in his headphones.

"We really gonna hold hands with that Bear?" asked Baxter, his rear seater.

"A-firm. The world's a funny place, Bax Boy."

"Any funnier and I won't be able to stand it." Baxter reached down and stuck the Garfield cat on the instrument panel shield. "I'm just glad we aren't heading for the beach."

"You would say that." Eisley jammed the brakes down hard and advanced the throttles to full military power, then into afterburner. His twin Pratt and Whitneys roared live fire; his needles were in the green. The missiles hanging from the Tomcat, the 20-mm rounds coiled up in the nose, were live and ready. He looked over at the cat officer, gave him thumbs-up, and saluted. "Here we go."

The cat stroke threw Eisley's head against the backrest. In seconds they were rocketed from zero to one hundred and forty knots. The Tomcat sagged as it ran off the metal cliff of the *Kennedy*'s flightdeck. Eisley kept his eyes off the waves and rotated the nose up eight degrees. The wings bit air and they were flying. He slapped the gear handle up and turned to join up with his wingman. Minutes later, both fighters were orbiting at thirty thousand feet.

"Bull's-eye, Cutlass two zero two is at base plus fifteen with two turkeys."

"Roger, two zero two," came the voice of the officer on board the high-flying E2C radar plane, "stand by for vectors to your intercept."

"Cutlass lead's ready to copy."

"Target, zero one zero, range two twenty on an inbound heading. Go get 'em and keep the bugs away."

"Cutlass flight's turning," he replied. "Fucking escorting the enemy," muttered Eisley as he looked off his left wing. Somewhere out there, the Bear with the zapper was inbound. Why had he drawn the job of keeping it safe? There was an Alpha Strike going into Dahr Nema. That was where he should be. He glanced back at his wingman. Across a river of five-hundred-knot air, he saw Cotton nod.

Together, the two fighters burned north.

"Okay, Bax," Eisley said, "no reason to be subtle about it. The bastards are probably expecting us or something. Light 'em up."

Baxter switched the powerful Hughes radar out of standby and sent a beam of energy through the sky.

A white fog of vaporized propellant cascaded down the dark green body of the rocket. *Al Infitar*'s superchilled fuel hit the heat waves still rising from the desert sand. The air-raid alarm siren began to wail as the stork-legged service gantry fell away.

"Stop that noise," said Reiner, the launch director. He mopped his brow despite the intense, air-conditioned cold in the firing bunker.

"They didn't believe, did they?" asked Dr. Wei, the warhead specialist. He chuckled silently and shook his head.

"They will," said Reiner. Five missiles, each armed with a deadly cargo of uranium isotope, lay protected in their hardened shelters. No air raid would reach them under twenty feet of sand and eight of concrete. The one on the pad would be fired before the Americans ever came near. The attack would fall on an empty launch pad; the missile would be on its way, unstoppable. Reiner smiled and snorted.

"Yes?" said Wei.

"Let the Americans have the deaths of Jews on their hands for a change. Let them see how they like it."

The air-raid Klaxon fell silent. Only the hum of equipment fans and the nervous shuffling of feet could be heard within the blockhouse. A distant crump of detonating high explosive shook the concrete floor.

"Downrange radar five is off the air."

"Station eight is not answering!"

"Fools." Reiner's hand hovered above the button that would begin the automated firing sequence. Once started, computers would initialize the rocket's ring laser guidance and arm its isotope warhead. *Fools!* he seethed. Did they think it was all a bluff? In twenty minutes, a cloud of intensely radioactive dust would fall like gray snow across Tel Aviv.

The blockhouse went silent as twenty pairs of eyes focused on this one, culminating motion. The finger, slick with sweat, pushed the button in with a soft click.

"Arming sequence is completed!" shouted the technician at the warhead desk. Above the row of green lights, a digital timer counted down the seconds to ignition.

"Aircraft over the runway!" The hammer of an antiaircraft cannon sounded, then another joined in. A third.

The timer fell through twenty seconds. Ten seconds; five.

The thick plate-glass window was packed with faces as a sputtering glow erupted from the base of *Al Infitar*. A shock wave blasted out from the flame pit, followed by billows of white smoke. Then, with gathering speed, the dark green rocket broke free from the earth on a pillar of fire. Its lusty roar drowned out the feeble sounds of earthly battle as it rose into the dusk sky.

"Depressurization is complete," said Taskaev.

"Telemetry!" Kessel shouted over the Bear's intercom. "I have—"

"Yes, yes, just get it done," said Ermakov. He glanced over at the American fighter to his left. Its pilot waved. Ermakov thought for a moment, then shrugged. He waved back.

The sound of the big hatch sliding open on the Tupolev's spine rumbled through the airframe. Ermakov set the autopilot and took his hands from the controls just as a prickly, static-electric field charged through the cockpit.

"Again?" said Taskaev.

Ermakov glanced at him over his oxygen mask. "Again." The static charge grew, and once more sparks began to leap from the instrument panel to the windshield braces. Ermakov felt a jolt through his flightsuit where the back of his knee touched something conductive. He looked out to his left at the American fighter. "Say what you will," he told Taskaev, "they build very pretty airplanes."

"Especially tonight."

"Look!" said Ermakov. A brilliant globe of fire was rising in the south, trailing a ribbon of exhaust.

"I've got it! I see it!" Kessel shouted. "Just fly straight. Straight!"

Stingray was ready. Kessel trained the crude aiming device at the rising ball of light. Why couldn't they have a proper gunsight! The Bear trembled slightly, throwing off his aim. "Hold us still!" Kessel shouted. Why couldn't someone make a targeting computer to do this? If only that Pasvalys woman hadn't thrown everything off track with her unspeakable behavior! Why did he have to aim like some medieval archer . . .

A green light came on in the illuminated reticle. The sensor on his aiming sight was picking up its own reflection from the distant rocket. Kessel swiveled in his seat to follow it and tapped a foot switch. The lights dimmed as Stingray fired.

A stream of high-energy particles lanced across the distance at light speed. *Hold still,* said Kessel as he followed its upward progress. *Just a little more. Hold still!*

"First-stage separation!" the range officer said as the signal was downlinked to the launch bunker. The rattle of antiaircraft guns was sporadic now. It was lucky the whip antennae connecting *Al Infitar* with the ground station had not been hit. A strange calm fell across the desert as the attacking planes departed, leaving SAM sites and the Dahr Nema radar station blazing. The long runway was pocked with deep holes and littered with time-delayed mines.

"Pitchover maneuver in eight seconds. Second-stage ignition has begun." A cheering went up in the bunker, as much for the successful flight of the rocket as for their great fortune to sit out the air raid inside the most secure of shelters. Two feet of solid concrete covered with ten feet of sand over their heads made them immune to anything but—

A warning bell rang. "Second stage has stopped!" the telemetry officer shouted. "The second stage—"

"What?" Reiner stood up and walked swiftly over to the flight-dynamics console. There it was. Under a flashing red light, a message scrolled across the display, along with the precise instant of engine shutoff.

Al Infitar was still moving under the impetus imparted by its first stage, but it was slowing like a ball thrown straight up. *"Mein Gott."* Reiner looked up at the roof of the bunker.

"Mein Gott."

"I got it!" shouted Kessel. The burning dot of the rocket's engines had gone dark. With it still registering on his laser aiming device, he recorded its slowing, then, its tumble. "I got it!" He tapped the foot switch and Stingray shut down with a spooling-down whine of power converters and turbopumps.

"Very good," said Ermakov. He hit the switch that closed the sliding hatch above the particle beam, then looked over to Taskaev. "You see?" he said with a grin. "Like I told you the last time. Nothing ever happens on these test flights." He glanced across at the American fighter pilot. *Why not?* he thought with a shrug. Ermakov waved.

Al Infitar picked up velocity as it dropped back to earth. The desert complex of Dahr Nema was just a dark discoloration on the unbroken desert, surrounded by rising smoke plumes from knocked-out radar and SAM sites. The smudge became more distinct as the crippled rocket fell through sixty thousand feet, through fifty; at twenty thousand feet, the arming circuit came back on. It was not bothered by the fact that it was descending on its own launch site and not Tel Aviv. All it knew was that its internal laws had been satisfied: the barometric sensor had recorded its upward passage, and now it was recording its fall.

At five thousand feet above the launch complex, the firing sequence began. A bright blossom of orange flame opened directly above Dahr Nema.

Moments later, radioactive snow began to fall across the desert.

Eisley waved back at the Russian sitting so near, yet as remote as the man in the moon. Or was he? The Bear wagged its wings as the sliding hatch cut into its back began to close. Eisley returned the salute. "You know," he said as the big bomber turned for home, "they sure build them pretty."

"Who?" asked Baxter.

"The Russians."

"I never thought I'd hear you say that."

"Times change."

"I wonder what they're packing inside that Bear?"

Eisley turned the Tomcat toward the *Kennedy*. "That," he said, "is something we'll probably never know. Don't forget. They're still the enemy. Whatever's inside that big old ship, it's got to be their biggest secret, right?"

"You still think so?" asked Baxter. "I mean, about them being the enemy?"

Eisley looked south toward the remnant glow left by *Al Infitar*'s demise. "Maybe. Maybe not." He glanced back at Baxter in the canopy bow mirror and shrugged. "I guess we'll have to wait and see, shipmate." Eisley keyed his transmitter. "Cutlass two zero two is headed for the boat."

EPILOGUE

"Anything happen yet?" Gallagher asked the front-desk guard as he walked by. It was the day of the United Nations deadline for Iraq to withdraw from Kuwait. The watch springs of war had been wound tighter and tighter for half a year; now everyone waited with one eye to the nearest television for the words *We bring you this special announcement. . . .*

The guard shook his head and nodded at the radio beneath the polished wood desk. "It's been on all day. Ever since I came on shift. Nothing yet. I sure wouldn't want to be in Hussein's shoes right now, you know? Except he probably has this ace up his sleeve, just waiting for us."

"I don't think so," said Gallagher as he passed by. "So long."

The guard huffed. *Docs,* he thought with a shake of his head. *What do they know?*

Light streamed in through Building 111's glass doors. Gallagher walked across the quiet lobby, his new running shoes squeaky on the polished tile. He slipped his sunglasses on and stepped outside.

Winter was northern California's finest season; a clear, warm sun hung in a cloudless blue sky while a cool, gentle breeze caressed the Livermore Valley, sending waves of movement through the new grass on the hills. There wasn't a hint of fog against the Diablo Range, and to the east, brilliant flashes telegraphed from the spin-

284

ning wind generators atop Altamont Pass. It was perfect weather for flying.

He turned around and looked up the sheer facade of Building 111. Its gray concrete looked archaeological, an ancient fortress that had outlived the hatreds, and the nations, that had inspired it. At level seven, where he had just left William Hewlett Enstrom of the Kratos Foundation, he saw a curtain fall closed. He waved. "So long," he said out loud as two quick beeps came from his Saab.

"Hey, ace," he said as he folded his long legs into the car. "Ready for your next lesson?"

"So? What did he say?" asked Sara Avilar. She snapped off the car radio as Gallagher started up the 900. Her black, curly hair fell in rings around her deeply-tanned face.

Gallagher sniffed her perfume. It was patchouli, of course. He opened his window and put on a long, serious look. "He wants me to come work for the Foundation. Scouting flesh. You know. The best and the brightest." He looked up at the wall.

"Scouting?" said Sara with a raised eyebrow. "There's a better word for it, isn't there? How about *procurer,* or—"

"Throttle back. I told him I'd get back to him this afternoon." He put the car into first and moved out from under the cool shadow and into the golden sunlight.

"You mean you'd actually consider it? After everything that's—"

"It's a job, isn't it?" he said simply as they drove out toward the main gate.

"What do you mean, *it's a job?*" she demanded. "That's like saying it's only Tuesday. You *do* know what day this is?"

"D day. Why?"

"Wrong," she corrected. "It's D day *and* it's Martin Luther King's birthday. Remember him? *I have a dream?*" She looked away from him, out her window. "How could you even think of going back to work in there?" She shook her head. "You've been so clueless since you got back. It's just as well you didn't fly at Yverdon. You probably would have forgotten how to . . ."

He shot her a quick look.

She bit her lip. "I'm sorry, Wyn. That was cruel. But it's true. You know better than to trust them again."

"Maybe you could just relax a little. At least when you're this side of Berkeley. You know. Don't worry. Be happy."

"Zero probability. I just can't figure you, Wyn. How can you be so calm? There's a war coming. A *real* war. Any minute. Maybe it's already started. Not like those games you play onscreen. I can't turn off the radio or the TV without thinking I'll miss something important. You're acting like it's all going to just work itself out." Sara pursed her lips. He could be so damned infuriating sometimes! Especially since he returned. She looked over at him, trying to decipher his mask. "Did you leave the journal article? The one your friend sent?"

Gallagher nodded. He picked up on the way Sara pronounced the word *friend*. He looked over at her, and for the briefest of instants, her face, her hair, her eyes, belonged to another woman. "Enstrom reads Russian. He should get to the interesting part before too long."

The main gate appeared as they rounded the last corner. He slowed as he came up next to the guard booth. He handed over their white day passes. A plastic card was attached to them.

The guard nodded at the white papers, then flipped them over to see what Gallagher had mistakenly included. "Hey!"

It was Gallagher's green Q-1 clearance.

Gallagher waved and gunned the Saab away from the booth.

"What was that all about?" asked Sara.

"A loose end." The turbo spooled up as he made his way down North Greenwood to the freeway. He swept around the curve of the westbound ramp. Five minutes later, he was pulling in front of his hangar at the Livermore Airport.

He unlocked the combination lock that fastened the steel door. He no longer trusted keys. The hasp clicked free. "Give me a hand?" he asked as he put his shoulder to the steel doors.

Together, they pushed them open. A flood of clear, warm light bathed the crimson plane inside. On the bulbous nose of the Sukhoi

29 was written *Silky Sue II*. The word *experimental* appeared beneath the cockpit rail.

"A Sukhoi 29. I still don't know how you got your hands on it," she said as he removed the canvas canopy cover. "Or how the Danes let you out with it. Or how you managed to con the Air Force into loading it up and hauling it all the way over here. I mean, I hadn't even *heard* of a Sukhoi 29. The 26, sure, but—"

"It was an exchange." He opened the long, teardrop canopy and removed two parachutes. He tossed one to Sara Avilar and buckled on the other himself. "Flies just like the 26, except you can do it with a friend."

"Yeah," she said as she strapped on the thinpak chute. "I bet."

"Come on." He took hold of the polished propeller and pulled the two-place Sukhoi out into the sun. "Let's aviate."

She hopped up on the knife-thin wing and stepped down into the Sukhoi. The front cockpit swallowed her small frame. It was huge. Her feet barely touched the rudder pedals, and with its steeply raked seat, the tall control stick was chin high.

"Clear!" he shouted from the aft cockpit. The Vedneyev radial started with its traditional whoosh of compressed air. With a belch of blue smoke and a deep-chested rumble, Gallagher taxied the craft out to the runway, did his run-up checks, and secured the crystal canopy.

Gallagher pressed the transmit button on the stick. "Sukhoi Two Sierra Uniform is ready, Runway Two Five Right."

"Two Sierra Uniform is cleared for takeoff," came the prompt reply from Livermore tower.

"All yours," Gallagher said to Sara.

She nodded and slowly fed in the throttle, her feet still on the Sukhoi's brakes. The engine roared and the ship began to inch forward. She released the brakes, and the Sukhoi 29 accelerated down the tarmac like a gunshot.

Sara stabbed the brakes, steadying their path until the small rudder became effective in the stiffening slipstream. She hauled them off from a three-point attitude, then leveled off fifty feet above the runway. As the golf course at the end of the runway flashed under their red wings, she pulled them into a vertical climb, straight up, the big engine singing a high, happy song. The Sukhoi was in its element, climbing strongly into the cool blue sky. Sara rolled around a perfect vertical axis, and with a push on the stick, she brought them level, heading east toward Altamont Pass. The practice area was just on the other side.

"Not bad," Gallagher said as he glanced down at the ground. They were coming up to Lawrence Livermore; it looked like a square island of geometry against the green fields all around it. Building 111 was perfectly identifiable. A sudden notion flashed through him. He wiggled the stick. "I've got it," he said, taking control back from Sara. He banked up hard on a wing, rolled, and pushed over into a dive. Building 111 was dead ahead.

"Wyn!" she shouted. "They'll shoot us down!"

"No chance." He rammed full throttle home. "I told him he'd hear from me this afternoon."

"What? You mean . . ."

"I'm not going back, Sara." The Sukhoi was stiff with speed as it plummeted toward the concrete waffle standing above the Lab. It never occurred to Gallagher before, but it looked a hell of a lot like a tombstone.

William Enstrom leafed through the obscure Soviet journal, angered at Gallagher for dropping off his Q-1 clearance. Didn't he understand what it meant? It was his admission to a secret elite; an underground kingdom of people who fought the real battles, manipulated the real controls. How could he simply toss it away? Still, the diamond-coating machinery in prototype was worth a hundred Gallaghers. Enstrom, and Kratos, would benefit a great deal from its ultimate manufacture. *Amazing,* he thought with a derisive snort, *the Russians actually dreamed it up first.* What would they be able to do with it anyway? They needed a machine to grow potatoes, not diamonds.

He saw the title of a small, half-page announcement:

INNOVATIVE SIGNALS PROCESSOR DEVELOPED AT SERPUKHOV INSTITUTE.

Researchers at Serpukhov have developed an image-recognition system that compares a potential target with up to 1,000 stored patterns and determines a match within one second.

He looked up, his eyes wide. "No."

The hybrid optical processor uses light for information handling. A video camera captures a scene, which is scanned electronically into an acousto-optical device.

"No!"

A sound pricked his ears. He looked over at the window. The glass was buzzing. Was it an earthquake? Enstrom stood up and made his way to the glass. He swept the curtain aside.

A small red airplane was flying impossibly low, level with the seventh floor! It was a small crimson circle sprouting two thin wings. It was coming straight at him. "NO!"

As he started to duck down beneath the windowsill, the plane suddenly reared up on its tail. With a yowl from its slashing prop and a slap of pressure against the glass, it climbed out of sight. A picture rattled off the wall and crashed. *Gallagher!*

He quickly found his place in the announcement, skipping to the very last sentence.

It was signed *Academician E. V. Pasvalys.*

"They're going to nail us!" Sara yelled as they climbed back to a more sedate altitude. "I can't believe you did that!"

"Some folks just need an unambiguous message," said Gallagher as he leveled off heading east once more, pulling the propeller control back from its maximum-noise setting.

"Tell me about it." Sara had been as unambiguous with Gallagher as she knew how. Even after his return. He still hadn't caught on that her admiration of him was not entirely professional.

"How about a slow roll?" he said, gripping the control stick. He raised the Sukhoi's nose a few degrees and fed in aileron and rudder. The ship slowly banked, the altimeter frozen at four thousand feet. Over they went, more, more, until they were inverted, and the green hills marched by directly overhead. "By the way," he said, "are you doing anything after our session? You know, for dinner?"

"Are you asking me out on a date?" she said as she hung from her shoulder straps. "On the day the war's going to start, you're finally asking me out?"

Finally? "I know it sounds kind of politically incorrect," he said as they rolled back upright. The blood rushed from his head, but it was only partly due to gravity. "We could say it was in honor of Martin Luther King's birthday. Or anybody you want. You can pick."

"I think I can fit you in. We can watch CNN at my place and wait for the world to end."

Gallagher recalled the photos of the Russian Bear and the exploding Iraqi missile that Parrum had shown him. For all his years at Livermore, everyone had been panicked at the thought of a Russian technical breakthrough; what about a *human* breakthrough? Wasn't that what it was really about? "Sara, something tells me it's not going to end anytime too soon."

"Fine. We'll get a pizza. I've got a sleeper couch. You can—I mean, it's not all that comfortable, of course. I mean, it's not a bed. . . ."

"I'm sure we can work around it." He felt a huge weight lift from his heart. It was dull and gray and made of reinforced concrete. Gallagher slapped the stick into the right corner, and the Sukhoi rolled like a mad top. He recovered level and slightly off heading. The Sukhoi rolled so damned fast! "So the answer is yes?" he said as he faked the stick over, nudging them back to the correct course.

"What do you think? My stick." She took control and made an equal and opposite roll to the left. The rollout was precise, on rails. Perfect.

"Not bad," said Gallagher.

"Better than yours. Wyn, serious stuff. I want you to know you were right for not going back to the Lab. The most important thing is to realize that you have this choice."

"Which choice?"

"It doesn't matter what you do. Number one on the agenda is to know you can be a creator or a destroyer. I'm glad you figured out which one to be."

Gallagher stared at the back of Sara's head for a moment, remembering. "Someone else told me that the most important thing was to find your home."

Sara looked up into the canopy mirror and saw Gallagher's face framed in its silvery reflection. "She was right, too." She saw him break out into a smile.

"Why am I always half a step behind?"

"Don't flatter yourself. So how does pizza at Chez Avilar sound? Just right for the end of the world?"

"Not the end," said Gallagher. "The beginning."